With Tha

M. J J L

A New Revelation

A.S. Jenkins

AuthorHouse™ UK Ltd.
500 Avebury Boulevard
Central Milton Keynes, MK9 2BE
www.authorhouse.co.uk
Phone: 08001974150

© 2010 A.S Jenkins. All rights reserved.

No part of this book may be reproduced, stored in a retrieval system, or transmitted by any means without the written permission of the author.

First published by AuthorHouse 1/18/2010

ISBN: 978-1-4490-3910-3 (sc)

This book is printed on acid-free paper.

Prologue

Rome was a particularly busy city at the start of the Sixteenth century and all the Vatican Church was in a blind panic. The pope had great ideas within the great city to make changes to its chapel, changes that would shape history forever.

The morning dew had left a slippery film of moisture on the courtyard cobbles; as the priest ran towards the chapel he feared he would fall but nothing could stop him. The fear of failure had gripped him even more so; a mere twisted ankle would just slow him down. Nothing but nothing could stop this determined priest. He had to be there; he had to make a good impression on his peers, and get there before the painter got there. It was imperative to him in completing a good first impression.

But he was late. The painter had already arrived and gotten started, but this wasn't your normal redecoration.

He had to get on with the normal running of the chapel and not let the hustle and bustle of the painting get in the way of the day to day activities.

As the high priest approached the confessional he noticed a sandaled foot sticking out of one of the many pews. It was a third of the way back and a chill riddled his spine. As he approached, the foot was quickly pulled back within the pew. The priest started to walk towards the lowly figure as quickly as he could, even though his traditional gown was very restrictive.

He had a fear that was unknown but at the same time very familiar, this scared the priest, who was still relatively young to be in such a high place within this particular chapel. He was overseeing the latter part of a very important commission in the chapel. A prominent painter and architect was completing a work of national importance, and the smell of paint and oil was overwhelming, almost nauseating; the young priest was thinking that it may have been this paint and oil combination that had resulted in him seeing the fore mentioned foot, as a figment of his already active imagination.

As he got to the pew in question he saw no one. He quickly turned and continued to wait for morning confessions. The chapel was vast in the sense that he felt all alone but also very vulnerable. His steps echoed throughout the vast chapel; the only other sound was that of a giant scaffold being dragged from time to time, breaking the endless silence.

The priest was making his final preparations before entering the confessional and so hung his stole over the edge of the door to indicate that he was ready to take parishioners for confession. The reason for his nervousness was unknown to him and he furiously rubbed his rosary so much he feared it would break; his heart was in his throat and as he swallowed and gulped down the lump, he heard someone approach the confessional.

The priest composed himself, and readied himself for the task at hand. The heavy oak door closed and the strange figure sat down ready to make his confession.

He lent forward and slid open the meshed opening to address his parishioner. There was an eerie silence before the stranger spoke.

'I'm sorry father it has been some time since my last confession.' The voice was deep and had a confident sound not like the normal tone of a person in confession, but a strong type, a type that wouldn't seem to need to confess to anything.

The priest was ready. He had composed himself and was trying hard not to be violently sick; the paint and many oils that the painter was experimenting with to paint the vast ceiling were so overwhelming. Many priests had refused to work under such conditions, but the Pope had insisted on the work, even stopping the building of his own tomb for the commission of the work on the chapel.

'Do not worry, my son. What is your confession today?'

'Like I said, it's been a long time since my last confession, father.'

The lowly figure wouldn't move on from this fact, the priest was feeling more relaxed by the fact that the stranger in the booth was confessing to his lack of attendance so the priest pursued it further.

The priest turned to try and make out the figure knowing full well he was really forbidden to do so. He tried so hard to see but only managed to get the stranger's silhouette, and this chilled him. The dark figure wasn't giving anything up and was facing the priest head on, seeing his every move. His piercing eyes, through the meshed opening, sent yet another chill; this was unfamiliar to the priest, he was having doubts about his real motives for being there.

Was he a spy sent by the pope? After all, he was very anxious to get the chapel back to its normal activities; or was it a sinister character trying to catch a glimpse of the renowned artists work?

Again the priest composed himself, the nerves getting the better of him, and he felt the stranger knew it too.

'Ok, my son. How long as it been since your last confession?'

There was a deadly silence. The figure cleared his throat and said with conviction, 'It's been one hundred and fifty-seven years since my last confession, father,' and with that said he thrust a heavy sword through the oak panel piercing the priest's stomach.

The priest stooped forward, seeing some part of a scripture engraved along the double-edged blade, but his own blood poured down the blade obscuring it before he could read it, then he lost consciousness. The sword was pulled back with the same speed and ferocious force.

The priest fell to the floor of the confessional, his lifeless frame left in a heap.

Once out of the booth the dark assassin stood over the priest; a streak of morning sunlight beamed through the gap between the assassin's muscular legs, giving the blood a florescent glow, before he simply picked him up like a rag doll and slung the body over his large shoulders like a hunter would do with his prey.

The assassin stood momentarily before the vast chapel, like he was in prayer, paying his respects, bowing his head as he did, then he turned and quickly left, as quickly and as undetected as he had arrived.

The blood poured from the confession booth and the morning sunlight gave it a translucent look, like of the finest red wine ready for the high priest to drink…

Chapter One

Psalm 27 v 1-8: 'The LORD is my light and my salvation –
whom shall I fear?
The LORD is the stronghold of my life –
of whom shall I be afraid?
When evil men advance against me
to devour my flesh,
when my enemies and my foes attack me,
they will stumble and fall.
Though an army besiege me,
my heart will not fear;
though war break out against me,
even then will I be confident.
One thing I ask of the LORD,
this is what I seek:
that I may dwell in the house of the LORD
all the days of my life,
to gaze upon the beauty of the LORD
and to seek him in his temple.
For in the day of trouble
he will keep me safe in his dwelling;
he will hide me in the shelter of his tabernacle
and set me high upon a rock.
Then my head will be exalted
above the enemies who surround me;
at his tabernacle will I sacrifice with shouts of joy;

> *I will sing and make music to the LORD.*
> *Hear my voice when I call, O LORD;*
> *be merciful to me and answer me.*
> *My heart says of you "Seek his face!"*
> *Your face, LORD, I will seek.*
> *Do not hide your face from me,*
> *do not turn your servant away in anger;*
> *you have been my helper.*
> *Do not reject me or forsake me,*
> *O God my Saviour.'*

As Miles Leonard walked, that very Psalm was repeating itself over and over. As he stepped up the darkened alleyway, the rain was piercing and the seventy-seven year old was struggling to see clearly.

'If I see tomorrow I'll get a CAT scan,' he thought to himself.

He and Derek Greyer had arranged to meet here earlier but now he'd started to regret it. He could see Derek's car, a black Bentley Continental. As Miles walked past it, Derek poked out of a recess in the alleyway wall and startled Miles.

'Hear and pay attention. Do not be arrogant, for the Lord has spoken. Give glory to the Lord your God before he brings the darkness, before your feet stumble on the darkening hills.' Miles was nervous but was not afraid of Derek.

'Don't give me your petty scripture; it has no valid petition against me. You're a weak old man. I give you one thing, you have great faith and a lot of patience. But I'm immortal. You will die soon. And your son, Paul, looks like he'll be in God's glory before you, Oh great Milo.'

'Oh, we're using our formal titles, eh Deygar.'

As Deygar stood there covered with designer labels, draped in wealth and with his gloating – the man was so full of himself, so full of arrogance – Miles had to say something just to take the chip from his huge padded shoulder.

'I know God will bring good from my son's life-threatening illness.'

'There it is again your great faith. If I had a son to pass on my knowledge–'

Milo butted in. 'What knowledge?'

'As I was saying, great knowledge, I would be questioning God and asking why, not seeking the good that can come from it. Just face it; you have no son to pass on the mission. It's over. This town and great city is mine. Who is going to stop me?'

Milo was struggling for something to say, to put Deygar in his place, but with his burden he was low on comebacks until his heart quickened and his faith rose.

'Someone will stop you, I have faith in that.' He could hear himself saying the words but was wondering where this declaration of faith was coming from. He also wondered where was this 'someone' who will stop Deygar, perhaps it was prophetic what he was saying, he hoped so for the sake of the church and the city.

'Only what you call a miracle will do. What, with you in your late seventies? God only promises three score and ten. You're on borrowed time old man.' Everything that came from Deygar's mouth was to bring Milo's faith to a dangerously low level. Deygar continued his insults to bring the seventy year-old down and it was starting to grate on him.

'You spend years training a son to replace you and it looks like it will be a complete waste of time.' Deygar stepped in closer to Milo. 'He is going to die soon; the cancer is terminal isn't it?'

Milo was at a low point. Faith-wise, with every word that came from Deygar, Milo struggled for faith.

'If only your father could see you now.' This was Milo's attempt to strike a blow to Deygar's ego.

'Yes, yes. If only my father could see me, he would be proud of what he accomplished before his untimely demise.'

'Proud? 'Proud of what?' You and Paul were born within months of each other. Your destiny should have been brotherhood in Christ not enemies of darkness and light.'

'Yes but you put a stop to that when we came of age, when you killed my father with your sword.' Deygar was starting to lose his edge and the coolness was being replaced with anger and rage.

'He was an object of mercy who should have known wrath. We both knew that your coming of age would bring your father to take control of the dark Lords and try to influence the government of this city.'

'That's why I'm pleased that I don't have to fight anymore, unlike my father, because my opponent is going to die naturally. I do believe Paul to have been a great warrior when having a great teacher and father but who's to know eh. It was never meant to be.' Deygar's ego was back and Milo's faith was showing signs of weakening. Deygar could tell and was most pleased with himself. 'You have eighteen months before the stars and moons rise, and then we will rise in power and take over.'

'You and your superstitions: 'stars and moons.' What are you on, Derek?'

Deygar reached for the hilt of his sword under his long designer trench coat. Milo froze, stepped back and reached for his sword.

'Hey! I thought this was going to be a bloodless meeting,' Milo said worriedly.

'For me perhaps.' And Deygar pulled his sword from its sheath several inches. Milo does the same, but with great fear; beads of sweat begin to appear on Milo's brow.

'Scared Milo?' Is that sweat I see? Nervousness: that can only mean one thing – you are fearful of me; you are doubting your very faith. You are a weak old man and now your faith is weakening also.'

'Raising my sword is my last option, Derek.' Milo called him by his correct name, the name given to him by his mother and father, but it did nothing to calm him. 'I'm sweating because this jacket is too hot.' With that said, Milo swept off his jacket and pulled his sword clean from its sheath. Deygar, taken by surprise, stepped back and fell over the kerb stone on the edge of the footway.

Milo just laughed to himself and replaced the sword into its sheath. He picked up his jacket and turned to start walking towards his car. Deygar, feeling stupid, pulled himself up, pulled the sword free and struck Milo from behind, but even with Deygar's speed Milo removed his sword, turned and guarded his neck just before Deygar's sword hit it. Their swords clashed and they both stepped back, a sword's length between them.

'Still need the practise don't you, Derek.' Milo's faith had risen to new heights; the heat of battle always quickened his heart.

'I have all the practise I need right here.' Deygar was determined to teach Milo a lesson for the embarrassing fall he just had.

Milo's chest was pounding, and he began to cough. Deygar took the opportunity to strike again.

Their swords clashed once again; they were nose to nose, both clearly seeing each other's eyes and more importantly each other's swords. Each of their swords were inscribed. Deygar read the cutting edges of Milo's sword; it read, '*Keep this at your side at all times, God'sword*'. The last part was deliberately mis-spaced to spell Godsword.

Milo reads Deygar's and it read '*For the days are coming when darkness will rise up*'. As they both read each other's swords they were quickly reminded of their missions and both stepped back, replacing their swords as they did so.

'I should strike you down right here right now, but it seems unfair with me being so young compared to you, a man of many years. I think I'll have more pleasure watching you die naturally.' Derek went to turn away momentarily, but then started to shout out his last statement to give Miles another faith-bursting remark. 'My father is remembered for dying at his peak, in battle where true glory is found, whilst you will be remembered as an old man clutching his chest, coughing his last breath.' He started the short walk back to his car and over his shoulder said, 'You won't die tonight.'

Milo's chest began to slow and his breathing was returning to a normal pace.

Deygar was still full of himself as he got into his car.

'Eighteen months, Milo. Be ready.'

Milo could see Deygar's every move in the mirror-finished wheels of his Bentley. Milo stayed motionless for a moment just in case he was bluffing.

Deygar removed his jacket and sword then threw them into the boot of his Bentley, and got in. Deygar's arrogance was still prevalent and as he started the massive six and three quarter v-eight, it roared into life and startled Milo.

Milo felt a little safer now and headed toward his car whilst Deygar drove slowly away. Milo got to his car, a Ford Mondeo ST200. 'A humble car for a humble man,' he muttered under his breath as he pointed the remote key fob at the car. 'bleep! Bleep! Click'.

Milo removed his jacket and sword and placed them into the boot with a bit more respect, because of the enormous responsibility that carrying such a weapon had. Milo understood the role he played; Deygar on the other hand treated the sword as just the tool for the job, easy to replace.

Milo looked into the distance through the rear-view mirror and noticed Deygar's car making the turn from the alleyway. Milo felt shaken by a meeting that had seemed to be a waste of precious time but made more of an impact for the undoing of nerves and faith than as a productive exercise.

Milo glanced back and saw himself in the mirror. 'I am old but I will seek another.' And with that thought Miles Leonard began to pray. 'Who can I find Lord, my son is so ill, please give me discernment in these days. Lord, speak to my son, he's weak in body but he's strong in mind. Continue to be with him and strengthen his heart at this time, Amen.'

Chapter Two
The Morning After

1 Thessalonians 5v4: 'But you brothers, are not in darkness so that this day should surprise you like a thief. You are all sons of the light and sons of the day.'

Miles began his day as usual, with a healthy breakfast, vitamins and then his morning walk, to commit his day to the Lord.

After his meeting last night Miles was struggling for words, his mind a rush of emotions: the mission at hand, his son's health, but the more he dwelt on his circumstances the more his faith was rising, which puzzled him. Why should this give him a great rush of faith? A normal believer would be at the depths of despair.

Miles began to pray, 'Lord, I know that we have to go through times of trial. I know it creates faith but this desert time is very hard on my son. Please grant this, my prayer of mercy, heal my son, heal my son; he has a mission, a destiny to fulfil.' Miles was at the end of his hope for his son Paul, and was worried for his church. 'Please, Lord grant me this, my only hope, my hope is in you alone, Amen.'

Later that morning Miles went to the church that his son Paul had planted almost twenty years ago with his father's blessing, but Miles worried about this even though scripture says not to; it was a big venture to take on at such a young age.

Paul was a youth pastor and went into assisting his father, Pastor Miles, then was given the vision to start again even though people told him that it was a foolish idea when he already had a church his father would eventually retire from and pass on to him.

Nevertheless, Paul had a vision and Pastor Miles honoured that by passing his church on to an elder that was an existing pastor and came with him to be a mentor and a help for Paul.

But Miles never expected this, his son to be dying of cancer and with a church of 450 strong members. However, the church was full of faith and really on fire for God, but he knew the time was coming when he would have to appoint a new pastor, a new visionary to lead the church after Paul goes on to glory.

Paul's understudy, Jason, had been taking on a lot of the day to day running of the church in these later days of Paul's illness since he found it hard to get around. Paul, still with good solid judgment and a sound mind, found time to seek God through the scriptures and wrote amazing sermons for Jason to bring to the church in preparation for what he called 'going back to the maker'. Not only that, Paul came up with real words from God for the church that were confirmed by others.

Jason had a unique gift and excitement about him that really lifted the church to new heights of faith and understanding of the scriptures.

Jason was in his mid-thirties and was married to Lorraine with two children, Luke who was six and Jessica who had just gone two. Their relationship was strong. They met in prison – Jason was a prison chaplain which he went into after leaving Bible College five years earlier.

He hated people calling it a prison; it was a young people's detention centre. He enjoyed his work and you could tell; everyone got on well with him, even the people who had no or little faith in God.

Lorraine was the manager of the catering section and head cook. She had been doing the same kind of work since leaving school; she had received her degree in cookery and hotel management whilst on placement in a big fancy restaurant nearly ten years ago. The detention centre would be a challenge.

She saw no difference in the work, just that the customers didn't complain much, food was never sent back if it wasn't right and once the guests were in their rooms they didn't have the key to get out again.

Jason hated her attitude to her work but it was just Lorraine's way of coping with it.

Jason was very active in the centre and found time to create a library and young offenders' fellowship, and that was the time when he met up with Paul.

Paul immediately saw the potential in Jason, and was very impressed by the work he had done at a relatively young age. Jason had confidence by the bucket load and Paul had a burning question on his mind only after their second meeting with one another.

Paul asked Jason his burning question knowing the answer full well before he asked it. Paul's gifting in the prophetic was amazing and sometimes quite scary.

Paul asked, 'Do you have any other burning ambition left, any other goals? You have achieved so much at such a young age; is there anything else for you to do here at the centre?'

Jason had always secretly hoped for a real man of God, a man of destiny, to ask that question and there it was ready for him to answer. He had rehearsed it over and over in his mind. He knew of Paul and the amazing church that he had the privilege of leading and was ready for the next chapter of his life to start.

'Yes, yes I do still have a burning ambition to lead a church of my own one day, but that may be a few years down the line.' Jason was so excited that he just had a permanent smile on his face.

'Well, what about becoming my assistant, being my understudy as a part of your training to fulfil that ambition?' Paul couldn't believe the excitement of one man, his joy filled the room.

'It would be fantastic. I know it's what I want to do, but I still want to pray it through and talk it through with Lorraine first, maybe her discernment is what I need to give me balance. I'm an emotional wreck. I'm so pleased with a new challenge. I mean my youth work is good here, don't misunderstand me, but because I've done a good job – well I hope I've done a good job – it more or less runs itself.'

In the last two years Jason's work had exploded and he ran two young offenders' fellowships at different centres corresponding between them on email writing sermons and working through studies for them.

'All that work isn't hard for me to pass on to my understudy at the centre; he too has had a vision to continue the work I had started. He used to joke about it, 'when I die I'll be doing this job', but now he hasn't got to wait for that now, eh.'

Jason always made a joke of every situation. It was his way of getting past his shyness, if you could believe that.

Paul was still amazed by his excitement and told him to go away and pray it through and for him to talk it through with Lorraine.

Jason did just that and Lorraine was so pleased and impressed with the offer that she said she would see what God wanted her to do. Lorraine ended up doing what God had called her to do years previously and that was to support her husband in his calling and she eventually founded the 'Pastors Support Network', now it was a nationally recognized organisation with male members joining in too.

Lorraine and Paul's wife, Anne, founded the 'Women of the Clergy' support group and she now finds herself just as busy as Jason. The pair so looked forward to the challenge of working for a busy church but nothing could have prepared them for the next chapter that was about to unfold.

Miles, Paul and Jason had arranged to meet in Paul's office in the afternoon.

It was one of Paul's good days and he felt quite well considering his condition and arrived before Jason, but Jason wasn't far behind and the pair were puzzled at this unprompted meeting; the monthly senior leaders meeting wasn't due for a few days.

'So what's this all about, Dad?' asked Paul.

'We need to both talk to Jason. I think it's time that we come clean and tell him of our unique situation here at the Good Hope Centre.'

The name of the church was a specific need of Paul's. He didn't want a traditional name; he wanted a name that spoke to the people that counted, hence the Good Hope Centre.

'Paul, I want you to introduce me to Jason in the M.D way if you don't mind. I think it's time that we do, considering the unique circumstances of our church and your health.'

Miles was very nervous but he hid it well; it was one of his many gifts.

'What do mean introduce me? I've known you nearly nine years Pastor Miles and what's this M.D thing all about, eh?'

Jason was truly puzzled by Miles' behaviour.

Miles and Paul took a quick look at one another and nodded to confirm to each other that it was time to come clean and tell the whole story of the church and the true destiny of the father and son vision.

'Jason, we are going to tell you something that might come as a shock. My father, Pastor Miles, I know that he's not a pastor but we all still call him a pastor; it's kinda stuck. He has two roles in the church or he had when he was full time at his old church.'

He was Pastor, yes; Jason nodded along leaning in on his chair, trying to follow a conversation that so far he didn't totally understand.

'Well, his other job was, well…' Paul was stuck for words so Miles took over.

'My other job was more of a 'spiritual cleanser'. I would pray and take on a more active, active…' Now Miles was struggling for words. The pair just couldn't sugar-coat it; they just had to come out with it.

Paul stepped up the game and started at a place where his father could take over at any point.

'You know Pastor Miles as 'Miles Leonard' but he has another name which his father, 'William Leonard', my grandfather, gave him; it is Milo. Milo is his M.D name; M.D. stands for Master Disciple.'

Jason looked even more puzzled by this new information about Pastor Miles and what was all this M.D. stuff was all about, he thought.

'What's this all about M.D? I thought an M.D was a managing director, now it's a Master Disciple?'

Jason was getting truly confused and he started to get all nervous and move about in his chair, loosening his collar.

'Ok, Jason. Calm yourself. There's a lot we haven't told you,' Miles said, trying to calm Jason's nerves a little before the real news came.

Paul interrupted, 'It was for your own good that you didn't know. It's a secret that most of the world doesn't know anything about, and we want it to remain that way. So this is just between us here in this office, okay Jason?'

Jason nodded, but looked very confused by this.

Pastor Miles got up – 'I think it's time for a coffee.' – and went to make three cups: black with plenty of sugar in; they'll need it before the days out.

Jason sat up thinking it was just a big wind up and was waiting for the punch line. Once Miles had handed the coffees out they all sat waiting for someone to speak first. Miles glanced to Paul then Paul glanced to Jason. No one was going to make the first move and make true eye contact with each other.

In the end Jason spoke up. 'I can't continue. This is your meeting and you both are telling me the big secret that nobody else knows.'

'Ok, the other role,' Pastor Miles started this time, having the most experience in this matter. 'It's like I said, like a spiritual cleanser but I don't just pray–'

'Yes, I heard it's an active role as well,' Jason interrupted.

'Well, it's a lot more active than you think.'

'Come on tell us, then.' Jason was now getting a little impatient.

'I'm a Master Disciple, which means I protect the church from principalities and powers.'

'What? I know that we have to pray about principalities and powers and God protects us. What do you do that's so different, eh?'

Miles had to try and calm Jason down. He started to pace up and down the room and this unnerved Paul.

'Whilst you're up, Jason, will you lock the door please. We don't want to be disturbed.' This request made matters worse and Jason wanted to know why.

'Why lock the door, eh? What's the problem?'

Paul tried to calm him down, 'It's ok, Jason. Trust us. We are still your friends, you know. We just don't want anyone else to come in the room. It will all be revealed. He just wants to show you something that will make this all become clearer, ok?'

Jason calmed down once again. Paul had amazing gift of reading a situation and once Jason had locked the door Pastor Miles continued.

'Oh Jason, could you also get me that dusty old bible from the top shelf of Paul's book case.' He tried to reach but the shelf was too high. 'Use the chair if it's too high,' he said, knowing first hand that the shelf was to high, and he would need a chair.

So he placed the chair directly under the bible on the top shelf. The pressure of the chair and Jason's weight triggered a counterbalance; he heard a noise and wondered what it was then paused for a moment.

'It's ok, Jason, just creaky floor boards,' Paul added, now knowing what Miles had in mind.

So, he continued for the dusty bible and grabbed hold of it, but the bible wouldn't budge. He just managed to push it back, and with that the old bible tilted. A few more pulleys and counterbalance weights move around making the whole section of wall behind Paul's desk move to reveal a stair case going down.

Jason jumps from the chair startled by this. 'What's going on here, eh?' He moved to unlock the door and leave.

'Don't go, Jason. All will be revealed soon. Just come.' Pastor Miles called Jason over and tried to give him some reassurance to continue and trust the pair in this 'new revelation'.

Miles helped Paul down the stairs to the secret room and Jason followed reluctantly. The way down was dark and this unnerved him. Miles and Paul got to the bottom and the passive inferred detectors triggered the lights at the same time. Jason made his last step down, which also triggered the mechanism that replaced the wall in Paul's office; this startled Jason to the point of almost a heart attack.

Jason stood motionless in front of a huge room filled with an array of fitness equipment, running machines, rowing machines, a free weights bench, a load of dumbbells and barbells and a large punch bag hanging from the ceiling, looking rather used and abused. Jason stood amazed then thought, 'Is this it? This is the big secret – a gym?'

'No, Jason. This is not the big secret. It's what the gym is used for that's the secret.' Miles was worried for Jason; was this going to be too much for him to take on board?

'Well, it's for keeping in shape isn't it?' Jason's question sounded obvious but it was a gym and what else is a gym used for, he thought to himself.

Jason tried a different approach, with humour. 'Ok, which one of you is Batman, then? Well, it can't be Paul. No offence, Paul,'

'None taken.' Paul said.

'So it's you, Pastor Miles, or should I call you Milo.' Jason started to walk around and as he went he kept talking of Milo being a Batman superhero character. 'No, no. I've got it; you're a spiritual wizard type who goes around solving crime and keeping our city safe at night.'

Jason was hysterical and Paul was worried for his state of mind. 'Dad, Pastor Miles, sorry, maybe this wasn't a good idea.' Paul's concern for

Jason had Miles worried but he couldn't go back now; he needed to know to whole truth.

'Jason, calm yourself please. You're not far off with the Batman comment. Yes, I am a sort of spiritual wizard like Gandalf but I like to think of myself as a spiritual warrior and a defender of this church, but the rule is that it's a role, and it should go to the next in line, my son Paul.'

The pair looked to Paul and Paul looked ill. The chemotherapy and radiotherapy had taken its toll on him, and Jason looked back to Miles thinking the worse.

'No way! You want me to become a Master Disciple thingy – whatever that entails? With whom am I supposed to be at war, eh? I'm not prepared for this kind of work. I'm a pastor, just a normal run of the mill pastor. I visit the sick, preach, serve the people of God.' Jason's breathing was out of control; he was starting to have a panic attack. He dropped to his knees struggling for breath.

Miles quickly moved over to him. 'Calm yourself, Jason. Breathe! Just try to breathe normally.'

'It's… easier said… than done… you know.' Each word that came from Jason's mouth was blasted out with a burst of air, air that Jason needed to regulate his breathing.

'Jason, calm yourself.' Miles had to reassure him quickly. 'It's something you know nothing about, so why would we ask you to do something that you clearly don't fully understand or have full knowledge of.'

Paul managed to find a paper bag for him to breathe into to regulate his breathing, which slowed the panic attack down. Jason composed himself and sat on the weights bench still breathing into the paper bag, which he nodded his appreciation to Paul for.

'Is it ok for me to continue, Jason, or do you want a break?' Miles asked.

Jason just nodded, still breathing into his bag.

'Ok, hear it comes, the real reason for this gym and, Jason, we're not going to ask you to become a Master Disciple, so you don't have to worry. So are you ready for this new revelation?'

Jason pulled the paper bag away and said in a deep and clear voice, 'Yes, I am ready for the truth, for this new revelation.'

Chapter Three
A Secret Revealed

*Psalm 40:11 'Do not withhold your mercy from me, O LORD; may your love and your **truth** always protect me'.*

'Jason, I am a warrior and I have had battles with the enemy. I have killed and we know that killing is a sin and I am answerable to God but he has appointed me to this role, as this church's Master Disciple. I will explain but for that we must go back in history and start with our Lord Jesus.'

Jason was very worried but at the same time intrigued by this new information and felt very privileged to be the one receiving it.

'Ok, are we all ready?' The pair both nodded. Pastor Miles commanded the highest authority and the two of them listened intently. It took Paul back to when he was a small boy watching his father preach; he said on many occasions, 'That's what I want to do when I'm bigger, Daddy.'

Jason's face lit up when Pastor Miles mentioned Jesus' name and found comfort in something familiar, with all the secrecy and this talk of a new revelation.

Miles continued with the pair intensely looking on. 'Ok, in Jesus' time there were Master Disciples even though they didn't call themselves that. They knew they had a role to play even in the early church. You see, Jesus had enemies, many of them, but there was one that was paramount to Jesus being handed over to the Roman Soldiers.' 'Judas,' Jason shouted out, like he was in a Sunday school class expecting he would get a prize for getting the answer first.

'Yes, Jason – Judas. Judas was the main reason for all that you see here today. This whole church, in fact, was built for the purpose of this mission and role of the Master Disciple. Well, once Jesus was handed over to the Roman soldiers and Judas had been paid his thirty pieces of silver for his involvement, he was convicted of his actions and riddled with guilt in the capture and possible death of Jesus.

'The next part of the story I think anybody could tell but there is one part that's been erased from the history books; it's the part after Judas has been driven to his death by Satan and his many demons.

'It's the fact that even Judas has his followers. The deed of bringing Jesus to his capture and death has brought him cult status and a small band of men – six in total – was to find his hanging body and what happened then needs more than faith to believe; in fact, it needs a strong stomach.'

Jason, at this point, had no idea what was to come next and there was nothing he could do to prepare himself.

There was no way for Miles to make this easier to say, so he backtracked a little to prepare Jason for the new revelation of Jesus and the enemies' plan on God's people and their eternity.

'We all know about the last supper and that the wine symbolises Jesus' blood and the bread his body, well the six men that found Judas' body did the same.'

Miles was finding this more difficult than he first thought. Jason was sitting there with a look on his face that just said, 'Spit it out, man.' Miles just went for it. 'Well, the men didn't use anything to symbolise his blood; they had managed to find bread to use. Once they'd cut his body down and took it back to a secluded place for sacrifice, they broke bread and ate it, then took a sip, just a sip I might add, of Judas' blood.'

Jason sat bolt upright with shear shock written on his face and he quickly made a grab for the paper bag again, thinking he would start to panic again, but he didn't which took him by surprise; he was remarkably calm considering what he had just been told. Jason's whole belief system had been thrown into disarray and he just looked at Pastor Miles nodding his head. His body was saying to Miles that he was in shock but his whole being was calm, which scared Jason more; it scared him that he didn't mind that he'd been lied to his whole life, that these two highly respected pastors and leaders, that he knew, had known this the whole time, but as he thought about it all, it made sense. However, he was going into hysterics again; he started to move around frantically knocking the paper bag to the floor and then stepping on it so it popped, which startled everyone. His breathing was getting out of control. He would soon pass out or worse if he didn't take control of himself. Paul started to panic a little for Jason's state of mind if he didn't pull himself together. He looked around for another paper bag, but Jason had burst the only one.

Miles took control. He grabbed hold of Jason by his shoulders and shouted, 'In the name of our Lord Jesus take hold of your servant and the servant of your church and sent him free.' Within seconds Jason was calm, coherent and sitting on the bench to listen to the rest of the story.

Paul was in awe of his father. He had a real gift and authority in God and in spiritual matters that most people wouldn't understand or wouldn't believe.

Now that Jason was calm, Miles continued. 'Once this act had happened, this created the Judas Cult. The six originals didn't realise this until it was obvious that they couldn't get ill, and worse; they were living beyond there years. The men regrouped then formed the cult, preying on believers for their blood to quench their thirst for life. You see, these Dark Lords were immortal. They tried to keep it a secret for over a thousand years, but a few times it got out. The elite would go out and slay them, fearing they would tell more people the secret of their long life. People feared these Dark Lords and they've played a serious part in history, in the crusades, and throughout most of the church's folk law and myth.'

'So these Dark Lords were vampires, and they obviously still are a risk to us if the Master Disciples are still needed.' Jason voice sounded fearful and he dreaded to hear more but at the same time was intrigued by it all.

Paul felt he needed to answer that remark. 'No, Jason. We feel that the whole vampire myth was just a smoke screen to divert people from the Dark Lords. It was taken to extremes – you know, biting necks to drink blood, they can't be in contact with daylight and that nonsense with turning into Bats. No, Jason; they have become, throughout history, normal looking people, but with a need to be everything that we believers are not – they're greedy, selfish, full of pride, deceitful and most of all: evil. They are indwelt with Satan and are very dangerous. That's why the Master Disciples are needed.'

Jason just paused with the new information that he'd received and took a deep breath, getting prepared for the next part; he could see Pastor Miles was eager to start again.

'Jason, the last of the original six men who cut the body of Judas down lived to over nine hundred years old, and like most of the men they had a numerous amount of wives and partners and created a great number of offspring. We're not sure how many of them were told of the secret of their long lives but they had to gain trust and be careful of the people they did tell.

'Like everything, we don't know for sure because most of what we know has been passed on by family and trusted members of the Council of Reference.'

Jason interrupted. 'Did I hear a mention of a Council of Reference? What is that and why are they involved?'

'Oh, Jason, the Council of Reference was founded over four hundred and fifty years ago and ran a lot of churches throughout the late eighteenth century. When there was a sudden rise of Dark Lords and most of the clergy left the churches to gain employment elsewhere, a great number of churches fell to the Dark Lords, and that's the true reason for the fall in numbers, not what you're told, like the rest of the world.' Jason looked even more confused; Pastor Miles needed to go further into history.

'You have heard of the Knights Templar, the Priory of Zion, the alleged bride of Christ and the possible blood line myth, haven't you?'

Jason just nodded with raised eyebrows, thinking to himself this was a test and should he be taking notes.

'Well, all that nonsense was in fact, nonsense made up by the church to protect the world from the absolute truth. Everything was constructed to make a compelling argument throughout history. Even the Dark Lords themselves would contribute to the cover up, trying desperately to protect the secret. They would leave clues to the whereabouts to the Holy Grail, the sacred bloodline, even give names to high ranking members of the illuminati, a shadow government created to make major decisions, but it was all a charade. The real decision makers were the Council of Reference, a line of spiritual titans that would intercede and would overrule the illuminati's authority. The church was still the controller and distributor of a majority of the world's wealth; they had the control, but were a secret society – a kind of puppet master. Yes, it sounds underhand but it was the way it was done. Yes, yes, you knew about it; sometimes you would even catch a glimpse of the strings but you would never see the puppet master himself. The greatest of illusionists were the Council of Reference and could still be; we don't know.' Pastor Miles winked at Jason, knowing full well that would take some serious thought, or maybe he would take Pastor Miles' word on the subject.

'As you can see, Jason, it is very important that it remains a secret and this information cannot fall into the wrong minds, the type of minds that can be tempted. You see, that's what these Dark Lords use, weak minded believers, just like Judas before them; he betrayed his beliefs and was tempted by greed. You do remember the seven deadly sins; well that's what these Dark Lords use. Apart from their physical actions, the sins are their best and most used weapon of choice to use on believers.'

Jason had a burning question; his mind couldn't think of anything else. 'I have a question to ask if I may, Pastor Miles.'

'Yes. Ask away, Jason,' Miles said, intrigued by Jason's new found enthusiasm. 'How does a Master Disciple destroy a Dark Lord if they are immortal?'

'Good question, Jason, and we will get to that important point in due course. Throughout history the M.D. found out the hard way, with many Master Disciple being killed. The best way was to remove their heads from their bodies. Many people have had a lot of different theories.'

Jason's face had a look of panic all over it. 'Beheading!' He shouted out. He began to panic again, but Pastor Miles put a stop to it before it started,

'Get a grip, Jason, and pull yourself together man.' Pastor Miles' tone was firm and commanded respect, and Jason quickly calmed himself.

Pastor Miles continued. 'A good sharp strike to the back of the neck, the part where the spinal cord connects to the head would bring them down, but in most cases I've known, it's best to remove the head totally to make sure of the kill. There is an alterative to killing them.'

'And what is that?' Jason asked, intriguingly.

'It's very rare, but they need to denounce the work of the evil one – Satan – and fall to their knees, seeking forgiveness for their evil doings and become a believer in Christ.'

'Has anyone ever done that, that you're aware of Pastor Miles?'

'No, Jason, not in my life time.'

'You see the mind is a fragile thing and once corrupted by evil it can dwell there forever, for an eternity in most cases'.

Jason gave a long sigh and paused for a moment before he spoke again. Then Miles got up and walked over to a picture on the wall; it was a picture of a waterfall and was a calming influence on the room until Jason found out what was behind it.

Miles pulled the picture and behind it was a cabinet, so Pastor Miles pulled out one of the drawers and then grabbed a case. It was about the length of a violin case but slimmer.

Miles brought the case over to Jason, sitting patiently, then he placed it on Jason's lap. Pastor Miles lent over and unclipped it and then let Jason open it for himself.

'Go on then, Jason. Open it. See for yourself,' Paul said, wondering how Jason was going to handle this one.

Jason's fingers were shaking and he felt very nervous. He had no idea what was in the case. All he kept thinking to himself was that it was too slim for a head to be in it, so what could be worse? He opened it and there it was, in its shinning glory, Pastor Miles' sword. Jason gasped but then looked deep at the sword and was taken aback by its beauty. The sword was samurai in its style and the handle was made from an ivory-type material and was engraved with angels, archangels and cherubs. Right at the top was an engraved lion: its head at the head of the sword's handle with its mouth open in mid-roar, symbolizing Christ as the head of the church.

Jason was in awe of such a weapon and then realized it was just that – a weapon that was designed to destroy – but he was still struck by its beauty and that this mighty piece of art should have been in a gallery or a museum, anywhere but not actually in use.

'It's ok, Jason. You can take it out of the case,' Pastor Miles insisted.

Jason was starting to get a bit flustered and began to ramble on. 'This reminds me of a film that I've seen; you know, Paul, the film with Sean Connery and Christopher Lambert in. What was it called?'

Pastor Miles was dumbstruck at what Jason was saying out loud.

'You know, Queen did the soundtrack for it. *Highlander* – that was it. They had to cut heads off men that lived forever.'

Paul was worried especially now Jason had a sword in his hands and was waving it about. Perhaps it wasn't a good idea to give the sword to Jason to hold in the current state his mind was in. Miles took control of the situation after seeing the look on Paul's face.

'Ok, Jason. Just calm down and place the sword back in its correct and safe position, back in its case, eh, Jason.'

Pastor Miles nodded his head to Jason, trying to reassure him of the situation.

As Jason placed the sword back, Miles came out with some wise words for them both. 'There's no glory in death, any death. A lost soul is still a lost soul if one doesn't have faith in God. It is the death of deaths. There will always be a way out of any situation for people who have faith and truly believe.'

Wise words that rung true in Jason and Paul's mind. Paul especially found comfort in those words.

'The most important thing to remember is to never go back on your beliefs. Never betray your belief system. Our faith is greater than anything that these Dark Lords can throw at us.' Pastor Miles insisted on this.

Jason raised his hand to ask a question. Pastor Miles whole demeanour seemed to create a student/teacher relationship and Jason felt like the student now.

'You have a question on your mind, Jason?' Miles asked and tried hard not to smile at Jason with his hand raised like a young child.

'Why do the Master Disciples, and the Dark Lords, use swords for there choice of weapons? Wouldn't it be easier to use another form of weapon like a gun? After all, we now live in the modern world.'

'Well, Jason. That is a good question but easy to answer; as well as being tradition, it is also a weapon that is hard to trace. A sword is an elegant weapon that commands respect and requires a lot of training to use with any effect. Guns, you see, require bullets and they leave a lot of evidence. Plus, a bullet won't kill a Dark Lord; a sword will.'

Jason was struggling to retain his train of thought and asked Pastor Miles for a drink of water. He feared the worst and was waiting for the part when they would ask the doomed question.

Pastor Miles could sense the fear in Jason's heart so he tried to address it. 'The reason we are telling you this is because the way of the Master Disciple is that it can only be past on to family members and you know that Paul is too weak to take on the role of M.D.'

With that Jason jumped up from where he was sitting and shouted out 'There's no way I'm going to become this church's Master Disciple. I can't do it. I just can't.' Jason began to panic. He was starting to go into a kind of shock. His hands started to shake, his head was spinning inside and then he just passed out with the shock of it all.

A few moments later Pastor Miles and Pastor Paul had managed to bring the stricken Jason round and tried to reassure him that he wasn't going to be the next Master Disciple.

'No Jason, the reason we have told you is that we want you to help us find the church's new Master Disciple, and as a new team is formed, we will defend this church to the end.'

Miles couldn't have said it any clearer. Jason felt better but was still very nervous.

Chapter Four
Appointed by God

*Hebrews 3:2 'He was faithful to the one who **appointed** him, just as Moses was faithful in all **God**'s house'.*

Four weeks later and Jason was still trying to get over the new revelation he had received from Miles and Paul. He had managed to tell his wife, Lorraine, which was just as shocking to her as it was to Jason.

The couple were coping well, considering the situation, and the two other pastors, Paul and Miles, were very pleased with the couple's maturity.

There was a scheduled meeting with the leadership team, which consisted of all senior leaders, with the exception of Paul – he wasn't up to it. The main subject in discussion Pastor Miles felt would make others feel uncomfortable, so present were the pastors, teachers, small group leaders and cluster group leaders. The meeting was to discuss the future plans of the church and mostly to bring people up to speed on Jason's pastoralship of the church which they had mixed feelings about; some were excited and others felt it was a lack of faith, giving in so soon and not being prepared to pray it through to the bitter end.

But Pastor Miles put some people's hearts at rest.

'I know that some of the team and members of the church feel that I'm giving up on my son, and I might add that Paul wanted to be here this evening, but I said that it would be uncomfortable for some of you, and now I know why, because it's a lack of faith with some of you and other members of the church. Paul hasn't been condemned to a death, if I may add, and I say 'if' my son Paul does die, its not death; its liberation of his soul. As believers why do we get so het up about death? It's our glorious beginning not our ending. We live on you know.'

Pastor Miles began to get carried away with the emotion of it all. Miles had great faith and truly believed that his son would get healed. Jason stepped in to try and calm the situation down before he started to preach a lengthy sermon.

'But the main reason of this meeting is that if Paul is healed, great, praise God, but in the meantime we still have to deal with the running of a busy and active church, and for the record I think Pastor Miles was right to take a lead on this and help us. After all, Pastor Miles is supposed to be retired, so we should be grateful for his time and his gifts especially with the emotional tie of his son being so seriously ill and the future of a church he planted twenty years ago. He is acting on the benefit of the church. And when I say church I speak of the people, the heart of any active church in service to this community.' Jason said it but he couldn't believe what he'd just said out loud. Miles was proud of what he had just said and was reaffirmed that Jason was the right man to lead the church on after his son's glorious meeting with the Lord.

Most of the people bowed their heads in shame, some nodded in agreement but one started to clap.

It was Rachel; she was a cluster group leader and was responsible for a number of small groups that met in homes in the surrounding area, mostly young people. She had great gifting and a heart for the lost. The pastors saw great potential in her.

Rachel then stood up and gestured to the others to do likewise. They all did it, with others clearly doing it in protest but this didn't bother Rachel and she clapped on regardless.

'I'd like to say something if I may.'

The clapping stop so Rachel could address them. 'I really respect Jason and the man who thought it was right to put him in place here, Pastor Paul. He is a great man, a man of honour, and mostly, a true man of God, and God couldn't do better by taking him from us if he wishes. God knew the plan before all this happened so we should not doubt Him either. Thank you.' Rachel sat down with a great smile on her face.

'Thank you Rachel,' Jason said and Miles nodded his appreciation also.

The meeting went on for another hour or so discussing other issues and the day-to-day problems of a busy church.

In closing, the last thing on the agenda was the true reason for the meeting.

'I have a request of you; you are the engine room of the church after all. Please pray about this issue. We do need to appoint an assistant to help Jason and myself in these last, last…' Pastor Miles struggled for the right way to say it. 'Well, we don't know when or how long we have with my son, Pastor Paul, I just thought it was a need that's all.'

The other leaders could see that Pastor Miles was getting upset and agreed to pray for an assistant.

'Just one more thing; the person we need has to be a person that is not already involved in anything in church, so can give a hundred per cent to the assisting of Jason and myself, that's all.'

Jason then closed in prayer and people started to get ready to leave but as people were moving about he made eye contact with Rachel and mouthed, 'Thanks for that.' Rachel leaned in, trying to hear what Jason was trying to say.

'Thanks for what you said,' Jason said again, as Rachel got within a few feet of him to hear more clearly. Jason whispered so others wouldn't hear.

'If you don't mind, Rachel, the other pastors and I would like you to stay for a moment after everyone else has left for a quite word.' Jason felt awkward for asking, knowing full well of the implications of why she was to stay behind.

Pastor Paul walked in after the meeting had finished and everyone had left and gave his father a big hug.

Pastor Miles, Paul and Jason sat down with Rachel. Rachel wasn't nervous at all; she was used to the pressure, after all, in her day job she was a manager and sister on a very busy intensive care ward at the local hospital and she was used to working under great pressure.

'So, what is it that you want to speak to me about?' Rachel's mind raced thinking what on earth could they want with her. 'Was it the standing up and the clapping? If it was, I'm sorry?'

'No, Rachel. That was fine and was greatly appreciated.'

Paul interrupted – 'What standing up and clapping?'

'Never mind. I'll tell you later, Paul. Jason was on great form tonight I may add.'

Rachel was a pastor's pastor, helping and caring for the needs of her leaders and she had great respect and genuine love for all of them. 'So how are you, Paul, really?'

Paul quickly realised that she was asking as a nurse, not as a regular person would ask just to be polite. 'Er, well, not too bad under the circumstances. I'd say I was holding my own, thanks Rachel.'

'Well thanks for staying behind, Rachel, so we could have a quick word with you.' Miles was nervous and Rachel could tell. It was unusual to see Pastor Miles so nervous addressing someone that he knew well.

'Well, there's something we would like to ask you, well put to you, well get your opinion on.'

'Come on, Dad. Spit it out man.'

Rachel was so shocked to see the father and son relationship acted out so vividly in front of her.

But Miles had every right to be nervous and so was Jason, just realising why they had asked Rachel to stay for a moment, but Paul wasn't; Paul was anxious to get the ball rolling, so to speak. Paul wasn't sure of his time left; his life line was ebbing away. Each day that passed without an active Master Disciple in place before he went on to be with the Lord, played on Paul's mind like a lead weight.

'So, what is it that you all want then?' Rachel was puzzled at this unprompted meeting and then put two and two together. The last request from the meeting was to pray about an assistant for Jason and Miles. 'But I couldn't possibly do it,' Rachel thought.

Pastor Miles stepped up to ask Rachel the burning question on all their hearts. 'Rachel we've asked you to stay for a moment just to ask you about your husband, Adam, and ask, if we may, if he was involved in anything in church lately.' Pastor Miles and the other pastors held their breaths a moment.

'Well, you know that Adam and I stopped leading the youth group when Grace was born last August.'

Miles interrupted – 'Yes, yes, but is he involved in anything that we wouldn't necessarily know about?'

Paul could see that his father was getting more impatient especially with the regular meeting running over.

Rachel also noticed Pastor Miles' impatience so she got on with it, totally unaware of what her answers would mean and where it could potentially lead.

'Well, Adam's involved in his prison work and the men's development group, but that's about it, but I might add, he is starting to reduce how much time he's devoting to them, especially with Grace beginning to be more active now that she's nearly nine months old.' Rachel was starting to get the idea now; they had Adam sized up for this new role.

'Well we would like to see Adam for a meeting, maybe tomorrow if that was alright with Adam and yourself.'

'Well, yes of course. I'll have to ask him first, but I think it will be fine. What time should I tell him to come? Don't forget he's at work till four thirty.' Rachel was speaking for her husband; she was also intrigued by this and couldn't wait to tell Adam.

'Well, ask him to be here for about five then. We'll be here waiting.' Pastor Miles was egger to get the ball rolling so to speak and didn't mind staying after five.

'But isn't that the time when you all leave?' Rachel's suspicions grew and she was more intrigued by the urgency of the meeting with her husband. 'What could this be all about?' she thought.

With that all arranged Pastor Miles closed the meeting without even praying, which even the other pastors thought was odd. Rachel looked to Paul and Jason, and they just shrugged their shoulders.

As Rachel walked towards the door she passed Paul. 'I wouldn't worry about it; he's just anxious for you to get home so Adam doesn't worry where you are, that's all.'

Rachel rushed home, so excited to tell Adam of the odd behaviour of the pastors and their strange request to see him. She pulled onto the driveway and the passive infrared set the security light on, which alerted Adam, he then came to the front door to greet her.

'Hi, Hon. Long meeting, ah? You're a little later than usual.' Adam noticed Rachel had something on her mind.

'I'll put the kettle on, we'll sit round the table and talk about it, ok?' Adam started to think it was bad news, and Rachel could sense it a mile away; the stricken look that his face had turned to was a dead give away.

'No, Adam, the meeting was fine; it was what happened after the meeting that freaked me out and the reason I'm later than usual.'

'Why, what happened then, Rach?'

'Jason asked me if I would stay behind after the main meeting with the other pastors, then Paul came in and sat down with us all. I thought they were going to ask me how I was doing or words to that affect, but no; they started asking me about you and what you were doing for the church at the moment.'

'So what did you say to that then?' Adam was nervous at why they would ask for him.

'I told them about your prison work and the men's development group.'

'Then what?' Adam thought the worst 'Maybe I should have told them about the men's group and asked before I set it up.'

'It's not about that. The pastors want to see you tomorrow at five for a meeting.' 'What's it about, Rachel?' Adam always got nervous around the pastors when dealing with them in a professional capacity.

Adam and Rachel had been married for five years and in that time had lead the church youth group very successfully. It was a hundred strong and had fifteen other sub youth leaders and all those had a cell group; a cell group consisted of three to four (a maximum of six) young people, who all had to be organized by the couple every week as well as a mid-week home group meeting for around twenty other youth members that couldn't make the Friday youth meeting.

Rachel had already been involved in the church for five years before they married.

Adam joined the church in 1992. He always respected God, but never truly believed until that same year he lost a best friend in a tragic car accident. He began asking a lot of questions and found himself at church, and ultimately finding God.

As you could tell, the couple were very busy and since taking a long overdue break from things, the couple were now a trio with the birth of their first child, Grace.

As Adam lay there in bed that night, his thoughts went to the first time he was in church after that tragic accident, and with his first meeting with Pastor Paul, but Adam, not being of a church background, just called him, by the informal name of just 'Paul' and it stuck from that day on. Paul and the other pastors didn't really mind that much, they were just glad that the church was the first place that Adam had been to after the accident for good council and to reflect on his own life and where it was going.

That night Adam couldn't sleep. He tossed and turned for hours until he finally fell asleep, so anxious about the meeting the next day.

Adam sat in his car in the rush hour, traffic was building (it was a typical Monday morning), tapping his fingers on the steering wheel. His mind and thoughts pondered many things but one was clear, very clear – he was bored. He ached to find out what the meeting was all about, but that was at the end of his day.

'Ten years. Ten years. I know I've been there for what seems a lifetime already, but can something happen today, for goodness sake!' was the thought running through Adam's troubled mind.

Or was it a prayer?

Only a few nights before, his very own pastor, Pastor Miles, was in a darkened alley meeting with the Billionaire business tycoon Derek Greyer – a very cloak and dagger affair. But Adam was completely oblivious to that sitting there watching the traffic light sequence change for the third time without a single car moving. It was hugely frustrating for Adam; he had memorized the traffic light sequences for most of the city. Adam worked for the Government and had spent time in the city's planning department and had vast experience in the traffic management of the entire road network. Yes, he was very meticulous, and he would often admit it himself. But at times like this it was useful and yet annoying at the same time.

His mind raced and he found solace in mental arithmetic. It was sometimes the only way he found of alleviating the mindless boredom of it all. 'Okay, it's a thirty second sequence with four way traffic signals, plus two filter lanes that came on at peak traffic times, such as now.' Adam's mind raced, calculating all the figures allowing the eight second delay on each sequence for the traffic to clear to allow the next lane of traffic to move on. 'A potential four minute wait, or 228 seconds, again,' he thought to himself. He had a real knack for figures and could calculate multiple numbers in his head in just seconds. That's probably why the twenty-eight year-old was the youngest in his department.

His current job was Health and Safety consultant; he had other duties for the Government. He started his apprenticeship when he left school at just sixteen with no formal qualifications he could call his own. Well, maybe a sports diploma; he excelled at sports or anything physical.

He had worked up from the bottom, literally learning the basics of building and maintenance and had worked on the roads for many years, constructing many of the city's road networks until a few years ago when he got into management. The promotion was long overdue, even for a man as young as him.

Many people noticed the potential in him, right from his first completely managed, engineered, full road construction project. His meticulous nature rubbed off into many parts of his life and it was only now he had started to calm down and mellow a little. That's what fatherhood does to you; he had become a father for the first time earlier that year, and it had its advantages. He could sometimes and only sometimes be a little disorganised like he was this morning.

After a twelve minute wait he was moving at last and on his way to work. He would pass many of the guys he worked with when he was an apprentice, occasionally they would still wave or stop him for a quick chat.

He had a lot of respect for what he called the 'backbone of the workforce' being the guys on the ends of those shovels. It was often a thankless task working in all weathers under massive pressure to perform with strained budgets and elevating costs. But Adam often fought their corner and it was the main reason for his current position: to keep their welfare his main priority. The respect was mutual; the men on the roads would really appreciate a visit from Adam when on a safety matter. Well that's what he called it in the office. They only knew he'd be there for a chat or a quick cuppa in the site hut.

In the eyes of others he had it made, but recently he'd been a little bored with it all. He'd pretty much gotten out as much as he could get out of his job and, at the end of the day, that's all it was – just a job. He had never called it a career or thought of it being a particularly noble task; he just knew he needed to be there for the men that had been there for him when he was younger.

But now change was on the horizon. But would the change be of benefit, and whom would be the benefactor?

It was finally time for the meeting and Adam had, had a terrible day at work to top it off, but after he'd finished his day job he was on his way. He decided to give Rachel a call.

Adam called Rachel from the car on his way to the church on the hands free.

'Hi, Rachel, it's Adam. Just thought I'd give you a quick call to say I was ok and on my way to church.'

'Thanks, Hon. Are you nervous at all?'

'Yes, just can't think what this is all about, Rach.'

'Don't worry too much. It can't be too bad. At the end of the day they are men of God. What news can be worth worrying about from a team of pastors, eh?'

'Ok, Rach. Thanks for the encouragement. I needed it after the day I've had.'

'Why? What's wrong?'

'I'll tell you all the details later. Let's just say I could have just quit, that's how bad a day. I'll see you later. Love you.'

'Love you too.'

Rachel was nervous but at the same time excited for her husband and just couldn't wait for him to come back and tell of what went on at this mysterious meeting. But no man was as nervous as Adam. He drove his pride and joy, his classic VW Golf Gti, in to the church car park. Adam loved his cars and although his Golf was a little worn around the edges, the car was in good condition for its age, apart from a little rust around the front headlight. The car was what Adam called the 'shopping trolley'; it had done all the running about that a family needed to do – over a hundred and thirty thousand miles but it still drove like new. Adam had a real issue with new cars and felt so strongly about it that he only drove cars that had genuine character. He felt that the Golf Gti was the car that summed him up – relatively young, very reliable, and a bit quirky. And that's all that Adam could think of – cars. It was one of the subjects that could subdue him; it was the only subject where Adam was a true genius.

As Adam got out the car Jason was there to greet him.

Jason knew Adam really well and knew how to calm the nerves. Jason nodded to Adam and said, 'Still got that old Golf, eh?'

'They are good cars. They don't make 'em like that anymore, and if they did I'd just buy another one just like it. Hiyah, Jason. Good to see you.'

'It's even better to see you, and I can speak for Paul and Miles when I say this. We are glad that you have come today.'

Adam was surprised by how Jason made Adam feel; he made him feel like a special guest, a member of royalty, the only thing missing was the red carpet, Adam thought.

The walk up to Paul's office was a nervous one, but Adam held it together.

Pastor Paul, Pastor Miles and now Pastor Jason, quickly followed by a nervous looking Adam, gathered in the already tension-filled office. Before anything was discussed, the Pastor's were on edge, especially Pastor Miles.

But how was Pastor Miles going to broach a subject that had been kept secret to non-family members for over six generations? More importantly; how was he going to ask a man to do a job without telling him the secret – the absolute truth?

'Sorry if I'm a bit late, guys.' Adam had no problem with addressing the pastors that way and neither did the Pastors. It was a warm release from all the formality of church life, and was one of the reasons that they liked Adam and Rachel so much.

'No problem, Adam, and anyway you're not that late, only a few minutes and it's only expected when you've just finished work,' said Pastor Miles. He could see that Adam was nervous so he spoke softly so not to unnerve him.

Adam just nodded in agreement.

'How is your work, anyway? Is it going well?'

'Well I could have easily quit after the kind of day I've had, and that's all I have to say about that, thank you very much.' Adam was trying his hardest to relaxed, but it was just coming over as aggressiveness and he was soon to notice it himself. 'Sorry if that sounded a bit rash of me. It's the work coming out of me.'

'There's no need to apologise,' Paul said, seeing the very thing, the very quality that Adam needed to have to become a Master Disciple: the ability to switch moods from a passive to a defensive personality in a moment.

Paul was excited and his father could read him like a book. Paul's whole body language had changed from someone nervous to a person who had the weight of the world lifted from his shoulders.

'Anyway, guys. What's this all about? You really freaked Rachel out last night with this request.'

'We are very sorry about that. It's because we don't want anyone to know about this little meeting, that's all. It's of a delicate subject.' Miles was quick to answer Adam but Paul quickly butted in to ask the next question.

'We have a strange request of you, Adam. You know about my condition and that even though we still have great faith in God that I could get healed from my ailments we still have the matter of business as usual to take care of.'

'So myself, Pastor Miles and Pastor Jason have been praying and seeking God on a number of issues and one particular, a special kind of 'helper' in the church and the wider community.'

'Helper? What kind of helper?'

Pastor Miles spoke up. 'You'd better sit down for this, Adam; this information is going to come as bit of a shock to you.'

Pastor Miles and the other Pastor's began to tell Adam the story they had told Jason just only a few weeks ago, and came all the same interruptions and the same shock to Adam's belief system.

Adam was seriously shocked by this new revelation, but at the same time intrigued by it – a similar reaction to Jason's hearing of the news.

But Adam questioned it over and over asking deep-rooted questions that challenged Pastor Miles to his core.

Paul stepped up and just came out with it, the burning question on all their lips. 'So what do you think, Adam?'

Adam just shrugged and said, 'Think of what? I don't know what to think after hearing that for the first time.'

'Jason told us of your skill and your clear gifting in areas that could be of benefit to all concerned.'

'Wow! I'm starting to get the picture now, guys. You know I'm a little slow to catch on after hearing that, but I think I know where this is heading. You want me to a Master Disciple, don't you?' Adam got up from his seat and started to panic a little. 'Paul, I'm flattered by the sentiment, and Pastor Miles, thanks that you would even consider me to be the replacement for your son in this role but what makes you all so sure of my ability? I've just become a dad for the first time, and that's been a new challenge to get used to. What makes you so sure? Please tell me, cause I can't see it, please.'

Adam was getting a little jittery and needed to calm down a little. Jason stepped up this time. 'Adam, if it's any consolation they only told me this news a few weeks ago and I was just has shocked by it as you.'

'Yeah, but did they ask you to become an M.D after they'd told?' Jason just nodded. 'See that's why I think I have the right to be a little more shocked, ok, Jason.'

'I'm sorry, Adam. It was probably me that lead the pastors to even consider you.' Adam paused in his stepping around Paul's office to listen to Jason confess to the true reason why Adam was there in the first place.

'You remember the time when you helped me to shed those few extra pounds that I gained when Jessica was born and I couldn't get enough time to go the gym, so you devised that little home exercise programme for me? Well, I told Paul and Miles that you kept really fit and you did a little martial arts when you were younger, and that you kept it up for your own personal fitness programme.'

Adam sat back down in shock. He was still: still in mind and body; no movement at all. It was like he was meditating on something and the pastors dare not disturb him in what seemed to be a deep spiritual thought. Pastor Miles dared to speak first and bring Adam out of his spiritual coma. 'Adam! Adam!'

Adam looked up to acknowledge Miles. That's just what he did – look, but it was such a look that disturbed Paul and Jason but not Miles; it reminded him of his youth and his fiery temper.

Miles continued like nothing had happened. 'Jason tells us that your garage is some sort of gym and that you train regularly.'

Adam's fiery disposition was tamed momentarily, as Miles got up from his seat and pulled on the same dusty old bible that Jason had pulled on, only a few weeks earlier, to reveal the secret passageway down to the Master Disciple training room.

All the pastors followed Miles' lead and headed down the staircase to the training room. Pastor Miles reached out his hand to Adam. 'Come, Adam. You will enjoy this I assure you.'

Adam got up from the seat and followed Miles down to where he saw a room so filled with equipment he thought he was in a professional gymnasium. He shook his head in disbelief and took a quick glace at his watch. He had totally been unaware of the time and over two hours had passed; it was quarter past seven.

'I'd better give Rachel a call. She'll be worried sick.'

Adam gave Rachel a call on his mobile phone, and within a couple of rings Rachel answered.

'What's going on? You've been ages. Are you on your way back now?' Rachel was so eager to know what had gone on; Adam was struggling to get a word in.

'I'm still at church, Rach. I've just lost track of time here with the Pastors.'

'Going well then?' Rachel interrupted, so excited to hear the news, but would she continue to be once she realizes what the news entailed and most of all would she understand the truth of it all or would it all come as a shocking conclusion.

'Rachel, I can't talk now. I'll be with you soon.' Adam had no idea how he was going to broach the notion of considering their offer or even how he was going to tell her the story he was hearing for the first time. He was struggling to even think, but now was a time to just listen to what the pastors had to say, so Adam focused his mind back on the situation at hand. He quickly shook his head to regain his focus and continued to look around the training room. Adam was awestruck; the training room was amazing. His mind simply forgot the agenda and walked gingerly over to the bunch bag hanging still, with just one thought on his mind: 'Let's see if I can get that moving.' Adam jumped over the weights bench and in one fluid motion completed a spinning roundhouse kick with such power the bag folded and swung out of control, then Adam simply bunch it to bring it to a full stop without any hint of movement. The pastors were amazed to see such a magnificent show of talent and gifting in a man that was such a devout believer and what society would deem a weak person because of it.

Adam apologised for his outburst, which the pastors were more than happy to witness.

Pastor Miles thought to himself, 'A man of God with a God-given talent. We will train him, and he will become a mighty Master Disciple: a Master Disciple that will complete the task at hand: an M.D that will end the evil Dark Lord's walk on earth forever.'

'What are you so happy about? What's with the huge smile, Dad?' Paul asked his father.

'It's just that I'm so glad that we decided to ask Adam. He is perfect. He has such skill and a talent that he will bring a new freshness and, most importantly, gifting to the role of Master Disciple. Did you see that kick, Paul? It was amazing.'

Jason and Adam had moved on to the running machine and he was asking how he and his wife Lorraine had coped with the news of seeking a new Master Disciple out from the church, to which no one else would have knowledge of.

'Adam, that is an interesting question and I've asked it myself a million times, but I always get the same answer back; it's God's mission and he will bring about order in the chaos. We just have to trust his judgement and also the leaders he has appointed to lead over us. God has obviously given us these leaders, because of their gifting and you can clearly see their importance; just look at the major attack on their faith with Paul's illness, and they still get up and fight on. I feel it a privilege to work with such men of God.'

Jason's speech had a profound affect on Adam and he quickly grabbed hold of Jason's arm and pulled him towards Paul and Miles, talking excitedly about the prospect of Adam becoming the new Master Disciple, but would the reality of it all be too much? And without thinking of the dire consequences, Adam spoke to the three pastors directly, and said, 'I've decided to take you up on your offer. It would be an honour to become a Master Disciple and be the protector of this church. I would like some time to talk it over with Rachel and get her blessing on this because I dare say it will have a profound affect on her spiritually as well, but at this moment my heart is saying yes.'

Chapter Five
To Make The Right Decision

Revelation 4 v 20 'Here I am I stand at the door and knock. If anyone hears my voice and opens the door, I will come in and eat with him, and he with me'.

THE MEETING WITH ADAM ENDED WITH Milo praying; now he and the others were allowed to call him by his M.D. name, but only when they met.

Adam was more nervous than ever as he walked towards his car. 'How am I going to explain this to Rachel?' was all Adam could think of. His mind was racing with thoughts of letting down the pastors, church members, the community and most of all God. But Adam hadn't got long to think of something. The church was only a ten minute drive to the family home and he knew that Rachel would be waiting with baited breath to hear of what went on in that fateful meeting.

Adam was trying to rehearse some kind of speech but as he pulled up on to the driveway the passive infrared sensor picked up the car's movements and the security light came on. With Rachel's alertness being heightened by her anticipation of Adam's arrival, she was out the front door and next to the Golf's driver's door before Adam could get out the car.

'So, how did it go then? Go well, eh?'

Adam had no choice but to just put her off for the moment. She was holding Grace and she was fast asleep. Rachel, being a complete bag of excitement, had lost track of time and not put her to bed at her normal time of seven o'clock.

'It went well. I think I just need to get in the house, eh, so we can chat it through around the table.'

Rachel immediately knew it was serious. All their major discussions happened around the table in the kitchen with a strong cup of coffee at hand. She then immediately took Grace to bed once Adam had given her a kiss goodnight. Within ten minutes of getting Grace settled, Rachel demanded to know what had gone on at that meeting.

Adam was struggling. He'd only just been told the truth himself a short time ago and now he had to go through it all again, barely believing it himself and it would seem harder to someone who wouldn't be seeing the training room as they were being told. So he plucked up enough courage and began to tell Rachel the story he had been told by their trusted pastors only hours earlier.

'Ok, Rachel. What I'm going to tell you may come as a bit of a shock.' That was an understatement if there was ever one, but Rachel sat there still, with, what seemed to Adam, a holy calmness and tranquil attitude that had to have come from God. Any normal person, hearing this, would probably pass out with the shock of it all. So Adam twittered on for over an hour telling Rachel all about the Dark Lords and their rampaging throughout history and especially throughout the time of the early church and for the need of a defender: a warrior so filled with the power and might of God to defend them and protect the church.

Rachel sat there amazed by Adam's excitement and attention to detail to a new truth he had just heard and trusted straight away; and then to tell it with such conviction was inspiring to her. As Adam was getting to the crux of it all Rachel soon remembered the previous meeting with the pastors. Rachel interrupted and was so excited to tell Adam.

'That's it! That's what that meeting was all about.'

'What meeting, Rach?' Adam was puzzled and had lost his train of thought.

'The meeting asking us to pray for an assistant to the pastors.'

'It's not an assistant, it's a new M.D. to replace Paul as Pastor Miles is worried about Paul not pulling through. I know Pastor Miles and, him being a thorough man, he is even planning a replacement for his own son. What an honour.'

'Why would the church need a managing director? It's not a company or anything, is it?' said an utterly puzzled and confused Rachel.

Adam tried to explain the best he could: 'No, Rach. In church terms an M.D. is a Master Disciple.'

'Well, how come I've never heard the term before? I've been in the church most of my life and I have never heard of a Master Disciple.'

'Rachel, what I'm about to tell you and everything else you are going to hear tonight must never be discussed with any one. Do you understand me?'

Rachel took notice of the seriousness of Adam; his eyes were piercing. He looked full of emotion, like he was ready to cry.

'Ok Adam.' Rachel poised herself, ready for more revelations.

'You have never heard the term M.D. because it's never been discussed with a non-bloodline church leader or member.'

'What do you mean a non-bloodline church leader or member?' Rachel was getting more confused and then she got up from her seat and started to pace around the kitchen.

'Well, you know that Paul's got cancer and it's terminal?'

'Yes, Yes.' Rachel was getting more wound up by Adam backtracking.

'Well, Paul should have been the M.D. because his father was pastor of a church and so was Paul's grandfather. Their family goes back seven generations of pastors and church leaders. So it's the first time in history that the role of Master Disciple has been offered to a non-bloodline church leader.'

Rachel paused for a moment. She stopped pacing around and thought of what an honour it would be for her husband to fulfil a role, a position in the church, that could potentially affect future history. Rachel was getting a little ahead of herself and was being carried away with the emotion of it all.

Rachel walked over to Adam, gave him a hug and said, 'What an honour. What a privilege to be asked – such a role for the church and community.'

Adam was awestruck. He couldn't believe Rachel was excited about it all. But once all the excitement had gone Rachel soon realised the seriousness of the role of Master Disciple and was scared for her husband and fearful for his life.

'Adam, there's no way that you've agreed to this. Just because you know the secret doesn't necessarily mean that you will do it, because that's bribery.'

'Rachel, I told them that my decision will be made up by the mutual agreement of both of us praying about it and seeking God.' Adam soon realising that what he just said was a lie. In his heart he wanted to be the next Master Disciple. He hated lying to Rachel, but there was a time when Rachel had misled him too.

Before the couple met, Rachel's grandfather had set up a trust to be passed on to her in the light of his death: a trust fund that had to be kept secret until Rachel was married. The secret was a property that had an estimated value of over 1.5 Million pounds, but it couldn't be sold. The property was an old people's home but Rachel hated that term and liked to call it 'a rest home for the seriously over-worked and under-appreciated', or the term that was family friendly was 'The Home'.

Rachel had managed to gain the qualifications to successfully manage and run the home through no intention of her own when gaining her degree in nursing and nursing management. The home had successfully been running for years whilst Rachel's grandfather, William Winters, was still alive and ran for a further ten years after he died, with Rachel still unaware of any secret will or trust.

The couple found out on their wedding day (May 17th 1997) when a letter was read out during the announcements and reading of the cards; it read:

To the happy couple,

This is a message from your grandpapa. I hope this message finds you well, Rachel, my dearest and only grandchild. I know that I did spoil you, but I felt that my legacy should live on and I know I was especially close to you. I have left you both a little something that I know will be of some help in those hard years to come when the thought of children and a family of your own are in mind, but with the hardship of the extra finance I now feel that this is the appropriate time to give you this. The home that I ran and owned for over forty seven years is now the rightful property of the newly-wedded couple here before you all today. Whatever Rachel's new married name is; I hope it's a strong name.

I hoped you picked your husband well and remembered what we both said.

Please forgive this, my dear, I just wanted you to get the right man first, a man of integrity, Rachel. I know that was the most important item on your ideal man list.

I would like to thank a few people myself at this point if I may: my solicitor for writing up the complex will for me and having it in your possession for all these years – a speech for a wedding that hadn't even taken place – and most of all for keeping your word for so many years; you to are a man of integrity and honour.

With thanks always,

W.A. Winters

You could have probably imagined Adam and Rachel were more than surprised by the news and very shocked to learn that the couple had just inherited a place where Rachel had spent many years of her youth, running around the fabulous grounds, playing hide and seek with members of staff and, most of all, spending time with her beloved grandpapa.

But with all that water under the bridge, this new news had come as even more of a shock. Rachel was beside herself with the worry of it all, the way Adam seemed set on becoming the new Master Disciple – it troubled her. The fact they'd only just become parents for the first time and were having to adapt to a new way of living was one thing but this was a total life shift; their whole belief system, the way they lived their lives, would change forever.

But the couple sought the Lord on it and prayed throughout the night to seek the face and thoughts of God about an issue they already knew the answer to.

Within the early hours, the couple came back together after seeking God in different rooms so not to get emotionally tied to one another.

The very next morning the pair woke from the best night's sleep they had had for a long time. Grace slept through without making a single noise, and both came to the same conclusion.

'Yes, Adam, you are a very gifted individual and have many talents with many of them God-given. You will make a great defender and Master Disciple. It will be an honour to be your encourager in this your God-given calling.'

Adam's response was of similar content but with a slight change: 'Rachel. Yes is the answer I got from God but I kind of knew when I was first told. After last night, praying it through, that did it for me and confirmed that this was my calling, to become a Master Disciple.

The couple hugged and a still moment came over them, standing there in the bedroom. It was like God was there in the room with them getting in on the group hug. Adam and Rachel felt greatly blessed by the way God had communicated to them and confirmed it by his presence in the room.

Later that morning Pastor Miles gave Adam a call from the church office; He already knew Adam's decision. He had also been seeking God throughout the night with amazing accuracy, his great prophetic gift at action yet again.

'Ok, Adam. When do we start the training then, Eh?' Pastor Miles didn't even give Adam a chance to say that he'd decided yet.

Taking Adam by surprise, he just responded with 'Yes, ok then. We'll start when you are ready, Eh!'

'I'm ready now. Come to the church and we will begin your training.'

'Pastor Miles, er, I still have a job to go to you know. I thought this was a volunteer role for me, not a full time gig, Pastor.'

'Well, what did you expect? A phone call for when we needed you? This is not the movies. It's not Batman and Robin. We don't know when the Dark Lord will attack and we don't have an M.D. signal.'

'So you want me to give up my job to be the full time M.D. of the church? Man! This is fast becoming the biggest burden to carry – knowing a secret, having to replace a dear family member into the role of a warrior that I was not born into and now you want me to give up my job? That's great! Just perfect!'

'Adam, I think you'd better see me at some point this morning and we will talk it through then.'

'Ok Miles. Would lunchtime be alright with you? I'd hate to clash with your break time, I know how busy you are with everything else going on, with Paul and all the rest of your schedule.'

'No, lunchtime will be fine. This is important. It's the most important issue that's on my agenda anyway. So I'll see you then. Bye!'

'Bye, Pastor.'

So Adam went to work as normal, but his mind was filled with doubt and was weary about the future. What would they do as a family if Adam had to give up his job and be the Master Disciple 24/7, on call to defend the church.

Once Adam was at work he decided to call Rachel and get her views and most of all pray about this situation that had arisen.

'Yes, Adam. What is it?'

'It's Pastor Miles. He's made a suggestion. Well, I should put it a different way – he's made a change to the M.D. role at church.'

Rachel was getting rather impatient. 'Well? Spit it out.'

Adam was reluctant to say, especially after Rachel only just hearing the initial news of the M.D. role. 'Well, it's the fact that it would probably be better if the person asked to fulfil the role would be prepared to do it full-time.'

Adam waited for the shock factor to be taken on board, but Rachel was silent, which surprised Adam and he started to worry.

'Adam, I love you. Didn't you realise that when we both prayed last night? We'll just have to release some of the money from my work at the 'home' to cover some of the salary that you won't be bringing in, that's all, and the church will probably give you something, well I hope so, with you risking your life and all.'

Adam was so relieved to hear Rachel sounding so encouraging and supportive to the discussion that had just turned the family's life upside-down in every way possible.

At lunchtime Adam went to see Pastor Miles at the church. He was so excited to see the pastor now that he had all the green lights to start his training.

Adam explained the phone call to Rachel and the two of them laughed. Adam continued to tell him that he had considered handing in his notice at work and would be giving the whole idea of working two roles a month's trial just to see if he could maintain the two together.

'Adam, there is a meeting that I would like to call for tomorrow night and I would like Rachel to come to it and settle her thoughts and worries. That's all, for now, then once you have finished work we will start your training. Please forgive me for my lack of patience.'

Adam was unaware of the urgency of the situation and also the fact Derek Greyer existed as a Dark Lord.

The very next evening, the time had come for the meeting at church. Even Grace was in attendance; a babysitter was out of the question. It would have probably been someone from church, and Adam and Rachel didn't want too many awkward questions about the reason for this secret meeting.

As Adam and his family pulled up into the church car park, Adam noticed a lot of familiar cars, so he parked next to Pastor Miles'. Adam tried to make light of the situation by talking about the pastors' car: 'Mondeo ST200, eh! Not as fast as this thing, eh Rach!'

Rachel took no notice. She was too busy thinking of the meeting.

The family car – as Adam called it – was a Subaru Legacy Quad cam turbo estate and it had been beefed up by a company called Prodrive. They were responsible for the world rally team's cars. It was a very fast car and Adam was immensely proud of it. And once again, it reflected another side to Adam's personality – an old car but practical and quick.

But at this time Rachel wasn't ready to talk about cars and their performance; all she could think of was the impending meeting with whoever was there.

The couple carried Grace (asleep in her car seat) and as they all walked in to the pastor's office, to their surprise, all the pastors and their wives were there also looking very nervous as well; this put Rachel's heart at rest.

In attendance were Jane (Paul's wife), Margaret Leonard ('Mrs Leonard' – no one called her by her first name) and finally Jason's wife Lorraine.

Rachel felt really at ease with the other wives there and sat next to Lorraine.

Pastor Miles spoke first.

'I'm glad all of you could make it at such short notice. This is probably the single most important meeting of this church's history and I find great honour to be part of it.'

'You are all aware of the discretion of the nature of this meeting. Adam, all the pastors and their wives have been brought up to speed on the issue of you succeeding Paul to become this church's new Master Disciple.'

Rachel was starting to get very nervous at what her husband was getting himself involved in, as she looked at Grace in her car seat, sleeping soundly, unaware of what her father was about to embark upon.

Pastor Miles noticed Rachel's tension and said, 'Rachel, I bet, if I was a betting man, you've been thinking a lot about this, in the short time you've had to think that is. So tell me what are your worries?'

Pastor Miles didn't need the gift of discernment to figure that one out; it was written all over Rachel's worried face.

There was a short pause. Rachel then cleared her throat and said, 'Of cause I'd be worried. I was shocked to hear this new revelation and the facts of this Judas cult and then even more shocked to find out that you needed my husband to become a guardian for the church.'

Jane and Lorraine nodded and twittered on in agreement, both acknowledging their own experiences in finding about this new revelation.

Rachel was putting a lot of emphases on her husband, sort of claiming ownership on him. She held a tight grip on Adam's hand; the other was on Grace's car seat. She felt she was losing everything, and then Paul's wife, Jane, spoke. She had a quiet, delicate, angelic voice that always calmed and brought about a stillness to any given situation. She was a spiritual giant. She had to be; her whole life had been spent preparing for this and to find her husband couldn't do it due to the cancer was neither a blessing nor a relief. It was the ultimate catch 22 – a healed husband with a high risk of death as a Master Disciple, or a husband with cancer who would have to deal with the illness for years.

Rachel just looked at Jane and immediately felt guilty.

'Please forgive me, Jane. I was just being selfish.'

'No, Rachel. No matter how spiritual we are, we still need to protect the ones we love. It doesn't make us less of a believer. Trust me, I was just the same when I was first told.'

All the wives nodded in agreement and even Lorraine spoke out saying that even Jason knowing such a secret was bad enough.

Rachel started to cry in relief. Jane reassured her saying, 'We are all here if you need us. We are the backbone of prayer for these guys and they need us just as much as the church and community need them; you just don't forget that, Okay Rachel!'

Just then Grace started to cry.

'It's strange how a baby can sense when their mother is upset,' said Pastor Miles.

Pastor Miles then asked Jason to open up Adam's new office.

'I think we need to stretch our legs a little. Jason, would you be so kind as to show us down to Adam's new office please?'

'It would be an honour,' said Jason. So he grabbed the bible and released the mechanism to open the secret door that was the rear wall of the office and started to go down stairs. 'Ladies, would you please follow me down.'

Rachel looked shocked but quickly picked up Grace, who was now settling off again; she was so intrigued by the other partners rushing down the stairs to the training room that Adam had spoke about so enthusiastically. She couldn't have been held back by anyone or anything.

Once everyone was down, the training room came alive with light for all to see. Rachel's face was alight with excitement and a smile from ear to ear.

Some of the wives started to chat among themselves.

'I haven't been down here in such a long time,' Jane said to Margaret.

'It's been at least twelve months, Jane.'

Lorraine quickly stood next to Rachel; it was also a first time experience for her seeing the training and she was clearly nervous about the whole thing.

They all gathered around Pastor Miles, waiting for him to address them.

'I know this is a lot for the both of you to take on board, Adam, Rachel, but this will be your office from now on, if you still want it to be?'

Adam looked to Rachel and the pair nodded to Pastor Miles. 'Yes, Milo, now that I can officially call you that. It would be our honour for us both to defend and protect this house of God in His name and through His Son with the assistance of His Spirit.'

Pastor Miles closed the meeting with a prayer.

'I thank you for these people who stand before you now. Bless them in and through your name oh Lord and bless and honour their hearts that hold such knowledge dear to themselves and only share their worries and anxieties with you. So bless them I pray in the name of our Lord and saviour, Jesus. Amen.'

Adam and Rachel said their goodbyes and then left to get Grace to bed.

Once home and Grace was all tucked up in bed, Adam took time out to seek God on the next stage. He spent over three hours in the study just trying to get focus on the idea of being the sole person responsible for the whole community. Rachel's excitement was soon dampened by Adam's actions and the seriousness of the situation took its place.

Within an hour of Adam going into the study the phone went and it was Lorraine.

'Hiyah! It's just me, Rachel – Lorraine. I just thought I'd phone to see how you were. It was a nervous experience, eh, seeing the training room.'

'No, not at all, Loraine. I thought it was really exciting. It's now that I've got really nervous. As soon as we got back and sorted out Grace, Adam's gone and shut himself in the study to seek some focus on it all.'

'I wouldn't worry, Rachel, our Jason did the same but he was in his office at church. He was there half the night. I was so worried. At least Adam's there, eh. It could always be worse.'

'Thanks, Lorraine. Thanks a lot for the phone call. It was really appreciated. I feel a whole lot more relaxed, if that is at all possible with what we've taken on, eh.'

'Ah well, God Bless. Have a good evening and see you soon, eh.'

'Thanks again, Lorraine, and God bless you. Goodbye. See ya!'

The very next day Adam had decided to give Rachel a break and take Grace out for the day – a 'daddy and daughter day'. Once in the car the pair reached the bottom of their road and for a split second Adam didn't know where to go. 'Free time and no idea how to spend it,' he thought. Then it dawned on him. 'I know where we can go, my precious,' he said, as his eyes poured over his beautiful Grace.

The 'Home' was on the agenda and Adam was grinning from ear to ear. He hadn't been for a while and the last time they'd visited the Home it was to show off Grace to all the staff. It had been over six months and at that moment Adam was struck with guilt.

That was that! He'd made up his mind; they would go there and maybe pay a visit on something else whilst there.

From time to time Adam had helped out at the home and had frequently helped out Joe, the grounds keeper, a life long friend to Rachel's grandfather.

As the pair approached the Home, the tall iron gates were closed as always. So Adam wound down the window and typed in the security code to access the main gates. Once opened, Adam could see Joe in the distance driving along in his converted golf buggy along the half mile road to the main car park. He pulled along side to greet him.

'Hi there, Joe. How's things mate?'

Joe turned with a startled look all over his face. 'Oh, it's you, Master Adam. And look who's here then.' Joe jumped from his buggy and ran round the car to give Grace his normal greeting to a baby – the obligatory pinching of the cheek and the squeaky voice. 'Who's a beauty, eh, eh?'

Joe was a wonderful man who had one of those work-worn, weary faces but with a smile that could heat the coldest of hearts. He seemed to live in his tweed jacket and wellies. In fact, he was always impeccably dressed (well, for a grounds keeper); he always wore a shirt and tie, what ever the weather, and his straw-like, wiry hair poked out from beneath his flat cap.

Adam hugely respected Joe. He'd worked at the home for over thirty-eight years, full time. He and his late wife Katherine shared a cottage within the grounds of the home for over forty years together. To say that she was warm-hearted would have been an understatement; she had a molten lava heart that overflowed into every life she touched and she would kill you with kindness; she would bake cakes for England. But unfortunately the beautifully large-hearted Katherine fought a long battle with cancer and died in Joe's arms at the age of seventy-two. She was buried within the grounds of their humble cottage which Joe tended to every morning before he started his duties. Joe's immaculate temperament and his impeccable character shone for the two of them now; he was a pillow of strength – all noble characteristics that Adam envied, and longed to gain in his old age.

Joe got back onto his buggy and went about his duties as he always did without query or complaint.

Once the pair had pulled up to the home Adam gave a swift wave to Julie working in the front office.

The home was like a cross between a Victorian school and a hotel; it had about seventeen self-contained flats in the grounds and Adam had a few of the old stage coach garages for himself – what he called his 'hobbies' space. But he felt he had to show his face in the office at least to show Grace off.

Julie had only seen Grace a handful of times, so it was long overdue to see her again. Adam always struggled with the attention a baby brought, feeling even more pressure to succeed as a parent, especially now in the new secret role he found himself in.

Julie cooed and cuddled Grace for as long as Grace could stand before she let everyone know it was enough. Julie could sense the genuine reason for the visit; Adam had itchy feet and wanted desperately to get to his garages round the back of the home. It wasn't a long drive round but Adam placed Grace (now settling down again from another ordeal of face pinching and all round cuteness that no normal baby could tolerate) back into the car. He drove round past Joe's sheds and up to the many old stagecoach garages at the rear of the home.

He opened the garage door to see a dusty sheet over a car; Adam quickly pulled the sheet off to reveal his immaculate 1991 BMW M3 Evolution Sport, one of the last ones ever made.

It was his twenty-fifth birthday present from Rachel. It was Adam's favourite car in the whole world; he had loved them ever since he was fourteen.

Adam walked around to the driver's door, opened it up, got in and started it up; it roared into life on its first turn of the key.

'First time!' Adam shouted. He slowly pulled the car out of the garage and left it running whilst trying to find the hose to his jet wash. After washing some of the dust off that the sheet can never guard against, Grace woke up.

'Ok then, Grace. Time for your first run in the Beamer.' Adam then quickly closed the stagecoach doors, turned off the ignition and locked up the Legacy. Within a few minutes Grace was back asleep again.

Adam was really enjoying himself with the open road ahead with his favourite car and his daughter by his side. He was a true petrol head; he loved everything about cars and the freedom they gave him, not in the selfish way, but his mind was free just to concentrate on one objective; he could give his all just to one pursuit.

Adam was grateful to God. He felt so close to God when behind the wheel because he felt his most relaxed. And with that in mind, Adam began to pray about the mission before him. Adam's mind wondered onto spiritual matters and felt a closeness he had never felt before; he was overcome with emotion and love for his Lord.

Just as Adam was getting the car straight round a fantastic right hander, he felt his phone vibrate in his pocket. Adam quickly pulled up in a convenient place to answer it. The caller ID read 'Rachel'.

'Hello Rach.'

'Where are you? We need you quickly. It's Pastor Miles.' With that the phone went dead. Adam, thinking the worst, turned the beamer around and headed for home. But this time the drive was very fast. The car behaved like it should and Adam's driving was a little panicked but he held it together. His mind was racing like the engine was. Grace was being tossed around a little more than before but she was still sound asleep. A few minutes later he was back home, but as Adam pulled on the driveway, Rachel ran out clutching a medical bag.

'Adam, we've got to go to the church quickly.' The panic on Rachel's face was clear; something serious had happened. 'It's Pastor Miles,' was all she said as she jumped into the car.

Adam was clearly worried, but Rachel had turned into 'super-nurse' mode and that made Adam calm for the moment.

Adam had never seen Rachel in 'full flight emergency' mode before, then he realised that is was an everyday occurrence for her on an intensive care ward. He was a bag of nerves but Rachel was calm and professional.

He drove the car like a true professional; every turn was taken with just pure speed in mind – a confident driver but in total control of the vehicle.

Once at church Rachel just left the car with her medical bag in hand and shouted back to Adam. 'You bring Grace, ok.' She ran, rushing as she would for a patient at work when the life support machine would bleep warnings to the assisting nurses.

It was this nature, of the 'nurse' Rachel, which made Adam feel more nervous than he already was. Adam's mind was all a rush like someone had filled his head with cotton wool and decided to kick it like a football.

He quickly grabbed Grace's car seat and followed into the church after Rachel.

Pastor Jason was waiting at the door. His face was white with fear; he looked very ill like he was ready to pass out.

As Rachel passed Jason she shouted out again. 'Get him some water and sit him down before he falls down,' was the last thing Adam heard as she turned for the stairs to head for Paul's office.

'I'm ok, Adam. Just carry on. He's in the training room. Quickly! Just be quick!' Jason said just before he fell to his knees with the pressure of it all.

Once all were down into the training room, they soon realised the importance of Rachel's presence. Pastor Miles had been attacked; it was an obvious plan by some of Derek Greyer's hired men.

Pastor Miles was in a bad way. Rachel rushed to his side and straight away started to go to work on his injuries.

'Where does it hurt the most, Pastor?' asked Rachel, trying not to inflict more pain for Pastor Miles.

'My legs,' he yelled out in pain. 'It hurts everywhere. I can't breathe properly.'

As Rachel was tending to Pastor Miles the pair of them realised the importance of the role of Master Disciple. The two of them caught each other's eyes and just nodded: a sign that confirmed that her husband's gifting was needed in such a high position, such a high calling.

Rachel gave the pastor a high dose of pain killers to settle him. He was in immense pain, with a dislocated ankle, massive muscle damage to both legs, three broken ribs, bruising to his face and chest area; the list seemed to go on.

'A lesser man would have died from such injuries,' Rachel said. 'It just a good thing he's a fighter and an extremely fit seventy-seven year old.'

Once all was calmer, Pastor Miles called Adam and Rachel over.

'You two are a gift from God and…'

'Pastor, please save your energy. You are going to need it if you're going to start my training,' Adam said with a hint of anger in his crackled voice. He was now even more determined to complete his training as a Master Disciple.

'No Adam. You are going on aggression. Anger's not the way of the Master Disciple. Now that is your first lesson. You will learn fast enough. I pray you will learn at a pace that God allows you to, so not to go on your own strength, but to learn to hear God's voice in defence of His house and His people. You will learn many things – the skill of the sword, hand to hand combat, and you will receive the most powerful weapon of all.'

'What's that?' Adam asked, just wondering what on earth it could be.

'The power of faith.' Then Pastor Miles passed out and went into a deep sleep on the makeshift bed that they had made for him in the training room.

Chapter Six
The Training Starts

1 Timothy 4:8 'For physical training is of some value, but godliness has value for all things, holding promise for both the present life and the life to come'
1 Corinthians 9:25 'Everyone who competes in the games goes into strict training. They do it to get a crown that will not last; but we do it to get a crown that will last forever.

With Pastor Miles getting around with

the use of a stick, a whole three weeks had passed since the attack and Adam had started his training to succeed Milo as the next Master Disciple.

Adam and Jason were discussing the attack on Milo and were worried for the mental effects it might have caused. Adam had seen the marks inflicted before firsthand.

'Those marks on Pastor Miles' legs; the only way they could have been caused is with the use of a baseball bat, one of those aluminium types.'

Jason was disturbed by this and more concerned by what had possibly happened to Adam; his chequered past, showing its way through gradually, greatly worried Jason. 'Pastor Miles is a very fortunate man.

A lesser man would have died from that kind of attack, like Rachel said.' Jason's voice was breaking under the worry of it all.

'But Pastor Miles is no ordinary man; he is a Man of God, full of faith, and as a strength of character like no other,' Adam quickly replied.

'Rachel had said that it was a combination of fitness and faith and I like that idea.'

To the rest of the church Pastor Miles had had a fall. Paul and Jason were talking in Paul's office about what was going to happen when Pastor Miles was fully fit and well.

'I think we'll all have to rally around when the training really starts. At the moment it's all been book-based training whilst my Dad is getting fully fit. The past two weeks have been relatively easy for Adam. It's going to be pretty tough on both Adam and Rachel, especially with young Grace.'

'How long do you think it will take your Dad to train Adam, Paul?'

'My Dad said nine to twelve months. He's been a believer for ten years so spiritually he should be pretty solid. I know when I started my training fifteen years ago that's when my faith really grew and the scriptures started jumping out at me. I mean I've always believed the Word of God but your whole faith changes when your life literally relies on them in battle.'

Jason's face lit up with fear when Paul mentioned the word battle.

'I remember my dad telling me a story once of him just yelling scripture at a Dark Lord called Treygar and he was thrown over six foot to the ground, just by the power of the Word, eh!'

'Tell me more stories, Paul.' Jason felt a lot better hearing these faith-building tales. He needed to hear it more than Adam did; he needed the reassurance.

Jason was on the edge of his seat but at the same time scared of what he might encounter in this new faze of his spiritual life.

'There is one story that will never leave me; when I was young teenager – about fourteen or fifteen, not sure – well, we were driving back from my father's church one Sunday evening when we were overtaken by a huge black car. As the car passed us the rear window came down and a gun barrel pointed at us. A man lent out of the front window, ordering us to pull over.'

Jason's face showed what a thousand words could never tell.

'So my dad pulled over. I think he was more worried for his family than anything else. All I remember him saying was 'Marge if this is it. Get out of here as fast as you can. Paul, son, lie down and don't get up until I or Mom says so'.'

'So what happened to your dad?' Jason was so intrigued now nothing could pull him away from this tale.

'Well, I heard a lot of commotion and shouting and then a single gun shot. I was just lying down in the back of our car scared that I'd just lost my father. My mother lent over the seat, stroked my head and said, 'It's alright, Paul. Your Dad's coming back soon. He's nearly finished talking with the men,' thinking that would calm me down. But she was right. He got back in the car and showed me something that I will never forget. He asked me to hold out my hand and there it was a 38 calibre bullet from a revolver.'

'He was shot?'

'Yes, at point blank range, in the back of Treygar's car, Derek Greyer's father. And now, years later, you really understand scripture when you are put in that situation. My dad said, 'No weapon formed against you shall stand. No weapon! Do you hear?' I'll never forget that, never.'

Jason was amazed to hear such an amazing tale of when Paul was a young boy growing up with an amazing father like Pastor Miles; his faith had been quickened by it which he greatly appreciated.

With that story finished the phone rang.

'Hello Paul, it's Adam.'

'Oh, hi Adam. How can I be of help?'

'Well, I was wondering when we could get together to get started on the real training.'

Adam was so excited but at the same time fearful at what lay ahead.

'I will have to ask Dad – I mean Milo. If you give fifteen minutes I'll call you back.'

Adam hung up and just waited for the call from Paul, but within ten minutes Milo rang himself to just say, 'Adam, tomorrow at seven in the a.m. – the training room.'

And that was that – brief but to the point.

That Saturday Adam was as ready as ever he was going to be and arrived at the church at 6:49a.m. He was well watered and in the training room at 6:55a.m. where Milo sat waiting for him.

'Have you been here long, Milo?'

No response from Milo. His eyes closed and he appeared to be deep in meditation and prayer.

Adam just sat next Milo and he too closed is eyes to think on what lay ahead for him. Milo began to pray.

'Lord, I pray that you would be with us in power. We don't like keeping secrets and deceiving people, Lord. But we are sworn ambassadors for your kingdom and spiritual protectors for this, your church. Grant us clarity of mind, dilute our anxieties and worries. Let our minds just be focused on you and this, our mission. Bless and do likewise for Rachel and Grace and the families represented here and the further leadership of this, your church.

'We know that these are the last days that we read about in your Word. We know that the world has become something that you didn't create it to be. The evil that has gripped our world is polluting its people more so than ever. Lord work in us; let us be what you want us to be. We know our mission and we gladly take on the responsibilities that our mission brings.

'Just bless and give Adam the strength now Lord. Amen.'

Adam was moved by the prayer and sat in silence then Milo stood up to get started.

'Okay Adam. Let's get started, eh.'

Adam nodded with a slight look of excitement on his face.

'Okay Adam. If you can get warmed up, like you would do for a normal training session.'

Adam began to do his stretching exercises to warm up the muscles then went to the punch bag to bring his heart rate up to the optimum level. Once Milo was satisfied that Adam was warmed up enough, he got three cardboard boxes; each box measured roughly two feet long by one foot wide and one foot deep. Milo stacked them on top of one another so they stood just over six feet tall.

Adam looked confused by this but Milo soon enlightened him.

'Adam, come let's see what you can do with this little exercise.' Milo placed Adam in front of the stacked boxes. 'Ok Adam. Can you kick off the top box without disturbing the other boxes?'

It felt strange to Adam to be training with boxes, but he trusted Milo and his methods, so he tried.

Adam approached the boxes then he leaped up and turned in the air; his right leg swung out, the heel of his foot connecting with the top box, knocking it clear with immense power and absolute accuracy.

'Excellent, Adam. Just excellent. Have you kept up your kickboxing training?'

'Just a little, Milo. But I think it was your prayer before we started that did it for me. It really spoke to me, especially the part about diluting our worries and having our minds clear. I just saw the target much more clearly.'

'Ok Adam. Let's try again.'

Again and again, Adam did the exercise and each time he did it, he was spot on. He was now doing a combination of kicks: sweep kicks, kicking out the bottom box, then a reverse kick, flying kicks, roundhouse kicks and various combinations, including punching the middle box once the top one had been kicked clear then sweeping the bottom one before the top box had hit the floor. Pastor Miles was very impressed with Adam's skill and agility; he was already so accomplished in many of the martial arts, skills that were new to Pastor Miles.

After a few hours, Pastor Miles decided to call it a day; he was exhausted just watching Adam achieving amazing feats of dexterity and coordination.

'That's it, Adam, for today. It's been a pleasure watching and training you or should I say training me, cause I've learned a few things as well.'

'Thanks, Pastor – sorry – Milo.'

'Well, if you keep this up, at this rate we will have to speed up your training to the next level. The only thing I see slowing us down is this old man before you.'

'Don't be silly, Pastor. I just hope I'm as fit and active when I reach my seventies.'

Once Adam and Pastor Miles had finished in the training room, Pastor Miles decided to stay a while and do some work in Paul's office.

Adam felt so inspired by a man close to eighty that as he walked towards his car he said to himself, 'That man doesn't know when to stop.'

As soon as Adam got home, Rachel was quizzing him on how his day had gone. 'So how was it, then?' she was so excited but at the same time was quickly reminded of the danger of the intended training and what it was all leading to.

Adam quickly answered; 'Brilliant! Fantastic I mean. That man is an inspiration. I just hope I'm as fit and full of wisdom as him.'

Four weeks later, Adam and Rachel's routine had totally changed – work in the week, training at the weekends (even though Adam was doing some kind of exercise everyday) and the care of Grace had to be fitted in.

All of this was taking its toll on the family; they were exhausted and both felt that they should talk to the only man they could – Pastor Miles – so they set up a meeting.

Pastor Miles felt he should go to their home rather than the family coming to the church; 'Less formal that way,' Pastor Miles thought.

They were all sitting in the lounge drinking coffee. Pastor Miles felt he should cut to the chase and get to the point; all that small talk always annoyed them, especially Pastor and Rachel with all the church meetings they attended.

'Is everything alright with you both?' Pastor didn't give them time to answer. 'I know that the past few weeks must have been hard for you both, but Rachel let me encourage you by saying Adam is an excellent student and is teaching me a thing or two.'

Rachel quickly made her point known. 'I know Adam won't say anything; he'll just keep going till he drops but I can't see us maintaining this pace for nine months.'

'No, No, at Adam's rate we'll be all done in six months easy.'

'Well, even six months, Pastor. We're both finding it very tiring.'

Adam quickly made his point known. 'Rachel and I have been discussing the possibility of my working part-time for the church and part-time for Rachel at her rest home for the old folks and leaving my current job. We have both felt for a while that we do too much and financially we do quite well from the home. We don't have a mortgage and we own everything we have. Our jobs do give us great satisfaction and the money does help with giving to the church and life's little luxuries. Rachel will continue to work at the hospital for three days a week and the other days we will take care of Grace as normal. I will work at the home a few days a week. I know it will be tight for a while but we will adjust to it. It's like everything in life; you just get on with what you've got.'

Pastor Miles was shocked, thinking he would have to give a lot of thought to the problem and the pair of them had sorted it all out themselves.

'Well it's obvious that you've given this a lot of thought, eh.' Pastor Miles was giving his chin a little rub. 'Yes! Yes! I've got an idea; Adam, you work for church part-time and work for Rachel for a few days a week. Yes! Yes! I think that'll work lovely.'

Rachel and Adam just looked at each other and thought, 'Didn't we just say that?'

Pastor got up and just looked at the pair and winked, in his cheeky way. Sometimes he would just pretend to be old and forgetful.

'I must meet with Paul before telling you this. no! Actually, I'll give him a quick call.'

Pastor Miles was acting very strangely. Adam and Rachel had never seen him like this before. It was like he was a small child with a secret not sure if he could tell.

He quickly called Paul on his mobile, in the kitchen, out of ear shot of Adam and Rachel.

The pair were puzzled by all this, but moments later he came back into the lounge.

'We have the means in which we can put your plan into action.' Within two months the plan was up and running. Adam resigned from his Government job at the office and worked his month's notice. A job that brought Adam satisfaction; he had been there since he was eighteen. Most of his colleagues were very proud that he was going to work for the church, knowing full well that he was intended for a role in church, seeing the good in him there, but others mocked his decision. That was not going to put him off the call on his life.

The many that respected Adam and his decision to leave made a presentation for him on his last day, and even the chief executive was informed of his departure. After implementing many new ideas that affected the whole business and never wanting any recognition for it, they presented him with a time piece to be a constant reminder of all the good that he had done there.

Adam went forward to receive his watch and shook hands with the chief executive. Mr Powell shook Adam's hand (it was a firm handshake filled with genuine gratitude) and then gave him his timepiece.

Rachel and Grace had even turned up to see the proceedings. Rachel was welling up with all the emotion of it all and then Adam came back down from greeting Mr Powell and getting his award for 'faithful service', as Mr Powell called it.

In all the time that Adam had been there he had never witnessed a leaving like this. People had left before with many more years served and retired only to receive a normal run of the mill gold plated watch.

But Adam was astounded to see a Bretling Navitimer, a personal favourite of Adam's, with a price tag of over three and a half thousand pounds; it would have remained a dream, until now.

Adam was dumbfounded and Rachel was a mess of emotion after seeing what her beloved husband was giving up so he could fulfil his calling. Everyone there was under the impression that he was going to become a clergyman and wear a collar – the whole nine yards. But they were never to know the absolute truth.

Adam's training was going from strength to strength and he was also settling in quite well at the home. Rachel's work was also going well but still very busy at the hospital. Grace was doing well, crawling faster and starting to show signs of wanting to walk: going round the lounge by holding the furniture and sidestepping round the sofa and chairs.

Everything was working out quite well for them all.

The next time Adam was due for his training session with Pastor Miles, Pastor Miles said, 'Adam, it's exactly halfway through your training, and would like to say that it has been a fantastic experience for me and has opened up the power of the scriptures for me, as well as you.'

Adam nodded his appreciation and went to speak but was quickly stopped by Pastor Miles.

'It is time to give you something very precious. It is one of the most important tools to becoming a fully operating Master Disciple.'

The pair walked up to Paul's office where Pastor Miles reached under the desk to pull out a long wooden box. He placed it on the desk.

'It is time for me to do something that I thought I would be doing with my son, Paul, but as you now know God had other plans and that plan was for me to give God'Sword to you. This has been in our family for four hundred years. There are six of these, five of which are locked away in a metal locker buried in the floor of our training room. Only one God'Sword is allowed out at one time, because there has only ever been one Master Disciple appointed at one time.'

Pastor Miles motioned to Adam to open the box.

'It is your time, Disciple. Just Master it'.

Adam stepped up to the box. It had a metal plaque on the top it read: 'Trust in the Lord your God only and do not be Tempted.'

Adam opened the box to reveal a sword of such exquisite beauty, with the utmost highest craftsmanship ever seen. It looked like it should have been in a museum with its ivory handle, carvings of angels and angelic beings, and lion's roaring mouth with fire in its breath. The sword wasn't finished there; on the blade itself was inscribed with a small segment of Psalm 23 – 'The Lord is my shepherd. I shall not want…' – right down the centre of a double-edged sword.

Adam picked up the sword and turned it over; on the other side there was another inscription that read in larger writing: 'Godsword keep this by your side at all times'. Adam quickly noticed the play with words: 'Gods word' and 'God sword' – keep this by your side.

'It's amazing, Pastor. It is such a beautiful piece of art. It has to be worth thousands, if not hundreds of thousands.'

'Yes, Adam. It is worth something. Well, there is no price for His Church, is there.'

Adam quickly remembered its use and was humbled by its beauty. He tried to lighten the mood: 'Well it's better than my rod and staff.'

'What! I have one of them as well. Your rod, Adam, is a defence weapon only. It will fit in your coat or jacket at all times.'

Pastor pulled out a titanium, extendable baton; it only measured approximately ten to twelve inches in length but once Pastor Miles thrust it out to its full length it measured over four feet. 'Enough to defend yourself with, eh, Adam! It's lightweight and very strong. Go on, try it out on the punch bag downstairs.'

Adam quickly grasped the skills needed to flick the baton out and strike the bag in one fluid motion. Pastor was very impressed by Adam's quick grasp on these skills that took him years to master.

'Very good, Adam. You will always amaze me. Next week we will start your sword training. You had mentioned 'Kendo' a while ago. What did you learn?'

'I learned only sword and staff play, just the stuff needed to round my other skills off. I'd learned a lot of the kicks, punches and blocks from other martial arts I have studied. I felt a little weaponry was needed so I learned staff, sword skills and little with the Sais – they are like big, three-pronged forks.'

'How old were you when you learned all these skills?'

'I started when I was about seven or eight, onwards to about eighteen or nineteen, on and off. I'd get bored of it, leave, get in trouble, then my parents would encourage me to do something else. You know the old story to try and keep me out of trouble but some how trouble would always find me, plus I loved to watch old Bruce Lee and Jackie Chan movies as a kid; I still do.'

The sacred sword that Pastor Miles – Milo – had given to Adam was a new spark of inspiration that got him to find out all his old martial arts manuals, books and old VHS tapes from his parent's attic space. Adam's parents were an amazing couple, a source of inspiration as well. Andrew, Adam's father, a non-believer, ran his own building firm and had done for over thirty years. He was very strong and fighting fit for fifty-five. Annie, Adams mum, 'would like to believe'. She was head chef at a very famous hotel and ran the London marathon two months after giving birth to Adam. Fitness was her church. A true fitness guru, she had done over one hundred full marathons and countless others in her fifty-three years of life.

Once Adam had got the books and stuff home he started to read up on Kendo and various other martial arts.

A lot of Adam's skills were self taught. He would learn the basics from a qualified instructor then go it alone. He found that a class wasn't at the same pace level. He would get frustrated by the slower ones and others that would drift in and out, coming for a few weeks then they wouldn't come for a month; the whole class would then have to wait until they were up to speed. This frustrated Adam till the day he confronted his kickboxing instructor at the age of fifteen; the situation got a little heated and Adam knocked the instructor out sparring, just to prove his progress above the others.

Adam started to learn things from the books and manuals that he hadn't noticed before; a lot of the doctoring and head knowledge from the martial arts were very similar to passages from the Bible. Adam started to use the scriptures to inspire and to bring about a clear understanding of the truth and what he called 'dodgy' doctoring.

He got Pastor Miles involved in his investigations. He also found new insights into the arts and how God could play a big part in their meditation and quiet times. Adam and Milo would take time out from their physical training to train the heart and mind, and to seek God on one of the most important gifts – Discernment: discernment of what to learn and, most of all, of what not to learn. Some of the skills brought about anger and the fundamental status of the Master Disciple was about calm and understanding, and a righteous anger that was guided by God and not by the heart. Adam and Milo also devoted a lot of time to prayer and intercession, and developed a strong relationship. From time to time Paul would also join them in their prayer meetings and would often bring words of encouragement to the pair.

The words also helped Paul and Jason to develop their working relationship; this worked for sermons and words for the greater church leaders who were all still unaware of Adam's training and mission which always caused Jason great stress and worry. After a time Jason understood his mission and was humbled by the many gifted people around him.

That Saturday, Adam had the day off – some quality time with God. Rachel took Grace to see her mum and dad, so it gave Adam a chance to go up to the home and maybe get the Beamer out for a spin.

Whilst Adam was getting the Beamer out he decided to have a look in the other garage, the one he'd used for his motorbike. Adam sold the bike when they found out Rachel was pregnant with Grace. Adam ached for that feeling he got from riding; the speed the freedom all came flooding back. The bike was a Honda VFR 750, the racing term was the 'RC30' – a super bike that was capable of almost 85 Mph in first gear alone, but Adam feared an accident, so sold it to a collector.

As Adam walked into the garage he saw the locker in the corner next to the work bench were he stored his leathers, helmet, boots and gloves. He opened the locker and there, after almost a year, they were still hanging up, still as fresh as the day he put them away. Adam couldn't understand why they weren't dusty or looking a little older. He didn't look into it too much; he quickly grabbed them off the hanger and put them on. Amazingly, they fitted; all that training had got Adam back into shape and amazingly he had a little more room round the midsection.

Joe happened to be walking past, pushing his trusty wheel barrow. 'Hey, Adam. What you all dressed up for? Got ya bike back, son?'

'No, Joe. Just trying 'em on for old times' sake.'

'Do you miss the bike much, son?'

'Just a little, Joe. Just a little.'

'So, what brings you round then? You not working today?'

'No, Joe. Day off. Just come up for a mess about, you know, like typical Guys – have a mess with the car, bit of a tinker, time alone with my thoughts.'

'Say no more. I'll be out of your way. Missus and the nipper alright?'

'Yes, they're fine, Joe.'

Adam loved Joe's old way – the way he spoke and conducted his affairs – it was a generation that Adam adored being around: a much simpler time to live in. Adam envied Joe for a moment, the way he didn't know of the dark powers, the evil corruption and of his mission to protect the church as a Master Disciple.

Joe carried on. On his way, as Joe walked away, Adam's mobile phone went off. He quickly ran to the car to get it. He quickly glanced at the screen; it was Pastor Miles.

'Hello. How can I help, Pastor?'

'Adam, where are you?'

'I'm at the home, Pastor. What's wrong?'

'Can you get back to the church right away? It's urgent! Something has come up. It's not good. Just get here quick.'

Pastor Miles hung up. Adam feared the worst. There was no time to put the car away so Adam quickly got out of the bike leathers. He thought to himself, 'If I had a bike I'd be there in minutes.' The next best thing was the beamer; it was a lot quicker than the Golf anyway.

Several minutes later he pulled on to the church car park. Pastor Miles was there waiting, holding a bag and a long trench coat over his other arm.

'Quick, Adam. We have to go now.'

Adam noticed the sword and it all felt very real indeed. Milo jumped into Adam's car.

'We go in your car. He won't be expecting that.'

'Expecting what?' Adam was getting very nervous. 'Go where?'

'Just drive out of the church, take a left and carry on till I tell you.'

Adam grabbed the sword and placed it directly behind his driver's seat which happened to be on the left, so from behind it looked as if Milo was driving.

'So what is it, Pastor?'

'Milo! My Name is Milo!'

Adam was starting to worry even more. He had never seen the pastor like this; he looked like he was ready to explode but he also had a spiritual sense about him, a presence that commanded calm and Adam felt at ease for the time being.

As Adam drove on, listening to Milo's directions, he began to speak of a phone call that he'd had just moments before he called Adam at the home.

'Deygar has called me. He has only done this a few times and he can never be trusted to be unarmed, so be on your guard. He wants a meeting with me but my spirit says that I shouldn't go alone. I know that we haven't completed your training, but if you have any doubts, just leave me there with him. Don't sacrifice yourself for my sake.'

'What are you talking about, Milo? There's no way I'm going to leave you.'

Within a couple more turns here and there, they were in the heart of the industrial area, right on the edge of the city limits. It was a familiar spot. There wasn't a single person to be seen for two or three miles, and a big plus was that there was no CCTV. This all came as a huge advantage to Deygar, being in such an isolated place on a Saturday.

As the pair drew close Milo spotted Deygar's Bentley Continental.

'That's him, Adam. I should really have told you this at the end of your training but it seems a little late for that. I have to give you your Master Disciple name; we can't be calling you 'Adam' in the heat of battle now can we. Paul and I came up with 'Seth'. I hope you like it. Roughly translated it means 'appointed by God'. I do hope you like it.'

'I do, Milo. It's perfect. Thank you.' Adam played the emotion of it all down a tad.

Milo seemed nervous as the car drew closer. Adam got within a hundred yards of Deygar's car and turned the beamer round to face away in case of an emergency getaway.

'Good thinking, Seth.' Adam thought it was strange to be called Seth so quickly after just being named by Milo; he just hoped he could remember it when Milo called it.

'You stay here, Seth. I'll go; I will call if I need you.'

'But, Milo, you don't have a sword; you're not armed.'

'I know, but you are. I'm placing my trust in you.'

Adam felt the enormous pressure of being there, but in his heart he felt ready.

Chapter Seven
The Encounter of Deygar

Exodus 23:22 'If you listen carefully to what he says and do all that I say, I will be an enemy to your enemies and will oppose those who oppose you'

Milo got out of the car and started walking towards Deygar's, slamming the door behind him.

'You're late, Milo. You know I hate shoddy time keeping. I am a very busy man.'

Deygar looked over Milo's shoulder and noticed the beamer; Deygar was a big car enthusiast and had a substantial collection.

'It's been a few months but in that time you've finally found some taste in cars, eh! Well, that's an Evo Sport M3 BMW. Nice car. I'd like to add it to my ever growing collection once I've taken it from you.'

'It's not my car for you to take. It belongs to a friend.'

Deygar quickly remembered that the M3 only came as a left-hand drive car. He then realised that Milo wasn't alone. He was suddenly on his guard, wondering why Milo would bring back up.

Milo cut to the chase and pressed Deygar for the reason for the meeting.

'So what's this meeting really for, eh? You running dry on the believer's blood? It's an addiction with you trying to overdose yourself. It won't make you any stronger, just weaker, weaker in spirit.'

'A little bird tells me that you were attacked recently.'

'Well that little bird must fly slow; that was over three months ago'.

Milo knew what Deygar was trying to do; he was trying to aggravate him, make him lose his cool, but Milo wasn't having any of it.

'Well, it's good to see you up and about, especially a man of your age and condition.'

As he spoke Deygar was looking towards the Beamer, still wondering who the mysterious figure was. Plus, Deygar could clearly see that Milo was without his sword.

'Where's your long coat and what goes on underneath it? You are missing a vital piece of equipment for an M.D.'

'I've had to give it up you see – too 'Old'.'

'I wonder who's told you that, eh. Someone very wise I suspect.'

'If all you called me here for was to insult me I'll go because I too am a very busy man.'

'No, Milo. I've called this meeting for a reason. I am in need.'

'Oh? Mr Billionaire is in need? So what is it that your money can't buy? So, finally the scripture comes to you; you know the one about the camel, a rich man and that elusive needle.'

'Shut it, Milo. And less of the Bible lesson. I need Betrayer's blood! And I need it now.'

'So that's it, eh! You're weak. Your strength is failing you.'

'No! No not at all! I have all the strength I need to strike you down now.'

'So you would strike an unarmed man? Very brave. Very noble of you.'

Adam was getting very nervous just waiting for something to happen, until he saw Deygar reach for his sword. Adam grabbed for the sword behind his seat, he also had the extendable baton on his belt.

Milo stepped back noticing Deygar reaching down slowly to his side for his sword.

Deygar pulled his sword clear from its sheath.

'We can do this the hard way or the easy way; you decide, Milo. Just deny your faith and I will make it painless.'

'Strike me down, Deygar. It's no loss, for I will be in glory forever.'

'I'm already there; I'm immortal. Get ready to die Master Disciple.'

Adam got out of the car. The sword was behind his right leg hidden from sight. His left hand gripped the baton, ready to extend.

Deygar stepped back seeing a new face running towards them both.

'Who is this boy?'

Deygar pulled his sword ready to strike Milo. Adam leaped into action extending the baton and pulling his sword clear, blocking Deygar's sword just before it hit Milo.

'Who is this?' Deygar was full of rage and had a hate-filled anger towards Milo. He kept trying to strike Milo, but Adam guarded him from each deadly blow.

'Milo, step back. It's time to finish this, right here, right now.'

Milo could clearly see Adam's skills but feared the anger in him was too much.

Milo grabbed Adam's arm. 'Stand down, Seth. Your anger is getting the better of you.'

Deygar stepped back and for the first time looked scared and shaken, not his usual cool calm self.

'Thank you for your defence, Seth, but lower your sword.'

Adam was confused. He could clearly see that this was a trap to lure Milo here to kill him.

'Who is this?' Deygar shouted a third time.

'This is Seth, 'Appointed by God' and my new student and Master Disciple.'

'Excellent; two of you to kill or maybe just one and the other will denounce his faith.'

'How about it Seth? What would you say to a billion for a few pints of blood? Just believe in me, Seth, and you could be rich beyond you wildest dreams. Just think what you could do with a billion.'

'Don't listen, Seth.' Milo instantly recognising his tactics to lure Seth to deny his own faith. 'It's a trick to tempt you, Seth. He wants you to betray your beliefs.' Milo could see where this was going but Adam held firm.

'I am the richest man I know. You can take your money and shove it.' The anger was welling up in Adam again and Milo was concerned.

Deygar raised his sword again but this time it was towards Adam. Milo feared the worst; he was too angry to fight effectively – it was a battle of the hearts.

Deygar struck with his sword. Adam defended to the best of ability but was overwhelmed by how strong and powerful Deygar was. Adam was thinking that if he could just relive him of his sword he could take him down. He prayed in his heart; 'Lord grant me the strength at this, my darkest hour.'

Within a moment Deygar's strength seemed to diminish or was it that prayer that made Adam's strength increase. He took it as answered prayer and quietly said 'Thank you, Lord' in his heart.

Their swords clashed and then Adam hit out with the baton with his other hand, knocking Deygar's sword from his hand.

Adam kicked the sword towards Milo, and Milo stood on the blade so Deygar could not retrieve it.

Deygar was defenceless and had nowhere to turn.

'Seth they call you? You know that I am without sword or weapon. A Master Disciple's role is for defence only. The only way to make this fair is for you to put down your sword or give me my weapon back.'

Adam had no idea of what to do in this situation. With that pause Deygar reach into his jacket and pulled a gun.

Adam immediately recognised it as a Glock 34 – a 9mm semi-auto with a laser dot sight – and it was pointing directly on his chest.

'Ok!' Adam raised his hands. 'If you want to play it that way – I give up. There's no way I can beat a gun with a sword.'

'I should kill you both for this outrage, removing my sword in combat.'

'There are no rules, Deygar. You know that it's just because our new 'boy', as you call him, made a good tactical move on his part and you don't like it.'

Milo was just as surprised as Adam to see Deygar with a gun. It just wasn't the way of a 'Dark Lord', even one as bad as Deygar. 'Eh! What's with the gun? Come now.' Milo was scared for all their safety.

'Just give me my sword Milo and we will finish this.'

'You leave us no option, Deygar. Why the gun if you don't mind me asking?'

'You have your back up, in the form of a 'new boy' who is good with a baton and a sword, so I have mine, in the form of a semi-automatic pistol.'

Milo picked up the sword by its handle. It was an evil looking weapon with a black carved ivory handle in the shape of a dragon. Milo handed it over, blade first, just in case he was bluffing and had to strike in defence.

Deygar sheathed his sword, still pointing the gun in their direction. Then, as quickly as the gun could fire, he pulled the trigger twice – a bullet each for Milo and Adam. The pair feared for their lives, both praying that this wasn't the end for the two of them. But the bullets didn't make contact. They were flash powder rounds temporarily blinding the pair and giving Deygar the perfect amount of time to get away; he quickly jumped into his car and sped away.

Milo and Adam both fell to the ground, blind, clutching at their eyes, fearing what Deygar could do with them, so vulnerable and open to attack. Within a few moments Adam's eyes were starting to clear. He could see and hear Deygar's car rushing away in a cloud of dust.

'It's okay Milo. He's gone. Can you see now?'

'I barely heard the shot but didn't look away. I got the full extent of that flash powder stuff. My eyes are just a blur.'

'Don't rub them, Milo. I think there's a trace of CS gas in that stuff too, that will just prolong it. Stand up and face the wind; the breeze will blow out any trace of the CS without you putting it back each time you rub your eyes.'

The pair just sat for a moment until Adam could see a hundred per cent clearly before the pair headed back to the church.

Once at the church Milo had to speak to Adam about his anger and attitude but not before Adam got off his chest what he had got to say.

'No! Milo, I'm speaking first. There was no mention of guns. This is getting out of hand. For all we knew those bullets could have been real and where would that have gotten us, eh? I'll tell you, Pastor – Dead with a capital 'D'. And where would that have got the mission?'

With that said Milo slumped over his desk. He looked up to Adam looking down at the sword and seeing the scriptures.

'He couldn't afford to shoot us dead. He would have the full extent of the law after him. It's murder.' Milo was trying so hard to reassure Adam.

'Milo, people like Deygar probably own the police. He is one of the richest and most influential people in this city. *You* should know; *you* told *me*.'

Milo stood up. 'You still don't get it do you? We have secret, a secret that, if it got out, would cause panic throughout all mankind. Every continent, every nation, all the world would be at war with each other, and so does Deygar; his secret is part of it. He would be exposed. The whole ethos of the Dark Lord cult is selfishness and greed, all of the deadly sins, he is maybe one of the last 'Judas Cult' members so he can't afford the secret to get out either, so he has to go by the book, so to speak. Where else do you think he amassed his enormous wealth? Like his father before him, he has betrayed people for greed, killed people and, like his father, he won't stop until he tries to attack our church, God's people, then we can strike a defence blow for our Lord – a God of justice and of peace.

'You see, he has sold mortality to influential people in order to build a kingdom and gain world wide influence. If the world knew how he'd come across this power they too would have the upper hand, but he could never tell if that secret was made known because he would have no power.

'You see, Adam, he needs betrayers' blood every tenth year of his natural life to maintain an immortal existence, but to keep from dying he has to drink blood from a believer who is willing to betray their beliefs or kill a believer in battle whose faith has failed them. Doubt, temptation and lack of faith all can lead them to destruction and, as it says in the scripture, we are protected by our 'shield of faith'. We must put on the whole armour so we will not suffer the consequences of being without faith.

'And that's why it's important to keep your 'cool', as you would put it. Be calm; let the power of God flow through you. Anger is a step closer to losing your faith. Then you are running on your own strength and understanding and lastly 'emotion'. So, don't go there, okay?'

Adam left the church a few minutes later, after the pair had prayed and thanked God for keeping them safe. The battle with Deygar, however, was far from over.

Adam pulled on to the driveway. It was then he realized that he had come back in the Beamer and left the Golf at the home. Rachel's car was parked up; they were back from Rachel's mum and dad's.

Once in the house Adam found Rachel in the kitchen busy cleaning from giving Grace her dinner.

Adam tried to play the whole events of the day down until later.

'Hi, Rach. Good day?'

'Not bad. Yourself, dear?'

'Not bad either, until I had a call from Pastor Miles. That's why I'm late and I've come back in the Beamer. I didn't have time to take it back. I'll do it tomorrow at some point.'

'So the Golf's at the home then?' Rachel could sense that Adam had something on his mind but was prepared to wait till Grace was safely in bed.

Within the hour Grace was fast asleep and Rachel wanted to know what had gone on.

'So, what went on today? I know you, oh so well. There's something that you're not telling me.'

'Ok Rachel. Pastor Miles had received a call from Deygar. He is the Dark Lord that I am to protect the church from. Well, he wanted to meet Pastor at the edge of the city, you know, the industrial zone. Well, I took him in the beamer.'

Rachel was shocked then went running upstairs to wake Grace.

'What's wrong? What is it, Rach?'

'We're taking that car back now. How many people own a 1991 M3 Evo Sport, eh?'

Adam quickly realising the gravity of the situation. The whole family got ready to take the Beamer back to the home. Rachel didn't let Adam out of her sight for a second, constantly watching him and around him for any danger.

They were quickly on their way to the home, but it was all too late; Deygar had already assigned someone to trace and follow the Beamer. Being a very distinctive vehicle, it wasn't hard to find the whereabouts' of such a rare car. He was desperate to track down the mysterious Master Disciple, and Deygar's spy didn't take long to track him down. It wasn't long before Deygar knew everything about Adam and his family.

A week or so later and Rachel had started to think she had overreacted over the Beamer being traced, so things were back to normal – or as normal as it could be for them.

Adam wasn't too happy at the prospect of seeing Deygar again; the whole gun issue had given young Adam a bit of a scare, so he decided to go and see his dad, Andrew – 'Handy Andy' to his close friends, who knew of his amazing skills and knowledge of all things gun related. He was a gun guru. He knew everything there was to know about guns and ammunition.

As well as martial arts, Adam's dad introduced him to firearms and reloading. However, all that knowledge that Adam had picked though was to be wasted because by the time it came for Adam to apply for his firearms certificate, all small hand guns and firearms had been banned. But now that knowledge could be finally used for good, so he decided to see his dad for some advice on a weapon that he had in mind, just right for the job.

When Adam got to his parent's house Andy was mowing the front lawn.

'Hiyah, Dad.'

'Hiyah, son.' Andy turned off the mower and walked over to Adam. 'So what brings you here without the Rachel and Grace, eh?'

Andy could sense something; this was a father - son moment, so he decided to go to the workshop up in the top garden round the back.

On the way, Adam popped his head in the kitchen to say Hi to his mum. Even though Annie did it for a living, she loved to cook and bake healthy cakes for Adam to take home for Grace.

Once in the workshop, Adam started to talk but tried not to say too much on the current situation. Andy wasn't a believer but even if he was he could still not tell the whole truth.

'I'm a little scared at the moment, and basically I need a gun to protect my family.'

Andy, like a true father, went on the defensive.

'What's wrong? What's the problem? Why do you need a gun to solve it, eh?'

'That's not all, Dad. I need you to make some special ammo for it too.'

Adam totally ignored is dad's questions.

'Like I said, son; what's it for? What's the problem?'

'There's no problem, Dad. I just need a little protection round the house, you know.'

'I don't know. Enlighten me.'

'Dad, you have seven shotguns. I just need one.'

'Son, I go shooting; it's my hobby. I don't have them for the time when someone tries to break in to our home.'

'Dad, what about that gun you've got by the side of your bed with those special bullets, eh?'

'Ok. You got me there, but I have a licence for those.'

'So do I, Dad. Eighteen I got my shotgun certificate as well because I couldn't go for my full firearms certificate.' He paused. 'Okay Dad. I'll tell you but don't go telling mum, she'll just worry.'

'So dads don't worry?'

Andy was really wound up by that, but decided to let it go.

'Someone tried to carjack me the other day in the Beamer and shot two rounds of flash powder to attempt to blind me whilst driving, but I managed to get away – just. I was wearing my sunglasses.' Adam hated lying but had no choice. He could never tell Andy the truth, he just wouldn't understand.

'Well, its no good me telling you to sell the car is there. I know how much the Beamer means to you. So, what do have in mind, son?'

'I haven't giving it much thought, but I think a shortened, pump-action shotgun, 8-10 rounder that shoots those little bags, like the police use – you know – the ball-bearing shot bags; just enough to knock someone down; not lethal. Do you remember the cartridges we made for your berretta 9mm? We took the 9mm casings and half filled them with rock salt then topped them off with melted wax tips so they would hold together.'

Andy just smiled along, nodding as Adam excitedly told the story.

'Do you remember we took them to the gun club and we shot Mick in the chest wearing that body armour? He still hit the deck clutching his chest, severely winded.'

'Ok. That was a nice trip down memory lane, son, but where am I going to get a weapon like that without too many people asking questions, eh?'

'Couldn't we go and see Mick at the gun shop? He's an experienced gunsmith. Surely he'll know of something along those lines.'

Adam was excited by the chance of seeing Mick. He hadn't seen him for at least ten years.

'A lot of the guns you've mentioned were destroyed years ago during the dangerous weapons amnesty. I'll call Mick and see what he can do. I don't know why you don't come shooting with me again; it would be fun.'

'I'd love to, Dad. But, as you know, I'm very busy at the moment and any free time I get, I try to fit in my health and fitness routine, just like mum does.'

'But remember, son. I'm not condoning the use of a weapon on anyone, but this is to keep your family safe, and if it does happen again don't be a hero, call the police.'

'Ok, Dad. I'll try to keep that in mind if there is a next time.'

Adam's phone rang in his pocket; he stepped outside to speak in private. It was Rachel calling.

'What is it, Rach?'

'Adam, I think I'm being followed. There's been a black Range Rover behind me for nearly the whole of my journey. It was two cars behind me but now it's right behind.'

'Where are you?'

'I've stopped at the main traffic lights on Station Bridge Road. I'm coming back from my mum and dad's.'

Then Adam heard a scream down the phone.

'What is it?'

'They've just nudged the car.' Rachel was starting to panic. Grace was in the car totally oblivious to the gravity of the situation.

'Lock the doors. Don't get out. Try to drive the car, through the red light if you have to, Rach. Just stay in the car. Don't get out under any circumstances. I'll get to you as quick as I can.'

Rachel quickly did what Adam said, locking the doors by pushing the door lock down with her elbow, triggering the central locking system, locking all the doors in a spilt second. A man stepped out to approach Rachel in the legacy; he tapped the glass to alert her.

'He's trying to get into the car.'

'Rach, don't panic. I'm on my way.'

She desperately tried not to make eye contact. Her hands started to shake. She quickly remembered what Adam said; she put the car in gear and drove through what seemed to be the longest red light in history.

Adam ran to the car, quickly saying goodbye to his dad through the workshop window. He got into the Beamer and plugged his phone into the hands free holster fitted to the dash board.

'Are you moving yet, Rach?'

'Yes, I am moving at high speed but the man is running back to the black Range Rover.'

'Are they trying to follow you?'

'Yes! Yes! Where are you, Adam? I need you here with us.'

'Never mind that; I am on my way to the big shopping mall near to your parents. Get to there, Rachel. They won't dare to try anything with a lot of people around. I will meet you there. In the meantime, try to lose them. The Legacy is a much quicker car than any Range Rover. And remember to stay calm; you are a great driver. Don't let me down.'

With that said, Rachel began to pray quietly in her heart, 'Please, Lord, help me drive this car, and please protect us and others on the road. Protect the innocents, Lord.' That's all Rachel could say – 'Protect the innocents, Lord.'

Adam furiously drove the Beamer as fast as he could and still kept a running relay with Rachel on the phone.

'They're still behind me. I've got Grace in the car, Adam. I'm so worried. I'm scared they are going to ram us off the road.'

'Ok, Rach. Just try to keep it together. There's just a few more turns and I'll be at the shopping Mall.' Adam was nowhere near but he had to give Rachel some hope. This was getting out of hand and Adam feared the worst.

'Where are you, Rach?'

'I'm just getting on the duel carriageway.'

''Ok, Rach. This is good. Try to outrun them. Use the turbo pressure switch on the dash.'

'No, Adam. I hate that thing; it's too fast. It always scares me when you use it, and anyway I've never used it. I don't know how.'

'It's easy, Rach. Just turn it on.'

'No, Adam. I'll just try to lose them some other way.'

'Listen, Rachel, it's the only way of distancing yourself enough to lose them. Just listen; turn it on and the car will do the rest. Trust me.'

'Ok. What button is it?' Rachel relented. All she could think of was Grace and getting to her husband safely.

'Rach, press the red button next to the water spray button on your right of the steering wheel.'

'Ok, Adam. I've pushed it. Now what?'

'Ok, now the turbo pressure will build up until it's at maximum. A red light will come on to tell you this. Is the needle at 2.5 bar on the turbo pressure gauge yet?'

Rachel was frantically looking for the turbo pressure gauge the car was fitted with. There were all sorts of clocks and gauges: oil temp, water temp, fuel pressure, rev counter and the only one Rachel used on a regular basis was the fuel gauge and that was half-empty.

'Oh, found it. It's nearly there. The red light has come on. Now what?'

The Range Rover was still at the rear bumper of the Legacy but not for long.

'Ok, Rach, when you're ready to go, make sure there's nobody in front of you. When you are ready to go press the right-hand button next to the pressure gauge. There's a two second delay so you can get both hands back on the steering wheel safely, then all that turbo pressure will be released at once. It will be very fast so just hold on.'

Rachel was very nervous about doing such a dangerous thing but it was the only way to lose the very determined men in the Range Rover, and she was worried at what they might do if she was to stop or eventually run out of petrol, which could still happen if this plan didn't work.

Rachel was getting herself ready to press the button, to release all that pressure, when the Range Rover made their last ditch attempt to stop them by ramming the rear of the Legacy. The car slid to the side of the road but Rachel held the car with immaculate car control, the four-wheel drive system fighting to control the rear shunt. With that last attempt, Rachel hit the button to get away. She couldn't afford another rear end shunt like that.

And within five or six seconds the car went from 70 to 120mph and was still accelerating, leaving the Range Rover behind.

'Adam, how do I stop this thing? I'm doing nearly 140mph.'

'Take your foot off the accelerator; that will release the remaining pressure through the dump-valve and bring you back to normal road speed.'

Once at a normal speed Rachel had a quick look to see if the Range Rover was still there – she'd lost them. Rachel felt very proud of herself and then headed for the shopping mall to meet Adam, who was just pulling up on to the second level car park, in the purple zone, overlooking the road where Rachel was turning off to meet up with her husband.

When the pair saw each other Rachel just lost it; the emotion of it all just hitting her as she got out of the car to greet her husband. He ran towards her – big hugs all round for the pair and a big thank you to Adam for talking Rachel through it all.

'Thanks, Adam. I couldn't have done it without you.'

'No, Rach. I'm sorry I wasn't quick enough to come to your assistance.'

The whole issue had brought about serious anxiety for Adam; they were on to them. Whoever they were, it was no coincidence that he had had a run in with Deygar and then this happens. Adam felt they needed a rapid response vehicle of some kind to get to people in an emergency. Adam's mind was starting to consider the whole situation would have been a different story if it wasn't for the speed and skill of Rachel in the highly modified Legacy.

The pair of them went to see the pastor to tell him of what just happened to them.

Pastor Miles was shocked at the story and praised God for the safe delivery of them both.

'So what do you have in mind for a rapid response vehicle? 'Cause you know you are more than welcome to my Mondeo ST200.'

'No offence, Pastor, but your car is slow compared to the Legacy and we want something quicker than that. We could already have the quickest car in the form of the Legacy, but you'll never beat the traffic problem. I couldn't get to Rach in time even in the mighty Beamer and that's got 238bhp. We need something that cuts through traffic – a bike! A super fast bike!'

'It's all getting out hand, Adam.'

'Pastor, what's getting out of hand? My wife and daughter were chased today – followed. For all we know, these people know where we live.'

'Calm yourself, Adam. Everything will be alright. Let's just pray together.'

Adam felt that prayer was the last thing to do, given the situation required a practical solution, but he soon succumbed and was quick to practise a calm approach; maybe prayer was the right way to go to achieve calmness.

'Lord, you know everything about us and, Lord, I pray that you will create an edge of protection around us all, especially around Adam and Rachel and their little baby, Grace. Protect them all and bring about a peace so they can enjoy a full night's sleep and rest. Bless and protect Grace. I know she is very young, but it doesn't mean that she still can't be affected. So bless little Grace, Lord. We know you love children. And let their home have a super natural edge of protection around it, for it is holy ground. Let no evil be able to stand near it, Lord.'

Adam and Rachel just looked at each other and smiled.

'Thank you, Pastor. It's just our lack of faith. Our flesh was starting to do the thinking for us both. We were very scared, Pastor. Thanks to your wise words, we know we can overcome any situation with faith,' Rachel said, but in her heart she echoed the same opinion as her beloved husband; we do need a response vehicle of some kind. And Adam felt the same way and let his thoughts rule his mouth, yet again.

'Yes, Pastor, but we still need a rapid response vehicle of some kind. Remember, prayer is one of the tools we use, but that sword plays a pretty big part also.'

'Just leave it with me, Adam. I'll pray it through on my own. I am hearing you and I do understand that it has been a traumatic experience for you all, but we have to continue with the mission at hand. God will succeed. We are on the winning side.'

With that said, Adam and Rachel left to go home for something to eat. They were still too shook up to stomach anything but they still tried to get some nourishment. Adam needed to keep up energy levels. He didn't know when he would be needed again.

As the couple retired for bed that night, Adam just said this to Rachel, as they fell asleep: 'I'm going to see 'Tatter'. See if he can help us with anything.' And so Adam prayed, 'Lord give us rest. Grant us a full night's sleep. Let no one disturb us as we sleep and, like Pastor Miles said, put an edge of protection around this, your house, Lord. Amen.'

Later on the next day, after Adam had finished his training with Milo, he headed to his brother's. Adam's mind was a rush; he had a plan, and an idea.

Adam pulled up at Scott's place. Everyone called him 'Tatter' that was because of his nature; ever since he was a small child he had messed with and taken things apart, fixed things and improved things. He had always been tatting with something, hence the nickname.

Scott lived in an old Victorian fire house with the traditional huge arched front double doors. He lived upstairs; all the space downstairs, where you would normally find the tender, was his garage and workshop. He even had the original fireman's pole; he still used it to get down from his room upstairs. It was a mess, but it was a really cool pad.

Adam rang the bell at the side door. Above was a camera; it quickly focused on Adam.

'Buzzzz!' And the door clicked open.

'Hiyah, bro. What brings you here?'

'Well, I need a favour. I know that you are a modern day genius, and I do know that you always like to rise to a challenge.'

'Just spit it out, man. What do you want?'

'It's a strange request, but I need you to make me a tracker, so I know the exact location of someone – and its got to be mobile – handheld if possible.'

'Is that all?'

'Oh, it needs to be able to have a GPS built in, if poss.'

Scott just looked at Adam and smiled. Scott loved a challenge but this wasn't going to make Tatter sweat at all; he just loved to make things.

'I've just made the finishing touches to my latest gadget and this is totally un-detectable to police cameras and Radar guns.'

'How come?' Adam waited with baited breath.

'I've invented a stealth box for my car.'

'A what? Did I hear correctly? A stealth box? What does that do and how does that work and can you make me one?' was all Adam could muster in the split second that he had to speak before his brother spoke up about the much-anticipated new gadget.

'I'll tell you but you can't have one yet. When the stealth box is fitted to a car it sends out a digital or analogue signal blocking the police's tracking signal and gives them a speed readout of zero mph and that's not all it does; it also messes around with VHF frequencies. I found out this part; when I tried it out, the TV screen started rolling, so then I figured out that even if the police record you, they won't be able to make out what's on the screen.'

'That's really impressive. How long have you been working on that?'

'Just a couple of months.'

'Just a couple of months? Man, you are a genius. Just a shame you can't patent it.'

Scott just rubbed his chin. 'This GPS system: does it need to be global, 'cause the software is huge for the entire world? For example, if it was just the city limits we can get all that information from a single CD rom from the city library, copy it, load it on to your tracker and – hey presto! – an LPS system: a local positioning system.'

'Cool!' was Adams reply. 'So you can get to work on it then?'

'Yeah, just need a few things first.' Scott rubbed his chin; this time he was really thinking. 'What do I need from my brother? Can't think! I *have* everything – damn!'

Adam started to have a little mooch around the place when something caught his eye around Scott's workshop area.

'Ah! What's this, Scott?'

Adam lifting a mobile phone sized object up to show Scott.

'Don't press the button on the side whatever you do.' Scott took the item from his brother and placed it back on the workshop bench. 'I shouldn't even have this, you see, they only issue these things to fully qualified pilots.'

'Why? What is it?' Adam was confused. It just looked like a phone with a lot more features on it – a lot like a radio scanner. 'That's it; it's a radio scanner. You listening to the police band?'

'I wish! This is a transender. It's what a pilot would use on a small aircraft or a large one if the plane went down in an emergency situation.' Scott switched it on. 'Listen.' It was air traffic control talking from the city's airport in the middle of bringing a 747 down to land.

'Okay control: bringing her down. This flight, 0003459, requesting to land on runway 6.'

'All's clear. You are in runway 6 flight plan and request has been granted. All clear, flight 0003459. Thank you.'

'Thank you, control, out.'

'That's amazing. Let's have a go.'

'You can hold it; just don't press the button on the side – that's that talk button – 'cause these things can be traced if illegally used. They have a multitude of uses. In the past one of these things brought down a 777 to land by a member of the ground staff. The whole power system had failed, even the backup systems. This type of equipment was their only alternative, but no one's to know that because it was all hushed up. You know the press would have made a field day from that kind of knowledge.'

'Well, how did you know it happened?'

'Well, I had this thing, didn't I. Eh, I've got an idea; if you can track a signal with this I could use it for the LPS system.' Scott was excited to have a project but was getting a little carried away with himself. 'So, how many receivers you gonna need?'

Adam thought for a minute. 'Do I go for two or three? Well, it's no good just having one. Make two to start with – one for me and one for Rachel, so we will know each other's exact location. It will be the ultimate mobile phone.'

That was it for Adam; this would give Rachel peace, having a handheld piece of equipment that would give her the reassurance that she so desperately needed.

So with that sorted, the next thing on Adam's agenda was to see his father to see if he had come through with a little extra protection in the form of a gun.

Once Adam had left his brother's he thought he'd better phone ahead to see if the folks were at home. There was no answer so Adam decided to go straight home. He tried calling again later but there was still no answer.

Later that evening Adam's father called back.

'Hi, son. You called earlier?'

'Yes, Dad. I was wondering: did you manage to see Mick?'

'I gave him a call; he's working on it. I'm seeing him later in the week. He couldn't talk much; he was on his mobile, so I was brief.'

'Ok, dad. Call me when you go. I would like to come too if that's ok.'

'That's fine. Mick would like to see you. It's been so long.'

Adam and his father had a way of communicating in code over the phone if there was anyone listening on a phone scanner, so there was no way that they could understand what they was talking about. It was a little childish but they were talking about an illegal weapon after all.

'So I'll come at TT2at,' said Andy then he hung up; no response; no answer; nothing from Adam.

Adam put the phone down. He knew what the code TT2at meant and was excited.

'Who was that on the phone?' Rachel was surprised by how short he was on the phone.

'Was that your dad? How come you didn't say goodbye? Have you had a falling out?'

'No, of course not. It's our phone code. It's a childhood thing. Anyway, I'm seeing him on Thursday at around teatime to see if we can get some extras for our defences.'

'What do you mean extras?'

'You'll see. Don't worry.'

Rachel was a little worried. She had no idea what Adam was up to with has dad, but she was reassured by the fact Andy was involved; it couldn't be that bad.

The rest of the week was pretty much normal – Adam, with work and his endless training and looking after Grace, and Rachel, with her work and taking care of their emotional needs which was becoming the new item on the current agenda.

But there was a man whose week had changed dramatically, Derek Greyer – Deygar. He was sitting in a huge leather chair in his extravagant office, clearly disturbed by the introduction of a new Master Disciple. Seth was on his mind and so was his family.

Chapter Eight
The Formal Introduction of Derek Greyer, aka 'Deygar'

Exodus 23:27 'I will send my terror ahead of you and throw into confusion every nation you encounter. I will make all your enemies turn their backs and run.'

Derek Greyer was sitting at his desk pondering the one thing that now occupied his evil mind – Seth.

His office was huge; the rear wall was literary a wall of TVs: eight 40 inch plasmas across and five deep; forty screens in total and they were showing the news in every major part of the world – CNN, BBC world news, Sky News and countless others. He had his finger on the pulse of the world, ready to strike on any disaster or tragedy that he could profit from, but not this morning. He could not escape the thought of Seth and the obvious skill he had learned from Milo in just a short space of time; or could it be that he had had him in the shadows, as it were, hiding him from Derek in an attempt to make a strike at the Dark Lord and wipe out the remaining cult members?

Derek quickly dismissed that thought, thinking that it was a form of attack. Their moral code, as it was noted, was that the prime duty of the Master Disciple was for defence only, not to strike out with a motivated planned attack.

This went on puzzling Derek for some time, but he had to concentrate on the day ahead, after all he was the CEO of a large company. His mind had to stay focused on here and now.

He glanced over to see his schedule; he had meetings for the whole morning. He had to think and bring his mind on to the matter at hand and get on with things. First on his list was a possible new client, Mr Gary Busher.

Mr Greyer's personal assistant showed Mr Busher through to his office.

Derek Greyer's office was situated on the fifty-seventh floor of Greyer International Tower. The office itself was the usual four walls (as you would expect from a typical office space) but Mr Busher noticed that the two main walls were made, from floor to ceiling of glass: super reinforced glass with no beams or strengthening rods. It gave a sense that anyone could fall out at anyone time. It really made Mr Busher feel uneasy and a little scared.

Mr Greyer was admiring the view from the immense window; his feet right against the glass, he glanced down. He focused on his feet then noticed the view straight down – fifty-seven stories – he gave a little smile to himself thinking that even if the glass wasn't there and he was to fall, he would not die. Mr Greyer wasn't in any hurry to test this theory but the knowledge excited him.

'Will that be all, Sir?' called out his PA.

'Thank you, Miss Jones. Just a coffee for myself, and for you, Mr Busher?' He asked, still with his back towards them both, but he could be rude to anyone; after all, he was the boss.

'Oh, a coffee for me would be fine, thank you.'

The bank of TVs, still switched on, now were muted. He couldn't bear to be out of touch not even for a second and this unnerved the possible new client, sitting at the mercy of Mr Greyer.

Gary Busher was a little nervous. He had every right to be; many had sought a meeting with the mighty Mr Greyer and had failed to do so, so he had to impress or he would face the music and never again have this glorious opportunity. This was his last chance and Mr Greyer knew everything; it was his business to know.

Mr Greyer finally turned to face his audience; it was silent for a moment while Mr Greyer checked out the possible new client. He looked him up and down like a farmer looked at cattle.

He had a study frame – an athletic physique, like a football or rugby player would have – but time had taken its toll on him. His eyes were heavy and he looked tired. Mr Greyer reached out a hand to shake. Mr Busher stood and did likewise; it was a firm aggressive shake on Mr Greyer side, but Mr Busher was feeling quietly confident on the inside and lightly tightened his grip. This was a good thing; Mr Greyer felt good about this one and told him to be seated again.

'Mr Busher, may I call you Gary?'

'Yes. Please do.'

The gesture wasn't returned; no one addressed Mr Greyer by his first name. Nothing but Sir or Mr Greyer would do.

'You asked for this meeting, Gary, and I kindly agreed to it. So what is it that I could do for you, or what is it that you can do for me?'

Gary Busher had fallen from the top of his game. He was a good businessman, family man and devout Christian. He had two sons and a daughter. His beautiful wife, Sarah, had developed cancer and it was only a matter of time. Gary sought God on this, but it just made him angry; the thought of working so hard in business and that the things he was involved in at the church were all a waste of time. And then when you'd think things couldn't get any worse, Gary's eldest son, James, got involved with drugs (a coping mechanism for his mother's illness) and had accidentally overdosed.

His business suffered Gary's constant hospital appointments and the ever increasing stress of his wife's cancer, and now the death of his eldest son had driven him away from the security of God's love and understanding to the huge leather seat in Derek Greyer's office. Only Hell itself was a worse place to be in.

And Mr Greyer knew all this; it was his job to know everything. He knew the buttons of his heart, now all he needed to do was press them in the right order and he'd have him eating from the palm of his hand.

'Ok, Gary, I know that your company made in the region of 25 Million this year; a good year you would say, but before you interrupt me I do know that a lot of that credit goes to your other partners, a Mr Greenwood and a Mr Leach, a very befitting name I'd say. Mr Leach: he has been taking a lot from your company, Mr Busher?'

Gary now had Mr Greyer's full attention.

'All I would say is dismiss him with a full year's salary and that would be the end of it. He has cost you too much, Gary.'

Gary was so intrigued by this new information about one of his most trusted partners and, most importantly, trusted friends.

'Please tell me; what he has done? Gareth Leach is a good friend and business partner. He has been a loyal friend during our most resent dark and troubled times, so please tell me. I need to know.'

Derek knew that Gary was ever closer to closing the deal with him; he just needed a little push, thought Derek.

Derek pressed the intercom button. 'Ah, Miss Jones. Please would you show the Doctor in now. Gary, all of your worries, queries and questions will be answered soon enough.'

A very smartly dress man walked into the office pushing a large medical trolley. He pushed it in front of where Gary was sitting and then slipped on a white coat and some very thick industrial rubber gloves. Then he stepped aside.

"Intrigued now, Gary Busher of City Aggregates 'Mr Greyer said standing up to make more impact'

'Your company recycles road materials, refines them and takes out all of that precious expensive oil which, in turn, you sell on for profit. You then resell the remaining road aggregate to build more wonderful roads with which you get a massive handshake from the said companies responsible for building the new roads. So, it seems you make a lot of money for what is in essence a waste product.'

'No, not at all, Mr Greyer. We also do a lot for the environment. We do get a by-product from the processing of the material which powers the non-nuclear power station right here in our very own city, Sir. Sorry.' Gary could see that interrupting him in mid-speech wasn't going down well. Derek Greyer's face was like thunder and with that his fist came down hard onto the mahogany desk. Pens and papers lifted several inches before returning back down again.

'As I was saying, you do make a lot from nothing, don't you, but I see a flaw in your company. So you recycle old roads, sell the oil, do your bit for the' – Derek raised his hands and did the quote gesture with his fingers – 'environment. But your company has no life expectancy: no future. One day the roads will be all in good order and won't need replacing so often. So, as a result, no recycle, no oil and now you say no by-product for the power station which gives us all the power we need in our precious city.'

Gary was afraid to speak and was still concerned about dear Gareth Leach and what he had done to deserve the sack. In his twenty-five years of business he had never had to sack anyone.

'Doctor please go ahead with the demonstration.'

The doctor pulled a white sheet from off the top the trolley to reveal a gross section of road surface. Paul could see the layers clearly; the heavy road stone layer, followed by several other strong tarmac layers. From Gary's experience you could clearly see it was from a motorway or heavy construction type, the type that lasts for years and rarely breaks or fails.

The doctor walked towards Gary carrying, what could only be described as, a chemical type glass beaker; the type used in schools or labs. It was half filled with an orange looking liquid.

He held it under Gary's nose.

'Please smell.'

It smelt citrusy, like lemons, oranges and maybe a little lime.

'Fruity, yes?' the doctor said back to Gary.

'Yes, fruity.'

The doctor took the beaker of fluid and poured it over the section of road and within seconds the thick layer of road had completely melted through. There wasn't even half a pint of liquid in that beaker and it melted a good section of road right down to the core level.

'My plan is to have this stuff manufactured in my new factory just up the road from your recycling plant; handy eh! Thank you, doctor. That will be all.'

As the doctor left, he quickly removed the gloves and threw them on top of the section of still melting road. Gary noticed that the gloves didn't melt.

'Oh, the liquid can be transported in anything made from rubber or silicon,' was the doctor's last remarks as he left.

'Thank you, doctor. As I was saying, I am going into business making that stuff. I just need a partner. You see, I have no market for a road dissolving liquid but you do, Mr Gary Busher. You could make a lot of money here today.' He knew that was the only thing on his mind right now. The hospital bills were mounting up and the level of care his wife was needing was round the clock and very expensive. All he wanted was to see his wife well again and he would do anything to see that.

'My plan is to have a tanker full of this stuff – let's say – spill on to the Northwood expressway into the east end of the city, dissolving not one of the major routes into the city, but three. As you rightfully know, Mr Busher, that's a raised elevated section and would damage the westbound and northbound routes of the Northwood expressway, crippling the city for months. They would need a contractor of good reputation and if they didn't accept, you would have me as a good advocate, being the most influential man in the city.'

Gary was speechless and had long forgotten about dear old Gareth Leach; his mind was all in disarray. The greed of it all was settling in.

'Gary, you might have a multi-million pound business but you have a lot of overheads. Your costs are mounting up. You live in a modest home and drive a modest car for a millionaire. Just think – there would be no limits to your wealth. You could buy anything or anyone. You could buy out the companies that build the roads and then nothing could stop you. Nothing!'

'Ok, what's in it for you, Mr Greyer?'

'Now your talking, Mr Busher. All I want is thirty percent to start with, for the first two years but as you grow I would like to grow. It's our little vested interest, you see. I supply you with the market; you pay me what I'm due. So after two years I would have fifty-one percent of your company. I know, before you say it, that's a controlling share but I will never wish to buy you out and in ten years you will be worth an estimated 6.8 billion. Not your business, I might add; *you* will be worth that. I have it all worked out your 25 million this year becomes 50 next. Do you see where I'm going with it? The growth of your business only depends on one thing.'

'What's that?'

'We need the doctor again, Gary. I'm sorry.' Buzzzzz! 'Send in the doctor please, Miss Jones.'

Mr Greyer pulled out a file from the desk and placed it in front of Gary; he could see it was a business contract but Gary was more concerned at why the doctor needed to be there. To maybe witness it? Surely it was a job for a lawyer, not a doctor.

'Please, Gary. We need one last thing from you. Could you roll up your right shirt sleeve? You see, the doctor needs a blood sample for a blood screen. It's a health check thing. I do it with all my new business partners and it is an annual requirement. It's in the contract.'

Gary was a little taken aback by this but he could see why Mr Greyer wasn't prepared to take on a partner who could possibly drop down dead at anytime.

'I can assure you, Mr Greyer, I am in good health for man of my age. What's with the blood?'

'Let's just say, I do like to know about the health of a partner as well as their wealth. Let's just say I have a vested interest.'

Gary nodded reluctantly, took off his jacket and rolled up his sleeve.

'You know the drill, doctor.' Derek stood up and started to take his jacket off and roll up his sleeve. 'I wouldn't expect you to go through it if I didn't set the example, eh.'

'That's not necessary, Mr Greyer.'

'No, I have to. You'll see why in a moment.'

The doctor pulled the syringe out and placed a large needle into it which disturbed Gary.

'Don't worry, I won't be using such a large needle for you. Mr Greyer's body is somewhat made from granite. He his very muscular and the normal needles just bend up and it makes it more difficult for me.'

Gary quickly thought, 'And more painful for Mr Greyer.'

The doctor had drawn off 25ml of blood and placed a small piece of cotton wool over the incision. 'Please, Sir. Hold your arm up for a little while, thank you.'

'You're next, Gary,' Derek said smiling.

'I will need a little more blood from you, Gary, but not much more.' The Doctor pulled out a 50ml syringe then placing a smaller needle in it, he then tapped the chosen area to raise the vein in Gary's arm. The needle went in and the blood started to fill the syringe. It stopped once it got to the 35ml level and again he placed a small piece of cotton wool to stop the flow of blood continuing. 'Thank you.'

Gary's blood-filled syringe was placed in front of him on the desk for the pair to clearly see. Mr Greyer's was still held tightly in his hand. Mr Greyer then did something odd; he pulled an old fashioned type cartridge fountain pen from his desk. He took the syringe and squirted a little blood into a clear glass inkwell. He then drew some with the fountain pen, just enough to sign the contracts.

The look on Gary's face said it all – 'We're signing the contract in blood'? Gary was fearful. The whole meeting was an eye-opener and he felt a conscience come over him. He had a quickening of God's power. He was reminded of a sermon he had heard over three years ago about the whole subject of selling your soul for a price that can't be paid for.

Derek could sense a nervousness rise within Gary. He had to move in quickly. 'Please, Mr Busher. Would you do the honours and sign? This contract will ensure your success and I do have a surprise for you once you have signed.' He knew that would intrigue Gary. 'A surprise?' What could it be? There was nothing that could surprise Gary other than any help for his beloved wife Sarah.

Gary grabbed the pen from Mr Greyer's hand and a moment of trepidation came over him.

'Gary, I know about your wife. I know about the illness. I'm sorry to pry, Gary, but I had to do my homework. I didn't mean any harm but I can help. Believe me, Gary, I can help.'

'Let's sign up,' Derek spun the contract round towards him, grabbed the blood filled pen and quickly signed the bottom line of the contract in his own blood. By this time Gary had forgotten all about the blood-filled pen and when the contract was turned to him he also signed and dated the contract with blood.

'How? How can you help my wife?' Gary was now hooked. The sermon was long forgotten. He was just thinking about Sarah and helping his family.

'Now that we are official partners let's shake on it.'

Gary's mind was focused on one thing and one thing only. He shook but the only reason was to speed up proceedings. He just wanted to find out how. His heart was screaming – Just tell me! Just tell me!

'Gary, you are now family and I consider you and your family my family. I will help you in a way that no doctor or medical institution could ever do.' He turned to his doctor. 'Please collect the vile labelled 'Busher' from the lab.'

Now it had just hit Gary like a train: he had that vile made up the whole time, maybe this Mr Greyer has a softer side, but he could not be more wrong – he was pure evil. Gary, however, couldn't see it. Derek had only one motivation and that was the blood sitting in that syringe on his desk: the blood of a betrayer. Derek Greyer had won again and received the prize and now he was a real threat.

The doctor passed the small vile to Derek and then held it out towards Gary but quickly pulled it back before Gary grabbed it.

'Now listen, Gary. This is for your wife, Sarah, and only for her. Once you have given this to her she will feel tired and want to sleep, but she must not. You must get this liquid into her whole immune system. This liquid will flush out the cancer in her and heal her. It is a miracle liquid and costs a fortune but I know you are good for it now we are partners.'

'Why? How? What is that stuff? Why isn't available to everyone who has cancer?'

'Gary, this may not work and this 'stuff', as you call it, is a homemade remedy made by me, so there is no way of getting it until you are in the 'family', lets say, and I know you will not tell of this part of our little meeting today. If that is all, we must conclude our meeting. We have overrun a little.' Derek reached out his hand again. The pair shook hands. 'I hope all is well with your wife. Please do call if there are any changes with Sarah.'

With that said Gary nodded his appreciation and quickly left, clutching the glass vile in his hand, egger to give it to his beloved Sarah, hoping it would work, hoping it would indeed heal her. But what Gary Busher was carrying in his hand was just a diluted sample of Derek Greyer's own blood, mixed with a small amount of steroid. He would never reveal the true ingredients to anyone. He had it memorised for total security. The blood mixture wouldn't make her immortal, it would indeed heal her and in Derek's mind that is all he wanted at that time. He had no feelings, no emotion. Derek's motivation was just a selfish, self-gratifying notion to remove blood from one vessel to another vessel and he had it in the palm of his hand.

He had an hour to kill until his next meeting so as he continued to watch the wall of TVs. He would watch screen after screen, hoping something would catch his eye. Then he would quickly pick up the phone and there he would claim more wealth from misery. In that hour he made eleven phone calls and netted a few more million for the ever-growing empire.

His next meeting was with the head of a processing company (DigiLab Holdings, which Mr Wong was the CEO of) that he owned in a kind of 'ghost chairman' position so other companies wouldn't know of his involvement. The company had lucrative contracts with many of the country's hospitals and other privately funded medical centres. Their work primarily involved x-ray films and other scanned images.

The business was to take the used films and dispose of them in a more environmentally friendly and safe way. However, with the hospitals and medical centres unaware, the company produced silver from the disposed films. That made this business a very, very profitable business indeed.

But there was a spanner in the works and Mr Wong was there to answer for the drop in the current market and the impending financial losses.

Buzzzzz! 'It's Mr Wong, Sir.'

'Show him in, please.'

Mr Wong quickly sat down. 'Hello, Mr Greyer. Morning good, ya?'

'Yes, morning good. So tell me what's going on, eh.'

'As you know, we are the largest company in the world that does this–'

'Sorry to stop you, but I know we're the largest company. I own it.'

Mr Wong was nervous and had gone into his rehearsed speech as usual.

'Is the digital age crippling us? That's all I want to know.'

'No no, sir. People are still using tapes and cameras and so on, sir, but not in the same quantities.'

They also dealt with deposable cameras and a video tape recycling scheme – another branch of their business in order to profit from the silver locked within all those old VHS tapes that litter our homes. It too was profitable and had minimal cost involved.

'How is the plant, Wong?'

'Good Sir. Good sir.'

'Just tell me the figures.' Derek was getting a little impatient.

'Last month, sir, we were down by 0.2 per cent, sir.'

'Okay, Wong. I heard 'down' in that statement didn't I?'

'Yes, sir. Yes.'

'So what are we doing about it?'

'We are still making silver from the waste film from the processing plant and all sources are delivering on time.'

'You haven't told me anything remotely good yet. So what you should do is lose people so that we can break even this month.'

'Sack people, sir?'

The look on Derek's face said it all – smiling, knowing how he would affect hundreds of peoples lives with just a stroke of his pen. 'Yes. Sack people. Is that all Wong?'

'I was wondering if there was any chance I could get a little more of your amazing tonic, sir. I have been feeling a bit low lately. A little pick-me-up to get me well, so to work for you even harder, sir.' He wasn't stupid, Mr Wong; he knew what strings to pull to get what he wanted too.

'Yes, Wong; a clever move. You are obviously learning something working for me. You give, then you get, that's a good working relationship.' But he sensed something else. Derek wasn't stupid and Mr Wong had a severely sick wife as well. He thrived on misery. Greyer was pure evil and he used it to push his key players throughout his many businesses.

'Yes, it's my wife, sir. She is really sick, sir, as you know. We have being seeking many professionals and they have diagnosed a brain tumour. It's inoperable it doesn't look good, sir. I was wondering if you could make some for her too.'

'Wong, I am sorry to hear that, but I don't think the tonic would work on that kind of tumour. It may only give her a limited time, a year maybe, I don't know.' He knew damn well that it would work; he just wanted something again and was using the ill wife to get it, just like he did with Gary Busher. He was pure evil, pulling on the heart strings yet again. 'But perhaps I could strengthen the tonic. It just might work, but would you do me a favour?'

'Yes sir. Yes, anything, sir.'

'I need you to arrange a meeting with Bill Barns, the Microchip Manufacturer. He knows me well. I tell you what I want – either forge our businesses or wipe him out. I want his share of the computer market; after all it's the rise in the computer market that the processing plant is losing money. Everyone switching to digital cameras and not developing photos anymore. We do still have the contract with the hospital and all their x-rays and used film screens?'

'Yes we do, yes. It is a very profitable contract, sir.'

'So hurry, Wong. Make it happen. I would like to get ahead of the game. Barns Tech will be ours, Wong. It will be ours; your wife's health depends on it. Deal with it Wong!'

Derek turned in his chair to open a drawer. It was filled with his so-called 'tonic'; around 40-50 vials of his own blood sat in a refrigerated section of the office furniture and you would never know it was there. He quickly gave Wong a single vile.

'Normally I would never let you out of my office with that, so be careful with it. That is a super strength version, so be extra careful. Don't lose it; you won't get another one and this one is for you now.' And Derek quickly threw Wong a vile to drink, whilst he was still in Derek's office, in front of him, to witness him drinking it. 'Now I hope that is all, Wong. I am going to take the rest of day off.'

'But that's not bad for a mornings work 12.25 million without breaking sweat, so only 0.2% loss on one of my businesses but I'll get that back tomorrow, eh.' Derek smiled only proving, yet again, that he had no feelings; no emotion.

Buzzzzz! 'Miss Jones, I am taking the rest of the day off. I'll be back at the Manor so please no calls. I wish not to be disturbed. I have another matter to take care of so I'll be giving that a lot of thought this afternoon.'

The issue still burned in is soul. 'Seth' was another problem that needed dealing with asap.

Derek took his personnel elevator down to the private garage in the lower basement and decided on the Bentley Continental. The whole basement was dedicated to a few of Derek's cars. He had many highly marked-up cars, rare and very expensive. Amongst them were an AC Cobra, a Mercedes AMG SL and a Ferrari 250GT California; that alone was worth over 1.2 million. He had every kind of car; cars deemed too expensive to drive. He didn't care; money and obtaining it and, most of all, spending it was like a drug to Derek Greyer. He thrived on it.

Once he was home, the Derek Greyer facade was gone. His study was like a mirror image of the huge office at Greyer international tower, but his home also contained an equally huge training room, which he hit as soon as he arrived. He felt he should sharpen up his skills after seeing Seth's. He had to admit it; Seth had shaken him up. He defiantly needed to step up his training.

The equipment that littered the gymnasium in his vast mansion had started to gather dust. Derek had let his fitness drop knowing full well that he could easily kill Milo. His son, Paul, was no match; even if Derek didn't kill him, the cancer would do the job for him.

He had an arrogance that emulated from every pore of his evil body and this made him smile – but only for a moment, then his thoughts dwelt on Seth and his much-needed reason to dust off the equipment and start up his training again. Seth worried him. But then he gently rubbed his chin and a smug smile danced across the face of Derek Greyer. He had a plan and he was keeping that plan a secret… for now.

Chapter Nine
Seth 'Tools Up'

Ephesians 6:17 'Take the helmet of salvation and the sword of the Spirit, which is the word of God'.

THE PROXIMITY SENSOR WAS BUZZING, ALARMING the whole household to amber status.

'Adam, why have you set that for? It's noisy. It could wake grace.' Rachel seemed to have underestimated the resent following and chase episode. The car and Rachel's skill and bravery were all factors but most of all God was with them both. Adam, however, was a nervous wreck and was taking control of his home, upping the security of the family home.

'Rachel, if someone comes walking down the driveway we will know won't we. That's all, Rach. I'm not trying to worry you but you seem to be handling the recent goings-on a whole lot better than me'.

'Yes, Adam, but we can't live in a constant heightened level of worry and anxiety. It will just overwhelm us and wear us out for when we need be on alert. Trust in God's favour. Practice that faith; God has called you to a great commission. I now believe that and I will stand with you and trust God for you, if I have to, but please turn that buzzer off and give me a cuddle.'

Adam soon realised she was right and just he needed to trust more in God. His faith was the most important weapon he had, but as Adam went to the alarm control box the buzzer sounded, startling Rachel.

'Who's that?'

'It's Dad. He's come to pick me up. He's early.'

'Why? Where you going?'

'Don't worry. I won't be long and don't answer the door. Check it out first and keep the phone close by. And double lock this door when I leave. I will call you when I'm on my way back.'

Adam closed the door behind him and then heard Rachel lock it. As he walked up the driveway towards his father, he checked his pocket for his mobile phone; it was there. A little pressure was released from Adam's ever-increasing stress-filled mind.

'Hi, Dad.' A little anxiety was on show and Andy could see it clearly. Just like any caring father, he could always tell when his son was feeling it a bit. Even though Andy wasn't a believer he still had those father-like instincts and he could tell.

'Shall we get going then, son?'

The two of them were soon on there way to Mick's shop.

'So have you had any more incidents like the other week?'

'No, but Rachel thought she was being followed the other day. I think it was on Tuesday. Anyway, how's Mum?' Adam just wanted to change the subject. He hated to tell lies to his father and felt it was always bad practice to lie in general anyway.

'Mum's fine.' Andy was short with his answer. He also was worried about his son's family and hoped this visit to Mick's was a good idea.

'Do you think Mick will come through with something?'

'Knowing Mick, yes, he will come through with something.'

A few twists and turns and within ten minutes they were at Mick's shop. Adam quickly got out of the car and walked briskly to the door, making sure he got to that door first. He was aware that Rachel was home alone without him there to protect his family.

He pressed the security buzzer on the huge metal door the CCTV camera quickly turned. The sound of the motor alerted Adam and he looked directly towards the camera's lens. The intercom crackled and popped with the sound of Mick's voice.

'Who is it?'

Andy reached forward to press the intercom and get into the camera's gaze. 'It's your old friend, Andy, and his son.'

'Come in.'

The door buzzed open. Adam pushed the door and soon felt the immense weight of it, like the enormous weight and responsibility of carrying a weapon. Was he making the right decision? Was he going against the code of the Master Disciple and the result was to upset Milo? After all, he was doing all of this behind his back without his full knowledge. This quick thought disturbed Adam for a moment, but it was soon lost when hearing Mick's voice for the first time in ten years.

'Hiyah, mate,' was Mick's patter. A typical cockney originally from north London, he moved twenty years before to set up on his own and has never looked back. 'Long time no see, eh Adam. How are you? It's been years, mate. I hardly recognised you on the CCTV monitor. You still doing all that kicking and chopping martial arts stuff, eh?'

'Yes, Mick. Still practicing and keeping fit. Still keeping sharp, eh.'

'So, what can I do you for, mate?'

'I would like a protection weapon, something non-lethal. I was thinking of the pump-action shotgun that fires those little bean bags, like the police use.'

Mick nodded along. 'I know the exact thing you're talking about. But, Adam, Mate, the ammo for those things are pricey, but if you're dead-set on one I can get a load custom-made.' Mick was getting excited by this. It really perked him up and he quickly got carried away. 'Come with me. I've got a pump-action gauge that I'm cutting down in the workshop. Come this way, my fellows.'

He had all sorts in that workshop. It was like an Aladdin's cave of the gun world. There were carbines, rifles and lots of shotguns. He even had a semi-automatic shotgun that even Andy got excited about and quickly grabbed.

'How much, Mick?'

'No, it's not for sale; it's for a special client.'

'Who? Al Capone?' Andy said with huge grin.

Mick laughed. 'No, mate. Here's the weapon for you.' He handed over a shortened pump-action; a 'Gauge' was the term used by professionals and the police but mostly criminals. 'This is the ideal weapon to convert to a 'beanie baby', mate, I can tell ya.'

'A beanie baby? Is that a name you've given it, Mick?'

Mick nodded with a cheeky cocky grin across his face. He seemed more excited than Adam. Adam was a little worried but once the weapon was in his hand he felt reassured by having a form of defence that was non-lethal.

Mick could see that Adam was interested in the 'beanie baby'.

'Hey, I'll tell you what I can do for you; that particular weapon was on order from a regular and he only called me earlier this morning and changed his mind and diverted his deposit on a carbine rifle. So if that's what you want, I can have it converted no probs for you in a couple of days and throw in a couple of boxes of ammo. So, the balls in your court, as they say.'

Adam looked towards his father for permission. He just frowned and raised his eyebrows, like fathers do, then tilted his head towards Mick. Adam then took control and went ahead with the deal.

'Yes, Mick. Wrap it up, as they say.'

'Are you sure, son? This may upset Rachel knowing you have a weapon in the house.'

Andy had every right to be concerned for his son, but was using Rachel as a pawn in his little game of guilt chess

'Rachel is the whole reason for being here and especially now we have Grace as well. I want to protect my family.'

Adam felt a surge of adrenalin talking about his family and most of all the true reason for the extra protection. He quickly rose to his feet to the surprise of Mick and Andy which gave them a shock.

'Ok! Sorted! How much, Mick?'

The question took Mick by surprise. He scratched his head, trying to rack his brain for a figure that would not insult Adam or Andy and, most of all, wouldn't leave him out of pocket. 'Adam, just give me four hundred quid, mate, and that includes converting it and the 100 rounds of ammo for it. Is that a good figure?'

'Yes, mate. That's fine.'

Adam reached for his wallet and got ready with the cash. Andy looked over and felt obligated to provide for his son and his family's wellbeing. He pushed his way in and threw in two hundred pounds towards the gun. Adam was surprised by this.

'You don't have to do that, Dad.'

'Yes I do, son. I still worry about you. Tell me you're not in trouble, please. You would tell me if you were?'

'No, Dad, I'm not in any trouble. It's just a precaution, that's all. Rachel was followed and it has really spooked me. She's a nurse; people die on her ward and some people take it personally. She has been threatened a number of times, Dad, and that part of her job worries me, that's all.'

'Then why doesn't she give up the nursing? You make enough from the retirement home, don't you? And you make a good living.'

'Well, Dad. We have been waiting to tell you and Mum together that I have quit my job to work for the church two to three days a week and work at the home for the rest. We decided this a while ago and it means we can spend more time as a family.'

'You quit your job? That was a great job. Why? That was a bit selfish. What about Rachel's job? Instead of buying a gun to protect your family why not Rachel quit and get out of that job and you keep your old job? I will never understand you pair.'

It wasn't the place for an argument and Mick was a little embarrassed. He walked into the armoury to find the ammo for the 'beanie' and made himself busy.

Andy had always had a problem with the level of commitment Rachel and Adam had for church. With Andy not being a believer it made it harder for him to understand what Adam had done, what he had signed up for and, most of all, what exactly he was doing for the church. Andy, being a hands-on worker and being in the building trade for over thirty years, had a massive problem with made-up jobs that just didn't achieve anything, in his opinion.

'Dad, calm down. All this happened after I gave up my job and Rachel still loves her job. It's only for a few days a week. You see, what we are trying to achieve, at some point, is being self-sufficient. With me working for the home, the money we earn stays in the home, if you know what I mean. You always said if you're going to make money why not make it for yourself. This way we have started that process, so just let me get this item from Mick so I can finish what we have started. It's just so that I feel okay. It's added security, that's all.'

The weapon in question held eight non-lethal rounds (about the size of teabags) and could knock over a twenty stone man easily, once Mick – the 'Gun genius' – had altered it and adapted the chamber.

Mick came back to the pair of them when it had all calmed down.

'Ok, Mick. I need just one more little favour. Could you drill a bevelled hole in the butt of the handle?'

Mick gave him a look that could only suggest bewilderment.

'Yes, Mick.' Adam took the weapon from Mick and tried to show him his idea. 'You see, if you drill a hole here…' he pointed to the bottom of the handle '…I could wear the gun on a belt and hide the thing down my trousers and if the need arose for its use I could access it quickly.'

Andy and Mick gave a quick look. Adam soon realised what his so-called idea could look like, and he may have given the game away.

'Why would you want quick access? That would also indicate that you would be carrying this weapon around with you a lot of the time. Please explain, Adam,' Andy said with a stern tone in his voice.

Mick was also nervous of Adam's intensions with this converted shotgun. Basically, it was a very dangerous weapon in the eyes of the law.

'It was just an idea, that's all.' Adam racked his mind for a viable explanation for this. 'The idea was to hang the weapon behind my head board on our bed just for quick access and so I wouldn't be messing around looking for a gun in the dark. You get it? You see what I'm getting at? You should know, Dad, you used to have a speed loader with rock salt filled shells and a 357 Magnum by the side of your bed.'

Andy blushed and nodded towards Mick. 'Yes I do admit it and maybe now it was a foolish thing to do, but it doesn't mean you have to repeat history. I thought you were a little wiser than me.'

'Maybe you are right, Dad, but you did it for that macho reason. I'm doing for the safety of my family. Rachel was actually followed. It was not made up, Dad. It did scare her and I would appreciate you not worrying Mum about it, thanks, Dad. So, with that explained, Mick, I'll see you on Thursday.'

'Yes, mate. Fine. See you then.' Mick looked towards Andy and said 'I do see the point of hanging a weapon on a hook behind the headboard, especially with small children crawling about.'

With all that sorted out, Andy went for mooch around the shop looking at a auto shotgun and was tempted, himself, to purchase a weapon but felt restrained to do so. The pair left Mick at the shop and were soon on their way home.

Andy was quiet on the journey back to drop Adam off, but as the pair pulled up to the driveway he turned to say 'Please be careful and if you need me for anything just call.'

Adam knew that could only mean one thing; he was saying if indeed you are in trouble, I'm here for you. I'm in your corner. Adam nodded. 'Thanks, Dad. I do appreciate that.'

With that said, Adam got out of the car. He hated lying to his father and felt riddled with guilt. He went inside to try to relax a little (the whole evening had worn him out), but his plan to relax was short lived, when he found Rachel upset in the kitchen.

'What's wrong, Rach?'

'It's Pastor Paul. They've rushed him to hospital. It doesn't look good. They've just rung me to start praying.'

'Let's just do that, eh Rach.'

'Lord, we have no words to explain this and we don't understand why Paul has Cancer but just be with him at this time. Be with the doctors and nurses caring for him. Let him still be a witness for you. Give him great peace–'

Adam stepped in. 'Give him health, Lord. Give him health. We don't want him to have cancer, Lord. We rebuke it, Lord, in your name. Just bless Pastor Miles and Margaret as they would worry and stress. Lord, strengthen their faith. In your name we ask it. Amen.

'Sorry, Rachel. I just don't want him to die. I just felt it right to be direct and just say what I truly mean.'

Rachel came round to where Adam was sitting and gave him a huge hug. 'I know. I was thinking the exact same thing.

'So why all the secrecy with your dad?' Rachel quizzed Adam about his resent shopping trip.

'Don't go mad but I've brought a weapon.'

'What type of weapon?' Rachel was nervous by the news of another weapon in the family home.

'A gun.' Adam was awaiting the huge reaction but was surprised by Rachel's subdued attitude.

'Why a gun? You already have a sword. What happened to faith?'

'My enemy has a gun. I just feel, 'like for like', that's all and anyway it's just for defence.'

'What do you mean, just for defence?'

'It won't kill; it's a beanie gun. It shoots little teabag sized bags that just knock a person over. If it gets a bit rough and I need to escape I have that back up.'

'But why, Adam?'

'Deygar pulled a Glock on me and Pastor Miles. I didn't want to scare you as it turned out to be flash rounds to temporally blind us so he could escape. For all we knew they could have been live rounds. So I did what I felt was right to do.'

Adam was filled with adrenalin and the whole episode was quickly replayed in his mind. Rachel could see Adam was clearly shook up by this and reassured him.

'Ok, Adam, I'll have to make my peace with the gun. Just do me this small favour; just keep it out of harm's way and mostly Grace's.'

The very next morning Adam went to the church to see if Pastor Miles was there. After his night with Paul, Adam would understand if he wasn't, but, as ever, he was there bright and early and was eager to get on with Adam's training.

Adam felt awkward telling Milo about the gun, but as it turned out he was fine about it; not clear on what it was, could have been the reason for his sudden change of heart. But their encounter with Deygar, with his semi-automatic pistol, had shaken him up also and he was still open about the whole subject of the gun/sword debate.

'Together, Adam, we will be a powerful force, but as soon as we lose sight of God, our vision is blurred and the mission is lost. We will fail as ambassadors for God. You see, Adam, we must keep this a secret, but at the same time keep a relationship with God. I know it must be hard at the moment having no one to share and lift the burden but it is important for God's people that this remains a secret.'

It always amazed Adam that Pastor Miles could sense when Adam was troubled without even saying anything to suggest so.

'So, how's Paul?' Adam was eager to find out what had happened the previous night at the hospital.

'It was a scary night, I can tell you, but Paul's a fighter and he is bearing up.'

The pair of Master Disciples went on and trained for a few hours as normal but their hearts pondered for Paul, still in hospital, and they remained in a reflective mood. There were moments of long silences and they felt in a real place of solitude, quietly praying as they went about their duties.

The remaining months of Adam's training went smoothly and Grace had started to try her first steps. Rachel was doing fine, especially now they had the LPS system working and they could pinpoint their exact location to the nearest metre. The tiny screen would show a grid reference and even a street name. Scott had done well and it gave Rachel reassurance and made her feel at peace whilst out in the car with Grace.

The six months was coming to a close for Adam and on the last day, even though Pastor Miles said you'll never stop learning, their official training time together had come to a close and they would spend the time together in prayer and exercise purely maintaining what they had started over six months ago.

'Mind exercise and body Exercise', Milo call it.

They had all arranged to meet in the training room; Pastor Miles and his wife, Margaret; Pastor Jason and his wife, Lorraine; and finally Rachel and Grace; they had thrown a surprise for Adam.

'Surprise!' they all yelled as Adam walked down the stairs to the training room.

'So, what's this all about, eh?' Adam was taken aback by the sentiment of it all.

'It was Paul's idea to do this for you, and we have a surprise for you later,' said Rachel with a huge grin on her face. 'But now let's eat.'

Pastor Miles felt great that they were all together, but missed Paul. 'Let's raise a cup up to my son, Paul, and pray a blessing on him.

'Lord, we raise our cups and remember Paul and his loving wife at his bedside right now and we just pray that you restore him and build him up in faith at this time, in your name Lord. Amen.'

As the evening went on Adam was getting more anxious about his surprise. Then the top buzzer sounded, alerting Pastor Miles that there was someone at the main doors of the church.

'Ok, everyone, it's time for Adam's big surprise. So if you would follow me up.'

They all went up to see the reaction from Adam; they quickly put a blindfold on him so everyone could get up there before he saw the surprise.

There was a huge box waiting on the car park near to the main doors to the church.

The box was all bound up, secure, so Rachel started to cut through so Adam could see what was in the box, fully.

Once all the binding was removed and the box taken off, all that remained was the packing and the plastic cover for Adam to take off. They quickly took off the blindfold.

'Wow! What is it?'

'Take it off then,' they all said loudly. All were just as excited as Adam was. Adam quickly pulled the plastic away to reveal a MV Augusta F4 Motorcycle, complete with leathers, gloves and a helmet, all matching.

Adam fell to knees with shock and just turned his head round to see everyone.

'Why, I don't deserve this.'

Milo stepped up. 'It's not brand new but it was the best we could find. We asked Rachel for the specification required, so thank her for this. We all chipped in and decided that you needed a vehicle to get from place to place quickly, so we got you this.'

'It's your favourite, right Adam?' said Rachel with a concerned look on her face.

'Rach, it's fantastic, honest. I would never have guessed this was the big surprise.'

'We've had some modifications made to the bike.' Milo was eager to show Adam.

'Come on, Pastor. Let him take it for a spin,' Jason said, quickly passing Adam his brand new helmet.

Adam soon got himself kitted out in the leathers and got on the bike. Rachel went over to him carrying Grace in her arms; she was nearly asleep. 'Please, Adam, go steady. You haven't ridden for a few years and this bike is very fast. Don't forget I ordered it.'

'Ok, Rach, I'll try,' he said and gave Rachel a quick wink.

Adam pressed the bike's starter button and it roared into life. He selected first gear and made his way to the car park exit, but first he familiarised himself with the MV's controls before hitting the main road. Then, with a blink of an eye, he was gone. Adam buried the throttle and hit 60 mph in less than three seconds.

Rachel heard the bike and thought, 'I said go steady on that thing' then quietly prayed to herself.

'We'll wait for him to come back, eh,' said Margaret

'We'd better get inside. Knowing Adam he'll be ages. It's been a while since he's been on a bike and, to be honest, he deserves it.'

As Rachel said it, her heart was filled with worry; the worry wasn't the danger of the bike. It was the true reason for the bike that filled her heart with such dread and fear.

It didn't take Adam long to get his bike confidence back, riding the MV. He was loving it and was soon getting his knee down in the corners and muttering to himself inside his helmet: 'Man! This is the business! The handling is fantastic!'

In the twenty or so minutes that Adam was gone, he soon realised that he ought to get back, especially as the party and surprise that everyone had planned was for him.

When he got back the car park was all deserted; everyone had gone back inside.

He got back to the party and was quickly questioned by Pastor Miles. 'So how was it, Adam?'

'It's absolutely fantastic, and I would like to thank you all again and especially Rachel for all your hard work and for everything that you are going through. It must have been a shock for you, especially with your work, having Grace and everything that goes with that and the news of my new career change.' Adam was skirting around the whole Master Disciple title and all its responsibilities. 'So I just want to say a big thanks and that I love you so much and I could not have done any of this without you. So, Rach, I love you and I thank God for you.'

As the evening was drawing to a close and guests started to leave Adam was also aware that Grace was now fast asleep and tucked up in the corner of the gym. It was time for them to leave too. He didn't want to appear rude, as he was the guest of honour, but Grace needed to be in her bed and Rachel was at work the next day.

Adam rode the M.V. home, still not believing it was his, and Rachel drove the Legacy with Grace still fast asleep.

The very next morning Adam left home for church eager to get on the M.V. to see Pastor Miles. The journey to church took barely minutes; the bike was impressing Adam every second he rode it.

In the office, Pastor was in the study quietly praying. Adam walked in tiptoeing his way past, trying not to disturb him, but Pastor knew he was there.

'Morning Seth.'

'Oh, morning, Milo. Sorry, did I disturb you?'

'No, not at all. We had a great time last night, and what about that surprise, eh?'

'Yes, it's still sinking in.' Adam was having to pinch himself whenever he thought about the bike. He still couldn't get over the generosity of everyone.

'You know that you can't wear your sword on your back when riding on the bike, well, not without being arrested anyway. I have another surprise for you.' Pastor Miles went over to the wall to open the safe behind the picture and pulled out a case and handed to Adam. Adam quickly placed the box on the table and opened it; it was a shortened version of his sword, especially designed to fit into the M.V's frame. Milo was keen to show Adam how it fitted into the bike's frame to conceal it. The pair quickly walked to the car park. Milo took the sword from him to give him a demo.

'You see, Adam, the sword fits in here. Did you notice the faring was slightly flared out to allow the sword to be fitted. There's a sheath fitted inside so there's no chance you will damage anything to the inner workings of the bike. And did you notice the handle on the sword, on its very end, was an exact copy of the damper control switch, so you can leave the sword in and it locks within the bike. It is only released when you press the correct button when the ignition is turned on.'

Adam was taken aback again and was soon thinking of when, how and who had done all of this work to the bike. Even with all of his car and motorcycle knowledge, he couldn't tell that the bike had been altered at all.

Adam quickly took the sword from its new home in the bike and tried it for its weight. He quickly thrust it either side of his body, spinning the sword through and around his hands, changing direction so quickly that Pastor Miles could only see it as a blur.

'We have everything we need now, Milo. It's great and I even had a chance to test the LPS system just the other day; Rachel was at the shops so when I called her I knew she was at the shops before she told me. It really freaked her out. It's a very vital piece of our equipment, Pastor Miles.'

'Adam, would there be any chance that we could have a system here at the church, like a central base unit where we could oversee everything?'

'I like that, Pastor. That's a great idea. I will see my brother and ask him. He always likes a challenge.'

A few weeks into their new prayer and exercise program and Adam and Pastor Miles had wondered why it had all gone quiet in the Deygar camp. And just then there was an urgent news flash on the TV.

'We're sorry to interrupt your program, but computer micro-chip tycoon, Bill Barns, was involved in a tragic accident in the last few hours. He and his wife, Janet Barns, were killed instantly when their leer jet crashed near Montego Bay, Jamaica. Their pilot, Captain Graham James, was also killed, leaving a wife and two children. We'll have more on this story as it arises.'

Pastor Miles gave a raised eyebrow look, like there was a link with the fact that they were only just speaking about Deygar and his lack of activity recently. Then Pastor Miles quickly recalled a newspaper article he had read recently; he started to walk around the training room nodding his head as he walked, muttering under his breath.

'What is it, Milo?'

'I don't know if there is a link but, Adam, hear me out. The article I read was about Mr Chan Wong, whose chairman of DigiLab Holdings, who had approached Barns Tech with an attempt to merge the three companies, but there were complications with the final contract and they ended up with lawyers fighting it through. Now, with the chairman and his wife both dead, it would mean the contracts would be void and the companies could merge as a result of the accident. I don't know;

maybe I'm reading in to this too much; maybe we will know more on the news later.'

'Or you could try the internet. That's constantly updated. But first, let's backtrack. You mentioned only two companies, DigiLab Holdings and Barns Tech. What's the third?'

'Adam, it's Greyer Industries. They all come back to him; DigiLab Holdings was his company (well, his father's from back in the early eighties) to which he sold for millions to still have a controlling role as a ghost chairman, but only I'm privy to that knowledge. Money, eh! It can bring its little perks like insider trading and the knowledge that no one can stop you because you're the boss.'

'How come you know all this Milo?'

'I knew his father well. He knew my business and I knew his. It was a way of control for us both; a way of keeping our distance, if you know what I mean. Back then it was a simpler time.'

Milo was reminiscing, thinking of his youth and – just for a moment – being a little envious of Seth's youth, courage and eagerness.

'I have it, Milo. If what you say is true he could have a hand in five of the world's wealthiest companies, but this is the worst of it; he could potentially be the unseen controller of all that wealth and power.'

'It's not that, Seth, that bothers me the most, it's the reason. It's not a human trait, it's an evil one. The more he relies on the blood of a betrayer for greed, power and, most of all, immortality, the more he takes on the character and traits of the Devil, the king of lies, the true betrayer; that's who we are up against.'

'But we need to be sure. This is all theory and speculation. We have to find out for sure, concrete truth. We can seek God on wisdom but in what direction and wisdom in what area exactly?' said Adam as he looked at the computer screen, with his head in his hands.

Adam was onto something with that last statement, but Milo didn't respond.

'Milo, I thought it was a believer's blood that sustained his immortality.'

'Not necessarily. It can be anyone that betrays their own beliefs, whether it's business, personnel or religious, but he needs Christ's own blood to give him a life that won't end – immortal living – and the only way he can get that is to kill a believer or betray a believer. Let's say, a weaker form 'diluted' from the real stuff, the powerful stuff.

'As believers we not only share in Christ's suffering and blessing; as believers we share His blood type, so to speak. We share His life and we share in His death.' Milo's eyes lit up with every word he spoke. You could clearly see his faith at work in him and through him. It excited Adam to the depths of his core.

Milo jumped into step. 'That's it! He can't sustain his immortality. He's running out of time. He gave away his plan. 'Eighteen months'; that was it. The stupid fool even told me. I can't believe he told me.'

Adam was all confused, nodding his head with a scrunched-up face. Adam was more than confused; he was a little frustrated, but he did not interrupt Milo mid-flow. He was a having total recall of something and Adam feared he would lock up if asked at this point.

'That means he's got less than a year to find new blood in the form of a believer who is prepared to betray, or worse, kill one of us in battle.'

And that was it; the pair of them looked at each other with a fear that stopped them in their trains of thought. Adam dared not say anything; he was clearly troubled by Milo's last statement. It finally hit home for Adam that it could be any one of them or anyone from the wider church, which was the worst case scenario for Milo.

'Only we know him as the evil 'Deygar', Dark Lord of the 'Judas Cult',' said Milo, 'but what if he's using his wealth to pull together others in the cult? If there are any left, they could form an alliance. With enough wealth, they could go on forever.'

Milo was struck with discernment at what Adam had just said. 'It's not the blood he wants, Adam. That's it; he's trying to find more members, very important members, key members.'

'We need to find out for sure, Milo, and I think I know how we can do it.'

Milo was excited and his faith was growing even stronger, until Adam came out with a statement that shook him, to his core.

'We should bug his office, Milo.'

Chapter Ten
More Knowledge Please!

Proverbs 10 v 14 'Wise men lay up Knowledge: but the mouth of the foolish is near destruction'.

WITH ADAM'S NEW AND EXCITING IDEA, Milo had reservations; he had a moral issue with the whole idea of spying.

Adam tried to explain: 'He is a billionaire; he can dig into our pasts and he can pay off police. He could do anything. How do you think he managed to have Rachel followed and chased and scared half to death, eh? It's money, Milo, and he has plenty of it. We could get the edge on him here, if you just let me.'

'How? I'm not 'Q', ya know.'

'No probs. My ever faithful brother, Tatter; he could knock something up in minutes. He's an electronics' genius.'

Milo didn't enjoy throwing a spanner in the works of Adam's ideas but he had one burning question.

'How do we get close enough to Derek Greyer to bug him, eh?'

'Simple; we fake a correspondence from a business partner or something. Businesses are always trying to impress with gifts and stuff like that; my idea is to send something from Bill Barns from Barns Tech, you know; fake the postmark from before the accident and I could deliverer it on the bike like a courier. They won't recognise me. I'll have my helmet on and he won't see the bike forty stories up, and I'll be wearing old tatty leathers.'

'Why Bill Barns, eh?'

'Because if he's as evil as you say, he will be more likely to keep something like that as a trophy and may not throw it like most business people do when they are sent stuff, that's why.'

'Genius, Adam. Simply genius. Get to work on it. Tell ya brother. He is now on the payroll.'

Adam was soon at his brother's place explaining what he wanted and he was excited by the latest project.

'More James Bond stuff, eh! Fantastic!'

'And, more excitingly, we're going to start paying you for your strokes of genius.'

'We? Who's this 'we', eh, Adam? Are you in the spying business or something?'

'No, Scott. I'll start to pay you on a job per job basis.'

'Cool!'

It was a dream come true for Tatter, being paid for is inventions.

'All I need is an idea of how small I should make these.'

'Just go with small, like a paper weight, just so we can know that it would be placed somewhere close,' said Adam without giving the game away. 'How long, Scott?'

'Give me few days, mate. I'll have it sussed then. Hey, do you want this to configure with your LPS and computer system?'

'Do I! Yes, that would be fantastic.'

Tatter noticed the bike leathers and gave Adam a double-take. 'You brought a bike, Bro?'

Adam was excited about the bike but how could he tell Scott the real reason behind having such an item, when it was really a company vehicle? He would never understand. But Adam underestimated Scott; on the surface he was an unbeliever, yes, a total atheist, but on the odd occasion he would utter the little prayers that would more than convince a non-believer near to him that he was a fully-fledged believer. He would often brag about the work his brother and wife did for their local church, but if only he knew the half of it; it was more than work – it was a fight for survival.

'An M.V badge I notice, eh. You'll have to show us this, Bro.'

Scott walked Adam out to check out the bike, but just gave it the once over. He was eager to get started on the latest gadget, especially now he was in business.

The day that Adam longed for all week – the day when all the leaders, Pastor Miles and Jason felt relaxed – had finally come; Sunday was the day when the whole flock was under one roof and safe.

Since Jason's new revelation, his sermons have been delivered with more passion and compassion for the flock, realising the importance of keeping the faith and encouraging the church to search the scriptures in more depth for themselves, and for the pastoral care of the people on the edge of faith to protect them, watch after them, and nurture them.

Ultimately, he wanted a self sufficient church that was strong in faith and understanding; stronger than just the four walls of a physical building; as Jason put it in his sermon 'the building could fall, but the church would still be there standing bolt upright.'

Adam had been a little cautious of late and today he wasn't as relaxed as he'd liked, and he had good reason; the church was expecting a lot of new people; it was new members' day.

New members' day was a concept dreamt up by Paul when he was fit and well, a few years ago. The concept was to help people fit in and feel part of something. The church was forever growing and the numbers were hard to manage from time to time. The home group leaders had the difficult task of checking who was new to the church and, more often than not, the person that they would ask had been coming for years which would create a very awkward moment.

So the new member's day was born. It provided a platform for new people to be seen and be formally introduced to the church. They received a certificate of membership and shook hands with all the leaders. It was a very exciting day for a new member; they felt special and it gave people a warm holy glow.

Paul's words were: 'It was one of the single most important meetings for new people to feel part of something, not apart from.'

Adam gave a quick look at his watch. It was 5.45; fifteen minutes to go and the place was packed. The first two rows were all seated. The first row had all the leaders in it then directly behind them were the new members. Adam gave a quick glance over to Pastor Miles; he looked nervous for some reason which was reflected by Jason. It was his first new member's service. Adam felt it was his responsibility to be on high alert for some reason, he just felt it was right. He was unsure if it was God telling him or his own intuition; with both, he guessed, he couldn't go wrong.

With just five minutes to go Pastor Miles signalled Adam over.

'Adam, I don't know what it is, but I feel uneasy in my spirit.'

'That's weird. I was feeling a little on edge, and I feel that God is saying now you have called me over that I should sit near the leaders just for tonight. I was going to ask you first because I know you always sit at the end of the first row.'

'No, Adam. If God's told you, who am I to get in the way? Be obedient. Do as He said.'

Adam felt increasingly on edge but, at the same time, he felt a surge of the Holy Sprit fill him with hope and reassurance.

The service started with a nervous Jason in the lead position conducting the normal run of announcements and prayer requests, and thanking the church for their constant prayer for Pastor Paul.

'Paul sends his love and prayers for you all. He has been feeling better and has been walking around the hospital. He has been a constant inspiration to me and tonight's service, being my first new members' service.'

The music started and the congregation stood to worship. The sound was great and very loud, with everyone in good voice. It was like the church couldn't wait to start. The excitement was electric; there was defiantly something happening tonight.

Adam gave another glance over to Pastor Miles. He wasn't singing; he had his eyes tightly closed, his face all wrinkled up and his fists tightly clenched, waving them above his head, deep in prayer, but not normal prayer; this was battle prayer, and Adam knew something was going to happen.

Adam continued to sing but had one eye on Pastor Miles. During the third song it happened; a man came walking down the aisle towards the front.

Adam knew straight away that something wasn't quite right with this man. He had a fiery look about him and his fists were also clenched as if he was about to have a fight. Adam could clearly see the adrenalin was flowing.

Adam had seen this look many times before but did anyone else notice it? Pastor Miles was still in deep prayer and this guy was getting closer.

As he got to the front he stopped just in front of the pulpit, where Jason was stood, but even he didn't notice. He eventually caught a quick glance but carried on with the service. He glanced over to Adam. Adam acknowledged this with a wink, like 'I've got it sorted, don't worry.' And Adam had. He slid the extendable baton down his sleeve, holding it just in the palm of his hand, ready just in case it all kicked off.

Adam made a move; he just took two side steps and met the man standing at the front, his face like a furnace, blood red and ready to explode. Adam could feel the tension radiating from him, his jaw firmly clenched.

Adam could take him out right there but there was no way he could do that in a service, so he did it the meek and mild way.

'Do you require prayer, sir?' Adam said, as calmly as he could, still holding the baton firmly up his sleeve.

A pause, then the man spoke, 'Are you Pastor Miles?' The man was speaking through gritted teeth; it was like he was being controlled by an evil sprit. Adam felt uneasy, but he had to deal with it the best way he could.

The singing and the worship continued thankfully for Adam.

'I'm not Pastor Miles but if you want to come with me we can see him in private, if that's alright with you, sir.'

'No. I was told that he sits there, where you are sitting. Are you Miles or not?'

Adam feared the worst. Was it a contract killer here to kill Pastor Miles? Adam quickly sizing this guy up. He was a big guy, around the twenty stone mark, heavy set and quite muscular. There was no way Adam could take him down in church, not without taking a few rows of people with him. Adam dared not look over to Pastor Miles who was still deep in prayer. Then, thinking quickly, he came up with an idea.

'No, I'm not Pastor Miles. He wasn't feeling well. He's next door. I could take you to him if you wish.'

'Yes. Take me to him.'

The man quickly turned to walk back down the aisle. Adam quickly indicated to Pastor Miles and he broke from his prayer like he knew what was going on. He gave Adam enough time to follow on after them without the man seeing him.

Once next door, in the fellowship hall, Adam felt he could drop the nice act.

'Hey, what is your problem?'

'Hey, where's Pastor Miles?'

'I'm right here.' Pastor Miles walked through, just behind the man.

'Hey, you were just to my right the whole time. Hate liars!' With that, he threw a punch towards Adam. Adam blocked it and brought the man down with a swift sweep kick to his legs and restrained him. It was over in a blink of an eye. The man didn't know what had happened to him.

'Who are you, and why did you come tonight? If you cooperate with us, you won't have to with the police.'

Pastor Miles saw a real street edge to Adam's attitude and felt confident with him being there.

The man instantly calmed down. The fiery temper had gone. 'Okay, I'll tell you, but will you promise to let me go?'

'There's no promises, mate. Talk!'

'You're breaking my arm.'

Adam had him in a typical police hold with the suspect on his front with his arm up behind and just the right amount of pressure on the shoulder socket.

Pastor Miles was getting a little more nervous, quickly checking no one could see what was going on, but Adam had it all under control, even though this guy out weighted him by at least six or seven stone. Adam was using the best weapon he had: his voice and confidence.

'I'm not breaking your arm.' Adam's voice calmed a little. 'If I was a copper you would need your arm resetting into this shoulder socket by now. Firstly, your name.'

'Okay, okay. My name is Dave, Dave Smith, and that is my real name before you ask.'

Pastor was observing this whole engagement on the floor unfolding and was struck with the notion and the phrase 'Mind Control'. Dave was the victim here, not Pastor Miles.

'You're hired help, aren't you, Dave.' With that said Adam gave a little more pressure to his arm until he felt the shoulder pop. His arm was dislocated from its shoulder. Dave gave out a scream, but no one would hear; the music was too loud to bring any attention to them.

Pastor Miles stepped in, feeling Adam had gone to far, his anger guiding his motions.

'Steady on, Adam. Please, he's in pain.'

Adam was angry that Pastor was trying to defend him – a possible hit man.

'Do you realise, Pastor, that if you had sat in your regular seat and not heard God tonight and confirmed that I should sit there in your place, what do you think would have happened?'

With that said Adam started to frisk Dave. 'Are you carrying? Are you tooled up?' 'Carrying what?' Dave asked.

'You know; a weapon.' Adam's theory and hunch had lead to his right side jacket pocket. He pulled out a gun of some kind, but it was no weapon that Adam recognised, and Adam knew weapons well.

Adam turned Dave over and placed the weapon under his chin. 'Tell me what this is. Now!'

Pastor Miles was scared at what he was witnessing – a side to Adam that let Pastor know that this seemed all too familiar, and Adam had been in this kind of situation before.

Dave was in fear of his life. He soon realised that Adam was more than able to carry out his threats and back up his words.

'It won't do what you think; it's an animal tracking gun, the type that game wardens use to inject projectiles into an endangered animal.'

'Why, and who set up the contract?' Adam's questions were coming thick and fast.

Adam picked Dave up on to his feet. 'This is going to hurt.'

'What's going to hurt?'

With that said, Adam pulled Dave's arm so hard that it was slammed back into the shoulder socket. Dave let out an almighty scream that someone had to have heard.

Pastor Miles was still looking on in wonder and shock at what had just happened. He ran it back in his mind again like an action replay in a football game.

Adam had just brought a possible hit man out of a busy public church sanctuary, tackled him to the ground, dislocated his arm from his shoulder and disarmed him.

'I should call the police, Adam.' Pastor Miles wasn't thinking straight.

'And tell them what exactly? Tell them a man came into church to shoot you with a tracking device to which he hasn't done and no one witnessed? I'm not defending the guy but it won't tell us nothing if he's locked behind bars, and for what? It wasn't even assault, well maybe. Call them, Pastor. They'll probably end up taking me away in hand cuffs.'

Pastor Miles looked hard into Adam's eyes. Adam gave a quick wink like 'trust me, Milo; I know what I'm doing. We're probably better off letting him go. He'll lead us to his contact and we will all be the wiser.'

Dave's face went pail with fear. 'No. I'll tell you what you want. I need sanctuary. Please, please; you have to forgive me, you're a minister for God's sake.'

'Fitting words, Dave. 'For God's sake', eh! Don't play with us, Dave, for your sake. Start talking, mate.'

The three all pulled chairs as Dave started to tell his story.

'Well, I'm a bit down on my luck. Fate – whatever you would say – but I hit rock bottom. I used to do door work and minding and the occasional muscle for debt collecting.

'I've racked up quite a gambling debt and need fast money so these two guys found me out. I never met them before. I don't know their names before you ask, so I'll continue. Well, these two guys offer me ten large – ten grand, if you don't know.'

Pastor Miles was looking a little confused but was struck with the realness of it all. It shook him to his core.

'So I took the job. They gave me the gun and the details: where, when and who, and to come back when the job was done–'

'Stop there. Come back? Come back where? Where did you arrange this job?'

'At this bar.'

'What bar?'

'The Old Mabel Tavern.'

'What time, Dave?'

Dave paused for a moment, checking his surroundings and the possibility of an escape. With an old man clearly in shock and in a church he felt he had nothing to lose.

Adam sensed something with Dave and quickly acted on a definite prophetic word from God; he was going to go for an escape attempt at any moment.

Adam quickly put the gun against Dave's arm ready to pull the trigger. 'Maybe we inject you with a tracker, eh, so they – whoever *they* are,

Dave – follow you instead. I know that you're thinking of escaping. He might be an old man but he can move when he has to.'

Dave was clearly disturbed by Adam's ability to read his thoughts.

'No, no. I'm not going anywhere. It's cool. You obviously have ability and you know your way around a weapon and you can use your hands in a fight. I'll yield. I won't put up a fight.'

'We'll see,' Adam thought.

'Firstly, Dave, tell me how you unload this gun.'

'You first need to disengage the trigger. The thing is still ready to fire, you see.' Dave leant forward to demonstrate.

'Not a chance!' Adam was quick to see what Dave was trying to do.

'No, I wasn't trying to take it off you.'

Adam quickly worked it out for himself, pulling the trigger action back, then he broke the gun in half a lot like a flare gun. He pulled out the tracker, a very small bullet about the size of a multi vitamin tablet. Adam then threw the weapon back at Dave. Dave sort of grabbed it in nervous fumble.

'Okay, the question still stands; what time are you meeting your contacts?'

Dave was in a situation where he had to give up the information. It was clear to him now, that this was the winning team. Maybe it was true that they weren't as well financed as his contacts, but image wasn't everything that it was all cooked up to be. It was becoming very clear that these two men were working for the greater good.

'After the service, around eight.'

'That didn't hurt at all. We're coming.'

'No, that's a bad idea. They won't like that at all.'

'We're coming whether you like it or not.'

Reluctantly Dave went with their plan, with the threat that if he didn't Adam would turn him in to the police or worse, his hired contacts.

The plan was to carry on as if the job had been carried out, to give Adam and Pastor Miles the edge they so needed.

Dave and Pastor Miles went together in his car with Adam following behind on the bike. Once they were a street away Pastor Miles dropped off Dave so it wouldn't look suspicious to anyone in the bar. Adam drove ahead and quickly noticed a black Range Rover with a private registration. It read 'DEY 10'; not obvious who that belonged to.

Dave walked up to the bar and then proceeded to the table where the two men were sitting.

'So, Dave, how did it go then?'

'It went well. The old man was feeling a little unwell so this guy took me to him to this quiet room out of the way. It was a piece of cake.'

'So you shot him with the tracker gun?'

With that question asked, the other guy got a tracking device out of his pocket and switched it on. It immediately started beeping and gave what they thought was Pastor Miles' location, but it wasn't. The tracking projectile was on Pastor Miles' desk back at the church, and that was the place where they figured Pastor Miles was.

'Fantastic job, Dave. Here's another five grand. We like people who deliver in our rapidly competitive business.'

The quiet one of the duo was a wall of a man: 6'8 and weighting at least 21-22 stone. He reached into his pocket again to pull out a mobile phone and gave it to the talkative one.

'Another gift from your new business partners. Keep it with you, mate, just in case we can throw some more work your way, okay, Dave. We will be in touch.'

With that said Dave got up to leave.

'Not staying for a celebratory drink?'

'No, it's probably best if I'm not seen with you, if we're going to be working together again.'

'And again, Dave, you surprise me with your level of professionalism. Yes, you are right. You should go.'

Dave quickly walked towards the door, left the bar and then proceeded to the street where Pastor Miles had dropped him off. All being observed by Adam who was watching, sitting on the M.V. and then the two men came out and walked towards the Range Rover. They too were quickly on their way, with Adam following behind on the bike, remembering to keep well back so not to be noticed.

After several miles, they exited the city and were in the countryside, heading towards a large manor house. Adam quickly turned off the lights on the bike to appear invisible to the vehicle in front. The Range Rover stopped in front of some large metal gates and an arm reached out of the vehicle to type a code into the security system to deactivate the alarm and open the gates. The vehicle then proceeded up through a heavily wooded area until reaching the top of a hill where the large manor house sat.

Adam had seen enough. He turned round and headed back to the church.

Once back at church he headed for Pastor Miles' office. Pastor Miles was sitting at his desk and Dave was in front of him, on his knees crying.

'What's wrong, Dave?'

'Once they find out what really happened they'll kill me. They gave me a phone to keep tabs on me. You may as well have shot me with that gun, Adam.'

'Dave, don't worry. They won't kill someone who does good work for them. To them, you've done a good job. How are they going to find out?'

'Like, when there's no movement from the tracker.'

'Dave, I was thinking about that. I do have a great idea. We are going to post that tracker all over the place using the postal system as way of moving it around. They'll be following shadows.'

Dave was reassured by Adam's idea and felt a little calmer by it.

'Dave, we will be praying for you and your safety. Keep in touch. Take the church's number but use your own phone not the phone that was just given to you,' said Pastor Miles.

Dave broke down in tears. 'I can't believe you can trust me after what I tried to do. I was hired to shoot you.'

It was Pastor Miles' time to shine now and Adam stood back and didn't dare step in. This was Pastor Miles gift: loving people and not judging them, whatever they'd done.

'Dave, that's why I'm a pastor. I learn to see the good in people – their true destiny, there true calling and most of all forgetting their pasts and seeing there true potential.

May I suggest, Dave, you do the same. You'll find that doing good is far more beneficial than doing bad, for temporary things, such as money.' With that said Dave pulled out the envelope containing the five grand and threw it on the table.

'You can use it far better than I ever could.'

'Dave, we forgive you. You don't have to give us the money. You need it; you are in debt.'

'Dave, you are clearly emotional at the moment. We will keep hold of the money for you, if you change your mind or do need for anything, just ask, please.'

'No. If you say that you forgive me I have no debts. You are good people, Godly People, and I do feel honoured to know you both and please pray for me won't you. That wasn't just church speak was it?'

'Yes we will both be praying for you, Dave. When we say we're going to pray that is exactly what we will do, Dave.'

The very next day Adam got the call he'd been waiting for from Tatter.

'Got that stuff done, Bro.' Scott said excitedly over the phone. He sounded more excited than Adam.

'I'll pop round on the bike. I'll be there in ten, mate.'

Adam gave Pastor Miles a quick glance and said 'We're on!'

Pastor Miles gave a disapproving frown towards Adam but just nodded and said 'Carry on; the Lord is with you and your plans.'

Adam quickly put on his bike leathers, gloves and helmet, and was soon on his way. It was a glorious day for mid-March; the sun was shining and Adam was extremely excited at their new challenge. When he arrived, Scott was outside washing his car.

As soon as Scott heard the M.V's engine roar up he dropped the sponge back into the bucket of soap suds to admire Adam's new toy. All Scott said once Adam had removed his helmet was 'Quick?' And Adam's answer was simply 'Oh Yes, very.'

'Suppose you've come for that stuff?'

Adam just nodded with the biggest smile on his face. Scott could just sense Adam's excitement and was envious of the possible challenge that lay ahead for his brother.

Once inside Scott showed Adam the stuff he'd been working on. Scott had built a paperweight, pen and stand, plus a paper knife. He'd been busy but it was the complexity of it all that struck Adam. His face was alight with excitement. The paperweight in particular was amazing. It was a large oversized processor chip from a computer encased in resin plastic glass and virtually unbreakable. Amazingly it was totally self-powered thanks to a solar panel used to top off the chip inside. And it was voice activated. The pen acted as back up for the paperweight 'bug'. When the person was too far away, the pen boosted the signal, thanks to a proximately sensor inside the top. It would never be found. Even when the ink cartridge ran out it still wouldn't be seen and was powered by a kinetic movement sensor stolen from a wrist watch.

All of the items worked independently. Even the pen stand and the paper knife had sensors so that if the knife was placed in a drawer it would be backed up by boosting its signal from the bug and vice versa. Scott had out done himself this time.

Adam was awestruck with only one question on his mind: 'How did you do all this so quickly? You could work for the FBI or MI5 or something. It's genius.'

'Well, we had trouble with the moulding; the liquid plastic glass would melt the complex electronic parts, so we coated them with liquid Teflon. It's so cool.'

'Hold up a bit, Scott. I heard a 'we' in that last statement. Who's the *we?*'

'Hey, Adam, I'd love to get all the credit for this but I'm sorry, I've got a mate who does plastic injection moulding. He's a genius too.'

Adam was worried to hear that a third party was privy to their plans.

'Who is this guy and can he be trusted, Scott?'

'He's cool. It's Dave from the plastics factory from across my work. For all he knows it's for my boss. He doesn't even know that it works. To him, it is a paperweight, pen, stand and a paper knife. No worries, man. Chill!'

Adam was quickly struck by the name. Could it be? No, he was telling himself, but God does work in mysterious ways. Could it be his Dave, the Dave who had surrendered to God after trying to inject Pastor with the tracker. Adam quickly put it to the back of his mind, packed up all the stuff and gave Scott a brown envelope.

'Okay, if you're cool with this mate of yours, Dave, so am I. I'm sorry for doubting you.'

Adam left Tatter's and was soon back at church showing Pastor Miles all the amazing stuff Scott had come up with. He was amazed and was really getting behind the whole idea. There was, however, something truly puzzling Pastor Miles and that was how were they going to fake the post mark. It was a major problem in their plan. Adam put it to one side for the moment and took the bullet from Pastor Miles' desk.

'We should post this today. They could be tracking it as we speak.'

Pastor Miles came straight back with 'Post it to where?'

Adam's quick thinking again: 'Just post to our self for a few weeks. It will keep them on their toes for a while.' And just as Adam walked towards the franking machine in the office it hit him. 'We can fake the post mark ourselves with the franking machine.'

'No we can't, Adam. That machine's state of the art. It's a digital machine that records all dates and it can be traced back to this building by the post office. We would be breaking the law. No, find another way, Adam.' Pastor was quite adamant about it.

'No, Pastor, not this one. The one downstairs in the training room. I noticed it down there when using the gym. It's the old type that you can roll back the dates manually and it can't be traced and we can fake a post office stamp mark easily.'

Pastor Miles looked worried but he had to admit the plan just might work.

Chapter Eleven
Deygar's Upper Hand

2 Chronicles 20 v15 'Do not be afraid or discouraged because of this vast army. For the battle is not yours, but God's.'

Back in Derek Greyer's office, the man himself was sat in front of the bank of TVs (watching numerous TV news channels in a hope of finding misery somewhere to reap more money from) when he was interrupted by a stressed Mr Wong.

Derek Greyer didn't even turn around to address him. 'You're late.'

'Sorry, sir.'

'So is it all complete this time? No more fowl ups?'

A nervous Mr Wong said, 'Yes Sir.'

'So where is it then?'

Mr Wong handed Mr Greyer what looked like a mobile phone but it was the long awaited tracking device he had been waiting for, for over 18 hours, and it had been held up, something Mr Greyer never experiences.

The device was state of the art, with voice activation and it only operated when Derek's voice spoke into its microphone.

'Power!' And the screen lit up and the device started to beep. 'I take it, Wong, that beep is the mark.'

'Yes, that's the person with whom you asked to track for business purposes.'

'Yes,' was all Derek could mutter. His excited grin was as evil as ever and growing more sinister by the second. 'What's the range of this thing?'

'Well, sir. On its own it's around a 30-40 mile radius, but alongside your laptop computer or a GPS equipped sat nav, like in your many cars, it will be able to track globally. It is state of the art, sir.'

'Good. Now, so what's the latest on Barnstech? Does the company now belong to the lawyers?' He didn't give Wong time to answer. 'The contracts now are void. Only the company name is property of the lawyers. I have 38.5 billion already invested in this. It's all mine, now pay the greedy sharks off and let's get on with this. That's your job if you want it or put someone else trustworthy in place and let's start making money already. Go!'

With Mr Wong gone, Derek started to work on his computer but first he buzzed his secretary. 'No more calls today. I'm in conference, thanks.' Then he pressed the remote to close the blinds in his vast office and walked over to a large wall safe. He pulled out a large oversized phone and brought it over to his computer, plugged it in, then started to tap keys on the keyboard. He then placed a headset on so he could talk through his computer and then via the oversized phone, which looked very much like an army issue satellite phone.

'Okay. I have done what you have stipulated before contacting you. When can we meet?'

It was unusual for Derek to have to answer to anyone. His voice had a worried tone like he was the pupil and he was talking to the head teacher.

The voice said 'We can't just yet. Like I said before, contact me next week. No other form of communication, only on the satellite phone and computer like always. Until then, goodbye.'

'Before you go, Number 2, why no names? Why all the code and secrecy?'

It seemed very brave to ask such a question. Derek's voice came over all nervous and anxious.

'Don't question my actions again, G.D. We have to. That's all. Goodbye.'

It was highly unusual to see the mighty 'Deygar' treated and spoken to like this, but it didn't seem to bother him. He quickly placed the phone back in the wall safe. The blinds were re-opened; he picked up his coat and left his office. As he walked past his secretary, he then said, in his normal tone, 'I'll be out for the rest of the day. See you tomorrow.'

As Adam rode the shiny elevator up to Mr Greyer's office he was a little nervous. There wasn't a direct lift to the top so he had to get off at the forty-third floor and walk to another bank of elevators to ride the rest of the way. Only Derek Greyer himself had an elevator that took him from the basement level personal car park area to his office.

Adam was getting a little hot around the collar. The warn bike leathers and smell of patchouli and oil was overbearing and he had to keep the helmet on because the building was filled with CCTV. He didn't want to blow his cover.

He finally got there, through the glass doors and towards the secretary sitting at her desk, busy taking calls and writing letters. Her eyes immediately meet Adam's. His visor was up to stop it misting up. Adam put on a deep voice to mask his own.

'Hello. I have a parcel for a Derek Greyer's office. It requires a signature please.'

'Ok. Did you sign in, in the building downstairs, in the lobby with security?'

'Yes, I showed them my I.D. and signed in. Why?'

'We have a strict policy here: no despatch riders in the building with their helmets on.'

Adam was done for. There was no way he could take off his helmet and risk running into Derek Greyer. He had to think fast.

'I'm sorry, they just let me through. I couldn't carry a helmet and the parcel as well could I. Well, it's my first time in this building. I have only been working for this company for a few weeks. I'm still getting to grips with all the rules and stuff. I can only say that next time I'll know better.'

The nervous Adam awaited the stern-looking secretary's answer.

'Well, I should report you. Seeing that it is your first time I'll overlook it this time but next time, don't forget and there are lockers provided for helmets. Mr Greyer's out of the office so I won't say anything if you don't.'

'Don't worry. I won't say anything.' Adam was feeling a little easier thanks to her kindness in letting him off about the helmet. Downstairs, the fake I.D. and the sob story about not being able to take off his helmet due to a resent operation to the back of his head (which would mean disturbing his staples from a recent bike accident), apparently, an often used reason for dispatch riders for not removing helmets, had all worked a treat.

Once all signed for, Adam was on his way, but then the secretary called him back.

'Excuse me, rider,' she said looking down at the scribble that Adam had called a signature, trying to make out a name, but it was impossible to make out (Adam showing off his recent Latin/Greek translation skills of unpronounceable words).

Adam stopped in his tracks. 'Oh what is it now?' he thought.

He approached the desk. 'Yes?'

'The post mark on this is nearly four weeks ago.'

'I'm sorry I don't post them, just deliver them. It must have been held up at the post office. Have you ordered anything for your office that could be electrical? 'Cause sometimes they x-ray for bombs and stuff. That could have held it up. We see all kinds of stuff going on with parcels nowadays, miss.'

'Hey, I thought you'd only been doing this job for a few weeks.'

'Well, got to go now; deliver more stuff; pay the bills, ya know.'

Adam quickly got back in the elevator and finally let out a sigh of relief. 'That was close,' he thought.

He quickly made it down to the forty-third floor to change elevators and get out of that building as fast as he could, but remembering not to bring attention to himself by rushing too much.

Once outside, Adam managed to get well away from the building's CCTV cameras and got to his bike, but before he could ride off he needed a breather. He took his helmet off to take in a full breath of fresh air – well, as fresh as you could in the city.

As he took a quick drink of water his mobile phone rang.

'Adam, come back quickly. I have Dave here and he's in a right state.' Milo sounded worried. Adam feared the worst but quickly composed himself and rode as fast as he could back to church.

Once back in Pastor Miles' office Dave was in a bad way and Adam had seen it all before.

Adam pulled off his helmet and gloves and this further alerted Dave; he was having some kind of panic attack.

'Dave, Dave, it's me. It's Adam. Calm down. You are safe. Don't worry, just try to calm yourself. Breathe! Breathe!' Adam tried his best to calm Dave but it just seemed to make him worse.

Pastor Miles stood up. 'In the name of Jesus, calm this man, Lord.'

Dave immediately calmed and just sat down as calm as calm could be. It even impressed Adam.

'Dave, what is it, mate? What's troubling you?'

'They know. They know that I'm working with you. They know – those two guys know – they just know. They keep ringing that phone they gave me and then hanging up just as I'm going to answer it. They know. They know. I'm a dead man.'

'Give me the phone, Dave.' Adam quickly checked the received calls list on his phone; there were no calls listed. Adam was worried. 'I was worried about this. They are playing games with your mind, Dave. Dave, look at me.' Adam was very intense looking into Dave's eyes. 'Tell me the truth. This is important. Have you ever done drugs? Dave, tell me the truth.'

'What's that got to do with it?'

'Just tell me, have you?'

'Maybe, maybe I have. So what?'

'How have you been sleeping, Dave?'

No response from Dave.

'Have you been eating enough, Dave?'

'So, I've been a bit stressed lately and forgot to eat as much, and a few late nights don't hurt anyone from time to time.'

'Dave, I believe that all this is in your head. It sounds like you are suffering from anxiety and are severely stressed out. You need to sleep, Dave, and to eat right. Get your head in gear, mate. You'll be ok. We are still praying for you. Maybe you should start praying yourself from time to time, mate. It really does help a stressed heart.'

Dave's whole being was lifted. It seemed he was released from a pressure that was far beyond just physical or mental, but spiritual.

The next few days were pretty normal as far as Pastor Miles and Adam were concerned, but for Dave it was close to miraculous; he prayed like he said he would and he had totally given himself to God, which gave Adam and Pastor Miles a real faith boost.

And, in the meantime, Derek Greyer had been to his country manor to continue his much overdue training with Seth in mind. The mystery surrounding him intrigued him the more he thought of him and – most of all – his advancement in sword skills and martial arts. How did he come into contact with Milo and what was their plan? Deygar didn't have time worry too much; his plan was getting into gear now and he didn't need distractions. He would have to but Milo and Seth to the back of his mind for the time being.

As Derek Greyer stepped from his treadmill, unusually, the phone rang. Everyone knew not to call Mr Greyer at home especially when he had implicitly requested 'No calls'.

He quickly picked up the phone, preparing to yell at whoever had the audacity to call him, but didn't get the chance.

'I'm so sorry, sir, before you yell, but I thought I'd better call you. It is urgent. I have received a parcel from BarnsTech and it's nearly a month late, looking at its post mark. It came yesterday but I was too nervous to call, so I opened it this morning and found gift items and a sealed letter from Mr Barns himself. I am so sorry again, sir.'

Derek just stood there in silence. 'No, you were right to call. I'll be right in. Thanks.'

Within twenty minutes Derek was there. He quickly took the parcel into his office. He saw many boxes but decided to open the attached letter first, and it read:

Dear Mr Greyer

Thanks for all the interest in our two great business empires merging. We do realise that it had gotten out of hand and we, as a company and more personally, would like to give you these one-off, specially commissioned pieces to grace your office, just to prove that there are no ill feelings between us as business men. I hope in the distant future we could form a business partnership, that would be mutual and beneficial to all parties involved, but at this time I would like to thank you for your offer.

Many Thanks

B Barns, BarnsTech Ceo

P.S... I do hope that we can successfully do business together in the future.

With that read, Derek let out a roar of laughter. 'Yes! Yes! Yes! I know exactly where those are going.'

He quickly grabbed the Microchip paperweight and placed it on his desk. As for the fountain pen, he slipped that in his inside jacket pocket and grinned. As for the pen stand, that was also placed on top of his desk. The paper knife was placed in the top drawer.

He sat there grinning for the rest of the day, totally unaware that the letter and all the items were all faked for the benefit of the Master Disciples' mission.

At 7.17am the phone rang at Adam's house.

'Hello.' Adam held out the cordless phone to try and make out who was calling from the caller I.D. It was Scott.

'Yes.' Adam said with a tired tone.

'It's there and it's working. One question: Why Derek Greyer?'

Adam awoke fully and sat bolt upright in bed, Rachel was still sound asleep. 'Never mind. I'll tell you later. It's working? How do I listen in?'

'Use the LPS, but you have to type in a code – 0748. It's the same code for the computer base station.'

'Cool! Thanks for all your help. I'll see you soon.'

Adam hung up the phone and immediately called Milo.

'It's a huge result for us. We will know his next move. We can sort of relax a little with this in place.'

Milo was coming round to the idea, finally. Adam thought 'Praise God'.

That was exactly what they all did on Sunday at church. Everyone was there, even Dave, and it was electric. The power of God was amazing and filled everyone with a new found faith. It even brought Paul out of the hospital to share in some much needed fellowship.

But as with everyday as a Master Disciple, it had its challenges, and the following Monday morning's training session was no exception.

Whilst Adam was training alongside Pastor Miles they had the computer on listening to Deygar's office through their newly-placed bug, neatly placed on Derek Greyer's desk.

He was on the phone. Adam and Milo could barely make out the secondary person but could hear Derek so clear it was like he was in the same room.

'Okay, G.D. I will arrange to meet you. You have proved yourself. But one condition – no weapons. We are from one, after all. Don't forget.'

'Okay, Number 2, but where shall we do this?'

'Take the satellite phone with you and call me on the corner of the industrial estate, Oak Lane West, corner of the city, in one hour.'

'So you're in the country already?'

'One hour!'

Adam and Milo just stared at one another.

'What was that all about, Adam?' Pastor Miles was shocked to hear Derek being spoken to like that.

'He was talking on a satellite phone.'

'So what?' Pastor Miles was being so naïve.

'Well, he could have being talking to Deygar from anywhere. That's why he was surprised when he said he was in this country and arranging to meet him in one hour.'

'So what do we do now, now that we know that piece of useful information?'

Adam answered 'Nothing. Let's just hope he takes something with him so we can hear that meeting.'

The pair carried on with their normal training and eagerly waited for Derek to meet the mysterious voice, hoping he would be considerate and take the fountain pen or something so they could listen in.

Exactly fifty-nine minutes later Derek made the call.

'Good, I hate bad time keepers. Punctuality is one of my many rules. I take it that's your Black Bentley Continental. Well, listen; drive that thing round to unit 4 and drive inside.'

'Okay,' said Derek, but it was too late, he had already hung up.

Adam and Milo were still listening. Thankfully, Derek had the fountain pen inside his jacket pocket; they could just barely make out Derek's voice.

As Derek pulled up to unit 4 the giant steel shutters went up and he proceeded inside, the building tightly gripping the wheel of the Bentley as he drove. Once the car was clear of the shutters they went back down. The shutters hit the floor with a huge bang that startled Derek. For the first time Derek Greyer was a little scared and he had every right to be.

He saw the shadowy character walking towards the car and reached for the handle.

'Hello, Mr Greyer. We finally meet.'

'Hello, Mr Williams. The honour is all mine. Thank you for finally agreeing to meet with me.'

'It's been a long time coming for me, Mr Greyer. I knew your Grandfather; he tried to contact me also, but I declined his offer.'

Adam and Milo were awestruck. He knew Deygar's Grandfather?

'Hey, he seems like a team player, Milo, and he's playing on Team Judas.'

Milo was troubled by this new outcome and was thankful Adam had gone to the trouble of planting those bugs.

'We could be in serious trouble with this guy. I've got a very bad feeling. I'm discerning a frightfully evil character here, Adam.'

'So, what's your Lord Name, Derek?'

'Deygar!'

'Very good, very scary indeed.'

'Mine is Hullem or Slayem. I have many an alias. Which one did you find me under?' Slayem had a smug grin and confidence that even unnerved Derek.

'Hugh Williams.'

'Ah, Hugh; good old Hugh.'

'I crossed-referenced some accidents that had been recorded over the past few hundred years and your name came up a few times. Your name came up as the only survivor when a boat sank whilst crossing the Menai Straight in 1664 and then again another boat sank in the same spot in 1785 and yet again the sole survivor was a Hugh Williams – an amazing coincidence. There was another disaster when, in 1820, twenty-four passengers drowned and only one survivor was recorded – a Hugh Williams. Fancy that!'

Adam and Milo nearly choked on their coffee.

'So this guy is over 400 years old and counting.' Adam was in serious shock at this, his first encounter of a true immortal.

'Ssshh!' Milo was getting impatient and was trying to listen in on the mysterious voice of Hugh Williams.

'So, after all this time looking for me, you have managed an audience with me. What's on your mind?'

'I belief we are the last two immortals left; the last of a once mighty force that ruled the dark world.'

Hugh was just listening intently at the words coming from Derek's mouth, nodding every now and again to give the impression of encouragement and to prove that he was indeed hearing the words spoken.

Once Derek had paused just enough for Hugh to speak, he gave a hand gesture to just say 'Wait a moment.' The pair paused for thought and then Slayem spoke – not Hugh – he was like a spilt personality. A real Jekyll and Hyde character, which unnerved Derek further.

'So what if we are the last two, Deygar? I could strike you down now then there'd be only one.'

He gave a look so evil that it stopped words from forming in the mind of Derek Greyer and rendered him speechless.

Slayem continued. 'You're giving me the impression that you want to join up as a team. Well, let's just say; I'm no team player. You see the only disadvantage to being an immortal is that anyone you team up with may die or becomes an adversary and in my line of work it's dangerous.'

'We could be a force to be reckoned with.' Derek's head was getting back into gear, but he was soon shouted down with Slayem's next statement.

'A force to be reckoned with, eh? I have studied over twenty-six martial arts; I'm deadly with a sword. I've spent over two hundred years in the Far East. And you want me to join with you?'

Adam almost passed out with the shock of hearing that Slayem was potentially a Grand Master in all of the major martial arts.

'There's no way I can bring this guy down, Milo. You've got the wrong guy. I'm the wrong guy.'

Milo had to intervene; he grabbed his hands and told him to calm down, fearing Adam was having a minor panic attack. 'Seth! Seth! You are thinking in the natural, not in the supernatural. Your faith will be the definitive factor here. God will assist you in your quest. I have tried to train out of you that kind of thinking that makes you rely on your natural abilities. God will help us both. Trust in your Lord and keep His word close.'

'How old are you, Deygar?' His tone was demeaning.

'I'm thirty-nine; forty in a month's time – natural years of course – but I am an immortal.'

'Deygar, you are young. You're naïve. You see me; I look as young as you but when your eyes have seen only a quarter of what I've seen then you can call yourself an immortal. So why work as two when I have achieved what I've done for nearly a Millennium. I think that you just want me for my vast – and it is vast – experience.'

Derek was failing and was running out of arguments for Slayem to stay and join up.

'No, that's not my motive. We both could benefit from teaming up: your experience and my knowledge.'

'What knowledge? You know nothing. What could you possibly teach me?'

'Listen to me, Hugh; I have created a multi billion pound empire in relatively a short lived life. What have you created?' Derek was getting a little confident with his barrage and was now attacking his achievements, or lack thereof, in his eyes.

Slayem held up his hands. 'So I don't boast a billion pound empire, but I manage quite well, thank you. You see, I'm not a greedy man. I may not have the billions but I will never spend what I have acquired throughout my life. If wealth is your quest, you will lose in the end. You see, with all that wealth brings unwanted attention. Shall I just give you this one piece of advice then I'll be on my way. If you want to be around for as long I, try to keep a low profile.

'How much is enough? Ten million? Twenty million? Where does it end? This will eat you up faster than being mortal.'

Derek Greyer was looking a little dishevelled and his confidence was going south.

Slayem held out one finger. 'Remember this one thing and you'll do well, you may even survive for a little longer: The key to long life is to downsize. Downsize your living; downsize your public profile; downsize your friends; basically live just for yourself and involve no one.'

Derek, at this point, was looking down at his shoes – £480 pounds worth of Italian leather loafers. He was slowly moving into depression.

'I don't understand. You want me to live a lonely, singular life with no meaning? No goals? No drive?'

'No, I didn't say that; have passion, but a passion to be the greatest warrior ever; to possess a life that will last forever; to have your immortal life here and now; to have your thirty pieces of silver and not feel guilty about it; defy your peers.

'Look at your car, for example. What did it cost? A hundred grand or so? I could live on that for a whole year in Thailand learning more skills, learning to be a better warrior.'

Slayem's thirst for knowledge excited Derek and he soon realised what he had been missing out on, chasing all the trappings of business like his father did, and it was his undoing. He thought to himself 'If only my father was better prepared for his battle, he would have defeated Milo.'

What then followed shocked Deygar to his core.

'Who is this Milo you think on? Your heart is troubled by this, isn't it?'

Derek Greyer was completely in shock and was also scared at the level of intelligence Slayem possessed. He had the ability to read minds or at least see what was troubling someone's thoughts.

Slayem let it go for a moment whilst Derek composed himself.

'You have to slay this man, Deygar. You do realise that, don't you? I can't do it for you.'

Derek looked to the floor in disgust; ashamed at the levels he had aspired to, as a so called Dark Lord of the Judas cult, in his short life.

'This seems to be a waste of my time. I can't stand around here giving the wealth of all my years of experience to a man who can barely call himself a Dark Lord. I look at you and see a weak man; a man who wouldn't have lasted ten minutes in just one of the many battles I fought during the crusades. You are an embarrassment. You should get yourself together and maybe give me another call in – let's say – five hundred years time; if you survive. See it as a test, eh. What do you say to that, the great and powerful Deygar?'

Derek was at an all time low but felt he at least needed to try and convince Slayem to stay for a little while longer.

'No! Slayem, wait. You're right. I could gain from some of your wisdom. In a way, I think I already have just from this meeting. I have learned so much and could gain more.

'I know that you really wouldn't gain anything from teaming up with me. My father knew when enough was enough. If he'd only been around long enough, maybe I would have gained from his years of knowledge but, as you know, he is no longer here to guide me, nurture me, but you are. Don't you have just one nerve in your body that would just say yes? Don't you want to help someone; someone who needs help rather than just helping yourself just once? Just once pass on knowledge instead of learning more? Teach me. What's a few months to man that's been around as long as you, eh? What do you say?'

'Did your father teach you anything other than gaining more wealth?'

'He taught me this: our mission is 'Keep immortals immortal'.

'That's right, Deygar. He's right. You've got lazy, greedy and most importantly there is a Master Disciple walking and breathing, full of blood, whose sole purpose is to protect his church and their precious believers, who could keep us going for a thousand years.'

Deygar was in shock. Were his ears deceiving him? Did he hear an 'us' in that last statement?

'Does that mean you will help me; help me avenge my father's killer and feed on their blood?'

Slayem this time heard a word that shocked him.

'What do you mean, 'their blood'?'

'There's two Master Disciples. There's the MD who killed my father, a disciple who goes by the name Milo, and his apprentice, Seth.'

The enraged Slayem couldn't believe his ears. 'So there's two Master Disciples and the one who killed your father he is still breathing? Why isn't this man running off a slow drip to feed your immortal thirst? Instead he's had the opportunity to pass on knowledge to another. His son will die for this outrage.'

'No, No, you don't understand; his son, the person whom he should pass on the knowledge, is already dying; he has cancer, so he has taken on a neutral – a nobody; an outsider from the flock.'

Derek was nervous to tell the full extent of it, but felt it would be better to be open about such important details, like a break in the code; a long established code dating back many centuries.

'The secret's been told to a neutral? This is an outrage. It seems that you need me a lot more than I need you right now, but I will help you in your vengeance.'

Deygar was crushed only moments ago but now felt encouraged by Slayem's harsh words. No one would ever speak to him like that, only his father, but instead of feeling worse, he felt inspired to recommit to the mission his father had spoken of many years before – 'Keep immortals immortal'.

The two Dark Warriors shook hands and agreed that Deygar make the kill of Milo and Slayem would kill his apprentice, Seth.

The pair of Master Disciples listening back at the church felt ill with the knowledge that had been provided.

'Well that's been his plan for the past eighteen months – contacting Slayem. I thought I was retiring. I'll need a sword then.'

Milo was at an all time low with the thought of starting again. He was, after all, a seventy-seven year old man; a prime of life that had well passed him; he was too old for such a quest and feared the worst. His faith was already failing him and Adam could tell.

Adam was trying to remember what Milo had just said to him about the natural and supernatural but he was finding it hard to put into practice after hearing that he'd be up against probably the toughest man in the entire world, who can apparently read your very thoughts.

The knowledge didn't have the desired affect; knowing such plans was damaging in Milo's eyes and had turned their hope into madness.

The pair had, had a week for the news of Slayem coming too assist in the killing of the two of them to settle in. Milo was quite optimistic and his faith was improving by the day. He was joining Adam in the training room, just relearning his defence sword techniques to start with, and then out of the blue he received a phone call from a distressed Rachel.

'Pastor Miles, I really worried about Adam. The past few nights he's really gone security mad, locking doors, rechecking them, and last night I found him walking round the house in the early hours. He really scared me, Pastor. What shall I do?'

'I know it's hard, but try not to worry, Rachel. I will talk to him and try to calm him a little. God has really been speaking to him the past few days. He is really being used by God and his body needs rest.'

'But I can't cope with him becoming ill with stress. I just can't take it, Pastor.'

'Rachel, you calm yourself down. We don't need another person worried sick. Let me pray for you, right now.

'Lord, take this anxiety and worry that's deep within Rachel right now and refill her with a strong and courageous faith, faith that could move mountains and reassure her of her calling to be a disciple. And bless her in her other roles as a mother to beautiful Grace and a powerful prayer warrior to her husband. Grant a peace throughout her household; let your spirit dwell there, Lord, in greater measure than ever. In your name, Lord. Amen.'

'Thanks, Pastor.' Rachel was grateful for the prayer and was most encouraged by it.

'And, Rachel, before you sleep tonight read Psalm 91 together.'

'Thank you again, Pastor.'

Rachel was on her way. The Pastor had always got a great way of helping, encouraging and nurturing all at the same time through a prayer.

The day went as normal. Milo didn't feel right to mention the chat he had just had with Rachel and they proceeded with their training. The computer was switched on the whole time but unusually there was no Deygar and Slayem chat. He was out of the office and he must have put the pen down some where else because all they could hear was the cleaner coming in to tidy his vast office at around 12:30.

The very next day, Milo felt he should talk to Adam about the lack of sleep he was getting. He could clearly see Adam looked terrible; the bags under his blood shot eyes were so obvious.

'Adam, come sit, sit down here. What is troubling you? Rachel called me yesterday beside herself with worry.'

'I know, and thanks for the prayer and the scripture; it really helped her get off to sleep.'

'It was supposed to help you both get some sleep, not just Rachel.'

'I just want to reassure you I'm not going mad. When I do finally get to sleep I keep having the same reoccurring dream, and the dream is about someone breaking in the house and taking Grace. I'm getting so bad with this dream that I've started to make gadgets to alert me.' Adam then turned up his trouser leg to reveal a strange looking strap around his ankle.

'What's that?' Now Milo was seriously worried about Adam's well being.

'Well it was part of one of those electronic muscle stimulating packs, you know, the kind that promise a six pack in two weeks; so I took one and strapped it to my ankle and then wired it to a sensor that works in conjunction with our alarm system. So when someone comes towards the house and sets off the security lights, via the proximity sensor, this thing sends a signal to my attractive ankle bracelet, giving me a little electronic shock to me Achilles tendon. It wakes me up so I'm ready to defend my family.'

Milo slumped back into his chair. He was worried and he had every right be. Adam was on the verge of a breakdown. His whole behaviour was unlike his usual self. He was jittery, chatty and was moving around a lot; he just couldn't keep still for a moment and kept checking his phone or his watch or the LPS system, and then it dawned on Milo that he was taking on too much too soon. All the gadgets he had on his very person were enough to take anyone over the edge. He was trying to be all to all people and Milo needed him back on his feet, well and his mind re-focused on the mission at hand.

Milo had to lay it out thick for Adam; he was tittering on the edge. 'Adam, you've got to start practicing faith and not all this madness.'

Adam was quick to point out the obvious. 'But the word says faith and actions.'

'Yes, but actions that won't harm you; actions that don't involve you sitting up half the night whilst wearing ankle bracelets that give shocks when a cat enters your garden. Can you see the madness of it all? Lack of sleep is bad. We need to be more alert than ever. You will see what your mind wants you to see without sleep and then the worse can happen; paranoia can set in and you lose control.'

Adam was curious about Milo's knowledge on the subject of mental health issues and it seemed all too familiar. 'It seems you've had some experience in this area.'

'Yes. I went through a very similar time when Paul was a baby and it drove me mad; a total wreck I was – so out there. I was scared of the scriptures, the radio was speaking to me, and I even thought Margaret was in on the attack, and that's what I thought it was; I was convinced it was an attack. I was so sure I was going to die without passing on the knowledge to my son – the next in line Master Disciple. As you could tell the pressure was truly on, and it was all created in my own mind. Please, Adam, see the warning signs and keep on top of it, please. I need you at your best.'

Milo's tone was of sincerity and he was truly meaning every word of it. He didn't want to see Adam in that kind of state. He'd been there and received the scars, the mental ones that can be easily be reopened.

Milo's words were words of help and you could clearly see Adam's mind relaxing and his whole body calming down, like someone had just put the air conditioning on in a hot car.

Milo suggested he take the next couple of days off, take Rachel and Grace out and come back on Thursday, fresh with new found focus, and for him not to worry, but the last part was difficult for Adam. From Adam's point of view he was the one chosen. He was an outsider to a family secret and, what worried him most; he was the only one who could possibly stop Slayem and Deygar. After all, his partner was a seventy-seven year old man. Milo was a wealth of hope and faith and knowledge of God that Adam truly believed could move mountains, but physically he could barely move himself around, especially when compared to Slayem.

The very next day Adam had decided to take the Beamer out and take Rachel and Grace on a picnic in the country and get away from it all.

Adam placed the picnic basket in the boot of the car and quickly glanced over to the far corner of the boot to see the LPS handheld, along with his sword and extendable baton. The only thing missing from his arsenal was the beanie gun. He was being especially cautious when Grace was in the vicinity and didn't want to upset Rachel on their only day off together in ages.

As Adam drove, Rachel was just grateful to be with her husband and was chatting away like a monkey in a tree, not giving her mouth time to rest and trying to take on board what Pastor Miles had said by encouraging Adam at any opportunity in his mission. Adam was loving their time together; it was just what they needed. Milo was very wise indeed, as Rachel had said earlier in their journey.

'It seems like our early married days back in BC,' (That was Rachel's way of saying 'Before Children') 'being out in the car and being a normal family.' Rachel was so grateful for the time together; the only thing giving the game away was the flashing light from the LPS system that Adam had placed in the centre consol of the car.

The afternoon was going great and once they'd stop for their picnic the family could truly relax and enjoy the reality of 'being one' with one another. The next amazing part of their day was about to unfold; Grace took her first unsupported steps. Being on a beautiful grassed area she felt so much more confident and a lot braver than usual, which gave the tired Adam and the weary Rachel a much deserved boost.

Chapter Twelve
'We Seek Help'

Psalm 121v1 'I lift up my eyes to the hills, where does my help come from?'

ADAM, TOGETHER WITH MILO, SPENT THE whole of the next two days training intensely; with Milo, at last, seeing sense and stepping up his own training, even though he was still trying to convince Adam he was officially retired.

As well as their physical training, the pair also continued to pray for God's protection and most of all His wisdom at this there most challenging time.

Adam had a burning question on his mind and thought he had already asked it in some kind of dream or something. 'So what!' he thought. 'If I have already asked this I've forgotten the answer.'

'Hey, Milo, are there any other Master Disciples around or anyone in the higher church who could help us?'

'Good question. There was once an MD. Council with over a hundred members. I was once asked to join a long time ago but unfortunately it, like everything else, died out with a lot of its members actually dying and some just got too old and retired from service.'

'You were asked, and you declined? How come?'

'Well, Adam, it was a long time ago. I still had my own church; Paul was very young and it was just bad timing, unfortunately, and so my plan was to train Paul to be my replacement and then within 15-20 years the Council was finished, no longer in service for God, but…' Milo rubbed his chin for a moment whilst the thought ran through his mind. 'It's a long shot, but I do remember a few still pray and intercede for active MDs. It's been a long time, before Paul was diagnosed, since I last contacted them.'

Adam was shocked to hear this and spoke out at his frustration. 'You knew this and didn't tell me? If I had never asked would I have never known, eh?'

Milo just gave Adam a quick cheeky wink and said 'Well, I'm old, don't forget.'

Milo got to work on contacting the MD Council. They communicated via the internet using coded email and creative ways of using scriptures to convey their requests.

Adam was glad; anything was good enough if they were going up against Slayem. The pair of them were more than convinced that he was pure evil and was more of a threat than Deygar. And Milo did say that they would need more spiritual help than physical.

'So where are you going?' Milo asked Adam as he grabbed his helmet and gloves.

'I'm going up to the rest home. I haven't been for a few days. I should really show my face once and a while.'

'The rest home?' Milo was intrigued by the sudden name change.

'Yes, well Rachel hated me calling it the old folks' home and Rachel calls it a home for rested mature people, so we settled on rest home.'

'So, I'll be off then. I've got the LPS if you need me, ok?'

So, Adam took the bike for a blast to save time and he needed to practise; you lose your confidence and your nerve the less you ride and Adam hadn't ridden for over a week, so a good blast is what he needed. He was really going for it, getting so low in the corners those knee sliders were getting red hot from running against the road.

Once at the rest home, there was a lot going on with many unfamiliar cars parked up and an ambulance with blue lights flashing and siren sounding coming towards Adam as he rode up the driveway to the main entrance.

Adam rushed in to find Julie, the home's administrator and manager, all upset and crying.

'What is it, Julie?'

'Oh, I'm so glad you came today.' And with that said she wrapped hers arms around Adam and just held him for a moment. This was unlike Julie – a firm and solid character who commanded authority. 'It's Mr Patterson; he's had a heart attack and we have had a break in overnight. Mr Patterson will be fine, I hope; it's his third.' With that, Julie broke down again. Just the thought of a resident dying made her cry again. It was the part of her job that she hated but unfortunately it happened from time to time. It came with that kind of work but it didn't stop Julie making people's last days there, their best ones; that was her motto.

Adam was guided to the office where they had the break in. He collated the damage and was convinced it was kids. 'Kids, I'll bet,' he said out loud.

'No actually,' said a deep voice, as it bounced around the air for what seemed like seconds within the halls of the old Victorian building.

Adam turned to see an out reached arm, and shook the hand.

'I'm DC Charmers. I gather you're the owner of this establishment.'

Adam was taken aback. 'No. My wife's the owner. I'm her husband, Adam. Adam Fuller.'

'Well, Mr Fuller, after your expert analysis of the situation, it wasn't kids. All that were taken at this time, as far as we can see, were confidential files.'

'Why would anyone steal files from a rest home?'

'That's exactly what I said, Mr Fuller. Missing files, one half-dead resident; that's a lot for one morning, don't you think, sir?'

'What are you saying officer?'

'Detective, please.'

And then it hit Adam: Why send a DC to a break in on a rest home? It all seemed very suspicious.

'If you are wondering why I was sent, it was because of the nature of the crime. They really meant business. Whoever it was got past your security system, cleanly broke the lock by spraying freeon, then tapping the lock cylinder, breaking it very cleanly and virtually silently. Very professional, don't you think, Mr Fuller?'

Adam was quickly racking his mind of all his old associates who could have pulled off a job like that and come to one conclusion – he was the only one he knew who could pull it off and he had a suspicion that DC Charmers was coming to that conclusion also.

'So what are you implying, Detective?'

'We've checked you out, Mr Fuller. You have quite a reputation; never charged with anything but still, just proves what a clever chap we have in our midst.'

'You can't say that. It's slander. I am an upstanding member of the community and have been for a number of years, I might add. So what if I was a bit of a 'jack the lad' as a youngster. It's now that I'll be judged, not my past. Ever heard the saying 'it's not where you've been but it's where you're at'?'

'Yes, yes. I've heard it all before, sir. Just look at it from a police point of view. With the evidence so far it looks like an inside job.'

'Detective, why would I rip off my wife's home?'

'I don't know why you would rip off your wife's home. That's why I'm here.'

'Come on, Charmers!' Adam was losing it and Julie had stopped crying to see a side to Adam she had never seen. It really surprised her to hear a chapter of Adam's life that was so private until now.

'DC – if you don't mind. I think I've earned it.'

'Since when has it been a crime to call the police when your property's been broken into, eh?'

Even DC Charmers was seeing that Adam was not handling it all well and tried to calm him down.

'Calm down, sir, please.'

'No, Charmers, no. You don't come round here and accuse me, who through marriage more or less owns the home that's been broken into.'

'This is the last time that I'll tell you, sir; don't call me Charmers. It's DC or sir, thank you.'

'May I suggests – 'DC' – you investigate this crime and don't keep bringing up my past. I, admittedly, may have been a bit of character in the past, and that's the key word here – Past, Detective – in that statement and this is in the present, so I assume you have my phone number, so you know where to contact me. I have to go and see Julie and tend to her, if that's all, Detective.'

DC Charmers was at last stuck for words and let Adam carry on tending to Julie, who was now fine and back to her normal self, after seeing Adam tear shreds off the DC.

'Julie, are you ok now? Well, if this guy starts hassling you, just give me a call. I'm off to do my own investigation.'

Adam started to walk towards the bike to head back to church, when he heard the LPS go off in his pocket. He quickly grabbed it. 'Yes. What is it?'

'Adam, just get back to church quick.' Milo sounded panicked.

'What is it? Tell me.'

'Just get back.' With that said, the LPS went dead.

Adam got on the bike, put on the helmet and gloves and started the bike with an almighty roar. As he pulled away the engine roar was so loud that the police standing around, including DC Charmers, turned to see and gave Adam a judging glance.

Within minutes Adam was back at church; the brake discs on the MV were glowing red. An unfamiliar car was parked up near the main entrance and Adam grew suspicious. He quickly pulled the extendable baton from down the sleeve of his leather jacket, just in case, and made his way up to Milo's office.

Once up the stairs, Adam opened the door to find Milo sitting at his desk with a stranger in front of him. His back turned with a serious glance on his face, as Adam passed to sit next to Milo.

Adam knew straight away it was 'Slayem'. He was sure of it, and he was right, but Slayem himself was totally unaware of their knowledge of him, so they had the upper hand – well, they hoped.

Milo's face was a picture of hope and faith, and Adam even noticed a little grin starting to appear now Adam had shown up so quickly. Slayem got up to introduce himself.

'So you are Seth?' He quickly sized Adam up, looking up and down at his frame, then said 'So where are your L plates, eh, apprentice?'

He knew who they were and this shocked the pair of Master Disciples.

Adam quickly grasped the baton tightly in his hand ready for a stand off, and with his other hand removed his bike helmet.

The thing that was running through Adam's mind was whether he had been there the whole time he'd been out at the Rest home. Was all that just a way of getting Adam out of the way, so Slayem could slay Milo in cold blood?

Adam quickly sized Slayem up, as he went in to shake hands, but as he got closer Slayem sat back down again, totally disregarding him. He quickly weighed him up; he was about six foot five and fifteen to twenty stone. It was difficult to work out the exact amount as he was wearing a long trench type coat, like the kind that Deygar would wear; designer type; expensive; perhaps hiding a sword or other kind of weapon. Adam soon realised that he only had the baton; his sword was on the bike and the beanie gun was sitting safely in the training room. The silence of the room was overwhelming, just starry glances and fixed expressions. Milo broke the silence.

'Ah, this gentleman has come to see you, Seth.' Milo just played along with Slayem's game. They had to act like they didn't know who he was and just carry on as normal, but Slayem's outbursts seemed so out of character.

'The thing is, sir, I don't know who you are, though,' Adam said, gritting his teeth through every word he spoke, still holding that baton so firmly, it was starting to make his hand ache with pain.

Slayem sat up in his chair. Adam was ready for anything; a sudden movement or strike against any of them and Adam was ready to block or strike with that extendable baton. It just took a micro-second to extend. A strike out to the forehead of Slayem would instantly knock him unconscious.

But he didn't do anything, he just said 'Oh sorry, Seth. I'm Mr Williams and I've come to see what I'm up against in the fight of your lives and the lives of this church, that's all.' His smug grin and charming attitude made Milo lose it.

'Get out now. This is holy ground. This is not happening. We all have our missions and we are abiding by our pledge to protect God's church and His people.'

Adam was amazed by Milo's faith and courage and stood up to Slayem. The pair were nose to nose; only the desk separated them.

Adam was amazed but fearful. There was only one weapon between them and Adam had it up his sleeve.

Then Slayem said 'Let's all calm down and sit.'

The three all sat down together. All eyes connected ready for anything.

'Now we are all seated comfortably, let's do a little experiment; if you are a Master Disciple stand up, and if you are a thousand-year-old-Master-Disciple-killer stay seated.'

Adam and Milo looked at each other with a panic, and no one moved momentarily.

Slayem edged forward in his chair. 'So there's no Master Disciples in this room, eh!'

Milo spoke out, but not as strong and confidently this time round, being a little tactful in his approach. 'Have you come to kill us?' The question commanded silence.

Adam's fixed expression on his face was that of a man who wasn't going to go down easily. He had a fight in him and Slayem could sense it too.

This excited Slayem to the depths of his evil core and he smiled towards the pair of them then said a statement that would chill Milo to his core.

'Oh no, I haven't come to kill you. I just want you to quit your mission or sacrifice yourselves. Or your last choice is to, maybe, just give me a couple of weak believers.'

Adam stood up ready with the baton to strike out at this evil thing in front of him. 'And what happens if we don't?'

Slayem then stood up to face Adam. 'Well, Seth, it would be better for you if you did what I say. You have a week to think it over. I won't come back here, but you will see me again.'

With that, Slayem got up and left the office. Adam was poised, ready to strike out if he tried anything, but the evil Slayem just left, to the astonishment of the pair of them.

'Milo, what just happened here? Was I dreaming? Was that just Slayem in your office threatening us? How did he get in here?'

'He said he was a friend of yours and he told me about Rachel and Grace and the old folks' home.'

Adam ran through all that had happened that morning: the break in, the missing files.

'It's all connected,' Adam shouted out and ran down towards the bike to race home.

Milo chased after him. 'What's all connected? What is it, Adam? Please stop! Tell me what's going on.'

Adam jumped on the MV and raced home. The journey was horrible. The idea that the whole little meeting was a way of getting to Adam's family; the attack on the home was away of getting him out of the way; the whole idea of it all was ripping him apart, and the idea of Rachel and Grace not being at home and just finding a note on the door or something was much worse. It was getting him so angry.

As he pulled onto the drive, Rachel's car was still there and all seemed well as Adam opened the door and ran into the lounge. His mission now was to find the two most important people in his world: Rachel, his beloved wife and his precious daughter, Grace. And the pair were there praying, Rachel kneeling holding Grace in her arms. Adam fell to the ground to join them in this holy embrace, relieved by their presence and well being.

Once finished Rachel could sense a problem and questioned Adam. 'What's wrong?'

'I just love you both so much.'

Adam was filled so much with the love of God and the love of any good husband and father. The shock of meeting Slayem had hit him hard, especially now he was holding the most precious people in his life.

'You're scaring me now. What is it?'

'Well, where do I start? The break in at the home–'

'Yes, I know about that. I've not long got off the phone with that DC Charmers, and what's his problem? I felt like a suspect. It was like we'd done it the way he was going on, on the phone.'

'I know, Rach. I popped down and saw Julie and I had my run in with DC Charmers, but I think I know who did it or who had it done on his behalf.'

Then Adam proceeded to tell Rachel of the meeting he had just had with Slayem and tried to calm her at the same time but unusually she did not need calming and she was a pillow of faith and courage. Rachel's faith had increased to beyond anything Adam had ever seen. She was amazing and acting like a real woman of God, and all she said was 'I will fear no man, and no man can escape the fear of my God. We'll stand firm in faith together.'

'Wow! Where did that come from?' Adam thought and was glad she was on his side.

Meanwhile, Deygar pulled up to the kerb in his Bentley next to the car he'd loaned Slayem for his little trip to the church.

'I've been circling for ages waiting.'

Slayem just got out of the car and got in the back of the Bentley with Deygar, abandoning the loaner car like it was trash. One of Deygar's associates got out of the Bentley and drove it back the office.

'So how long does it take to scare a man of God, eh?'

'Well it wasn't all a loss. I had that Milo in his office like you said, but Seth managed to get back before I could do anything. 'Men of God' – all they are now are very scared men of God, fearful of who I am and what I can do. I just want to thank you, Derek; I haven't had this much fun in years.'

Derek was glad he had found Slayem but was starting to think maybe he was now running the show. 'Was he the new boss?' he kept asking himself as the pair were driven back to the office.

As they entered the underground parking area of Greyer Towers, Slayem asked the driver to stop.

'Can I ask you for something, Deygar?'

'Yes,' said Derek, wondering what ever could this guy need.

'I need a car. It seems you have a few spare. I'll take that one there,' he said, pointing to a car in the third row.

'Which one? The Aston?'

'No.' replied Slayem.

Derek Greyer was a selfish man and didn't share anything, especially his cars; they were a no mans land in his world, as he walked sheepishly past the Aston Martin Vantage and onto the next car parked up – a Bristol Blenheim. And again there was a resounding 'No' from Slayem.

The next vehicle was a BMW M5 and that was the car Slayem had his evil eye on. Slayem headed off Deygar and hand slapped the bonnet of the car. 'This will do. This is all I'll need; quick and reliable and it fits in, not like the others, they stick out too much.'

'You've wasted a lot of money, by the way, Mr Greyer,' said Slayem, shaking his head as he walked on towards the lift.

Milo had to go and see Paul at the hospital. He'd been going like clockwork to see him, but he had an urgent call from the hospital. Milo feared the worst and called Adam to come for support, so Adam picked Milo up and the pair went together. Milo didn't say a single word the whole journey and Adam was fearful of the outcome. Was this the call they had all been waiting for, for the past year or so?

Once there, the pair walked down to the ward where Paul was. Those halls seemed longer than ever. Milo was weary and you could clearly see it on his face; a face that could break any minute; a face that normally held everything together for the greater church; a face that had told everyone to have faith, it was finally at breaking point. Adam couldn't do anything to help; he felt totally helpless.

As the pair made the final left turn toward the doors to the ward, Paul's doctor came rushing out, his face all a glow and his adrenalin was seriously up – way up.

'Come quickly.' The doctor pulling at Milo's elbow to rush him along. Adam was fearful; the curtain had been drawn around Paul's bed, trying to hide the fact that someone had died on a very busy ward in an attempt to calm other patients.

It didn't work, and Pastor Miles fell to the floor near to Paul's bed, not making the last few steps. His legs finally gave in. It was the last straw for Milo.

The Doctor yelled out 'No! Pastor Miles, your son is up and well.' He flung the curtain back to reveal a fit and well Paul eating a full English breakfast.

'What's going on?' asked Adam.

Milo was speechless, then the doctor proceeded to tell the pair that this is how they'd found him this morning, so they took him for a scan and the cancer had shrunk.

'Virtually gone! A miracle you'd say, eh Pastor.'

With that said, Pastor Miles fell to his knees again but this time it was with gratefulness not despair.

'A Miracle! A Miracle!' Adam was amazed. He had never seen such a thing close up. He had read about such amazing things but never had he seen it and he quickly grabbed his phone to tell the world, but was quickly asked not to in the building, so he quickly ran to get out in the open and make the call the whole church had been waiting, hoping and praying for, for so long.

As soon has Adam had hit the front door to get out, he speed dialled to call Rachel.

'Rachel, call the leadership at once. Great news! Great news – a miracle!'

Rachel was overwhelmed by Adam's excitement. 'What is it? What's the great news?'

'Paul is well. The cancer has gone. He's healed. He's in bed looking fantastic.'

Rachel was over the moon and was soon on the phone telling others of the great news – the news the church had been waiting for.

Adam rushed back in to see Paul. Milo was still praising and thanking God for this miracle.

'So, how do you feel?' Adam asked excitedly, so overwhelmed by the amazing miracle that God had done.

'I feel great, like a new man, and – before you ask – yes, I would like to go home now.'

Adam thought there was something else going on here. Paul wasn't just healed but transformed, perhaps a Prophet or Apostle.

Paul placed his hand on Adam's shoulder and then said 'God has poured his blessing upon you and will see it through to completion.'

Adam felt a surge of the power of God enter him and was taken aback. His feet shook and his legs buckled, having to take a couple of steps to steady himself.

Paul turned to gather his things and pack his bag ready for the off.

'Jane's picking me up. I called her before you came.'

'Oh, okay Paul.'

Adam still couldn't believe what was happening; Paul was acting so blasé about the whole experience, like it was an everyday event. Adam felt he should leave it; maybe it was Paul's way of dealing with it all. Death's door one day, completely healed the next – 'I don't know how I would deal with it,' he thought.

Milo turned to the both of them and embraced them like the shepherd would his flock, knowing this was a pinnacle event for all of them.

'This is a mighty miracle and it is for a special purpose; us three men of God will defend against the evil thriving in this city and crush it with the power of God's Anointing. The healing of my precious son was the first stage in God's plan; the next is His protection over our families, so our minds are focused on the mission at hand, so God's people can praise our Lord with new found faith and focus.'

Adam felt a little out of the loop with Paul's healing and now Milo getting amazing words from God, but he heard every word and wanted desperately to apply it to his life, especially the part about protection and his family.

That following Sunday, at church, was fantastic. The whole place was alive with the blessing and thanksgiving of Paul's amazing and miraculous healing. The church had their pastor back and he was on good form.

'My mid-life crisis was cancer and its curse was lifted by the power of God.'

The whole Church cheered and clapped and got to their feet just so show their appreciation to God.

It all came together; Jason's message was all about when we hit our personnel crisis and how God can bring about peace and having a faith with you through it can make all the difference.

And when Jason brought his message to a close, around ten people went forward for prayer and the closing song went on to be seven songs. People simply did not want to leave. The worship was amazing and Adam and Milo momentarily forgot all about Deygar and Slayem and really entered into a place of peace.

Chapter Thirteen
The Trinity is Formed

Mark 1v10. 'As Jesus was coming out of the water, he saw heaven being torn open and the Spirit descending on him like a dove'.
Matthew 8v13 'Go! It will be done just as you believed it would.' And his servant was healed at that very hour.

The following Monday morning was a normal affair for Adam. He got up, had breakfast and then went out to start the day at church.

But when Adam arrived he noticed Paul's car parked up on the church car park. Adam quickly got himself into the church and then into the training room where he found Paul and Milo.

'Shouldn't you be resting, Paul? It's a bit early for you to start training.'

'No, I've been doing that for months.'

Adam was truly worried by Paul's reaction. His frame had been weakened by all the treatment and there was no denying that. He could hardly lift the bar on its own on the bench press. Paul's frame had been robbed of his muscle and bulk and was now a shadow of his former fourteen stone stocky build, but he was unaware of it and he was not going to listen to Adam.

Paul felt out of it, and had for a long time, with Milo's frequent visits to the hospital or home to tell of the good news of the new boy – his replacement, an outsider – Adam, with his amazing gifts and clear talent, but Paul felt his cancer was a curse and clearly a reason to find a replacement Master Disciple. But now, with the cancer gone, he could concentrate on training again and getting back to being the one true Master Disciple and standing in his rightful place at his father's side.

'I have to train, Adam. There's a war ahead of us. I'm not like you. I have ground to make up.'

That was it, Adam now realising Paul's distress at being replaced.

Adam tried to reassure Paul and told him of the many times Milo had prayed for his son's healing and the frustration of not receiving it sooner. 'He had to find someone. Your church was in danger and he had to do what he felt was right at the time. He didn't know God's plan. Maybe it was God's plan after all, so we would help each other. Maybe God knew all along about Slayem and the power that three Master Disciple's would be against him.'

'Yes maybe; maybe that is the plan. Adam, would you help me train?'

'Paul, it would be an honour.'

The pair of them hugged and made plans for Paul's training and new health mission.

The two of them got straight to work and Adam took Paul to the health food shop for some supplements to get his weight back up to the standard to give him a fighting chance to defend against the likes of Deygar. Paul was an efficient swordsman and was trained in classic fencing. He had also dabbled in a little Kendo, before his cancer took hold.

On the shopping list were crash weight gain, whey protein shakes, muscle gain and Amino acid building blocks for muscle strength and other protein supplements. All designed for the speedy recovery of Paul's fitness and stamina.

The next thing was food, and a lot of it – fresh vegetables, fruit, as well as all those supplements.

Adam added 'God may have healed you, Paul, but I'm going to make you into a fighting machine that will defend his church like it was predestined.'

Two weeks into the hardest training that Paul had ever done, and it was clearly working; a stone of lean muscle to show for it, and Paul was feeling it.

Adam was more determined to get Paul fit and strong and took over Paul's training and dietary needs alongside his own training. Paul's plan was simple on paper, but hard in reality. It consisted of:

6am Breakfast:

A large bowl of porridge with half a pint of skimmed milk

Three bananas

Four rounds of wholemeal toast with peanut butter (reduced fat)

Then once that was done, Adam started on the supplements which consisted of:

Three heaped tablespoons of crash weight gain (vanilla flavour) in a pint of full fat milk, blended in the blender

Three 100mg Amino Acid tablets

One Zinc, vitamin C, D, E, tablets all washed down with a pint of water

One cup of black coffee with sweetener

With all that down, Paul had an hour's rest, then down to the training room to hit the weights for two hours, a slow session with big weights for the strength training to build muscle.

8:30am Snack:

A piece of fruit (apple or banana)

More water

More protein drink, muscle gain with skimmed milk

Rest for one hour

One energy drink ready for a two mile run

Then lunch, which consists of:

One whole chicken roasted (no skin)

Tin of tuna with Pasta

Two pieces of fruit

And then more supplements

Weight gain and muscle gain

Once lunch had an hour to settle down, it was straight into martial arts training to supplement Paul's sword work and give him more of an edge in combat. It would also burn excess calories from the supplements just leaving good old lean muscle tissue.

And then to finish the afternoon off, Adam would bring Paul up to speed on the computer system and LPS. Paul would then go home, rest, take the rest of his supplements and eat his evening meal.

That was a typical day for Paul for the past two weeks and it was nearly killing him, not the plan but the discipline, plus there was the muscle pain. It was, however, making him stronger and Jane had noticed a difference in even in that short time.

Jane was concerned about Paul (understandably, he was close to death after all).

'I know all this training is a good thing, but I can't still escape the fact he was nearly my late husband. Don't get me wrong, Adam, I think he looks great for all the training, but don't you think it's all a bit quick, to getting back to a fully active MD?'

Adam was trying to be sympathetic to Jane's concerns but it was Paul's eagerness to return to work.

'Hey, I tried to tell him, but you know Paul when he gets it in his head, you can't stop him. He's a determined and stubborn man. All I've done is guided him and equipped him for the job at hand.'

'I know, Adam, and I thank you for your guidance and being sympathetic to Paul's needs. I would be lying if I told you that Paul was okay about the arrangement with you and Pastor Miles, but since you have been training him he has begun to see it through God's eyes and he does see you as a gift from God. He prays for you every night – you and your family.'

'Well thank him for me. I do need prayer. I'm not the guy everyone makes me out to be.'

'Adam, I give God thanks for your abilities. You underestimate yourself. You have changed a lot in just a short time, just like with my Paul, and I do thank you again.'

With that said, she gave Adam a hug, kissed him on the cheek and said 'bless you, Gift from God.'

Jane felt better for talking to Adam and decided to get the other wives together to form a prayer network for all the leading men of the church, especially Pastor Miles. Pastor Paul and Adam had also had to build up their faith at this most difficult and testing time.

Whilst Adam and Paul had been training, Milo had been busy on the Slayem trail, listening to every word and tracking his every move through the bugs in Deygar's office. It was difficult; he was always up to something and he could only hear him when he was discussing his plans with Deygar.

One time, he heard them talking about a giant shipping container from Japan being shipped over. It belonged to 'Slayem' and it seemed to be very important to him. He was saying 'Please be careful and use your most trusted people. I don't need a mess up with this.'

The container was due to arrive in a week's time so the pressure was on for Deygar's team to deliver the goods and to be trustworthy.

He had also been seen driving around in Deygar's violet M5 BMW – quite a rare vehicle, easy to spot; the registration plate read M5DEY – not exactly conspicuous. Milo had an idea to bug it, but that was a job for Adam's brother, Tatter.

Milo had been busy; the MD Council had contacted him via an alarming e-mail:

Pastor Miles, thank you for contacting us. We greatly received your email. Praise God for Active members.

We, the former Council of Reference for MDs, have doubled our efforts with prayer and intercession for you both at this your most difficult and challenging time.

We are concerned for your safety: We have researched the person, whom you enquired about, and we cannot use their details over the internet. Email is widely intercepted and we cannot risk private information being made public. We will contact you via another means.

Thank you for your involvement in this issue. Our prayers and blessings be with you by the Grace of our Lord and God.

Milo was a little concerned by the news but had every faith that the Council would come through for him in time – and they did just that. Within a few days he received a letter, hand written and – more concerning – hand delivered, with instructions to destroy by fire once the information had been received and understood.

Milo opened it in his office, it read:

Dear Brother Milo,

We had no other way of getting the following information to you. Please forgive our concern in this matter but as you read this you will understand why.

Hugh Williams, 'Slayem' as you may know him, is pure evil.

He is second generation Judas Cult. His Father was apparently the founder and the very person who cut down the body of Judas and made the sacrifice and discovered the immortal powers of it. The other five original members were lost over time, and rumours say they were slayed by early Master Disciples, once their weakness was revealed by the Grace of God, and others fought each other.

At one time we believe (and our research is a little rough and flaky at times) that there were around one hundred members under the leadership of the father of Slayem.

But fear of the secret being found out more widely caused the founders only son, Slayem, to go on a mission to wipe out fringe members to keep the secret more closely guarded.

Even though Slayem's father is dead, he has still continued His father's mission. He is a danger to all, even other Judas members. We have been closely observing Derek Greyer for years and his father before him and we are still indebted for your involvement then, but at this time we fear his life. We fear he will just be used to get to yourselves and he will be killed to become the soul member.

We are praying for you Pastor and your new recruit and also for your church. May God richly bless your plans and give you the strength and the wisdom to complete your mission.

Amen.

Brother Anthony.

God may open their eyes to the evil that is Slayem.

The embodiment of pure evil, may they see his plans before he does. Give them spiritual insight to the deeds of this most evil being. May God bless and strengthen the families and leaders that are responsible for the running of the church, and Lord.

Give understanding to the Master Disciples that feel they can't ask for prayer because of the nature of its request, thus revealing this most precious of secrets. Amen.

Once read please destroy by fire. Do not make hard copies or photocopy.

The Lord will truly bless your mission.

Milo read the letter through a few times to try and take it all in. He then made a copy, knowing full well he shouldn't, for Adam and Paul to read with the instruction to destroy once read.

Milo had figured out some of the info about Slayem but this new insight into his past and more importantly his intensions were very concerning. Milo had also figured out the council's concern and knew that he wouldn't destroy Deygar when they were out of the picture.

Milo grew more concerned about their safety and then wondered why; why would he wait to kill us? Maybe Slayem was fearful of the prospect of a full-on battle with two Master Disciples; he feared our strength. Not knowing that we were actually three to contend with now.

Milo was encouraged by such a thought but also very fearful of it.

Milo thought he should have a quiet time with God:

Lord, hear my prayer. I'm truly scared, fearful. At most, I'm old and frail but have your wisdom deep rooted within me. Please give me the strength and health to succeed. Thank you for healing my son, Paul, and giving back my right hand man. I do appreciate Adam and his God given skills and it is now that I understand why Paul was ill; it was all part of your master plan. Give me more insight into your plan. Show me your hands and help me to fathom your ideas and thoughts. I'm grateful that you hold us all in the palm of your hand. Bless you, my Lord. Amen.

Once done, Milo just sat there in silence waiting on God to speak to him, whatever way he deemed worthy, but he was disturbed; Adam and Paul came back.

'I'm so glad you've came back. Read this,' he said and rammed the handwritten, hand delivered letter into Paul's hand.

Paul's face said it all. Once he had read it through Adam grabbed it.

'Cool! If that's true, why don't we just sit back and wait for them to destroy each other?'

'Adam, it won't work out like that way. How I see it, he'll wait until we're gone. He is using Deygar to get to us – fresh blood, nothing more to it. Then I believe he will destroy Deygar and move on. The council believe he could be the last of the 'Dark Lord' – no more Judas Cult; no more secrets; no more deceit. Maybe we could end all of this. This could be our time to complete the work the great apostle, Paul, started all those years ago.'

The fire in Milo's eyes was electrifying and was infectious. Paul agreed and Adam smiled and said 'But all this is theory isn't it. We need to prove it. All this secrecy about a container is really bugging me. He won't even talk to Deygar about it which now makes a lot of sense after reading that letter, which we have to destroy by the way.'

'You're right, Adam.' And Milo put the letter and the copy he made into the shredder then got the contents out to burn in his metal waste bin. 'Well, Adam, we only have a week and we will know what's in that container once and for all.'

Chapter Fourteen
The Waiting is Over

Titus 2v13 'While we wait for the blessed hope, the glorious appearing of our great God and Saviour Jesus Christ, who gave himself for us to redeem us from all wickedness and to purify for himself a people that are his very own, eager to do what is good.'

ANOTHER WEEK INTO PAUL'S TRAINING AND transformation into a fully-fledged Master Disciple was going well, but it was taking its toll on Adam. As well as his own training, he was training Paul at an athletes pace and he was feeling it. Rachel had asked if Adam could possibly have a day off, midweek, to take them all out on a family day. But Milo had him on his guard because they were awaiting the arrival of the mysterious shipping container due to arrive at any time.

Defied and frustrated, Adam took Rachel and Grace out for a spin in the Beamer anyway. They took Grace for a swim at the local leisure centre and then went on for a picnic in the countryside. Grace was walking quite confidently and was very aware of the stress her mum and dad were under. Grace was a very understanding little girl and always going up to her daddy to give him a hug and say 'Gob-Less' in her native baby tongue (meaning 'God Bless'). There was no fear of Grace ever forgetting that phrase; she'd heard a million times.

Adam was more than convinced that Grace understood what was going on and most of all she understood that God was real, even at fourteen months old.

Adam was grateful to God for having such a good mother for Grace in Rachel – a real woman of faith and a standard that was unshakable.

Meanwhile, at church Milo and Paul were listening in on Slayem and Deygar in the office, awaiting the arrival of the container that was intriguing them all.

A buzz was heard in Deygar's office.

'Yes?'

'Sir, the delivery has arrived at the main loading area, and requires a signature from yourself and a Mr Hugh Williams.'

Deygar grabbed his pen. It was perfect, as the pair listened back at church hoping it was the pen with the bug in, and it was.

The evil duo quickly boarded Deygar's express elevator straight down to the loading area to receive the container that had Deygar so intrigued these past few weeks.

Once down at the loading area, the place was a den of activity and noise; vehicles backing up, loud reversing beepers warning pedestrians and other users of the dangerous fork lift trucks travelling at speed.

Derek Greyer demanded a work force that was not just hard working but ever-efficient and was always striving for excellence.

A driver approached the pair as they paused and watched the ballet that was the loading area at its busiest time.

'Excuse me, but is there a 'Hugh Williams' around? I have an urgent delivery for him,' asked a large-set man, easily twenty-two stone of mass muscle, perhaps a former body builder in his early fifties. You could clearly see he could look after himself with many battle scars about his chiselled features.

'That will be me, Marv.'

'Sorry, sir. I could hardly recognised you in that suit. Since when have you considered yourself a business man who was serious enough about business to wear a penguin suit thingy?'

Derek was taken aback at the way this man addressed Slayem. There was no way that any of his employees would address him in that way. There was always respect and to know ones place in the running of things – especially 'business'.

'You know, Marv, you have to impress the new client. Don't you know how shallow people are, always judging you on what labels you wear or what cut designer suit one wears.'

'So, where do you want your container, boss?'

'Along that back wall, out of the way and near to that power supply.'

'Sure. You're the boss. Can you sign please and it will be off and powered up in no time.'

Within ten minutes the driver, Marv, had the container off and powered up, plugging it into the massive power outlet on the rear loading deck and then pulling down the huge power breaker. Suddenly, the container came alive; power fans and an air-conditioning system and the mightily huge steel door lit up like a Christmas tree, were all triggered. There was a digital display and Slayem typed in a code, covering the keypad with his free hand to not reveal the code to Derek.

But that was only half of it. It was a complex locking system that required the key holder – Slayem – to pull on two handles and turn them simultaneously. If any person not authorised tried to open it, it became the earthing point to a 50,000 volt electric shock.

Slayem turned to Derek at this point. 'It may not kill you, but it'll hurt like hell.'

It was at this point that Derek hadn't notice any signs saying 'Danger of Death' or 'Electric Shock' warning off potential thieves. Perhaps that was just Slayem's way. It seemed he loved death or any way of inflicting harm; he embraced it like a drug addict; you could sense the effect that being a Dark Lord had on him, so evil and so filled with the blood of lost souls; lost to an evil and thoughtless being; totally transformed by his own demons.

'I'm not all that bad you know, Derek.'

Derek let his mind wonder forgetting Slayem's amazingly evil gift of reading a person's thoughts.

'No. No not all. I was just away with myself. I was miles away.'

'I just find death the ultimate deterrent,' said Slayem, with his evil grin.

As the door opened and the pair were inside, all Derek could see were lots of steel cabinets, gun type steel cabinets, and then halfway through there was another door.

'What's through there?' Derek asked, his curiosity getting the better of him.

'You'll find out in due course. You're so impatient for someone who can live forever.'

'What are in these cabinets then?'

'Weapons. Lots and lots of beautiful weapons. Well, I am a collector after all. That's the only way I can ship this thing around. My official title is 'Historian and collector of armoury and weapons'. Well, I do have a PhD in the subject, which makes me Dr Hugh Williams, but I hate to brag.'

Then Slayem pulled out a sword, his favoured weapon of choice. The sword looked normal until he pulled it from its sheath; it was double-bladed, a lot like a two pronged fork.

'Why two blades?' asked Derek, wishing he hadn't asked, knowing that there would be a gruesome reason for a double-bladed sword. There was a reason and, like he'd expected, it was gruesome.

'You see, when you run a sword through someone and then twist – not much damage. But with a double-bladed sword, it tears their insides up so badly, there's less chance of surviving or counteracting in a fight. It also transforms into a Ronin Sword and – before you ask – a Ronin Sword is used a lot like a staff; you hold it in the middle and you can block and strike with ease. You see, the handle has a line through its centre and a release button.'

Slayem demonstrated the sword by pressing the button, making the handle separate into two halves then he twisted the handles round so the two blades were horizontal to one another. The handles clicked securely and the weapon was ready to use with deadly intension.

Derek's face lit up. 'That is amazing. Could I get one?'

'No, it takes years of training to use one of these things properly. In untrained hands you could cut your own legs or even your own throat, so maybe not for you, Derek.'

Derek's attention to that other door was getting the better of him and again he pressed Slayem for its contents.

'I can see you're anxious to see in here. Come; I think this will really impress you a lot.'

The pair went through another digitally locked steel door to reveal a room filled with more glass-fronted cabinets and much smaller drawers. Slayem signalled Derek over to a cabinet and grabbed hold of the handle to a drawer then pulled it open.

'What you are about to see will change everything you thought you knew about being a Judas cult member, for ever.'

The open drawer revealed a velvet-lined, padded inner with a velvet cloth over the centre, covering its contents.

Slayem quickly pulled the cloth off to reveal a single silver coin.

Derek felt weird and weakened by the sight of the coin for some reason, and not knowing its origin or significance scared him to his core.

'Is that what I think it is?' Derek's voice was a quivering mess of words and emotion.

'Yes! It is one of the very coins that purchased the life and execution of Jesus. Our leader and founding member, Judas, held this very coin; it was his contract and payment for a job well executed and carried through to the very end, and ultimately lead to his own death. It helped and assisted us to live forever.'

Derek was in awe of the coin, beckoning Slayem to allow him to hold it with his hands.

Slayem gave the coin to the nervous Deygar. 'A true Dark Lord once held that coin,' he thought to himself. And once received in his hand he felt a bolt of power so powerful it took him off is feet. He received such a feeling of evil that it disturbed him. He felt as if he had no control over himself. He felt he would gladly give up everything just to own that coin and to receive that feeling over and over again. The deadly sins had taken over him – to kill, to steal, to take, to over indulge, to covet and to serve his master, who now was Slayem: a pure evil being covered with flesh that happened to look like a man.

Deygar's mind a mess of jealously and rage. How and when did Slayem receive such an item?

Slayem was quick to answer his inquisitive mind.

'My father gave me that coin after my first kill. I was around fourteen or fifteen at the time and, I must say, it was the easiest kill ever. I just walked up to the man's home and slayed him. I felt bad at the time – well, after all, it was my first kill – but my father soon assured me it was part of being a Dark Lord and if I wanted the attributes of a Dark Lord I would have to kill and learn to take pleasure in it to survive a long, long life. He said it like this: 'Think of it as if we're the lion just picking off the weaker of the pack'. He was right; I would find it easier to kill and to find pleasure in it, hence all my weapons. This place also doubles as a blood bank and lab for me to feed on the long life-giving blood of the believer, so let's get to work on those MD's, Seth and Milo. One quick question, Deygar: do you own a battle suit of any kind?'

Derek shrugged at the ridiculous question. 'A battle suit? No, of course not. Why would anyone walk around in a silly suit? If I happen to be engaged in combat I'll be wearing what ever I'll be wearing; it could be a suit or a loose fitting pair of trousers and a long trench coat to cover up the sword. Why? What do you wear?'

'Well, I wear a mixture of a Kendo and Shiai uniform, plus a mix of my own modifications. My suit consists of 'Bogu', meaning Kendo equipment. The centre of the uniform is the 'Do' – the chest plate and main torso protector normally made from bamboo but mine is made from Kevlar, a lighter and stronger material. Then 'Hakama', meaning pleated pantaloons or skirt. Mine are modified to look less baggy, but I can still move freely. They are also Kevlar padded. Then the 'Kote', which are fencing gloves, and then on my feet are my 'Tabi'. Then the 'Tare', the waist protector. Then, what I think is the most important piece, is the 'Tsuki-Tare'. 'Tsuki' meaning throat and as you now know 'Tare' means protector. I'd say a vital piece of equipment for a Dark Lord, you see, a throat protector, but again modified Kevlar stronger and lighter. So who looks silly now?'

Deygar had a look of astonishment upon his face and now longed for a suit like Slayem's, especially his 'Tsuki-Tare'.

'So what are you going to wear, Deygar? It's hunting time.'

Chapter Fifteen
It's time for battle

2 Chronicles 20v15 'Do not be afraid or discouraged because of this vast army. For the battle is not yours, but God's'.

DEREK GREYER SLIPPED ON HIS LOOSE-FITTED Armani suit trousers and loose shirt and then threw on his favourite Armani trench coat to cover up the sword and other weapons. All the time he wondered if he was really ready for a showdown with Milo and Seth but he had singlehandedly sought and tracked down the mighty Slayem for back up, so no going back now.

Slayem did likewise and was eager to get started.

Milo and Paul, back at the church, were in a blind panic.

'Where's Adam?' Milo was worried. 'Check the LPS on the computer and then track him, Paul.'

'He's out of the city limits, Dad.'

'Just buzz him. Get him back now. There's two professional killers on their way.'

Adam answered the LPS. 'What's the problem, Paul?'

'Where are you, Adam?' Paul's voice was filled with fear. Adam could sense that there was a major problem.

'It's Slayem and Deygar, they are on their way to kill you and Dad – I mean Milo.'

'I'm on my way. I'm around ten minutes away, so hold them off till I get there. Lock yourselves in. And Paul; I hope you're ready because there's no going back.'

'God didn't heal me for nothing. I'm ready.'

Adam had his sword with him at all times and a few other items in the boot of the Beamer to protect himself.

'Rachel, we have to go. It's time. Once we're there, get out of harm's way and don't come back for anything until I contact you, okay?'

'What if…?' It was the first time Rachel had been truly scared for her husband.

'What if nothing, Rach. If they see you, you could be the target – you or Grace – they could hold you for a blood ransom. Sometimes it pays to think like them and what they would do to meet their objective. Just do as I say and pray for us all.'

Adam, Rachel and Grace were about a street away from the church when they stopped to let Adam out of the car.

Adam ran so fast toward the church. But as he approached Deygar's Bentley was parked up, empty, and the main door had been kicked off its hinges.

Adam was fearful and could clearly hear swords clashing upstairs. As he ran towards the sounds of shouting and swords striking one another Adam quickly prayed: 'Lord, please be with us in your house at this our time of dire need. Amen.'

Adam burst in the room to see Milo holding his own against Deygar, but he was beginning to struggle. Paul, however, was under Slayem's sword and he was ready to kill Paul when Adam shouted.

'Stop, Slayem. I'm Seth. I am your challenger not him.'

Slayem jumped towards Adam and struck him in the chest with a powerful kick throwing him six feet into the air. As Adam hit the floor he reached for the beanie gun strapped to his ankle and quickly pulled the trigger, shooting Slayem in his chest, thrusting his powerful frame into the far wall, indenting the plaster.

Adam quickly got up to help Paul to his feet. 'Are you ok?' Adam asked.

'Yes, just about, though.'

'Go and help your father.'

Milo's and Deygar's battle had moved downstairs into the main sanctuary and Milo was struggling to overpower him.

Paul quickly stepped in. The sight of him well and fighting fit and not suffering from the crippling effects of cancer was such a shock that he focused again, stumbled and fell over a chair.

'No, it can't be true. You were dying.'

'Yes, Deygar. The keyword was 'were', not anymore thanks to the life-giving Blood of Jesus.'

Deygar composed himself and got to his feet ready to fight but now with the two of them ready to strike back he was unsure and doubted his own ability.

Slayem didn't expect to get shot, so was a bit stunned by the close range shot to the chest. But the torso protector had done its job. Adam went over to Slayem nervously, his sword ready to give the fatal strike to end his immortal life, but Slayem flicked himself upright and kicked Adam again. He fell to the floor. Slayem's sword drew back to give Adam a fatal strike.

Adam again, thinking quickly, pumped the beanie shooting Slayem, and again the force of the shot threw him over the desk and into the wall.

Adam was convinced that the shot would disable him for a moment, so he could compose himself, but he was mistaken. Slayem was back on his feet with his sword ready.

Adam was weary and tired. Slayem jumped the desk that was between them and went for the kill. Adam defended himself with every sword strike. Adam was taken aback at the power Slayem possessed. His sword was huge and looked heavy, medieval in its design.

Slayem was trying harder and harder to kill Adam, and he was finding the going tough. He just couldn't get over the immense power and skill Slayem possessed.

'I thought you were good, Seth. Lose that ankle weapon and let me do my job.' Slayem was intimidating Adam, trying for a mind game technique.

Adam was having none of it. He struck Slayem with a powerful kick to his side leaving his guard down for Adam to go for the throat. Slayem's quick reactions guarded it just in time.

Adam's turn for the mind games: 'Don't let your guard down for a second. I'll take every chance I can.'

The pair stopped and paced round the room to take a break, sizing one another up.

'Just in case eh, Seth.' Slayem pressed a button on his chest protector and then a titanium collar sprung up from beneath his Kevlar collar; only his Adam's apple was exposed now, making a kill next to impossible for Seth.

Adam's mind was a mess. 'What do I do now? What I'd do for an actual firearm now; just shoot him in the head and it would be all over.' But even that wouldn't kill him, just slow him down for a moment.

Paul was downstairs in the main church and had more or less fought off Deygar, who ran from the church, back to his car.

Paul helped Milo back onto his feet. 'Let's see if Adam needs our help.' Paul was on a mission and Milo felt confident in his son's new found skills and abilities, thanks to Adam's quick training.

Adam and Slayem were ready to go again, their swords held aloft, when Milo and Paul rushed in the office.

Slayem, assuming the worst, that the pair had killed Deygar, quickly headed for the stairs, watching the three Master Disciples carefully as he slowly paced the stairs and out, only to find Deygar in the car ready to go.

'What's the problem? Let's go back and take them out.' Slayem's anger was clear; his face enraged by the adrenalin that flowed through his body.

'No. We need to go. There's three of them now. It's all different. He was at death's door a few months ago. It's impossible. It can't be true.'

Deygar's mind was a mess, trying to figure out why Paul was fighting fit and now apparently healed and fighting alongside his father.

'Let's go. We need to form another strategy, maybe a separate attack.'

Reluctantly, Slayem got in the car and the pair left to form another plan of attack.

Meanwhile, back in the church, the trio of Master Disciples were checking out the damage. Milo was shaken up pretty bad. Paul was ready to go again; the adrenalin still flowing, but Adam was thinking if he hadn't shown up just in time, the events may not have been as they were.

'Are you okay, Adam?' Paul asked, his voice cracking under the stress of it all.

'Yes, I'm fine. That Slayem is very powerful and skilful. He had me down in seconds.'

'I dread to think what might have happened if you hadn't shown up. It was also a good thing you had that beanie gun thingy.' Paul's voice was starting to break.

'I'll be ready next time,' Adam said with a glint of hope, rather than a statement of declaration.

Chapter Sixteen
The Wake Up and Rematch

2 Chronicles 32v8 'With him is only the arm of flesh, but with us is the Lord our God to help us and fight our battles.'

DEYGAR SKIDDED HIS BENTLEY INTO THE loading area of Greyer Industries, barely missing Slayem's huge container. The pair got out, Slayem punching the code into the armoured door with Deygar in hot pursuit.

Slayem's mood was a little hot to say the least, as he pulled open the steel drawers, pulling out several guns and ammunition.

'If he wants guns, we shall give him guns.' Slayem slipped several weapons into his belt.

'Wait! You told me not to use a gun and to be proud of the true traditions of a Dark Lord. Plus there's always the great risk of being caught by the police through forensic and ballistic testing. Bullets leave to much evidence – bullet cases, powder burns, shrapnel and hundreds more pieces of valuable proof that could all lead back to us.'

Slayem wasn't listening. All he wanted was the kill. Seth had dishonoured him and not fought fair as a true warrior should; now he would face him as an equal – both with guns.

Deygar couldn't reason with him. He was not listening to anyone but the voice in his head and that voice was pure evil.

Deygar took evasive action and stood directly in his path. 'No. I can't let this happen, Slayem. You told me, convinced me, taught me that the sword was an honour to carry into battle and deserved respect by the user, and the challenger. Seth isn't even using live rounds just the bean bags that police use in riot control situations.'

'No, Deygar. You are lazy. You're the disgrace here not me. If I want to finish this I can. You're not even out of your mortal years. I should be the one taking it easy in a huge leather chair. You are greedy, lazy and the one who contacted me to do your dirty work.'

Slayem loaded the Glock 34 with an extended magazine and tucked it in his belt along with the other two other guns, both Glocks.

'Don't worry about the police. You worry too much.'

Slayem then paused and took a moment, he soon realised that taking any kind of weapon other than a sword was breaking a tradition that he had tried to uphold for hundreds of years. He quickly placed the guns back to where they had come from and relocked the cabinet.

Slayem was hesitant and was dying to show Deygar his special recipe for death and destruction. He was quickly racking his brain and then it struck him.

'You use a gun, if I recall, with flash rounds. I know it buys you some time but that's all.'

Slayem quickly pulled open the drawer again to show Deygar the rounds he uses.

'You and your worrying about the police and all their little tests, ballistic tests and all the rest of them. You see, all those tests need evidence. I have invented a bullet that leaves no trace, no sign that a bullet was even there.'

Deygar was puzzled and had a look of bewilderment written all over his face and before he could lift a finger to ask the burning question Slayem continued in his rant.

'It's my own invention. It's a bullet made from glass and totally untraceable. It will be destroyed on impact leaving no evidence other than the dead body with a hole in it.'

Deygar's face was in shock at this news and again, before he could speak, Slayem was off again.

'Or I can use another of my inventions – a totally bio-degradable round and everything is gone, even the bullet casing; not a single trace of evidence is left. So now, are you convinced? Go and finish the job; take a weapon and shoot them and just make sure you bring enough blood for the both of us. Like I said; I should be the one staying in the big office taking it easy. I have been missing out on all this wealth with all its benefits.'

Deygar had heard enough of this and made his feelings known with a passion, well as much passion as an evil thoughtless man as Deygar could.

'No, Slayem. I won't take the gun. What about the code? What about the honour of the kill in battle? Shooting is murder. Slaying is our survival. That's the way it's always been.'

Deygar took a breath after his rant, amazed by his own words shouted out with such passion and conviction. He had to steady himself before he went on, but then Slayem got up, not with a look of anger, but with the look of a father seeing his son finally understand an ideal or a difficult maths equation.

'Finally! Good! Good, that's the answer I've been digging and searching for all this time – The Honour of the Kill. It is survival, you're so right.

Slayem grabbed Deygar by his shoulder, again amazing him with his shear strength and power, and said something that resounded in Derek Greyer's ears.

'We are the last of the immortals. We could go on and live on and on ruling the underworld and be the most powerful Dark Lords ever. We haven't long my friend. We haven't long at all.'

Deygar was intrigued by his last statement. 'What did he mean 'we haven't long'? We're immortal aren't we?'

'You see, with my skills in battle and your skills in the business world we could be unstoppable.'

It felt right for Slayem to say that but Derek couldn't help thinking that it was a one man show now and Slayem was running it from now on.

Milo was tidying up in the office when he felt he should be in the training room listening in on the evil duo. It could be a crucial time to listen in. He called Adam and Paul to join him also, but the three of them heard nothing but a constant phone ringing, not even his secretary answering it or the machine, which was highly suspicious. Adam and Paul were losing interest fast and got up to carry on with the clean up.

'No, I have a feeling I should be here for the duration,' Milo said.

'I have no objection, Dad. You can stay. If you feel God his saying wait, then wait.'

He was right. God was telling him to stay.

The pair of evil schemers were off to Derek's office to discuss tactics and their next move on the believers.

'So, if you want to wait a while until we attack again I understand, but you mentioned something in the car that intrigued me.'

'What did I say in the car?'

'Some thing about a separate attack.'

'Oh, I meant split them up and take them out separately. Who do you fear the most as a potential threat, Deygar?'

'Seth; he's quite handy and he's a lot more streetwise than Milo and his son, Paul.'

'Yes. Now you are thinking like a warrior; the strongest first and then we can pick off the weak later. I'm impressed Deygar, very impressed.'

'Plus, we have inside information on Seth, or should I say, Adam Fuller.'

Milo nearly choked on his coffee when he heard Adam's name mentioned but before he could shout him, Adam he was already there.

'So have you had time to go over the information I provided, Derek?'

'Yes; full name is Adam Fuller; married to Rachel; they have a daughter Grace – must be around twelve months old or older by now. Rachel runs and owns the Grange Retirement Home. Adam used to work for the Government but, as we know, now he works for the church as an assistant or what we would call a Master Disciple.'

'Excellent. So what's next Slayem?'

'Well I think we do something that will just bring Seth to us rather that go looking for him, and something that requires no thought on his part; no fear; no risk; something that he holds to his heart; something close; something precious.'

'I think the wife and daughter will have to play a part in this.'

With that said the phone rang again and Derek was quick to pick up.

'Your timing is amazing; we need you for a job.'

The line was a closed one and Adam, Milo and Paul could only hear Derek's voice.

'It's fifty large but it has to be tonight. We have to strike whilst the iron is hot… Yes, fifty each no probs… But it's tonight… Yes not over the phone, you never know… Yes, I will see you with the details… The usual place…' Then Derek hung up.

'We can't listen any more. We have to find out what he is planning. He mentioned Rachel and Grace. He knows everything. He must have been responsible for the break in on the home and the stolen personnel files.'

Milo tried to calm Adam but it was no good. He was fearful and nothing could get his mind from the thought of anything happening to Rachel and Grace.

'Don't panic, Adam. If it wasn't for you and your genius brother we wouldn't know this. We are ahead of the game. We just need to be on our guard now.' Milo tried to reassure him but it was a futile. Adam was in a dead panic and had to leave to be with his family. Milo signalled to Paul to go with him.

Adam was soon on the phone to Rachel to tell her to be on her toes and to double lock the house and set the alarm.

'Are you ok? I've been praying like mad.'

'It's ok, Rach. Just lock up and don't answer the door to anyone. I'll be home in a few minutes. Don't worry; I'll explain when I get home.'

Paul and Adam were soon at the house and quickly locked Paul's car in the garage, out of sight. Then there was some explaining to do with Rachel.

'What's going on, Adam?' With that said, Rachel gave Adam a great big hug. It was much needed.

'We were listening to Derek and Slayem on the bug and they happened to mention us by name. They mentioned the home. I think they're behind the break in. I think they're trying to get to you to flush me out in the open, emotionally, with my guard down, so I won't call on God for help – basically, cripple me spiritually but we have the upper hand; we know that they are coming and we will be ready. Paul and I will take shifts watching the house.'

Rachel couldn't really say much more but, reassured by Adam's great faith and strength in a potentially disastrous situation, she tried to settle in for the evening.

The four of them had a bit to eat, but a lot of the food saw the inside of a waste bin. Clearly on edge, the only one unaware was Grace who was tucking away at her meal as usual, but Adam was thinking about Grace; her just being a baby, totally unaware, totally vulnerable, totally innocent and at total risk. With that thought Adam broke down in tears. Rachel ran to him comfort but he tried to shrug it off.

'Leave me, Rach. I'll be alright. Not in front of Grace, she will pick up on it.'

It was soon time for Grace to go to bed and for Rachel to make plans just in case it went wrong.

The paranoia had got the better of Adam again and when it came to his first shift he attached his ankle alarm, which he had invented to alert him to intruders. Rachel noticed him pulling his sock over to keep it from sight.

'Don't bother hiding it. I've already seen it. What ever makes you feel relaxed enough, but please try and get some sleep. Good night.'

Sleep was the last thing on Adam's mind that night. His mind was racing, wondering who Derek was talking to on his phone and the fifty large each; for what job? What job could possibly need doing tonight that paid one hundred thousand?

Adam slipped in and out of a semi-conscience sleep most of his shift, to at least try and get some shut eye.

Paul was in the kitchen on his shift making himself a coffee and was then struck by what he thought was a torch beam of light coming from the woodland area at the rear of the house.

Paul quickly turned off the kitchen light to get a better view. As his eyes adjusted to the darkness he could make out a person walking through the woods towards the rear of the garden; Paul's heart was racing, not knowing what to do, whether to wake up Adam or go out alone.

He didn't need to make a choice. Adam was already awake and behind Paul, awakened by his ankle device.

'Oh it's you, Adam.'

'Who is it?'

Adam could make out two figures out there, walking behind each other to hide a set of footprints – a typical army tactic to reduce a trail left behind them to hide their numbers.

Adam feared the outcome of any confrontation between them.

'I don't know, and I'm not looking forward to finding out either.'

Adam turned towards Paul. 'Promise me, Paul; if this goes wrong please take Rachel and Grace away.'

'It's not going to go wrong, mate. Have faith.'

As the beam of light got closer so did the tension of it all, then the light was gone. The two of them, watching it all through the kitchen window, their eyes adjusting again to the lack of light, noticed one of the fence panels being slid out and two men climbing through then placing the fence panel back in place without a single sound. They were completely dressed in black combat gear; clearly army – or worse – SAS issue.

Paul got up to go. Adam quickly grabbing him back. 'No. Not yet, mate. Just check the front of the house. This little charade may be a diversion.'

Rachel came downstairs, clearly worried by something. Adam quickly sent her to get Grace ready for the backup plan of taking grace up into the loft area of the house and leaving all the beds filled with wrapped up blankets to give the impression that someone was still in them.

The two dark figures headed towards the patio windows. Paul was now on his feet, bolt upright, and heading also in the direction of the patio windows.

Adam gave chase to stop Paul from scaring away the possible attackers.

'No, Paul, we need them to try and at least break in. They've come this far. We need evidence that they were here. After all, it's our word against theirs.'

So Adam and Paul hid behind the archway that lead through into the lounge where the patio doors were, as the two dark figures attempted to get in through the glass doors.

Rachel was now in the loft area, praying like mad, whilst holding a sound asleep Grace, hoping that she wouldn't wake up and start crying, giving their position away.

Adam pressed the intercom button to talk to Rachel in the loft. 'Rachel, don't worry and please trust us and stay put until I call you on this thing.'

'Okay. I love you.'

'Love you too,' was the last thing Adam said as the two dark clothed men got through the glass and disabled the alarm sensor. The pair were ready with Adam getting hold of his Pro 34 sized baseball bat and Paul with a hockey stick.

The glass patio door slid silently open as the two men walked in. Adam, together with Paul, their weapons raised ready for the almightiest of swings, were poised. As the two stepped forward the pair struck out the bat and the hockey stick, hitting nothing. The two men were ready for the attack and had ducked. One gave Paul a kidney punch as the hockey stick hit the wall, sending shockwaves down Paul's hands. The other kicked Adam to the face, knocking him out on the floor, dropping his bat.

The man that had punched Paul lifted him up with one hand and pinned him against the wall by his throat.

'Hey, there's two of them here,' said one of the men in a thick cockney accent.

'Hey get up, or my friend here will break his neck like a chicken's.' He too with a thick cockney accent picked up Adam's baseball bat.

'Well, Mr Black. He had every intention of using this thing on us. What would you say to a bit of one's own medicine?'

'So, Adam. Where's the wife and daughter, eh?'

Adam was struggling for words. His eye and jaw were already swollen from the kick he received to his face.

'They're not here. They are somewhere safe. God told us you were coming, so we made arrangements.'

With that said the other man got hold of Adam's bat and swung it, hitting Adam's knees, bringing him down again, writhing in pain.

Paul tried to speak, which was difficult with his throat held so tightly.

'Yes? What have you got to say?'

Paul's word were limited but he managed to get out that Adam was telling the truth. 'God told us you were coming.'

Adam tried to speak up. 'Just believe us. We have taken precautions. How else could we know you were coming tonight?'

'They could be right, Mr White.'

'They might be right, Mr Black.'

'I'll go and check. Mr Black, you'll be okay babysitting these pair whilst I'm gone. Adam's not going to do anything; his knees are pretty much out for tonight's activities.'

Rachel could hear someone coming up the stairs and, after the noise of it all, she didn't necessary presume it was Adam. He clearly said he would call her on the intercom, so she kept quiet. Her heart was racing, fearing someone could hear it bouncing out of her chest, but the real miracle was that Grace was still fast asleep.

Mr Black checked the rooms for any sign of life, looking under beds and through the wardrobes, but he found nothing.

Adam was quietly praying that he wouldn't check Grace's cot; the mattress would clearly still be warm from a baby's body heat. He also prayed for the strength to get up and finish this task. 'Oh Lord. Amen,' he said quietly.

With that pray said he started to get up.

'Hey get back down here. Adam's on his feet.'

Adam quickly gave the man holding Paul by the throat a sweep kick, knocking the pair of them on to the floor. Adam was reluctant to use the beanie gun in the house for fear of waking Grace, but had no choice and quickly grabbed it from his other ankle and shot Mr Black as he ran towards him down the hall, sending back down with tremendous force, hitting the front door.

Paul quickly got hold of the hockey stick and held it ready to strike Mr White if he moved.

Mr White's reaction was one of shock and horror. There was no warning at all; he just shot him. He thought this Adam was a serious character, and not the man described to them and he now feared for his life.

Adam now turned his focus on Mr White. 'Now, what to do with you, eh?' He quickly looked at the collapsed motionless body of what he thought was his former partner lying in the hall way, but what he didn't know was that he was only unconscious from the force of the shotgun blast and hitting the door.

Adam had only a few moments to scare Mr White into thinking he was dead before he woke up.

'So, what I suggest is that you go back to your boss and tell of what you saw this night and know that this is not the way to do it. Leave the families out of it. Go! Just Go!'

Mr White just looked again at the body of Mr Black and ran back through the patio door, through the garden and into the woods, fearing Adam would follow him and shoot in cold blood in the woodland area.

Adam turned to Paul. 'Quick, I have an idea. Go to the shed and get a shovel and I'll go and check on Rach and Grace.' As he did this, Mr Black's body was still motionless, but Adam was afraid that he was faking it so quickly gave him another swift kick to the midsection – not one reaction. 'He's either a great actor or he's still out of it,' thought Adam, as he went upstairs. Adam didn't use the intercom just in case Mr Black heard. So he broke his own rule and opened the loft door without using the intercom first to find Rachel. A very scared looking Rachel hit him square in the face with a piece of timber that lined the floor of the loft, knocking him down the four steps he'd managed to cover on his short climb up.

Rachel panicked and quickly realised her error. 'Why didn't use the intercom like you said?'

'I'm sorry, Rach. It's because we have a man down there unconscious and I was afraid he would hear me talking to you. I didn't want to alert him to your whereabouts, but that doesn't matter now; he may have heard that.'

Rachel was so glad to see her husband that she didn't really register the fact there was a twenty stone hit man, unconscious, at the bottom of her hallway with a large bruised chest and an even bigger lump on the back of his head.

Adam quickly told her to go back up and keep Grace safe, who was still tucked up in her old Moses basket in the loft.

Paul came back with the shovel and a look of bewilderment written all over his face. Adam had collected a blanket on his travels and quickly filled Paul in on his amazing plan.

They just finished setting up the scare plan for Mr Black, as he woke up from the huge direct hit to his chest and head.

Adam quickly pointed the beanie at him and reassured him that there were real shotgun cartridges in the weapon now. 'A lesson learnt quickly by Mr White,' said Adam. Whose 'body' was now lying on the concrete patio covered with a blanket with a conveniently placed shovel standing next to it.

Mr Black's face was filled with fear. The bold, confident man of twenty minutes ago was now looking rather scared and worried, fearing for his own safety and well being.

Mr Black's mind was a cloud of emotion. 'What are you going to do with me, eh?'

'You're going to go back to your employer and give him a message from us, not to try anything like this again and to leave the families out it, or I will have to resort to killing someone else. You see, Mr Black,' Adam leaned in towards him and said 'I turn into a morally unstable individual and I would willingly kill for them, so I suggest you go now before I start getting upset, because I keep thinking what if this night had gone your way, eh, and you now would have my wife and daughter?' Adam quickly pumped the shotgun and held it under Mr Black's chin.

Paul stepped in on the tough act and said 'No, Adam. Don't do it. It would make a terrible mess and I'm not cleaning that one up.'

Adam quickly calmed down the act, although Paul thought it was quite convincing.

'Go, before I change my mind.' And with that said, Mr Black got up and ran the same route Mr White had ran only moments ago.

He was soon into the woodland area and, still fearing for his life, got to the place where their car was parked. He presumed that Adam had ditched it, to cover his tracks, so he made his way on foot. Upon reaching into his pocket Mr White's mobile phone had been completely crushed under the enormous blast it had received from the beanie weapon, so he couldn't even call ahead for help or a lift.

Chapter Seventeen
The Truth and Shame of It All

Proverbs 16v13-14 'Kings take pleasure in honest lips; they value a man who speaks the truth'.
'A king's wrath is a messenger of death, but a wise man will appease it'.

Rachel was soon downstairs and holding her hero in her arms. Adam quickly brushed aside that he was a hero; he was just someone that loved his family with a passion.

Paul quickly stepped in with his thanks and appreciation for the day Adam heard God tell him to get that gun, even though Milo disapproved of them.

'That's the second time that beanie thing has saved us from near death.'

The panic-stricken Mr White drove his high-powered car into Derek Greyer's private estate, totally forgetting the rule of no contact, especially contact with Derek Greyer's home. That was a big 'no no' in Derek's own rule book of hiring hit men or any one of the many people he had hired to carry out dirty work for him in the past, but Mr White had good reason; he had just witnessed the murder and slaying of his partner and was in quite a state of shock.

Deygar was furious and let rip on Mr White. 'What are you doing here at this hour?'

'Please, sir, let me speak.' Derek could see that he was a little shaken and it wasn't because of his rant at being at his mansion at the ungodly hour.

'Adam shot Mr Black with a shotgun, killing him.'

Slayem heard this and came in from the bar area almost spilling his double whisky and ice. 'Get a grip, man. He shot us with that thing; it only fires bean bags, like they use in riots. He'll be fine.'

'No. He's a big guy. He would have shaken it off. I was there. He was motionless.'

All three just stood there shocked. Slayem wasn't having any of it and shook his head in disbelief; Derek went to the bar to pour a stiff drink because they all needed it for what was going to unfold in the next few minutes.

Slayem's rage was getting the better of him and was he trying to convince Derek of an attack on the Master Disciples as soon as possible.

Derek was reluctant to go with his plan. He was now very nervous at the fact that Adam had killed Mr Black. So he told Mr White to get a stiff drink, and to rest and wait for his next assignment.

The pair's voices echoed around the large room as they shouted out their grievances.

'I'm a business man. I can't go around killing people willy-nilly, especially now Paul's back from the brink of death. We have three to fight and dispose of. I don't think I can do this.'

'You can and you will. What are you – a man or a mouse? That's what comes from hiring someone to do your own work. It's idle – bone idle of you. It's the old saying; if you want a job doing right, do it yourself.'

As the pair's volume came to a normal level Mr Black burst in, in a blind panic. 'They've killed him. They've killed Mr White and buried him.'

'What's going on here?' Deygar was furious and was outraged by this conduct. 'We have claims that you are dead, and you are clearly not.'

With all the commotion, Mr White heard. He came back from the bar and pool table area, only to be confronted by the sight of Mr Black. The pair looked at each other and said simultaneously, 'You're supposed to be dead.'

The pair were struck with horror; two professional, ex-army soldiers, who contract themselves out to VIPs, diplomats and celebrities as their personnel protection were foiled by an ex-government worker in is home with the help of an ex-cancer sufferer. The two of them held their heads low for the onslaught that was to follow.

But before Derek could get a word in Slayem said, 'Look at this. They are laughing now. They played you good and proper. Look, Derek, no more playing. Tomorrow we strike back.'

Before Derek could really go to town on Mr Black and Mr White, Slayem told them to go and get out of his sight before someone did get killed.

'Why did you send them away? I wanted to give them what for. It is an outrage that they could get away without facing the consequences of their actions.'

'I assure you, Deygar, you saying nothing will play on their minds more than death itself. They don't know when their punishment will come, whatever shape or form of punishment you see fit, and most of all, when.'

Deygar could see his logic and now felt so much more relaxed about the whole mess up, but what really troubled Deygar's mind now was how they knew that they were sending someone to get to his family on that night.

Slayem stepped forward and again freaked out Deygar with his mind trickery.

'The man truly knows God and he acts on what he hears. God told him we were coming, and that's why I must kill him – no one else.'

The morning after the night before: Adam's knees were swollen and he was having difficulty walking after his own pro 34 baseball bat was used on him.

Rachel was concerned and was begging Adam to get back into bed, but he wasn't having any of it.

Adam was convinced Deygar was hatching another plan against them and he would be right there when they were at their most vulnerable, especially with him being injured.

'All I'm doing today is getting you out of here. You and Grace are going to the home. There's an apartment in the top loft in the main building. I know it hasn't been lived in for a while but we'll soon fix that up and the fewer who know the better.'

'Wo there! We are going where? And why, may I ask, do you want us out of the way?'

'No, Rach. You don't understand. I don't want you out of the way. I want you out of harm's way. There is a difference – a huge one. I fear they will try again.'

Rachel wasn't having any of it. 'We are a couple, a family. All or nothing, we are one flesh, one body. Why separate us all?'

Adam tried to reassure her the best he could. 'It's not the best plan, Rach, but the only way I can protect my family – the only true treasure that's mine. Everything else can burn – the house, the cars; all we own can burn, Rach. You and Grace are everything and I can't lose you.' Adam grabbed hold of Rachel by her shoulders and pleaded with her just to trust him. She could clearly see that Adam was hurting emotionally as well as physically; his eyes were filling up and he was finding the whole responsibility of it too much to bear. Finally, Rachel relented and went along with Adam's plan and it was a good one. After all, Adam knew if ever she was followed, there was ample security. Any sign of her whereabouts could be kept a secret, keeping cars out of sight in the spare garages and, on a plus note, the loft had a 360 degree view of the whole surrounding area; she had a laptop computer, a mobile phone, plus the LPS system all at her disposal.

So, after breakfast they loaded the car out of sight in the garage. Adam was taking no chances just in case someone was watching the house. The car was mostly filled with Grace's most needed items; including the travel cot, chair, toys, food, clothes and mum with just an overnight bag of essential items. She wasn't making a big thing of it all.

'I'm not being driven from my own home by these people.'

'We aren't, Rach. We are keeping you and especially Grace out of harm's way.'

Paul was still there and it was now 9.45am. The phone rang; it was Milo to tell them that Slayem and Deygar were in his office and it would be a good idea to get moving now.

Adam couldn't get his leathers on to escort Rachel on the M.V, so Paul and Adam went together in Milo's Mondeo. The plan was to follow Rachel in the Legacy and have constant verbal contact with her on the hands free phone, just to keep Rachel calm. It was at this point Rachel felt the enormity of it all; simply moving from one place to the next was like a military exercise.

The two cars started off and it was all going well. They got to the first set of traffic lights and Paul could sense Adam's tension. Paul tried to calm him the only way he knew and prayed out loud.

'Please, Lord. Travel with us all this fine morning and place your Angels around us, Lord. Amen.'

Adam simply said 'Thanks.'

The lights went to green and they were off towards the edge of the city limits, towards the north end of the district heading to the home, when Adam thought he saw the Black Range Rover in his side mirror. Adam quickly grabbed hold of the driver's mirror to get a better look and prove he wasn't just seeing things. His paranoia getting the better of him again, he thought, but unfortunately he was proved right; it was the Black Range Rover of Deygar's. Adam read the number plate, DEY 10.

'What is it?' Paul was now worried by Adam's twitchy actions and dropped down the vanity mirror to see behind.

The black Range Rover had pulled up into the devoted bus lane and was clearly waiting for Rachel to pass so he could follow.

'Paul, Rachel's going to be followed soon by that Black Range Rover.' Rachel heard Adam say that over the phone and started to panic, as she looked into the driver's mirror and gave a fearful glance at Grace. She was smiling at her mum's concerned look, not aware to their imminent danger.

Paul was now cranking his head around to get a glance, but Adam soon told him to keep calm, as the two cars in convoy stopped again at yet another set of traffic lights.

'What do I do, Adam? Please, I'm scared.'

'Just keep driving until I say otherwise.'

The black Range Rover pulled out and got behind the line of traffic waiting at the lights. Adam could clearly see that they were three cars behind.

As the lights changed, Rachel drove as she would under normal driving conditions, straight on with Adam and Paul behind. Two of the cars behind them made a left turn so now there was only one car separating them from Deygar's car.

The four cars carried on for a few more miles until getting to another set of lights, but this time Adam told Paul to get into the right hand lane, to pull alongside Rachel in front. Adam wound down his window.

'Rachel, don't panic. Just drive the long way round. Don't go directly to the home until I say it's safe, okay? Okay, Rach? Talk to me.'

'Yes, I hear you. Just please be safe.' Rachel was concerned now and was fearful. Not knowing what was going on was ripping her apart with anxiety and stress. 'Please, Lord. Help us,' was all she could muster up.

As the lights changed again, the cars pulled forward and Adam instructed Paul to get behind the Range Rover, so now they were following them.

'So now what's the plan, Adam? We follow them, and for what reason?'

'You'll see at the next set of lights.' And as Adam had predicted all the cars were caught in the next set of lights, before the road opened up to the leading dual carriageway. So it was now or never for Adam.

Adam got out of the Mondeo as quick as he could with those injured knees, then quickly pulled out the beanie and smashed in the driver's window, throwing broken glass all over Mr Black.

'Hello boys!' Before Adam could utter another syllable, Mr Black floored the Range Rover, going round Rachel and through the red light, narrowly missing another car going the other way.

Adam quickly got back in the car with Paul. 'Go! Follow them and don't lose them. Rachel, go to the home now. You are now clear and safe.'

Rachel was relieved by this news but, again, was concerned for her husband's well being. 'Okay. Just be careful, and I'll be praying.'

Rachel was now safe and the black Range Rover was heading for the duel carriageway that would eventually lead them onto the motorway. It was really fast; the powerful, top of the range, Range Rover was nearly hitting the ton, and Paul was struggling to keep up.

'Come on, Paul, catch them. This is a quick car, Paul. Use it. Put your foot down man, we can't lose 'em. Come on!'

Adam was finding the whole chase very frustrating and ached to be in that driver's seat, but there was no way he could drive with his knees the way they were.

The Black Range Rover was getting further and further away and Adam reached over and placed his hand down hard on Paul's right knee, hitting the very sensitive accelerator of the ST2OO to the floor. Paul, finding it hard to control the car, and gave Adam what for. 'I'm not you, Adam. I'm not good at everything. I'm doing the best I can. Please!'

With that said the LPS went off. Adam quickly answered it. It was Milo back at the church. 'It's a trap. Get back to the church now.'

Adam didn't know what to do. They were stuck on the motorway and could not turn around anytime soon.

'What is it, Milo?'

'I don't want to panic you both, but Deygar and Slayem are on their way to the church.'

'Rachel, are you still there?'

'Yes.'

'Once at the home get out of sight and hide the car and wait for us to contact you.'

'What's wrong, Adam?' Rachel was now a nervous wreck and was at breaking point but Adam had no choice but to tell Rachel about Milo.

'It's all been arranged. It's a trap so they can get to Milo on his own.'

Paul's head turned towards Adam. It was a shock for Paul he had heard it all. Adam nodded to confirm to Paul. 'We have to get back to the church now.'

Milo had lost contact with the evil duo. Derek had obviously had left his pen in his jacket pocket in the office, so now he could not estimate their time of arrival and was genuinely worried for his safety and well being.

'We must kill Milo,' Slayem said. 'He is clearly their spiritual leader. There's no other way they could know of your plans last night. He is the main one who is most in tune with God. He knows our every move, so now we take him out of the picture and kill him.'

'It's been long overdue,' said Deygar, as the pair drove frantically towards the church.

Deygar's phone rang; it was Mr White. 'Hello, sir. The plan is going smoothly and they are following behind us as we speak. These two clowns are very much occupied for the foreseeable future.'

'Thanks, Mr White. Carry on.'

Mr Black gave a quick glance in the rear view mirror – no sign of the Silver Mondeo.

'I told you to take it easy. It's that car of Adam's missus that's quick. That Legacy is a really quick car.' With that said, the silver Mondeo streaked past them doing 135mph.

Adam and Paul were clearly worried about Milo, but the pair soon realised that they had no swords in the car. Even if they did get there in time they had no way to defend themselves, but the pair carried on regardless of the dangers that lie ahead.

Milo was scared and fell to his knees in the main sanctuary, holding his sword ready, knowing full well that his son and apprentice Master Disciple would not make it in time; so he decided to make a last, heart felt prayer to his Lord at this time of need.

'Oh, Lord. If this is my last mortal prayer to you before my last battle just let me say what a privilege it has been for me to defend your church all these years. Thank you for granting me a long and fulfilled life of servitude to your people and a much appreciated thank you for the healing of my son, bringing back him back from the brink of death; for that I am forever in your debt. I'm not going to ask for a miracle, Lord. Just let your will be done on this your day.' Milo paused for a moment and looked around at what his son had achieved – building an amazing place of worship – then said 'Amen.'

With that uttered from his weak dry lips, the church doors flung open.

Chapter 18
The Surprise

1 Peter 4v12 'Dear friends, do not be surprised at the painful trial you are suffering, as though something strange were happening to you.'
v14 'If you are insulted because of the name of Christ, you are blessed, for the Spirit of glory and of God rests on you.'

THE CHURCH FLOOR WAS COLD WHERE Milo was kneeling and all he could think about was his crippling arthritis – 'And at a time as this,' he thought. Milo's ears pricked up to the sound of a car pulling up at great speed and skidding to a halt on the gravelled area in between the shrubbery. He waited and said in his heart 'So this is it for me, Lord. I have done my best and you have sustained me all these years. Thanks, Lord. It's been an honour.'

Then he heard footsteps and the door slam shut. Milo went to get up and face his adversary toe to toe but the pair got to him before he could.

'Milo, get off your knees. We've got a plan.' It was Adam and Paul and they had got back just in time. Deygar's Bentley had just made the turn into the church car park.

The three Master Disciples quickly got themselves composed. Adam and Paul got their swords and hid.

Milo was most surprised to see the pair of them but it was no time to explain and have a party about it; they had work to do.

In the car park, the evil duo got their weapons from the boot of Deygar's car and then proceeded towards the church. They just stood for a moment before entering.

Once in the holy place of worship, Deygar was eager to unsheathe his sword ready for the kill. Slayem's was still under his long jacket.

'Anxious are we, Deygar?'

'This time I've come to finish this. Like I said, it's long overdue.'

As the pair climbed the stairs, quickly racing through their heads was the memory of last time and their battle with all three Master Disciples, but little did they know they would do battle again with all three, and Slayem was clearly going to let Derek Greyer make that all important kill of Milo on his own. He still hadn't reached for his sword.

Slayem opened the door to the office to be greeted by Milo, sitting at the desk, sword atop ready.

'I've been expecting you both,' Milo said with a new found confidence, but he was still very nervous at the outcome of this meeting. After all, Slayem was a formidable character and highly skilled, but he had noticed that his sword was still sheathed. The pair gave each other a quick glance. Slayem went for the hilt of his sword just in case – just a precaution in his eyes. He was uneasy being around such a highly filled man of God, even though he had such power and skill in the natural sense, but when it came to the spiritual he still got nervous from time to time.

Slayem stepped forward. 'That's why we are here, Milo. You always seem to know our every move; my associate is going to take your life in battle.'

Milo's mind was racing but he couldn't help thinking about the polite way Slayem said that Derek was going to murder him in a fight where there was only one winner. Milo hoped it would be the Lord celebrating the victory at this time.

All three Master Disciples could cut the tension in that room with a knife or even a sword for that matter.

'I know because God feels I should know. So if you have to take me that's your mission.' All three gave a quick glance around the room then Milo added, 'I too have a mission and I will uphold it even with my life.'

With that, Milo stood up, grabbed his sword and held it in the ready position.

Slayem stood motionless but Derek stepped back, he too with his sword ready for the first strike.

Slayem lost it. Derek was stalling. He pulled his sword from it's sheathe. The twin-bladed sword filled Milo with fear. His mind was fixed on what that kind of weapon would do to the human body, but then he quickly re-focused his mind on the situation.

'Seth and your son will be much easer to deal with, with you out of the picture. No more tip-offs. No more spiritual insight. Kill him Deygar or I will.'

With that said, Adam and Paul burst in with their swords ready. Paul made the first strike, hitting out at Deygar's readily aimed sword heading for Milo, blocking it and then he made a very strong kick to Deygar's chest. As he fell, Paul struck again giving him a well aimed punch to his kidneys, winding him as he hit the floor.

Slayem yelled out 'Seth! No!' turning the twin-bladed sword towards him and swinging it with no regard, without any skill or technique and with a mass of aggression. He yelled again. 'I'm going to kill you all.'

It was that evil switch that Slayem had and it was turned all the way up to maximum, bypassing low and medium all together. With his aggression turned up, he just swung out with his huge twin-bladed sword that Adam was trying to avoid at all costs. He moved around and, as he did, he gave Milo a swift kick, knocking him over the desk.

Adam was fearful for the welfare of Milo. Being a man in his age, a kick like that would kill a normal pensioner but Milo was no ordinary pensioner – he was a warrior and he was at work.

Adam blocked the strikes of Slayem but after just several massive strikes Adam was tiring. His knees were still swollen and he was in agony. He soon remembered the last time he had confronted Slayem; his power and skill had well surpassed his pitiful few years of training in a garage gym.

Whilst Adam was doing his best with Slayem, he noticed Milo get up from behind his desk, clearly hurt from the powerful kick from Slayem. But Adam noticed something different about Milo; he seemed Happy, as if to say he was glad to be there in the midst of battle, like a look of purpose – a look of focus and determination.

Paul was now the one getting into difficulty, with Deygar giving him a massive swinging drop kick, knocking him to the ground, but Paul quickly countered the next strike from Deygar's sword and managed to flick himself back up, kicking Deygar in the chest.

It was the best battle Paul had ever seen and gave him a burst of faith at a time when he needed it the most. But then Paul lost the rhythm of the fight and Deygar brought him down, as Deygar was ready to give the fatal strike with his sword.

Milo yelled out with his arms held aloft. 'By the power of God within me, bring these evil men down.'

With that said Deygar and Slayem were thrown across the office and into a solid bricked wall; slain in the spirit of God; rendered completely unconscious by His mighty power.

Adam and Paul were in shock to see this amazing act of God in its fullness; even Milo was taken aback by this show of God's amazing power.

The two evil men just lay there totally paralyzed by the power of God.

Adam quickly went over to Slayem's motionless body and was so tempted to finish it. 'Let's cut his head off now. Let's finish this right now.' And Adam grabbed hold of Slayem's sword. The massively heavy sword would easily remove his head. The shear weight of it would do the job even with his armoured collar on, but Adam had noticed that he wasn't wearing it.

Milo stepped forward. 'No, Adam, it would be murder.'

'But God slayed them for a reason. He always has a reason for doing things; you've preached on the subject several times.' Adam was getting frustrated by Milo's stalling. He didn't know how long they would stay down for. Adam was just trying to make good of a very convenient situation.

'Just get them out of here.' Milo was just surprised by this. In his whole walk with God this had never happened and he was totally confused. He had a moral obligation to the code of the Master Disciple – not to murder but to defend, even defend to the death, but never murder in cold blood.

Adam was getting more and more frustrated by Milo's stalling, but he had respect for Milo's many years of experience and insight. After all, he had been doing this for years.

Paul was still in awe of it all and it gave him a boost of faith he had never experienced before, but he was more confused about what to do next than the pair of them. They both had good ideas but he knew in his heart which one was the moral one and finally he spoke up and supported his father. 'Yes, we should just get them out of here.'

Adam hit a new low and struggled to hold back the anger of these men that lay at his feet. They had the power to end it right now, and especially after their plan to kidnap Rachel and Grace.

Adam pulled himself together and started to move the evil duo. He first moved Slayem's twin-bladed weapon by kicking it away from the motionless body and, in doing so, hit the release button that turned his sword into a deadly-bladed fighting staff.

Paul soon realised what it was and picked it up, admiring the quality engineering that the weapon possessed. Adam, quickly seeing this, warned Paul. 'It takes years to master that weapon so be careful with it. Try to collapse it and make it a little safer for us to move.'

The three quickly moved the pair downstairs and into Derek Greyer's Bentley. The two of them were heaped into the back seat and Adam quickly relieved Derek of the keys to start the car up.

Paul was getting a little nervous. It had been nearly twenty minutes and he feared the pair would wake up at anytime. The pair decided to take two cars, so Adam drove the Bentley and Paul followed on.

The two car convoy was soon into the countryside and Adam sensed that was far enough. He desperately fought the agonising temptation to kill the pair of them. 'Just cut their heads off now and it would be all over,' he thought. But he had to abide by the code if he was ever to make a true Master Disciple of worth and honour.

He could see Paul behind in the Mondeo, as he stopped and quickly pulled out the keys to the Bentley and through them into a neighbouring field with frustration.

As Adam walked towards Paul's waiting car, Paul could sense the mood and found it hard to understand what Adam was feeling. He tried to place himself in that situation; would he have such restraint? He felt he couldn't answer; kids – they change everything and he didn't have any. It was an evil plan of theirs to go after Adam's family and Paul found it an unforgivable act on their part.

On the drive back to the church Adam hardly spoke. He just called his beloved Rachel to simply say that he was safe, was out of harm's way and was on his way to see the pair of them at the rest home.

Once back at church, Adam was in serious pain with his knees now that the adrenalin had worn off. He was now wondering how he would ride his motorbike if he needed to in an emergency.

Adam just sat there in silence whilst Paul made everyone a drink; Milo was checking his chest in the mirror, fearing he would have a heart attack at anytime. Milo was still in shock and the gravitas of the whole experience had took hold of his mind. He had to sit down before he fell down.

The three Master Disciples were all suffering in their own unique way; Paul was busying himself; Adam was at an all time low and just wanted to be with his family and Milo feared the next move of Deygar and Slayem.

Paul quickly gave everyone a strong cup of coffee, even though Adam hadn't answered Paul when he had asked for it. He started to quiz his father on the whole slaying episode.

'Son, before you ask; I don't know how it happened. It just did. When Slayem kicked me I thought I was going to have a heart attack with the power of it, and then behind that desk I was immediately reminded of the Scripture of Moses, when in the heat of the battle he needed his arms supporting because, as you know; when his arms lowered they would start to lose and when his arms rose they began to win. I don't know why that particular piece of scripture came to me, but I was glad it did because it worked.

'So that's what I did; I raised my arms and just shouted out, and then you know the rest.'

Paul pondered for a moment then said, 'Yes. God showed up in power through you and floored the pair of them. Amazing! Praise God!'

Slayem came around first with a fuzzy, slight hangovery kind of feeling and struggled to get out of the rear of the neatly parked Bentley.

And then, he soon realised once getting into the front seat to drive away that the keys were missing, he didn't want to, but he had no choice but to wake Derek.

He lent over and gave Derek Greyer a hefty slap across his face to wake him.

'What happened?' was the response. He took a quick look around and soon realised the depths of their despair. 'Where the hell are we?'

Slayem shrugged his shoulders like a man without a single care in the world. Derek piped up with a great idea.

'Turn the key and check the sat nav. See where we are.'

Slayem gave him a look of 'I could have done that if the keys were in my possession, you fool,' but declined the pleasure of such a slapping down. All that was running through Slayem's mind was vengeance. The act of such betrayal was unforgivable, as if Slayem was capable of such of an emotion has deep as forgiveness that was way beyond him.

Derek quickly assessed the situation and acted. He reached over and opened the glove box to reveal a coded panel. He typed in 2168 and, with that, the Bentley's sat nav came on and the key fob started to beep loudly in the nearby field. Derek quickly located it, so the pair could compose themselves and get ready for their next encounter with the Master Disciples.

Slayem was angry and let out his frustrations on Derek.

'You have all this technology and still a seventy-seven year old man can run rings round the both of us.'

But what struck Derek the most was how the pair made it back to the church in time and the fact that they had lost their tactical advantage by losing their baring on Rachel.

Slayem soon answered him; Derek still forgetting his ability to read ones thoughts.

'Pastor Miles is a mighty man of God, knowing our every move – yes – but he won't next time we are to take him out. You see, this happened to me before, around two hundred years ago. A man of God had me frozen, motionless. Not like just now on the floor, but just standing, frozen, unable to defend or strike.'

Derek butts in to the story, completely taken in by it. 'You were vulnerable to the death strike to the throat.'

'No. Like then and like now; no man of God can spill blood on holy ground or on a church floor. We can, but they can't. And we will. At the appointed time, we will. We will!'

Back in the church, Milo was concerned for Adam's knees and decided to pray for restoration to his health. Milo also felt nervous and riddled with guilt for some unknown reason. So he prayed. 'Oh, Lord. Restore Adam's knees to their best and give him strength to continue his quest. Amen.'

Adam and Paul gave a quick glance and the pair raised their eyebrows, both thinking that the prayer was a little childlike in its simplicity and wording, but they soon swallowed whatever thoughts they were having because, before their very eyes, Adam's knees began to reduce in size; the swelling was retreating and the colour in Adams face was returning.

The former run-down looking Adam was now back to full health and feeling amazing. The pair of doubters had been lacking a little in faith of late and began to thank and praise God in their own hearts.

But before the three of them could go into a full-blown praise and worship session, the phone rang. Milo quickly got to it. It was Jason. He was back from his break and eager to get back to the fold, even though it would mean being a day earlier than scheduled.

Milo was quick to tell the others, once off the phone. 'Jason's back tomorrow and very eager. God has been speaking to him, apparently, whilst on his break.'

Adam was getting a renewed infusion of faith after hearing that Jason was back, and with his new knees he was feeling even more excited to simply be alive. With that, he got up and said, 'I'm off to see my family.'

'But wait, Adam. What if they decide to come back?' Paul was worried by Adam's actions – that Adam would just up and leave like that just after being part of an amazing miracle; his knees were totally restored by the power of God.

But Milo put his heart at rest. 'Paul, we are going to see many more miracles like that, and greater ones, before the work that God has set us apart for is complete in his name. So I'm not surprised by Adam's actions. So go and see your wife and daughter and bless them also.'

Chapter Nineteen
Their Next Move

Exodus 32v12 'It was with evil intent that he brought them out, to kill them in the mountains and to wipe them off the face of the earth.'

As Deygar and Slayem pulled up in the Bentley towards Manor House, the evil pair sat silently just pondering their thoughts. And as the car finally came to a halt in the huge driveway, next to the other multiple hundred thousand pound vehicles that decorated his vast estate. The pair got out and Derek Greyer slammed shut the door to his two hundred thousand pound Bentley, shattering the glass, not having a single care for it at all, which wasn't like Derek at all.

He was totally frustrated by what Slayem had told him. 'Why not on holy ground? Why can't we spill blood?'

'You misunderstood what I said, Deygar. We can spill blood; it's the Master Disciples that can't. That is why we are still alive, because of the code they can not murder us. It is still a huge sin to kill in cold blood. They can only kill in defence. Have you forgotten that fundamental part of being who and what you are, Derek 'Deygar' Greyer?'

Hearing his full name shouted out to him was a major wake up call for him and he soon realised why; he was on the verge of a breakdown of some kind. His jaw was clenched like it was wired up. His fists were in a constant readiness to lash out in anger with the slightest word said against him. Slayem could see the signs clearly and knew exactly what to do.

That weekend of Jason's return was amazing for the church. He presented the church with a major challenge to come together, pray and intercede against evil in their world; that was the main subject of his sermon in the evening service and the church's response was awe inspiring. That evening, an all night prayer meeting was planned and the church rose to such a challenge. It was to be held on the following Monday evening.

Even though people were due to work on the Tuesday, it was like God had empowered his people to even operate without sleep. Jason had come back with new passion and a stronger faith than ever. More importantly, the church could see and they were hungry for it.

Adam, on the other hand, was worried about the security of the believers in a church building all night. It was a very vulnerable time with Slayem and Deygar on their rampage.

Jason assured Adam that this was God's time and Adam's worries were planted in his mind by the Devil. He didn't have such worries, and all he said to Adam was to trust Him.

But something bothered Adam and he had a hunch. All wasn't clear somehow. So that night, Adam prayed before going to sleep.

The loft in the main building of the home wasn't the most modest or comfortable but the main thing was that they were all safe, and Rachel felt the same way after the initial couple of nights of getting used to it.

It was an open plan space with one separate room from the main living and kitchen area in which Grace slept in. Adam and Rachel had to slum it on a reasonably comfortable sofa bed but it just brought the couple closer together, stronger than ever. The pair prayed that if what

Adam was thinking was right that God would be able to communicate that to the others in time or just prevent the evil duo's plans, but Rachel suspected it also and confirmed this to Adam before he had a chance to tell her of Jason's thoughts on the whole theory.

The pair slept soundly and woke up feeling fresh and alert for the day ahead of them. Adam was soon on the phone, once he had shoved a bowl full of breakfast cereal down his neck. He could never function properly without his bowl of healthy muesli and chopped banana.

Milo was at the church early. After a rough night's sleep, he was starting to feel the pressure of the all night prayer meeting and see the magnitude of the situation. He imagined the meeting with the possibility of a full church at the mercy of Slayem and Deygar. He quickly switched on the computer and waited for the evil duo in question to start talking about their evil intentions.

The phone rang, startling Milo, who had fallen into a semi conscience state over the computer.

'Milo, are you at church already?' Adam asked sounding as fresh as a daisy.

'Yes. Had a bad night last night. Couldn't sleep; got this infernal prayer meeting on my mind.'

'Okay, Milo. I'll be there soon. Put the coffee on; I'll be there in ten minutes.'

Adam quickly explained to Rachel that their prayer before bed last night had started to come to fruition; Milo had, had a rough night and was feeling the pressure. Rachel gave a grin of acknowledgement but really she hoped the other part of the prayer would fall into place instead, but she had prepared herself for the outcome.

Adam was right to be on the defensive; to be the servant he had been called to be; to guard and protect the believers, who were the church.

Adam quickly put on his bike leathers. This time he wasn't taking any chances and prepared for the worst case scenario. His short sword, which fitted into the bike, was grabbed off the wall and so was his baton and beanie weapon.

All Rachel said was, 'I'll be praying for you here, okay.'

Adam nodded his appreciation and knew that her presence at the home was the conformation that he needed. It wasn't like Rachel to miss a meeting at church, especially one called by its newest leader, but she had to stay for the sake of their daughter, Grace.

Adam blasted the M.V. to church but, on the way, topped up the petrol tank just in case. Adam was just so on the ball this morning and felt confident, but also nervous about the whole day unfolding. But it wasn't like he had a choice; he just had to ride it out and hope and pray that the outcome was the one planned by the Almighty.

He was quickly at the church building and soon in the training room next to Milo, drinking strong coffee.

It was bad. In Milo's mind, it was like the pair had gone to ground – not a whisper from either of the evil duo. Milo had feared the worst, that the discovery of the bugs had alerted them. But then a sound came through, of singing, which reassured the pair. It was the cleaner doing her rounds.

Adam was pacing up and down, kicking the punch bag each time he passed. This unnerved Milo and then the pair heard footsteps; it was Paul, eager to start his morning workout. He too, was anxious about the coming day. Adam felt an enormous weight lifted from his shoulders. 'So it wasn't just me,' he thought.

'I'm sorry if I'm seem a little frustrated, but last night I couldn't get this over to Jason and now all three of us feel it.'

Milo was worried but still tried to use the 'great faith' line one more time. 'We have to practice what we preach sometimes, Adam. That's all.'

Adam was now angry and vented his anger towards Milo. 'But not to the detriment of using the greater church as bait.' Adam gave the punch bag a punch so powerful that the bag hit Paul, knocking him over the running machine. 'Sorry, Paul. I didn't know you were there.'

'I didn't know you felt this way, Adam. I'm sorry. What's on your mind? Please tell me.'

Adam went on to tell Milo that it was all too soon after their last encounter with Slayem and Deygar to be planning an all night prayer meeting, whilst the pair could potentially be in such a blind rage. It could be an offer the pair could not pass up. Basically, the whole church in one place all night was too tempting. It would be the kind of plan 'I' would execute if on such a mission, he went on to say. 'Think like them. Would you take this opportunity?'

All three in the training room were lost for words – it all made such sense. Milo and Paul had been blinded by it. It was so obvious, yet not conceivable, even by the evil standards of Slayem and Deygar.

'I just feel in my spirit that tonight's the night.'

'But, Adam; Jason feels its going to be an awesome night of God's work and power manifested in His glory.'

'That's the problem; we have no idea how and in what form that power will be coming in.'

Adam was frustrated by the lack of activity at church. No one seemed to be taking the proper precautions for such a potentially dangerous night in the history of the church and there was no one to talk to about his concerns.

So, he thought, I'll go to the home for a few hours and try to make some sense of it all, and give a piece offering to Julie, whom he hadn't seen for a while, to apologise for his lack of attendance for the past week.

They still had responsibilities to uphold and had to secretly defend themselves and the wider church against the threat of evil forces, which was the hardest of roles and the one for which they received the least credit. But Adam ploughed on with it and thought some kind of break would give him some clarity and, just maybe, God would reveal Himself to him in some kind of new revelation.

It was still a great clear day; the mid-morning sun gave a mirrored finish to the roads, the heat glistening from the brows of the nearing hills and bridges that lined the road towards the home. Adam gave the M.V. Augusta F4 the full beans and cleared his head. Driving and riding were the two greatest ways he could do this. Just to concentrate on one solitary activity was Adam's therapy and, within twenty minutes of riding, he was feeling great.

The bike came to a screaming halt on the home's car park. The brake discs glowing with the signs of excessive speed and use.

Julie had heard the bike pull up and assumed it was Adam, so she went out to vent her frustration at his lack of attendance.

But she knew him very well and, seeing him remove his helmet and his expression underneath, she immediately knew what kind of time he was having and that the bike ride had fixed it. She didn't want to bring Adam down again.

Adam was nervous at seeing Julie and had only had the chance to speak to her on the phone recently. One of the calls was to say that they'd have to move into the top loft and to not speak of it due to an issue with Rachel being followed. The stalker story had hurt Adam; telling lies was never easy for the couple but it was for Julie's safety as well as their own that she didn't tell anyone. So the stalker story made a lot of sense.

Julie greeted Adam with a hug and the guilt enveloped him like her arms, as she hugged him and reminded him of the lie.

'How's Rachel, Adam?'

'She's fine. You should go up and see her. She'd like that.'

'I was worried about giving her location away. You never know, do you.'

'You're right, as usual, Julie. I'm glad we entrusted you with this. We had nowhere else to turn. As you know, we couldn't go to any of our parents because of endangering their lives and we are safer here.'

Adam tried to play it down but the words seemed to just speak out without any control, so he just left it as said.

'So what brings you here then?'

'I just need to do some mindless work. No offence, Julie, but no-thought-required-work, you know.' Adam was digging an even bigger hole for himself and Julie laughed at him getting himself into a knot.

'I know what you mean,' she said and gave a wink.

'So is there anything for me that's urgent?'

'No. Everything is up to date.'

Adam was feeling even more guilt and it was confirmed to him when he went into the office and saw Julie's name written on the work schedule board. She had, more or less, doubled her workload. So Adam immediately stepped up and asked if there was anything to be getting on with whilst he was there.

Julie scratched her head and then remembered that Joe needed him for something and she had simply forgotten with everything else going on, which grated on the already guilty mind of Adam. So he quickly went into the gardens and checked around the sheds and garage area to see what Joe needed him for.

Joe was busy in a potting shed, totally engaged in his duties and didn't hear Adam come through the door.

'Hiyah, Joe,' he said, which gave him a little fright. Adam gave his apologies for not knocking first, but the old gentleman soon came buzzing over to greet his friend.

Adam, at times, had confided in Joe. His outlook on life would give him great insight into the many mysteries of life. Older people had there own outlook, and more often than not, he would find a great gem of advice from good old Joe.

But Adam sensed something wasn't quite right with Joe. He had a more than weathered look about him; more than usual for a man that had worked hard all his life, outside, in all kinds of weathers. Something definitely troubled Joe but he hated attention, especially towards himself which explained why he had worked such a long time on his own, tending to his chores, planting boarders, mowing endless gardens and many, many other duties; the list was as endless as were the gardens he tended.

So Adam skirted around the subject and waited until Joe was ready to say what was troubling him, in his own time.

'So, what is it, Joe, that you wanted me to do for you? Julie mentioned that you needed me for something.'

Joe rubbed his head, rubbing a little peat across his furrowed brow, fiercely racking his brain to remember what it was.

'Oh yes, Adam. I could do with your car taking out of the garage.'

Adam quickly remembered that the Beamer hadn't been locked up in the garage for a while and it was in the garage at the family home, which reminded him that he must go and bring it back to the safety of the home garages.

Adam was concerned for Joe and was extremely worried about him.

'Joe, the car isn't in the garage. It hasn't been for a while.'

'I know, Adam; I just told Julie that for a reason to get you down here.'

Joe pulled out a couple of chairs for the pair of them to sit down. What Joe was about to say was serious.

'Well, Adam, it's me health. I'm not doing too good, sir.'

A huge lump dropped down Adam's throat as he swallowed, fearing the worst.

'I've been diagnosed with prostrate cancer.' Joe raised his hand. 'Do not worry, sir, Adam.' He often went all regal at times did 'Old Joe'. 'They've caught it early, so it will be all fine. I'll be great, so you and Rachel don't need to worry yourselves, okay.'

Adam was shocked at the news and even more so at Joe's attitude towards such a crippling disease as prostrate cancer. 'Here's a man that's apologising for getting ill, seriously ill, and he is telling us not to worry. The man is a legend; he's here again teaching me a real life lesson from a generation that goes unnoticed so often,' Adam thought to himself.

'Is there anything that Rachel and I could do for you? Anything, Joe?'

'Please try to keep this between us. Julie doesn't need to know. She is a little stressed and could do without the extra worry about me.'

'And again, typical Joe, thinking of others before himself; amazing man of immense character,' Adam thought.

Joe gave Adam a little wink and Adam understood what he meant. It was a typical thing a man of his age would do – 'I don't want to be a burden to anyone.'

But Adam gave him hope and said, 'Now I have something to pray about at tonight's prayer meeting at church.'

Joe simply said, 'Thank you'. A man of simple faith – he just believed.

Not thinking, Adam said, 'Why don't you come tonight?'

'I don't know whether I could last the whole night, but maybe just an hour. It would be nice to go to church. I must say though, I've not always been a good boy. I've had my bad times.'

'Haven't we all, Joe. If we had to be perfect to go to church the place would be empty, hey Joe.'

Adam was starting to wish he hadn't said anything. He soon remembered what could potentially happen tonight at church, but Joe needed some reassurance from something and what could be better for him than an evening in God's house?

For an hour or so Adam worked in the gardens and gave Joe the help he didn't like to ask for, well until Joe said, 'It's okay, Adam. I like to work alone. You can go, and I expect you've got a thousand better things to do than baby-sit an old man.'

So Adam popped in to see Julie and tried to broach the subject of Joe's illness. He told her that the secrecy was to not bring extra stress on her; it was Joe's idea not to tell her.

Adam felt awful about telling Julie after giving his word to Joe. But Adam needed to let her know; it wasn't like she wasn't trained for such things. The home had many an ill resident. But leaving Julie upset wasn't part of his reason for the visit, and he felt awful.

After a few hours he got back to church and noticed Paul and Milo driving out together in Pastor Miles car, as he made the turn into the church car park. 'What are they up to?' he thought.

Adam went in to see Jason and asked where the pair of them were going. Jason just responded with, 'If they need you, they would use the LPS, so relax and chill for a while.'

Adam responded with a simply, 'oh!'

'Hey, want some breakfast, Jason?'

Jason gave a quick glance at his watch and noticed it was 11.30am.

'Adam, it's 11.30. I had mine two hours ago.'

Jason was clearly a busy man, so Adam went down to the kitchen to get something to eat; Adam had a real craving for a full English breakfast: eggs, bacon, sausage and tomato – the full works. But, when opening the fridge door, he was confronted with shelf after shelf of protein shakes. He lost the craving just as quickly as getting it and decided on a quick training session down in the training room.

Adam gave it his all and had such a good training session that, once he was all finished, he fell fast asleep in Milo's chair next to the computer in a heap of sweat, holding his punched blooded knuckles in his lap.

Milo and Paul were on a new mission and that mission was to cheer up Adam and try to lift his spirits, but he wasn't down at all, just frustrated by the lack of support from his peers, especially Milo. They went to a motorbike store to get Adam a gift that he mentioned a time ago; just a little something to say thanks. It was a typical way for a man to apologise, by way of a gift. They bagged up the items and then headed back to church.

The pair got back to church and Paul was so excited about giving Adam the bag of surprises that he was almost giddy, like he'd lost twenty years on the journey back from the bike shop.

Paul headed for the kitchen thinking he'd be in there stuffing his face on energy bars and protein shakes. And when he opened the fridge, his theory was confirmed; there were two shakes missing – one for before a workout and one after he'd finished.

'He's downstairs,' Paul thought.

Paul signalled Pastor Miles downstairs with his hands – an internationally known gesture which made Milo laughed out loud.

The pair went to Milo's office and noticed that Adam had locked himself down there, closing up the secret door, to not alert anyone to his presence.

Once all the relevant levers and pulleys were pushed and pulled, the pair were on their way down only to find Adam fast asleep. Paul went right up close to Adam to mimic him in his sleep. Milo was not so sure, so kept well back. He whispered, 'Be careful. You know what they say about sleeping dogs.'

'No way. He's well out of it.'

With that said, Adam leapt up, grabbing Paul by the throat and pinning him to the gym floor.

'What was that about letting sleeping dogs lie?'

All three started to laugh so much it brought Pastor Miles to tears. The three hadn't laughed like that for what seemed a life time and they soon realised that it was the thing the Master Disciples had been missing.

Once the three of them had composed themselves, they quickly told Adam what they'd been up to and gave him the bag of surprises.

Adam quickly opened it up; it was an assortment of vital body protection parts for Adam; including the all important spare spine for Adam's leather M.V jacket and various other carbon fibre body armour pieces. He quickly grabbed his jacket from the hook and quickly fitted them.

Adam was so impressed by their kindness that he got a little emotional.

'I'm sorry, guys. I was jumping the gun about tonight's meeting. I'll try to relax a little more.'

Adam went on to tell the pair about Joe and his unfortunate news and that he was coming tonight to the prayer meeting in hope of a miracle.

The three Master Disciples had a few hours to study and pray together and did so with their minds focused on the meeting that night.

Afterwards, the three spilt up and Adam went to see Rachel and Grace to make sure all was well and tell her of the unfortunate news of Joe. As soon she heard of the terrible news she was straight on the phone to other pastor's wives.

Adam wanted desperately to distract his mind and gave Grace a bath before putting her down to sleep. It seemed it was the right thing to do, and Adam felt like the responsible father that he was, under the circumstances.

'A father to one; it felt like a father to many,' he thought to himself as he poured the soft water over his daughter's head, washing out the baby soft shampoo from her beautiful blond hair.

Adam welled up. The emotion of it all was so overwhelming and he felt weakened by it, not strengthened by it at all.

He shook his head and re-focused his thoughts. He had to focus on what God wanted to achieve on this night, not what Adam Fuller wanted.

All three Master Disciples did what they could to distract their minds from the meeting that was about to unfold before them. Milo tried a little time in his garden but it had been so long since he had spent in it that it seemed like an endless task. The garden was in such a state that this only frustrated him further. He had exacting standards that only he could match; this again infuriated him in reminding him he should be retired and not being a Master Disciple in the first instance.

Paul did what he thought was best and went for a run. All the inactivity whilst on his cancer treatment made his new love of fitness his only outlet for stress relief, and it was now his best weapon against the forces of evil that now preyed upon them.

Time did what it always did, and ticked forever closer to that inevitable time of seven o'clock.

Adam kissed Rachel and Grace goodnight before heading out on the bike. He did so, not knowing the events that were going to unfold before them.

He needed to get there early but not too early to distract Jason from his duties.

Chapter Twenty
He Was Right to Worry?

*Matthew 6v27 'Who of you worrying can add a single hour to his life?...
v34 'Therefore do not worry about tomorrow, for tomorrow will worry
about itself. Each day has enough of its own.'*

THE CHURCH WAS FULL. NO ONE was expecting this kind of turnout for a Monday night prayer meeting, especially an all-nighter.

Adam was on edge. Earlier, before the church meeting had started filling up, he meticulously checked all the exits, fire doors and the alarm systems, and still he felt nervous; every noise or hand clap gave his heart a workout. His heart rate jumped from a relative 55bpm which was more than proof of a good fitness level, to an alarming 148bpm within seconds; he feared a heart attack if he didn't get it under control.

Adam gave a quick glance over to Milo to see how he was coping.

He was deep in prayer, even though he seemed fully focused on Jason. Adam had seen this look a million times and never let on to it. Milo had a glazed look towards his subject but his mind was elsewhere. And Adam knew exactly where.

Jason stood up and addressed the congregation by first announcing a wedding for the following weekend of Charlotte and Adam.

Adam heard his own name read out and panicked, then the whole congregation clapped, which unnerved him further. He quickly got up to look around and then was pulled down by the edge of his jacket by Paul, who quickly gave him the conformation that he so desperately needed. 'Mate, I thought it was you as well,' he said and gave Adam the reassuring wink he always gave when he was nervous.

The prayer service started and Jason lead the first session. The whole emphasis of the night was to raise the profile of prayer. His exact words were, 'We must be a praying people. Praying must be one of our primary focuses as believers.' He went on to say that the communication between his church and their Lord was the 'key' to knowing Him better. 'Better talkers meant better listeners.' It was an amazing way to communicate to people on a grand scale and it also meant that he didn't need to explain the main objective of the evening.

So he indicated to the worship leader to start to play.

With that the band struck up, the drums seemed louder to Adam, but it was understandable under the circumstances – he was a bag of nerves. He had to put it behind him and try to focus on the meeting. After all, he could get a lot out it if he was just to let his mind concentrate on what Jason was saying and not what his mind was shouting.

Adam remained seated whilst the rest of the congregation stood to sing. He lent forward and rested his elbows on his knees and started to pray. 'Oh, Lord. Help me to listen to that calm, still voice tonight and not the raging violent inner-me, shouting to leave my seat and check the exits and windows for a fourth time. Please, Lord. I am leaving it all tonight in Your capable hands. Amen.'

The worship was intense and vibrant and was lead by Jason's words of encouragement that, at times, were as powerful as a full length sermon. He was on great form and the two hours he lead his session were over in what seemed like moments.

Then it was Pastor Miles' turn and he was to lead session two. Again, he too had put his worries to one side and he was on great form, also starting this session with a sermon-like introduction. Milo went on for what seemed a few minutes.

Adam gave a quick look at his watch to check the time – 2.30am. He shook his head in disbelief. No way was it that time! Had he missed two hours? The meeting did start a little after its planned time but that was normal for a prayer meeting with all the people excited just to be there. Adam looked again; it really was 2.30am. His Breitling watch never missed a stroke.

Adam went outside; the bitter cold of that time of the early hours was enough to confirm the time. But he had to ask for a second opinion; he called Malcolm. 'Have you the correct time, Malc?'

He too rolled up his sleeve, after reluctantly taking off his extra think ski gloves, and gave Adam the time. '2.32am precisely, Adam,' He shouted back.

What had happened to the time? Where had it gone? Maybe it was one of the ways God was using to help Adam cope. After all, he did pray for help in the prayer meeting.

Again Adam shook his head to re-focus and went back into the meeting. Pastor Miles' session was coming to a close and, like all the other session before; they had a coffee break and quick biscuit to reenergise the lagging congregation.

But, strangely, the congregation wasn't lagging and, unlike prayer meetings of the past, when a session finished and people inevitably snuck away and left (at least to say they went to one of the sessions, so not to feel so guilty when asked later), no one left. Amazingly, people had called others during the first interval on their mobile phones, telling them of the amazing prayer and worship that they were missing out on. And more people were on their way.

What happened next, shook Adam to his very core.

Pastor Miles session went amazingly due to his honesty. He went on to talk openly about planning Paul's funeral and that, whilst doing so, he still persevered with Prayer, continuing in faith whilst, at the same time, planning for the practicalities of his death. Milo was so transparent and honesty to the point that members of the church started to weep for him.

Pastor Miles went on to say, with a huge lump in his throat, the emotion of it all was too much to bear.

'I shouldn't have planned for Paul's funeral. It was a lack of faith on my part and please, church, can you forgive my lack, my doubt in faith at that time?'

But that wasn't the thing that shook Adam the most; it was the presence of his wife, Rachel, sitting beside him. Adam turned to her and gave a smile – a smile of 'yes, you should be here and it's cool. God's peace is here.'

Rachel reached down, held her husband's hand so tightly and leant in towards him. 'Grace is fine. Julie is house-sitting.'

Adam let out a little snigger at Rachel's comment about the 'house-sitting'. The three of them lived in an old, open plan studio loft in a rest home for the elderly. Adam, however, felt the richer man for it. He was humbled by the way life had shaped itself and the outcome that was about to unfold before them. He was more convinced than ever that God was going to bring them out of this mission, to the other side, safe and with a deeper love and understanding of their faith.

The penultimate session was Paul's, and the whole church cheered him, as he rose to the lectern to start.

After a good forty seconds of cheers and applause, Paul brought the whole proceedings back to focus on the task at hand. 'I hope that was for His Glory,' he said, pointing up towards the heavens. Again, the church cheered and let out their thanks for his healing and it was very apt.

Paul's session was all on thanksgiving for answered prayers and for the congregation to start practicing; thanking for prayers that hadn't been answered yet.

But then some of the main leadership came forward. Rachel, one of them, spoke:

'Church, please stand with me. We feel, as a church leadership team, that we should stand with our elite: the leaders, Pastor Paul, Pastor Jason and Pastor Miles. And lay hands on them and pray for this next phase of church life and for their health and the health of their families.'

Adam felt awkward because he needed to be up there as well, receiving prayer, and Rachel knew it also. Pastor Miles looked up as Adam thought it, and caught his eye; Pastor Miles nodded to him to come over and join them.

The prayer time was powerful, and Adam finally felt part of a team, even though no one could ever know his real position in the church and what risks it carried. He was the appointed 'Guardian of the church'; the 'Master Disciple'; the fighter and defender of evil.

All these titles and many more were going through his mind, but the main one now was 'team player'. He couldn't do anything without Milo, Paul and Jason; all had a part to play, none more important than anyone else, but everyone vital to the mission.

Adam knew he would never stand in church to receive gratitude or applause from anyone for his mission. But he was soon enwrapped in a vivid vision, standing in heaven, receiving the recognition that he desired so much and for so long. He was there in the Almighty's presence, kneeling down before Him and being knighted with the Word of God that is sharper than any two-edged sword.

Adam came to and was sitting back down next to Rachel, drinking a cup of strong coffee and eating a biscuit.

'What happened?' Adam thought. One minute he was in a prayer meeting, seeing an amazing vision, then he was sitting down drinking a cup of coffee and nibbling on a chocolate biscuit.

All the leaders and their wife's and partners had gathered in a circle in the main fellowship meeting hall. They were discussing the prayer meeting and having a time of reflection. Whilst the others carried on talking, Adam shook his head again; had he missed a session? He quickly gave his watch a glance; it was 5.30am.

He gave a look over to a nearby window and saw the morning sunrise, which gave an orange glow across the floor of the hall; it was beautiful to see 'His Glory' in such a tangible and real way. A sun rise, he'd seen thousands before but this one had significance – a clear sign; someone had been watching over the whole evening.

Adam sat there imaging God sending angels from heaven to guard the church grounds, like sentries in a Holy army, several on each of the corners of the Temple – a real bible moment for Adam in the twenty-first century.

Adam turned to Rachel, whilst she was taking a sip of coffee, to ask the obvious question. 'What happened to me this morning?'

Rachel put her coffee cup down. 'Well, where do I start, eh? You have been on the floor for the past two, well nearly three, hours.'

'Amazing!' was all Adam could muster.

There worries were dumbfounding. Nothing happened and nothing could. After all, they were in church with hundreds of believers. Who and what could break through that wall of faith?

Chapter Twenty-one
The Countdown Begins

Ephesians 6v10-13
'Finally, be strong in the Lord and in his mighty power. Put on the full armour of God so that you can take your stand against the devil's schemes. For our struggle is not against flesh and blood, but against the rulers, against the authorities, against the powers of this dark world and against the spiritual forces of evil in the heavenly realms. Therefore put on the full armour of God, so that when the day of evil comes, you may be able to stand your ground, and after you have done everything, to stand.'

SURPRISINGLY, EVERYONE FELT RATHER SPRIGHTLY CONSIDERING they had gone nearly twenty-four hours without any sleep – well, nearly all.

The others teased Adam for having his three hour nap on the floor of the main sanctuary.

'It wasn't a nap,' Adam protested. 'It was a God-ordained, planned intervention. He did it to speak to me and ease my mind of the burden of worry.'

Paul could clearly see Adam was feeling a little frustrated by the others teasing him and quickly changed the subject.

'Well, Adam. I don't know about you but I feel like a mobile phone that's been over charged. I feel great, like I have slept.'

Adam turned to Paul with a look of surprise written all over his face. 'Its funny you should say that because I was thinking of a similar picture in my mind.'

Milo stood up. 'We need to be somewhere else a little more important like…' Milo indicated with his head, nodding towards the floor, his vision transfixed on the floor of the hall.

Adam quickly realised that Milo was alerting them all to the training room. All three Master Disciples got up and quickly made their way to the all important training room to find out the next move of Deygar and Slayem.

All three were soon down there and huddled around the computer. Once the computer had got out of hibernation mode and the listening devices had been dragged into action with the help of Milo with the computers mouse, they awaited the sound of two evil men plotting.

There was a simultaneous sigh from the three of them, as nothing came up, just the sound of a radio and a man singing along, very badly, to the music playing. It was a tech guy checking Derek Greyer's computer system and running scan and virus software, keeping all the high-tech systems in fine working order. But he had run into problems; the high-powered laptop he used to run system checks was running a little slower than usual and this troubled him. He couldn't ask Mr Greyer because, after all, it was only 6:20am.

Shaun Wanes was one of the only employees of Derek Greyer that he could trust in his office with access to his personal computer files and private information (well, this is what he was lead to believe. Mr Greyer still had very private information for which he had the most sophisticated password system known to man – bio-metrics; his own fingerprint could only be used to open such files). But, at this time, it wasn't access that was the issue. The high-powered laptop he used to check the computer systems throughout the Greyer building, at a moment's notice, seemed a little slower than usual.

This bothered Shaun. He was an absolute perfectionist and if his machine wasn't up to the job he was not happy.

The system was a hard-wired type, but he had access to a wireless system that, at times, he was reluctant to use due to the secret and sensitive personal information getting lost or intercepted. But the machine was using both systems simultaneously. The anti-virus check was hard-wired so he could not move the laptop yet, but he was going to move it off Derek Greyer's desk as soon as that part was done to see if it would improve the speed.

All three Master Disciples were sitting and praying that this techie wouldn't find the bugs left on the desk, because it could be a slight possibility that they were causing the interference with his laptop.

'Please! Please don't let him, Lord,' they uttered under their breath with every move he made in that office.

The current waiting time on the virus check was eight minutes so Shaun got up to get a drink of water from the cooler. As he walked past the desk he glanced over and noticed the paperweight from Barns Tech, with its oversized microchip inside. He picked it up for a closer inspection and was amazed by the craftsmanship and precision of such a beautiful paperweight, not knowing it was an elaborate fake.

As he held it for a moment he noticed the speed of the laptop increase a noticeable amount. He reached over to check the laptop's speed via the taskbar at the bottom of the screen and checked the system. The speed had increased by 24,000bytes per second. This bothered Shaun. He brought the paperweight closer to the laptop and his theory was proven when the laptop slowed down again.

He paused a moment, wondering why a paperweight would slow down his laptop. Shaun was running all kinds of theories through his meticulous mind. And, as he thought through the possibilities, the Master Disciples were waiting and praying back at the church, fearing the worst.

Would he or wouldn't he discover the paperweight's true function? Their work would come to a crashing halt if they were uncovered. Knowing the evil duo's activities was the reason they were so ahead in the race against good and evil.

Shaun cradled the paperweight, like it was explosive device or a precious stone, and gently placed it to rest on the drinks cabinet next to the huge bank of Television screens, out of harm's way and away from the laptop, so he could get his work done and get out of there before Mr Greyer was due to come in. If he was to find him still there he would not be pleased with him, and Shaun feared the ramifications of such an act of disobedience would result in him being fired.

The Master Disciples breathed a sigh of relief as Shaun completed his work without hinder or worry of the true inner workings of the paperweight. He was too concerned about running all the necessary anti-virus software and backing up the computer system before Mr Greyer's arrival.

As Shaun finished his work and packed up his laptop, he quickly remembered to replace the paperweight to its original place, to ensure of no suspicious activity; fearing Mr Greyer at all times and giving him the utmost respect was a major part of his job description.

As the door slammed shut, the Master Disciples let out an almighty sigh of relief. It was as if they had been holding their breath the whole time Shaun was in there.

Adam got up. 'I need a coffee or something. That has worn me out more than a 10K run.'

Milo quickly chirped in. 'What in 'hell' are those two up to? Does anyone realise how long it's been since we heard from them?'

All three looked at one another in shock and realised the magnitude of that statement: 'what in Hell'. The statement rang in their heads for the next hour as the three of them drank coffee, prayed together and encouraged one another.

Milo prayed. 'So now, Lord, go with us as we go about our normal daily routines. Be with us, Lord, and be one step ahead of us this day. Amen.'

Adam got up and headed for the training room. Paul could clearly see the look of concern written all over Adam's face and quickly followed him down there.

Once down, Paul found Adam 'getting kitted up', as Adam would say.

'What are you doing, Adam?'

Adam turned and answered. 'It's not going to be a normal day. I'm afraid it's going to be anything but normal.'

Adam went on talking as he put on his newly acquired body armour and biker's leathers and started to load the beanie weapon up with shells.

'why are you getting kitted up? Does Milo know that gun is in the church?' Paul persisted.

'For Battle. And, Paul, this is not the church, it's the training room.' Adam pumped a round into the chamber so it was ready to shoot then strapped it to his ankle before grabbing his helmet and gloves.

Paul could clearly sense that Adam was on a different spiritual plane than normal and he was more inclined to go with it and not dismiss it as madness today. Adam was confident and even looked slightly different; he would even go as far as saying that he looked a little taller than usual. But Paul couldn't put a finger on what it was; he was just 'different'. He was clutching at straws at the specifics of *how* he was different.

But then it hit Paul like a round from that gun strapped to Adam's ankle; God immediately spoke to him, saying it was the day of reconciliation and completion. The word Paul struggled with was 'reconciliation'. Reconciliation with whom and why? The word signifies a longing to resolve an issue, but this was a 'battle', as Adam had said. Paul had to regain his focus and put it to the back of his mind.

As Paul stood there pondering his thoughts, Adam walked towards the stairs to go back, then Paul turned and shouted, 'Now what do we do, Adam?'

Adam had got about halfway up the staircase and then turned to Paul. He said, in a quiet and calm voice – a calmness and a depth that Paul hadn't seen in a while – 'I don't know, Paul. I just feel that I should be ready.'

With that said, Adam turned and carried on, saying under his breath, as he stepped the remainder of the staircase, 'I just need to be ready for anything.'

Paul caught up with Adam in his office.

'What is it, Adam? What's bothering you, brother?'

The word 'brother' struck a cord in Adam and he broke. 'You see, Paul; you, Milo and Jason are pastors of this church, a church that recognises you and your mission within it. Who am I? I'll tell you what I am – I'm the 'Godly killer'. I have to slay evil blood-thirsty men who are set to betray believers and kill us and then arrange a false and untrue split in the church of God, like others that have gone before us throughout the church's history. And I'm scared and fearful for the future, for my family and what happens to them if we fail. Sorry – if *I* fail.'

Adam was truly scared and now doubt had crept into his heart.

Paul had to act quickly and say the right thing before it was too late for all of them. He grabbed Adam by his shoulders and met his eyes with his. 'Hear this; you are a son of the living God and you will protect this church with the gift that God has bestowed upon you – a strong and mighty gift that has been passed on – and your family will be surrounded by the Angels from the heavens. They will come to no harm.' Even Paul was in shock with the words coming from his own mouth.

Adam didn't say anything. He just felt so blessed by the words of encouragement. The pair of them received such a surge of faith that filled their hearts.

Paul was still concerned about what Adam had said. 'What was that you said about churches throughout history? Who told you that?'

'To be honest, Paul, I don't know. I think it was a word of knowledge. That's why weak churches close their doors, because some do literality have the life taken from them. It's probably where that phrase comes from: That church is dead.'

The pair stared at each other for a moment, both thinking about what was said then Adam grabbed Paul by his shoulders this time and said, 'Be ready, Paul. God didn't heal you just to be pastor of this church but also to protect it. You are my right hand man. We have to protect Milo and especially Jason, the future spiritual leader of this church. He has no skill in defeating this present evil. God has blessed Milo and given him a new wave of faith and power.'

Paul just stood there and listened attentively at the words coming from Adam's mouth.

'Even if one of us fails, we must protect Milo and Jason to the death and just pray that God makes up for any lack in our skills, faith or power.'

Deygar and Slayem were preparing for the conclusion: the battle that would see the end of the Master Disciples. In their soon-to-be-acquired city, free of believers, who could possibly be of any threat to their evil intentions?

All they focused their energy on was the long-life-giving blood of the Master Disciples, soon to be in their possession.

'Seth is mine, okay, Deygar. I will make the kill. The others I may help and assist you with but under any circumstances, you do not kill Seth.'

The evil duo were planning their schemes in the huge container of Slayem's, in Derek Greyer's loading bay, away from any listening devices. The pen was still in his jacket pocket on the back seat of Derek's Bentley and the paperweight was of no use all the way up on the fifty-seventh floor on his desk.

'He has humiliated me before and he will be tortured. He is to feel the pain of my thousand year reign as the last of the remaining Dark Lords.'

Derek Greyer was shaken to his very core and was fearful for his own life. He felt unsure about Slayem's motivation in agreeing, and finally succumbing, to meeting him all those months ago. He had to think carefully. He knew Slayem's ability regarding his thoughts and quickly went on to the matter at hand. He knew that he had to focus and join in with Slayem or he would read into it, or worse, read his mind and finish the job. He quickly shook his head. It was like he had no control over his very thought pattern. He stood up and raised his sword. 'I will honour my father's death and slay my father's killer,' he said, hoping that would be enough to wipe his current thought processes.

Slayem was no fool and knew every devious thought that Derek Greyer just had, but he didn't let on to that fact. 'So he thinks he's being used. Well, he's right on that one. Once all Master Disciples are down he will be the last to fall under my sword,' Slayem thought to himself, as he grabbed the last item of battle dress – that titanium neck collar.

Slayem was now fully dressed for battle with that deadly Ronin sword at his side. He quickly remembered to cover up the battle gear with the discreet trench coat he had borrowed from Derek's wardrobe. He to was dressed for battle, but more in line with the twenty-first century, with a smart dress shirt (designer of course), with loose fitting trousers and smart, but functional, hiking-style leather boots. After all, he needed to move around freely and not look like he was going into a medieval battle. He looked like a cross between a samurai warrior and the shop window dummy from the GAP. Slayem turned to Derek and simply said, 'Remember I was around before trousers and designer labels were even thought of, let alone invented.'

Derek shook his head again, trying to focus, his thoughts getting the better of him yet again. It was like Slayem's ability was getting stronger with every minute that went by, edging ever closer to the final meeting, and the battle that would decide everyone's fate, including Derek Greyer. At this point, he felt he was up against four adversaries.

The pair walked towards the cars. Their steps now felt more ready and assured than ever. Deygar was ready; his heart was in his mouth but he felt confident about the plan they had made.

Slayem, on the other hand, was over-confident and was dancing rather than walking towards the car. His steps were rhythmic, like a jig. He turned to Derek.

'Deygar, I know your thoughts and *we* are going to get through this. It's a good plan, and thanks to you, we will see the victory.'

Derek was dumbstruck. Maybe he was reading too much into it and maybe he had known all along that he could, at times, put his trust into others. Slayem was the first to receive his trust. After all, he is an imposing kind of character.

The two of them were ready. Slayem was driving the M5 BMW and Deygar was in his Bentley. They opened up an open phone line between the two cars and spoke, hands-free.

'Okay, are we ready, warrior?' said the confident Slayem.

A simple 'Yes' was the response from Deygar.

The two cars pulled out of the loading bay of Greyer Industries to play out their finely tuned plan, a plan no one knew about but the evil Dark Lords themselves.

As their day had started yesterday, for Adam, Milo, Paul and Jason the clock was of no meaning to them and all was a little confusing.

Paul called to Adam for breakfast. 'It's 8.30 want some breaky, Ad?' There was a moment's pause.

'What? I'm ready for some lunch mate.'

The all-night prayer meeting had taken its toll on them all, especially on the matter of the real time.

But then Adam jumped from his seat. 'It's the LPS; it's gone off in his pocket. That's weird. I'm sitting next to the very computer that sends the signal.' Rather than answer the handset, he used the computer. It was Milo.

When did he go out? Was Adam's immediate thought. And why didn't he say any thing to anyone else?

Paul rushed down to find Adam on the computer and then finally picked up the handset to speak to Milo.

'Where are you, Milo? And why are you out on your own without telling any of us?'

'No, I'm with Jason but I'm being followed by Deygar's Bentley.'

It wasn't the best of times to lecture Milo but Adam did anyway. 'What have we been talking about? We have, if I'm not mistaken, been talking about the importance of you two, and you are off driving together with Derek Greyer following you.' As Adam said it out loud, he turned to Paul and said 'Ambush! It's an ambush, Milo. Don't stop for anything. Run red lights. Just keep moving. We have you on the LPS system. Just stay in the car. Paul, you take the other Mondeo, that may confuse them a little. I'll go on the bike and get there quicker, before it's too late.'

'Why didn't we hear about this on the computer bug thingy?'

Adam reached over and noticed the sound had been pulled from the rear of the computer, not that it would have helped much. Paul quickly replaced it, only to hear the laughter of Derek Greyer and the sound of the huge, six and a quarter litre engine of the Bentley revving up, and then the slamming and crushing sound of metal as the car rammed into the rear of Jason and Milo.

Paul was in a panic and he couldn't do anything. 'No, Dad! No!'

Adam tried to regain Paul's focus and pulled him towards the car park outside. The fresh morning air invigorated him but only for the moment. His thoughts were with his father and Jason, helpless in a car together with an evil man intent on killing the pair of them for no other reason than for greed.

Chapter Twenty-Two
The Battle Begins

Isaiah 13v15 'Whoever is captured will be thrust through;
All who caught will fall by the sword.'

MILO AND JASON PRAYED LIKE THEY'D never prayed before, as the Bentley of Derek Greyer rammed them again, hoping the strength of the Mondeo would hold up against that mighty Bentley Turbo. With all its power, the little Ford hadn't got a chance of surviving long, so Jason increased the speed, running red lights and narrowly escaping a serious accident.

Milo reached over to the back seat to grab his sword, as Jason wrestled with driving the battered Mondeo, now showing more than enough battle scars at the rear.

As the car turned quickly into Britland Street, the whole rear bumper of the Mondeo flew off into a newspaper stand, hitting the seller across his chest, sending him into a pile of newspapers.

'Please, Lord. Just bless that poor man,' was all Jason could say under the circumstances. He was still trying to outrun Derek Greyer.

Adam was racing towards the signal on the LPS that was still flashing and beeping, guiding Adam on his way. The M.V's engine was screaming. Adam had to use the bike to its limit. His mind was racing at the same pace as the bike, fearing the worst and praying with every breath he took.

Paul was trailing behind in his identical Mondeo. He too was panic stricken with worry about the dire situation his father and Jason were in. With that thought, Paul's car was rammed into. It was Slayem in the M5 BMW. Not expecting to be hit, Paul was fighting to control the car. The puny power of the Mondeo was no match for the 400 horse power of that powerful M5 Beamer.

'Hey, I've got Paul, I think, in the other car,' Slayem called out. 'How are you doing, Deygar, with Milo?'

'I'm doing great. Milo's car will be disabled very soon and then they will be on foot, as planned.'

Slayem went in for the final attack on Paul's car; he slammed the Beamer into second gear, flooring the accelerator. The car quickly accelerated towards the rear of Paul's already beaten car. He hit it so hard that it sent it into a row of parked cars. The cars airbag immediately deployed, cradling Paul's face from the broke class and debris.

Slayem drove on in the beaten M5, its airbag also deployed holding his arrogant face with a smug smile. But with the M5's sheer size, it could take a beating and still be drivable.

Paul was doubtful his Mondeo could do the same, but he checked the damage and, amazingly, he was fine. That was a miracle in itself. He quickly gathered himself and called Adam on the LPS

Adam pushed the button on the grip of the M.V and answered.

'What is it?'

'It's Paul. I've just been rammed off the road by Slayem in the violet M5.'

'Does the Mondeo still work? If not, Paul, get a vehicle of some kind. They are trying to separate us for individual battles. And, Paul, God be with you.'

Paul could only respond with the same sentiment. 'And you also.'

Paul tried turning the key of the Mondeo with little faith. It had, however, survived the crash. The car started just in time, as the sirens of the police were getting close to the scene of the accident.

Paul quickly reversed the Mondeo and got the signal of Milo on the LPS. He was still moving. 'Thank God,' he thought as he raced towards them as quickly as the Mondeo could go, which wasn't fast; it was barely 30mph.

Milo's car had also seen better days and was limping its way from the main part of the city, away from all the hustle and noise of the city, now engulfed in the sound of sirens of the police and the ambulance services, attending to the accidents that trailed behind them in their wake.

They were in a heavily industrialised part of the city where there still lay parts that hadn't been redeveloped or discovered by Greyer Industries. This part was considered by many older folk as the original city before development had taken over the once-tiny city. It was still teaming with old Art Deco type buildings of the 1920s. Their beauty was recognised by the few and they were now subject to many a protest to either demolish or restore them. It was a crying shame but they took up precious space. The tallest was only eight storeys high; with certain people's small-minded ideals, that was not 'cost effective in this high rise modern age'.

Milo was worried for Jason. 'When we do stop, and we will, I need you to run. And listen; look at me.' Milo tried to engage Jason. 'Please run to church, any church, and don't turn back. The church has three heroes; we don't need a forth so get to holy ground. You will be out of harm's way in any church.'

Adam could make out Deygar's Bentley in the distance, gaining on them, carefully trying to avoid the debris of the fallen pieces of Milo's car scattered all over the road.

Milo's Mondeo was failing and was now crawling along with Deygar mercilessly ramming the vehicle, knowing full well that it wouldn't go much further, laughing as he did so.

'It won't be long,' he thought as he grabbed his sword from the thick pile carpeted floor of the battered two hundred thousand pound car that was fit for scrap now. The front was severally damaged and the rear was showing some battle scars, also narrowly escaping death. He lost the rear end on the same turn that Jason lost his rear bumper to the unfortunate newspaper seller, hitting a lamp column, knocking it down, landing onto a car stopped at the traffic lights. The people inside might have been seriously injured but, as usual, he cared for no one but himself.

The Mondeo of Milo's was only managing 8 mph now and it was now time for Jason to get out. The whole rear of the car was literality being dragged by the front wheels, the rear wheels locked up by the crushed panels of the strong modest Ford Mondeo that had held up to some serious damage by Deygar.

Adam raced past as Deygar went in for the last of his crushing hits of his car. Milo grabbed the wheel and shouted to Jason to get out and run.

'That's Adam on the bike. Get gone, Jason, and may God be with you.' Milo kicked open the door with his leg, as he slipped into the driver's seat.

Jason was on foot now and needed to move quickly to avoid Deygar seeing him. All his focus was on the speeding object that had flown past at over 60mph.

'We've got Seth here, Slayem,' was all Derek Greyer could shout out. He was in a panic now; he was clearly outnumbered and was seriously contemplating aborting the plan.

Both cars came to rest, as the Mondeo's engine finally gave up just a few yards from where Jason got out.

Milo was out of the car in seconds, sword in hand and ready for anything, but so was Deygar. His sword was drawn and also his trademark Glock Pistol. He quickly raised it toward Jason making his way down the street.

Adam was off the bike, his sword drawn, and could see Deygar's desperate attempts to even the numbers up, as he pulled the trigger. A loud gun shot went off and, as Adam ran, it was all moving in slow motion, as he saw Jason fall from the 9mm round striking his left shoulder, rendering him to the floor in a heap.

'No!' Adam and Milo shouted simultaneously, completely in shock. Derek had live rounds in his weapon.

Adam pulled the beanie weapon from his ankle and shot Deygar directly in the chest. As he fell, he got off another round from that deadly weapon, hitting Adam in the left leg, knocking him down.

Milo, fearing the worst, was confronted with the issue of who to run to first to help. Jason was the closer of the two but with that weapon still in Deygar's hand he needed to prioritise the removal of it. As he got closer to Deygar he got up, clutching his chest with his left hand, with the Glock still clasped in his right. He lifted it up to aim directly at Milo, as he did a little smirk arose on his face. 'Maybe this isn't the right way to go,' he thought as he clasped the gun, trigger finger itching ready to fire.

When Milo's faith rose up in his heart, fearing the death of Jason and Adam (he was all there was in terms of a Master Disciple), he shouted out these words: 'It is written that *no weapon formed against us shall stand.*'

Deygar pulled the trigger of the ever-reliable Glock (a weapon that can withstand any environment that can be thrown at it, even shooting under water), but it jammed up.

He pulled the trigger again and the same again – the weapon jammed up completely.

In a complete act of desperation, Deygar threw the gun, nearly hitting Milo. It hit a nearby wall and the Glock went off repeatedly, emptying out the gun's magazine.

Milo's faith hit new heights, as Deygar drew his sword, ready for the bloody battle that he intends to be victorious in.

Their swords clashed and, in the fury of swords clashing, Adam limped his way over to Jason. He was in a bad way. The bullet from the Glock had ripped through his shoulder, dislocating the bone, shattering it in two. There was blood everywhere and Adam tried hard to be calm. But he couldn't hide it; he was extremely worried for Jason. He desperately needed medical attention. If he didn't get it soon he would possibly lose his arm from the shoulder down.

All Adam could do was make him comfortable and try to reassure him. Adam got up; Milo needed him, so he placed a hand on Jason's head and simply said, 'Lord, protect Jason and be with us all now.'

Adam rushed over to Milo who was tiring. His sword was low and he was finding it harder to raise it with every strike from Deygar's sword.

Deygar was finding it hard to believe that Adam was fine after being shot in the leg with the Glock. Adam unsheathed his sword and Deygar noticed that the slider on the left knee of Adam's bike leathers was damaged but his knee was fine, still limping a little, but fine.

Deygar was in a dire situation and was in need of some help.

'Seth, your challenger will be here soon. I'm here for Milo and Milo only.'

Adam wasn't having any of it, holding his sword out in the ready stance. 'No Deygar. My job is to protect believers and Milo is a believer.'

The three of them turned when they heard the sound of the battered car Paul was driving with Slayem in pursuit.

Derek was safe in his mind now that Slayem was there and was quick to take full advantage of it, striking his sword towards Milo. But Adam was quick to react and guarded his strike with his own sword as Derek's sword dropped. Adam then gave Deygar a powerful kick into his chest, knocking him off his feet, dropping his sword as the steel metal clattered across the floor.

Paul was out of the car and was running over to defend his father but Slayem was right behind him, sword ready to strike out.

Adam thought quickly, seeing this unfold before his eyes, and pulled out the Beanie, knowing full well that it was ready to fire. He fired it directly at Slayem (clearly a God-targeted shot), hitting the moving target directly in the chest, throwing Slayem back ten yards or so into a rolling heap on the floor. Paul looked round to see Slayem on the floor.

Adam shouted out, 'Make the kill! Make the kill!'

Paul got his sword out to finish it, but Slayem was quick to kick himself back up onto his feet. He decided not to kill Paul straight away – his arrogance and ego forever at the forefront of his mind – and instead gave him such a powerful kick to the face, knocking him unconscious.

'I'll deal with you later. I've got the starter and main course to get through first.'

Adam was clearly in trouble and had to think fast. God needed to intervene quickly.

As Slayem stepped over the unconscious body of Paul, Adam feared he would make the kill of Paul quite final. Slayem reached his sword out in defiance.

'It's you I came here for,' Slayem said through gritted teeth. 'I'll drink of your blood this night, Seth.'

Adam was clearly worried that Paul wasn't moving and Milo was being gradually worn down by the sheer fitness and power of the younger Deygar. It would only be a matter of time before Derek was to make his first kill as a Dark Lord.

Adam had to think quickly and pumped another round into the beanie's chamber and fired it; it hit Slayem in his side, damaging his armour badly and throwing him on to the floor again. It was the final straw for Slayem. As he got himself up his anger was rife and he thirsted for Adam's blood.

Paul began to come around and raised his head to witness what was going on. He quickly got to his feet and rushed over in a daze (from the kick he received from Slayem) to help his father, who has been kicked down by Deygar. Paul's timing was God sent.

Derek stood over the worn-down, seventy-seven year old man, who was clearly showing his age, with his sword ready to make the kill that had been overdue in the mind of Derek Greyer for over thirty years.

Paul got there in the nick of time and struck Deygar's sword-bearing arm, slicing through his jacket, and first blood in Gods' favour was shed.

Paul looked down. There was clearly blood running down the edge of his sword and the reality of his calling hit home. He was quickly burdened with the enormity of it all. After all, he was a pastor's kid and he was a relatively calm man before he was thrust into the Master Disciple world – a world that had been alien to him until he reached eighteen and even then he wasn't told the full extent of the responsibility of it all.

Derek was taken aback when he looked at his arm and was fearful; his main sword-wielding arm was now badly wounded.

Adam and Slayem were now fighting; their swords clashing together. In between the swords clashing there was the odd kick and punch making contact with Slayem, but with Slayem being so heavily armoured it was having little or no effect. His chest plate and other pads were so good; all Adam was doing was just wasting much-needed energy.

Slayem was a little worried; Seth's fitness was good and he clearly showed a good level of cardio-fitness, but it was Adam's power that concerned him. Even with the pads he was having more of an effect than Adam first thought.

With a quick flick of Slayem's finger he turned his sword into the deadly Ronin sword, which would make it much harder for Adam to strike a kick towards him. He pressed another button on his jacket to deploy his titanium collar and make it next to impossible for Adam to make the all-important kill.

Adam continued to strike at Slayem, hoping he could wear him down, but the super-fit Slayem wouldn't let down his guard. Adam's thoughts were turning towards his family and what would happen to them if he was defeated.

A smile beamed across Slayem's face as Adam's thoughts betrayed him. Slayem's thoughts were on that subject also. 'As Seth doubts, his faith are being weakened,' were the thoughts on Slayem's mind, and he loved it. It was only a matter of time before it was all over for the Master Disciples.

Adam got an evil vision of what could happen – of Slayem slaying them in their sleep. Adam saw Slayem getting ready to strike towards him with that deadly sword, but Adam was filled with a holy anger. Seeing a vision that was clearly not of God had quickened his faith.

Adam guarded his attacker and then struck back. He hit Slayem's sword so hard in the centre that the grip broke and the Ronin became two separate swords. Slayem, dropping one of the swords with the immense power of that strike, was completely unaware of where it came from.

Adam quickly moved in and picked up one of the broken swords. Slayem stepped back and was clearly shaken from the power of that strike. Adam moved in and took his opportunity to get a clear strike; the two swords going like helicopter blades at Adam's sides, alternating from side to side to defend his front and face area.

As Adam moved in closer, Slayem stepped back again and then, with an act of utter madness, he moved in and tried to guard against the powerful strikes. His arm pads were hit and the sparks were flying. The titanium started to dull the edge of Adam's sword so he had to try another tactic.

Whilst Adam continued with Slayem, Milo had made his way over to Jason, who was in a bad way. The colour had completely gone from his face; he was very pale and clearly in shock. Milo gave a quick look at his shoulder and there was no way of stopping the blood. It was no use tying it up with a belt; his shoulder was shattered and he would lose his arm.

Deygar's Bentley was still running and could be driven. With care, Milo lifted Jason up and started to walk him towards the car.

One, maybe two, steps and he was on the floor. He was losing consciousness with the amount of blood lost and begged Milo to stop. The pain was so unbearable. So the pair of them just lay there in the shadow of that art deco building with its straight lines and light coloured stone steps, the fear of God running through their hearts.

Milo's heart was quickened by the sheer sight of the amount of blood that Jason had lost. He grabbed Jason's shoulder and he let out an almighty yell of pain and then, in what could only be called a miracle, Milo forced the bones of Jason's shoulder together and again Jason shouted out in pain.

The blood poured through Milo's hands, down his wrists and he started to pray. 'Oh Lord. We can't explain this to anyone, so only you can intervene, heal and repair Jason's shoulder now.'

The faith grew in both of their hearts and Jason's pain was the first to go. Jason looked over to see what Milo was doing and saw that the blood from Milo's hands was starting to go back into his shoulder. What happed next needed to seen to be believed; the two halves of his shoulder fused back together and, before Milo could say 'Amen', Jason's shoulder was completely healed.

Milo's hands were completely clean of Jason's blood and the pair just lay there in the shadow of that old building, thanking and praising their Lord.

Milo was quick to get Jason out of there. 'Okay, Jason. Go get in the car and go. We can't do that again.'

Jason just nodded, got into Deygar's Bentley and was gone.

Deygar was distracted by the sound of his own car being driven away by Jason and Paul took his sword and drove it into his chest. Deygar fell to his knees and his mouth quickly filled with his own blood.

Slayem saw this and shouted over. 'Get up! Guard yourself now. You are immortal. You can't die.'

With that said, Paul lifted his sword to take the death strike towards Derek's neck.

But Derek noticed it coming and moved just milliseconds from being hit across his neck. Paul was devastated at losing his chance to finish Deygar and feared that he wouldn't have the energy or the faith to complete his mission, but that doubt soon dissipated when he saw his aging father, still with a sword in his mighty hand.

With Slayem distracted for a moment, Adam took his chance and struck his sword across Slayem's neck, but that dreaded titanium collar stopped the powerful blow and not even the evidence of a dent was made.

Slayem was most displeased by the attempt at his life and gave Adam a powerful kick to his chest, knocking him over and making him lose his grip on his sword. Adam slid one way and his sword went another way. He was in trouble. If he didn't think quickly… Luckily, Milo did the thinking for him, risking his own life in the process.

Slayem was standing over the downed Adam, ready to complete his evil intentions. Adam grasped the ground in desperation for his sword in the hopeless few moments he thought he still had left just to show how strong his faith was in front of such an evil, but talented, adversary.

But that wasn't the intentions of Milo or God in Milo's eyes as he moved in on Slayem.

Milo raised his sword and screamed at the top of his voice. 'Young men will dream visions and drive out demons,' he yelled and guarded the sword of Slayem from striking Adam.

Slayem was immobilised and thrown back temporarily by the strong act of faith from Milo. Even though he had gotten a few scriptures mixed up in the heat of fierce battle, it had worked.

Adam pulled himself up from the ground and retrieved his sword. He toed up to Slayem, who was now intent on killing Milo for his 'outrageous conduct', in his mind.

'You will die for this, Old Man. Of all people, you should understand the rules of engagement.'

Slayem went on the attack on Milo with such anger; it was like he had only been playing with Adam up to that point.

But with the power of Slayem full on, Milo was finding the going hard and was tiring fast. Slayem was fast and showing no signs of letting up on his attack on the poor old Milo, who was showing his age. After all, he was a seventy-seven year old man. It was a misconception that people did forget his age due to his abilities, but now he was definitely showing his age.

Adam was stuck at the sidelines desperately trying to get in on the action, so Slayem would let up on Milo, but Slayem wasn't having any of it. But Milo was showing a brave front and went for a strike of his own rather than just defending himself. His sword, however, lacked the power and accuracy of Slayem's and he simply kicked away the sword and drove his own sword through the shoulder of Milo. Milo dropped his sword and fell to his knees, writhing in pain, holding the damaged shoulder.

It all seemed to go in slow motion for Milo and, as he glanced up to see the smiling face of Slayem with his sword held aloft ready for the final death blow, he readied his soul and simply looked into the eyes of his killer – a last faith strike to rock the very foundation of the evil Slayem.

'One day the Devil himself will take the back the power which you hold so precious, leaving you in total damnation for eternity,' Milo thought to himself as he readied himself for his eternity with his Lord.

Slayem, filled with the hate and fire of the Devil himself, drove the sword downwards towards Milo's chest. 'Death time, Old Man!'

Adam moved quicker than ever and sweep-kicked Slayem over backwards, so he didn't stab Milo accidentally and then ran his own sword through Slayem's side, cutting through his kidneys, the weakest part of Slayem's armoury. Slayem got up. It didn't seem to bother him that he was severely injured. To Slayem, pain was only an indicator that he was still alive. 'If there's pain there's life,' was his exact thought on the subject.

He did verify the injured wound by touching it, but only to inspect the blood on his glove – dark red Chianti, like Slayem's soul.

Paul and Deygar's battle was coming to an end in Paul's mind, but he feared it was getting to that all-important time; to commit a sin that still violated God's code. 'Thou shalt not murder,' rang through his mind like an old hymn.

Deygar was still without a weapon and was holding his chest and spitting blood by the measure. As Adam and Milo had been battling with Slayem, Derek Greyer was trying to negotiate his way out of death in the mortal, with the eternal damnation part to come later, but he had been ignorant to that part his whole life.

'Paul, don't kill me. Please don't do it, Paul. You've done it, Paul. A proven man of integrity, a man of honour and code, 'God's code'. Don't kill me. You are better than that, Paul.'

Paul's mind was an ocean of emotion and the waves were crashing all around him. He couldn't turn to his father for good council now or Adam for battle tips once a man was down.

'Come on, Paul. I am, after all, an unarmed man. You can't strike a man without a sword.'

Paul's mind was racing like a speeding race car without brakes. He kicked over Deygar's sword in an attempt to even the odds and to take a little of the guilt away from the emotional wreck that he was.

Derek's free hand was shaking at the sheer thought of grabbing that sword and giving Paul back the odds that he was so desperate to even.

'I have billions, Paul. I could make you rich beyond your wildest dreams, and you don't have to see me again,' Derek said as his hand edged ever closer to the deadly blade that lay just before him.

Paul's mind was now clearer than ever. The thought of money at a time like this turned Paul's stomach and gave the advantage back.

With that running through Paul's mind he said, 'You're dead right. I won't see you again.' With that said, the sword of Paul's came down with God-feared force and struck.

Deygar's head fell to the ground and his lifeless body fell forward into a helpless heap, his feet still twitching with the last signs of life fighting to live, but then it stopped dead.

Paul fell to his knees and cried out, 'Please, Lord, forgive me,' and broke down. The tears ran from his eyes like streams. His mind was now free of any thought, except that he had killed a man – taken a life away.

God had truly blessed Paul in the shape of his talent, his skill as a swordsman and, most of all, his healing, but all that had been robbed from him. The guilt and shame was too much to bear. This sin in Paul's heart ebbed away any further blessing from his Lord. It was all wasted on the evil that lay in Derek Greyer's heart and his intent on killing them all in order to further his evil rampage on their beloved city. Also, the possibility of further rampages with the now internationally travelled Slayem with him. It was all gone but Paul would soon realise that the killing of Derek was part of the master plan ordained by God and carried out by Paul, through God's Spirit.

On the other side of the street, Adam and Slayem's battle was looking like an impossible uphill task. Adam was wearing down by the second by the powerful sword of Slayem.

Adam managed to glance over to see the distressed Paul shouting out and crying out to God for forgiveness, totally unaware of the distress his own father was in with a severe shoulder wound, but the strong faith and determination of Milo was no match for the love of father and his son. So Milo managed to get over to Paul and try to comfort him in whatever way he could even with the injuries he had sustained.

Slayem's determination was stronger than ever. It seemed to Adam that he'd stepped up a gear seeing the severed head of Deygar laying there in the gutter. The darkened blood was like his soul – black and empty, the colour of an empty vessel void of any kind of emotion other than selfish greed and ambition. And you could clearly see it in the eyes of Slayem; there was no soul there at all, just the steely, grit-toothed, fire-filled face of a man who no longer had control of the actions of his mind.

The demon who had been so kind to him at the beginning of his journey was in complete control now, and it wanted blood.

'Deygar's dead,' Adam said. 'So, it just saved me the job.' Said the deviant Slayem. Adam stood ready for the next onslaught. His sword edge glimmering in the evening sun, with the sounds of sirens blaring in the distance. The police and emergency services were stretched to beyond there capabilities with the dozen or so accidents left in their wake.

With the possibility of there being no police intervention for at least the next thirty minutes, Adam had to work fast if he was to see through this and be reunited with his beloved family.

Paul had composed himself and had gotten to his feet. His father, Milo, was lying down on the ground. Paul had managed to stem the bleeding a little. He still needed urgent medical attention.

Paul wanted vengeance, but he was going at this all wrong and Adam could sense it. Paul's face was a picture of hatred and anger and it wasn't holy. Slayem picked up on this and exploited it, firing him up some more.

'So all I have to do now is kill you, Seth,' said Slayem, pointing his sword towards the maimed as he did so. 'Then, to kill the weak son of a dying man.'

Paul was enraged at the sheer thought of his father dying and went in for the attack. Adam feared the worst from Paul's actions. He had to back him up, whatever the outcome was.

Paul struck his sword; it made contact with Slayem's, only then to receive a kick to the face, knocking him to the ground.

With an overreached Slayem, Adam took full advantage and kicked his side, hitting the damaged kidney area.

The injured Slayem showed sign of pain, holding his side with his right hand, the left hand shaking a little with the flashes of pain reverberating down the shaft and blade of his sword.

It was like a game of chess for Slayem and he needed to prioritise his next victim. Paul was all fired up, but an angry man is a controllable beast in Slayem's mind. On the other hand, Seth was more composed and was very skilful.

'Paul first,' Slayem said to himself, as he went on the attack.

Paul managed to get himself back on his feet just in time to receive an almighty kick to the face, knocking him unconscious. Then he turns on Adam. Their swords clashed back and forth at a furious speed and then Adam got a fist in and punched Slayem clean in the face, knocking the speed out of him.

Slayem shook his head in disbelief. With Slayem distracted, Adam let loose with a foray of strikes. Slayem blocked each one with ease.

And then it was Slayem's turn, to turn on the heat and he let Adam take the full brunt of his power and accuracy. With every strike Adam stepped back, using his sword more like a shield than a weapon, then

Slayem got a strike past Adam's defence and made contact with Adam's shoulder, hitting the Kevlar padding on his leathers and going through it like a hot knife through butter.

Jason had managed to call the church from Derek's car on the way to the church, to warn the wives, start a serious prayer meeting and create a treatment room just in case.

Rachel and the other Master Disciple's wives and Lorraine met at the church to pray. Rachel soon got to work in the training room, making a makeshift treatment room down there and the others started their prayer vigil.

Adam was worried that Paul hadn't moved for a few minutes, and his shoulder was needing a little attention. It wasn't as bad as Milo's; the bike leather had taken the brunt of the impact.

Paul started to move. With a little grumbling and moaning Paul got up and the pair stood shoulder to shoulder to protect each other and move towards Slayem.

'Seth, it has been a pleasure knowing you and being under your teaching and instruction.'

'Paul, what are you saying?' This alarmed Adam. It sounded like it was his last will and testament.

'I'm not gonna see this through, Seth. I can feel it.' Paul was scared and was preparing his heart just like his father had done just moments before.

Adam had to help Paul see sense. 'Paul, keep it together, man, 'cause we gonna see this through. Where is your faith?'

'I'm sorry, brother.'

It seemed to Adam that Paul was sacrificing himself for the greater good, 'but what greater good?' Adam thought.

Slayem started to sidestep towards Milo, and Adam sensed something wasn't right. Paul was doubting his own faith. Slayem was heading towards Milo to finish him off and Adam was torn again. He had to think quickly. Slayem was getting dangerously close to Milo.

Then Adam did something that would help all parties involved.

'Paul, get it together, man. Your father is lying there,' Adam shouted in one last ditch plan to get Paul back into the here and now.

Paul snapped out of it, seeing his father down and hurt badly, and headed for Slayem with his sword at the ready.

Slayem, with a hint of a smile, even though he was in great pain with his kidneys, turned with his sword ready, thirsting for the first actual official kill for the Dark Lord. After all, they were one kill down. Deygar's body was still motionless with absolute no hint of any movement now or ever.

Paul drove his sword towards Slayem's throat. Adam watched on as he headed towards him to back him up. The sword of Paul's was heading dangerously close to Slayem and then, at the last second, he blocked it with his own and turned, giving Paul a powerful strike into his face with his elbow. Slayem's sword then came down and ran through Paul's thigh, tearing through his leg badly.

Paul fell to the floor in searing pain, shouting out in agony.

Adam, seeing all of this, as Slayem went down to kill the injured Paul, jumped over the downed Paul and gave Slayem a flying kick to the throat, kicking the titanium plate into his skin, giving Slayem a nasty cut to his precious throat.

Both Slayem and Paul were down and Adam went to the injured Paul and dragged him over to his father for comfort and to keep them all together.

Adam was mad; Slayem was just toying with them all. Out of the three Master Disciples he had managed to seriously injure two and Deygar had shot Jason.

Adam was in no place to start questioning God's grace, neither was he in any position to start doubting his faith.

Slayem could sense Adam's thoughts and this drove him wild because he didn't seem to be even a little bit put out by this. Adam's faith was getting stronger by the second.

The pair stood just staring at each other. Adam was focused on one thing and one thing only – the death of Slayem.

Slayem was also focused on the preservation of his immortal evil frame. He dropped his sword in deviance and beckoned Adam to fight with his hands.

'Let's fight like men, Seth, with our bare hands. It will be the ultimate show of a true warrior.'

Adam went with it, placing his sword down with the respect it deserved, knowing full well that it would only be with the sword that he could finish Slayem off forever. So, why entertain such a ludicrous idea of hand to hand combat with a man that has studied every martial art there ever was to learn?

Adam's faith quickening in his heart; he knew full well that the God he served could and would protect him. He took the stance of a fighter with Milo and Paul watching on in horror, their hearts full of faith for their friend and protector.

'Please, Lord. Let Adam know the fullness of his faith and gifting in You, protect him as he serves you and your church,' was the only thing Milo could muster under his shallow breath.

Slayem went at Adam with his full force and Adam blocked a number of strong strikes from Slayem. A multiple strike of punches and kicks came Adam's way with such speed. Adam was soon regretting his decision to fight without a sword and was wearing out fast. But so too was Slayem. Adam managed to get a great kick with his knee into Slayem's side, hitting his kidneys yet again, folding up the mighty Slayem. The anger filled the mouth of Slayem like a toxin; he'd spit fire if he could. He then gave Adam such a powerful kick to his throat that he went down holding his throat. He was finding it hard to breathe; with each intake of air came the pain of swallowing the lump of doubt in his throat. He was in trouble and he knew then that the whole ploy of Slayem to drop swords was a mediocre attempt to wear Adam out, ready for his impending death.

Slayem picked up his sword, knowing full well that it was just a formality to run Adam through with his sword, but before he got to that part he needed to say just one more thing to Adam.

Adam was sitting up and was slowly crawling backwards, using his legs to push himself back towards his own sword, still finding hard to breathe, his chest expanding with every fighting breath he took and searing pain. The doubt was creeping in his heart, but he could see the look on Slayem's face and he was not scared at all; this catapulted Adam into a survival mode he never thought he had in him.

His breathing stabilised and he got to his sword just before Slayem got to him saying,

'It has been a pleasure fighting such a formidable opponent. Such a shame you won't be around to see the mighty future of the Dark Lord's rising.'

The sword was in Adam's hand now. He had a full grip on it and was ready for anything. He flipped up onto his feet and his sword blocked the attack of Slayem. He was totally surprised by the sudden surge of faith on Adam's part.

Paul managed to shout out encouragement. 'Go on, Seth. Finish it.'

Adam gave a quick glance over, distracted by the strong words from Paul, and Slayem took full advantage of Adam's lack of concentration and struck his left wrist with such power that the sword shook with the vibrations of bones breaking and shattering under such force. But Slayem was more surprised than Adam when his hand was still connected to his wrist.

Adam stepped back, still holding his sword with his right hand, ready for anything. He quickly glanced under his damaged biker's leather jacket to reveal his severely damaged Bretling Navitimer watch, which had taken the brunt of that strike.

His wrist was still in a bad way. The screwed-down crown had pierced his wrist and it was swelling up fast. The very watch that had been given to him as a gift for faithful service from his former co-workers had saved his hand. If only they knew the true benefit of that gift now.

He puckered up, pulling his glove over the damaged watch to carry on; the mineral, scratch-proof glass had fallen into his glove, and as he grasped the sword with both hands, the glass pierced his left hand, alike the situation he found himself in, painful, but necessary to the mission.

Slayem was surprised by the sheer strength and determination of Seth and was readying himself for the next and final part of this battle.

Their swords clashed again and again. The battle was relentless and Slayem was using all his skills – the skills honed from centuries of practise in battles – and was shocked to find this relatively young man holding his own to the might of the most evil man on earth.

Adam struck up towards Slayem's face and, as he leaned his head back, Adam brought his sword down with such force and accuracy that he took off Slayem's left hand – the very same hand that he had attacked on Adam's mortal frame just moments ago.

As the lifeless limb hit the floor, the pain surged across Slayem's face. Milo and Paul looked on with the faith that Adam would soon bring this terrifying mission to an end.

Slayem's face was a picture of horror and sheer amazement that this little upstart would actually take a limb from him.

In sheer shock, Slayem reached down, picked up the severed, lifeless limb and placed it in his pocket.

Adam found this action quite strange and he stood there dumbfounded by the actions of a man who, a moment ago, was giving a speech before he attempted to kill Adam in cold blood.

Slayem, in his vast historic past, had lost many a finger or a thumb as swords clashed at the hilt, losing the odd appendage or two in the process. But in the past, he would simply pick them up and reattach them later. With time and his evil ability to fuse nerve-endings and muscle tissue, he would heal himself in no time. But now a whole hand was something new, even for Slayem. Nevertheless, he still felt hopeful at the outcome of this battle or why else would he pick up his hand.

Adam, saw this as the last act of a desperate man. He could also see that Slayem was suddenly feeling nauseous and immediately dropped his guard with his sword.

'Finish it!' Milo shouted out. Adam's mind was a wash of moral emotion. Should he kill an injured man on his last desperate attempt of survival or should he 'finish it', as Milo so rightfully put it?

After all, Slayem's right hand still had a sword tightly held in it and, most of all, he still had a fighting spirit.

Adam regained his focus once again. Paul surged on in prayer being careful not to shout out again and distract him. All he could do was pray in his mind – the only organ that worked without the painful reminder of his injuries.

Paul's helpless frame just lay there. He had suffered badly at the hands of Deygar and Slayem collectively. Some severe cuts and even a dislocated shoulder, as well as the badly injured leg were on Paul's injury tally.

Adam raised his sword in defiance. Slayem was on his feet and was losing blood at a rapid rate. Slayem was showing great courage but it wasn't looking good for the Dark Lord. God had definitely been on the winning side this day, even though the Master Disciples had, had a few casualties.

Adam was focused and was readying himself for the final faze of this, his toughest day alive to date.

Yet again the pair were in battle mode, their swords clashing. The pair were clearly worn out; the fatigue was a wash all over their faces.

Slayem wasn't at his best since loosing his hand and was desperate to finish this battle sooner rather than risk bleeding too much. The two of them were fighting the battle of their life. But only one would live on forever for eternity and Adam wasn't ready to meet his maker yet.

Slayem couldn't kick or strike out other than with his sword, and it was the same story for Adam; the pair had sustained many a battle scar. So it came down to an old fashioned sword fight to defend the good in Adam and the evil intentions of Slayem.

As the pair carried on with their battle, swords clashing around them, their thoughts pondered to another time and place.

All that was racing through Adam's mind was the future, seeing Grace all grown up into a beautiful young girl; his amazing wife, Rachel, pregnant again with the possibility of a son in the frame; the church expanding into the place that had been envisioned years ago through a prophecy, all to come into fruition.

Slayem, on the other hand, dwelled on the past and all the terrible atrocities he'd seen at his evil hands. But his heart had softened in this last few moments and he started to think on all the beauty he had seen: the smell of fresh paint in the Sistine chapel, the crusades he had been in, the Great Wall of China, all the marks of man that had embedded mankind, the moon landing 1969. His mind was trying to catalogue all the greatness of man. He was so desperate to see at what point he had given anything to benefit mankind, but he couldn't find a single thing, until he looked deeply at Milo holding his injured son. Fatherhood struck a cord in his heart, which made him pause long enough for Adam to sweep his legs from underneath him, causing him to fall down the several steps at the front of a closed-down building ready for demolition.

Slayem's body flipped and gambolled over and over; it seemed like he had given up, not even trying to break his fall with his one remaining hand. He then hit the bottom with a crack; the titanium collar that was there to protect his neck caused his neck to push against it, breaking it like a twig.

Adam rushed down to the severely injured Slayem. Milo and Paul had managed to crawl to get to the top of the staircase to overlook the final scene of Slayem's long life.

The human emotions that filled Adam's mind were at war, conflicting with one another. All the 'thou shalt not kill' sermons that Adam had heard so many times rung in his head like crashing cymbals. They were eating away at his moral code and he was being urged on like a boxer in a fight, being willed on by onlookers, who, if they were in the same position, wouldn't be able to do so for the same reason. Adam had paused. He was not an evil man at heart but he had to carry out this mission for the protection of the church and his own precious family.

To kill. To kill. The thought was tough. He'd trained for it, knew it was part of his mission, but he was now struggling with delivering it. The thought of taking a life away like clicking his fingers – 'snap' then gone – engulfed him like a plague. Here was a man who, only a year or so ago, had created life, and now he was preparing to take a life.

Milo yelled down. 'Do it! Do it now!'

Adam was an obedient believer and the only thing that was left to do was kill Slayem. So 'In the name of the Father, the Son and the Holy Spirit,' was the only thing running through Adam's mind as the sword came rushing through the air down hard. It was all going in slow motion for the faith-filled Master Disciple, Seth. As the sword made its final few inches through the air.

One last ditch of defiance from Slayem was his eyes turning to focus in on the man so dedicated on killing him. He looked Adam square into his eyes. Slayem blinked as the sword hit his neck, taking his head clean off.

Adam fell to his knees in a heap of sweat and relief, knowing it was all over, and that he could live on knowing that his family and, ultimately, God's church was safe.

He paused for a moment then soon realised that he had to move quickly; after all, the mess and mayhem littered the street. Adam quickly managed to get to the top of the staircase to gather up all the injured Master Disciples and make some kind of order in all the chaos. There were smashed and battered cars and two dead people without their heads still holding swords in their motionless hands.

Adam didn't know where to start when a vehicle approached at speed it was a luxury Grand Voyager with blacked out windows.

It stopped and the side door slid open electronically. A voice beckoned out. 'All of you get in, quickly.'

Adam was clearly worried about such a request, and then the voice said, 'We are here to assist you as requested by Pastor Miles.'

Milo managed a sentence. 'It must be the answer to my email, the 'Council of Reference.'

There was no response from the mysterious voice in the passenger seat of the people carrier.

Adam bundled Milo and Paul in then raced to his bike and followed on after the car with the precious but beaten Milo and Paul safely inside.

Within minutes the luxury people carrier pulled into the church car park with Adam behind.

Again, the door to the car slid open all by itself and the pair were ordered out of the vehicle.

All three were completely bewildered by what had just happened, and then the three of them just sat on the church steps, simply waiting for the next request from whoever had brought them. But there was no request, no orders, just an envelope thrown from the people carrier, landing on the lap of Milo with the words written by hand.

For the attention of the Guardians of truth

The Master Disciples had been through hell and back over the past few months and it had all come to this – the end.

There they were sat, beaten and battered, at the doors of their church after battling with evil Dark Lords, one of which was a thousand years old and a master swordsman, holding an envelope within which could be information that could unlock the truth of whether the Council of Reference was responsible for their safe removal from that battle ground.

This would truly reveal the more crucial state of their activity over the years. Their silence, their secrets, now uncovered – an organisation nearly as old as the church itself.

Instead of ripping the package open, however, the three continued to sit and ponder for one last moment, before someone realised that it was over and found them.

Adam was war torn and exhausted. He had only just managed to pull off his helmet and was just lying there breathing slowly, appreciating the fact that he was still alive and not in glory.

Milo was also glad that he was still alive and very much kicking, and was thanking God in the silence.

Paul was still fighting a fight in his mind; his mind still racing and playing over and over again the moments of his battle and the battles of his brothers in faith.

Within a few minutes, Rachel had wandered up to see who had driven off the car park only moments ago, only to find her husband, Paul and Pastor Miles lying at the church doors. She soon alerted the others and got help to get all involved downstairs and out of sight.

With all the goings on and panic from the concerned wives, Milo had completely forgotten about the envelope he had been given and it had been placed on the computer desk. Adam was fine in his own mind and was desperate for Rachel to tend to the most injured and most vulnerable. He told her to look after Pastor Miles first, being the oldest and most at risk, but Milo insisted on Rachel looking after the needs of Paul. His leg was in a bad way, after all, and, as Milo put it, 'he is the future of the church'. And he was right to tell Rachel not to spend any time on a 'relic like him'. After all, his time was well and truly over as a fully-fledged Master Disciple. He could finally now relax, put all this behind him and have the retirement that he had dreamed of fifteen years ago.

Adam sat trying to calm down again; the rush of adrenaline had filled him after the sudden rush down into the training room. His head was buzzing and he was in a serious quandary as to who and why they were all picked up so soon after the head of Slayem had fallen. Then he remembered the envelope and quickly gathered it into his hands, shaking as to what lied within its sealed edges. He quickly gave Milo a look of approval before he ripped into it.

Milo did so as he pushed himself up on the makeshift bed, being propped up with several pillows, carefully placed by the emergency stand-in nurse, Lorraine, who was doing an amazing job.

As Adam ripped into it, Paul looked over, leaning in his bed carefully, as Rachel was now stitching up his damaged leg the best she could do. She was the typical calm self she always was under the immense pressure.

Adam pulled out a handwritten letter; it read:

Well done, good and faithful servants of the most high God, yours in Christ Jesus.

We, the remaining members of the former 'Council of Reference', have arranged the surrender of Slayem and Deygar will not be a burden to you. Please ensure our trust and commitment to your work in this time of concern.

Please make sure you and your team are near to a TV this evening for Great news.

And again thank you, and well done for the liberation of God's people there and around the world.

Many thanks and blessings from the former Council of Reference.

Please destroy this transcript once read.

Milo was shocked to find out that the Council were still operating; still a functioning body after all these years.

Adam was intrigued by the TV remark and switched on the television and within minutes a news flash was announced.

'Sorry to interrupt our normal viewing with this news flash, but we go directly live to our city streets with our outside reporter, Daniel Radford.'

'We have come down into the deep end of our city limits to find the massacre of decapitated heads separated from their bodies with what looks like, at first, a fierce and bloody battle to the end with swords.

'This medieval scene wouldn't look amiss if it had came out of a book, but what is puzzling police, is that it appears one of the victims is none other than the billionaire businessman, Derek Greyer, and an unknown man.

There seems to be no witnesses, but the first man on the scene was this man: George Gregor.'

The eager journalist then turned to the smartly dressed man of mature years and asked:

'So what did you see, Mr Gregor?'

'Well I didn't see anything. As I have told the police already, I only heard the sound of swords clashing and two men shouting a few streets away, so I made my way here and then found the two men in question. Then I made the call to the police.'

'Thank you, Mr Gregor. The police have many leads to what could have possibly happened here. They are pursuing all avenues of enquiries; firstly, with all the damaged vehicles nearby. A recent car chase earlier may be linked to this incident, but the police haven't released that information yet. We'll be here as the news unfolds. Now it's back to you in the studio.'

Adam watched the screen with scrutiny and with a puzzled look written all over his face.

'There's something familiar about that witness. This is live isn't it? I'm heading down there.'

Adam quickly made his way down there. The sudden rush of adrenaline gave him a new mission to solve – the missing link to all of this, and George Gregor was it.

As he pulled up on the bike, Adam was confronted with a barrage of police and the film crew were packing up until more news broke on the story.

The whole street was taped off and it gave Adam a chill down his spine to see the bodies being taken away by the coroner's office and the forensic officers checking every single inch of the street for any piece of evidence.

There was nothing for Adam there, so he rode back to the church slightly upset and frustrated by the lack of control he had; he was now placing his trust in an unseen, unheard, never meet entity. Akin to his faith in God, it was so unbelievable; the similarities were mind blowing, and were, after all, the only way that any of them could have got through what they all just had experienced.

Milo questioned Adam on his arrival back in the training room, with the simplest of questions. 'Of whom, where and what?' But before he could answer, the computer started beeping. It received an e-mail, and it simply read:

It's all sorted MDs

See you all soon.

Conclusion
Rebuilding the Future

Jeremiah 29v11 'For I know the plans I have for you, declares the Lord, plans to prosper you and not harm you, plans to give you a hope and a future.'

NO ONE KNOWS THE END FROM the beginning; no scientist, no fortune teller, no medium, not anyone but the maker and author of our very existence.

Adam gazed up into the heavens with a thankful heart, not knowing where to start when it came to thanking God for all that He'd done for the church and the greater city.

It humbled him knowing the city's greatest triumph, was also its biggest secret.

The Council of Reference had outdone themselves with every angle covered by the 'keepers of the truth'.

The police had made the investigation their top priority, sending top detectives criminologist, crime scene forensics and it's own designated police chief, brought out of retirement, to head up the entire proceedings.

The billionaire's activities had brought many theorists to make their own conclusions and conspiracies to his involvement. Some surmising a hostile takeover, the depth of someone's deliberations were laughed away. 'The sword is mightier than the pen,' after all, was one of the journalist's take on the whole series of events.

But Adam's theory was one he could not share with anyone; the fact was that the whole investigation had been handed over to the Keepers of the Truth – the true Council of Reference.

The power and influence that the council had was limitless and there was no problem with the financial help required to clear up all the mess.

Milo, Paul, Jason and Adam were all on the mend. It had been the best part of a week since the 'surrender' – as the Council of Reference put it – of Slayem and Deygar and the police had made their enquiry to why their cars were on the scene.

The explanation into the reason their cars were there was that 'they were just in the wrong place at the wrong time,' said Jason. Pastor Miles car had been stolen and Paul's identical car was there parked up due to an urgent meeting in a nearby building and that was the nearest space to park it. 'It was unfortunate that the car that hit it had been driven by the unidentified deceased man, 'Slayem.'

Adam needed time alone, so he made his way to Paul's office. He made all the necessary pulls and pushes to operate the door that lead down to the training room.

It was a strange, small journey into the training room. But every step Adam took was a sudden reminder of the battle that had happened days ago. As he placed his foot down, his mind would recall a blow or a strike, and with each and every step down into that training room; it was like reliving it all over.

Adam clenched his eyes closed and, as he walked, they filled up with tears; he couldn't make out if they were tears of joy or tears of relief. But as he got closer to the far wall he managed to open one eye just enough to see a towel hanging over the weights bench. He grabbed hold of it and pulled his sword from its sheath. Adam ran the towel down the sword's blade, cleaning it and removing any blood from its precious edge, but he had already done it moments after their battle. It was just something he'd done without thinking; it was like he was reliving the whole experience again with every vivid detail. Then he opened the cabinet that Milo had originally pulled the sword from, for what seemed a life time ago. Back then Adam never realised the full potential of that first encounter and with it a responsibility that far out reached the boundaries of his thinking.

He then gently placed the weapon the bible speaks of so frequently on its stand and closed the cabinet door, turning the key.

Adam turned round to face the stairs and, ultimately, the way out and thought to himself, 'Will we ever need this again?'

He then hung the key on a rusty old nail on one of the many beams, with this thought running through his mind:

'Please let me forget where I have placed this key. I hope I never need it, ever again.'

Was it just a thought?

Or a heart felt prayer?

You be the judge…

Acknowledgments

FIRSTLY I WOULD LIKE TO THANK my Lord for giving me the most vivid dreams ever, for which this book was inspired from.

I would like to thank my wife Rachel and my beautiful children Grace and Zachariah for the endless inspiration they give me on a daily basis.

All the leaders and pastors at 'The Church at Junction 10' for their words of encouragement, the long and short sermons, for which I'll be forever indebted to.

Thanks to my family, when told I was writing a novel were as surprised as me, 'and this from a man who left school with no formal qualifications'. Was one quote, thanks again.

A big thanks to Gemma Till, my first victim in reading the early draft copies of my book, thanks for taking them from my shaky nervous hands, I know I held on tight for a while, thanks again for all the encouragement you gave me, when I was thinking the opposite.

All my friends, (can't name you all), for all the help and support you've given me, thank you. Especially throughout the dark times, when I was filled with self doubt and unbelief.

A big thank you to Author House, for which this novel would still be locked in a laptop for no else to enjoy. So thank you again for all your professionalism and advice for which I am indebted to you.

The entire Design Team at Author House, whose help was priceless and made the whole prospect of getting a book, published as much a pleasure to do, as write. I hope we work together again.

Hayley Sherman whose help on the editing was fantastic a huge thank you for your massive contribution in getting it to, not only look good but make sense. I hope we can work together on future projects.

Thanks to Hugh Mcabe for the use of the photograph, he took, that graces the cover of this book. You have a genuine gift, not only did I find an image worthy to be placed on the front cover, but I also found a friend. Thanks again. The picture is called "Cloaked Figure" and was taken in the Pere Lachaise graveyard in Paris.

Last but certainly not least. Thanks again to my Lord and God and to the apostle Paul, the first true Master Disciple, for all the inspiration your words in the 'good book' gave me.

Lightning Source UK Ltd.
Milton Keynes UK
31 March 2010

152155UK00003B/18/P